LOCK NUT

THE PLUMBER'S MATE MYSTERIES FIVE

JL MERROW

RIPTIDE
PUBLISHING

Riptide Publishing
PO Box 1537
Burnsville, NC 28714
www.riptidepublishing.com

Lock Nut
Copyright © 2018 by JL Merrow

Cover art: Christine Coffee, coffeecreatescovers.com
Editor: Carole-ann Galloway
Layout: L.C. Chase, lcchase.com/design.htm

ISBN: 978-1-62649-728-3

First edition
May, 2018

Also available in ebook:
ISBN: 978-1-62649-727-6

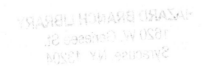

LOCK NUT

THE PLUMBER'S MATE MYSTERIES FIVE

JL MERROW

RIPTIDE
PUBLISHING

TABLE OF
CONTENTS

CHAPTER ONE

It was one of those chilly winter evenings that make it a pleasure to be at home in the warm. Me and Phil had just polished off a very nice lasagne, if I do say so myself, and were vegging on the sofa, Phil's hand idly stroking my hair. The room was cosy, the lights were low, and even the cats were purring in harmony.

I flicked on the telly and caught the news. Politics, the National Health Service, the latest Tory MP/rentboy scandal . . . I was about to switch it off again and suggest that me and Phil make our own entertainment, when something made me prick up my ears.

"A body has been found in a Hertfordshire canal. Police say they are treating the death as suspicious. The dead man, who was found near Pluck's End, has been named as Jonathan Parrot, aged twenty-eight, who lived locally but had been working in London's Camden Market. Police are anxious to trace a man seen pursuing Mr. Parrot through the market yesterday, described as white, in his late twenties, and of below-average height."

Phil and me both stared, appalled, at the telly, where an artist's impression of the suspect, sorry, *person of interest* appeared.

They'd made the chin a bit on the belligerent side, and the eyes were frankly menacing, but other than that, it wasn't a bad likeness of yours truly.

"Well, that's not good," I said weakly.

Then the phone began to ring.

CHAPTER TWO

I t all started at the wedding. It wasn't a bad one, as weddings go. The weather, for a miracle, stayed fair, everyone was dressed up to the nines—even me, thanks to some not-so-gentle nudging from Phil; my sister, Cherry; and my best mate Gary that had started to feel a lot like an intervention by the time they were done—and the service went off without a hitch (other than the intended one, that was). Some thoughtless git left his mobile phone on and it rang loudly in the middle of the vows, but hey, I had a lot on my mind that day.

It wasn't just my only sister finally getting spliced at the tender age of forty. I was having a few dad issues as well, seeing as both of 'em—that's the one that brought me up, and the biological one—had turned up in St. Leonards for the occasion, and don't think that wasn't weird. I wasn't sure how Mum felt about having her husband and her ex-bit-on-the-side in the same room, but there had been a definite whiff of sherry on her breath when she'd kissed me hello.

Plus, of course, there was the whole *there but for the grace of a few months* whatsit, seeing as me and Phil had our own wedding coming up in July. So, yeah, little things like phones kind of got forgotten. I like to think it lightened the mood, anyhow, having the chorus to "Why Does it Always Rain on Me?" suddenly blare through the church (Phil had been trying to get me to change my work ringtone to Handel's *Water Music*, but I'd reckoned it'd make me look like a poser. Or sound like one, whatever). It certainly got a laugh when Cherry spun round mid-*I do* to give me a death glare that really didn't go with the whole white dress and veil, pure-as-the-driven-snow look. And a louder one when the littlest bridesmaid, who'd been entertaining herself by pulling petals off her posy, turned and put her finger to her lips with a loud *Shush*.

The bishop who was marrying them cracked up. He was a jolly, Friar Tuck sort anyway, was the Right Reverend Peter Elwy, Suffragan Bishop of Westchester. (No, I don't know what one of them is, either. Although I'm pretty sure it's got nothing to do with Victorian women chucking themselves under horses.) Not what I like to think of as your typical Church of England thoroughbred: tall, pale, skinny blokes, with rounded shoulders and a chin that's receded so far that when they're preaching in the pulpit, it's back in the choir stalls with its feet up.

This bishop was shaped more like a football with a ping-pong ball on top. He was a last-minute stand-in for the (now ex) Bishop of St. Leonards, last seen skipping merrily off to Rome and leaving Cherry torn between panic over her wedding and glee over the improved career prospects of her husband-to-be, currently a canon. I wasn't sure how Greg had managed to get the Righteously Revved Peter along to officiate at such short notice, but he'd stopped Cherry having kittens, and I wasn't one to look a gift bishop in the mouth.

Cherry had been adamant she was going down the cute flower-girl route for her attendants, probably as an excuse not to have to ask our mutual sister-in-law Agatha to be chief dragon—sorry, *bridesmaid*—which I could sympathise with. That'd led to a shortage of potential candidates for the bridal party, what with Greg having no brothers and sisters and me and my big brother Richard having both failed to pop out any sprogs so far. Or, you know, cause the popping out of sprogs from others of a more suitable anatomy. Cherry had simply raided the St. Leonards Sunday School for photogenic tots and decked them out in poofy dresses and dinky little capes with so much white fur trim they were in danger of catching the groom's eye for his next adventure in taxidermy. The second smallest bridesmaid spent most of her time stroking her cape like it was an overbred cat and she was a budding Bond villain.

Cherry was sporting a fair amount of fur herself, but I was assured it was all fake, not from actual dead animals, so the guests would hopefully only be chucking confetti and not tins of paint in protest. It was a good choice for her—softened the remaining sharp edges, although she'd mellowed considerably over the last couple of years.

Not that I'd have said anything like that where she could hear me. I'm not daft. Or suicidal.

My mate Gary and his husband, Darren, cornered me and Phil after the service, while everyone was milling aimlessly outside the cathedral like a flock of sheep in posh hats, waiting to be rounded up by the photographer. Not that I'm calling the lady a dog, you understand, although come to think of it, she did have a bit of a bark.

Gary mock-swooned at the sight of me. "Tommy, darling, you look simply ravishing."

Phil coughed, although I had my suspicions it was more of a laugh. "Sure you don't mean ravished?"

I glared at my beloved. "Oi, you criticising?"

"Wouldn't dream of it," he said with a smirk, glancing around innocently. And promptly got his come-uppance when he caught the eye of the bishop, of all people. His right reverendness must have thought Phil was smiling at him and trundled over for a natter.

Gary patted my arm as the rest of us discreetly edged away. One sermon a day was plenty, ta very much. "Ignore the nasty man, Tommy dear. I said when I saw you—didn't I say, sweetie pie?—" Gary turned to simper briefly at Darren, then back to me "—who'd have ever guessed our little Tom-Tom would scrub up so nicely?"

"What am I, a secondhand satnav at a car boot sale?"

Darren cackled. "Nah, you're the hood ornament."

Which was rich, coming from someone a full fourteen inches shorter than me. More like twenty on this particular occasion, what with the over-the-top headgear Cherry had wheedled, threatened, and finally blackmailed me into wearing, along with the penguin suit, in my role as usher.

I'd tried to tell her I didn't have the first clue how to ush, but she'd shouted that down with a dismissive, *Don't be silly, nobody's expecting you to actually* do *anything.*

Cheers, Sis. Way to make me feel like a valued member of the wedding party.

Gary and Darren were wearing the suits they'd worn for their own wedding last summer: matching dark-blue dinner jackets, but in place of the crimson neck gear Gary's bow tie was yellow and Darren's, blue. Phil was looking seriously edible in a light-grey suit I knew for a fact had cost more than Cherry's bridal gown. Apparently one of the cathedral ladies had diverted her talents from cross-stitching cassocks. Or do I mean hassocks? I always get those two mixed up, although I know one means kneelers and the other means wizarding robes for clergy. And one's a railway station near Brighton. Anyhow, the old dear had managed to run up a simple lace gown that looked surprisingly elegant on dear old Sis. Especially with the fur cape and the beaming smile she'd been wearing all day, unscheduled interruptions excepted, of course.

Almost brought a tear to my eye, seeing her so happy. And Gary, who'd developed quite a friendship with her, had been leaking like a push-fit joint with a forty-year-old washer. I glanced over at a loud trumpeting sound to see him blowing his nose into his silk handkerchief, and felt a brief pang of sympathy for his dry cleaners.

Darren gave his husband a steadying pat on the shoulder, although as they were both standing up, it was a stretch for him. Then he turned to me. "I got a mate wants to consult you. In a professional capacity."

"Yeah? No promises, mind, I'm a bit booked up right now." February, coming after the January doldrums but still cold enough for pipes to burst and boilers to give up the ghost, is not exactly a quiet time for plumbers. I'd already had too many days off lately what with fittings for the flippin' suit and Cherry roping me into general wedding prep. She seemed to think I ought to thank her for letting me have a trial run for planning my own wedding later in the year, but to be honest, the longer I spent faffing around with seating arrangements and colour schemes, the more I was tempted to just grab my fiancé and catch the first train to Gretna Green. "What's the job?"

"She's lost her husband."

"Uh, sorry to hear that." I waited, but Darren didn't say anything else. "Hang on, you mean actually *lost*, lost? That's the job? Finding her other half? Unless she lost him down the plug hole, shouldn't you be talking to Phil?" After all, he's the private investigator in the family.

"Nah, the git's done a runner. And she wants you. Getting yourself quite a reputation, aintcha? She heard about that show you done at the St. Leonards Harvest Fayre, turning up a real live dead body in among the corn dollies and the homemade jam. Gutted she missed it, Lilah was."

I wasn't. The less I was forced to recall about that experience, the better. Not to mention, I was finding Darren's image of a "live" corpse a bit on the unsettling side. And yeah, all right, finding hidden things is sort of my speciality. It's just something I've always been able to do, and trust me, it isn't as much fun as it sounds. But it's hardly what I'd call a profession. For a start, the pay's pretty lousy. For which read nonexistent. And what people never seem to get is that there's limits to what I can do.

"I can't find people at the drop of a hat." Come to that, I wasn't even sure I could find *people*, full stop. Things, yes—and dead bodies, definitely—but walking, talking, living people? Okay, I'd found a missing toddler once, alive and well and snuggled up in a den in St. Albans park. And Phil too, in the early days of our reacquaintance, considerably less well and not at all snuggly, having been knocked out, soaked, and shoved into the boot of a car. But adults in so-called hiding aren't, as a rule, actually hidden. Not like buried treasure. They don't stay in one little hidey-hole, waiting for the bloke with the psychic metal detector to come and dig them up. People simply change their name, dye their hair, and get on with their life somewhere far, far away.

It's different, all right?

There had been one time, back last summer when me and Phil were desperately searching a burning building for anyone about to get crispy fried, that I'd felt like I could sense living people just because they were there, and not because they'd been stashed somewhere like a squirrel's winter pantry. But it hadn't happened since, and I'd been starting to wonder if I'd . . . not imagined it all, maybe, but, I dunno, chalked things up to my so-called sixth sense it hadn't earned?

I mean, I'd tried and everything, in the couple of months afterwards. I hadn't gone so far as to try to re-create the original setting, mind—if you've risked death by barbecue once, there's a definite sense of been there, done that, really *don't* want to try it again, ta very much.

But anyhow, there was a bigger objection. "I need to be close. So the only way I could find him is if she can tell us where he is, and if she could do that, why would she need me to find him? Seriously, Phil's the bloke for your average missing-persons' job."

"So have him in on it with you," Darren said with a shrug. "You don't have to tell Lilah it's him what finds the bloke."

I gave him a look. "What, so apart from the whole lying-to-the-client thing, you don't just want me to muscle in on my fiancé's business, oh no. I'm also supposed to drag him along, introduce him as some kind of spare part, and then expect him to do all the actual work? Exactly how well do you think that's going to go down?"

Darren cackled. "He'll be fine. He's a big boy, your Phil is."

Couldn't argue with that one. I cast a fond glance over to where I'd last seen Phil, then spotted him ten feet further off, now having a natter with my mum and managing to look only mildly like he wished he was anywhere but there.

"You've got to talk to him about it," I said firmly. Phil was tighter with Darren than I was, so I was honestly surprised he'd come to me first.

"Way ahead of you, mate. Already have."

Oh. See what I mean? "And he's okay with it? And hang on, how did you know that was what I was going to say?"

"Tommy, darling," Gary said with a fond yet pitying glint in his eyes. "You're a man of many fine qualities, but caprice isn't one of them."

"Oi, are you saying I'm predictable? That's halfway to *boring*, that is." At least, I was fairly sure that was what he was saying, not having the opportunity right then to look up *caprice* in a dictionary. Well, ask the internet what it meant, or if the signal was dodgy, Phil. Same difference.

Gary gave me the puppy eyes and put a hand to his heart—the left hand, so his wedding ring would show up nicely, because with Gary, that was *never* going to get old. "Would I?"

"Anyhow," Darren put in heavily before I had a chance to make a comeback. "Are we gonna talk about my mate or what?"

"Fine, go ahead." I didn't roll my eyes because I was too busy glaring at Gary.

Darren puffed out his chest. "Okay, so I used to know her as Dinky Delilah, but these days she's going by Lilah Parrot."

"You used to know her as— So, uh, she's an ex-colleague?" I swallowed. Darren's a market trader these days, hawking fruit and veg in St. Albans every Wednesday and Saturday and who knows where the rest of the week, but in his younger days, he had an apparently flourishing career in the sphere of dwarf porn.

Any remarks as to what a small niche *that* had to be were likely to get the commenter a swift nut in the nadgers.

"Yeah, me and Lilah, we made some great films together." Darren gazed off into space with a fond smile.

"I never knew you did straight stuff," I said without thinking, then snuck a glance over at Gary. He didn't seem bothered, although I wasn't certain I'd have been so easygoing if Phil started getting all misty-eyed about his sex life with, say, the bloke he'd been married to before he met me, let alone any past acquaintances of the female persuasion.

Then again, for Darren, it really had been just sex, hadn't it? Not even that. Just work. I wondered if he'd had a bloke back then, and if said hypothetical bloke had minded what Darren got up to in the course of his nine-to-five. Gary, if anything, seemed proud of Darren's X-rated past, so maybe any significant others back then had been too? I tried to imagine being chuffed about Phil shagging other men for a living, and failed dismally.

"Course," Darren went on, and I forced my attention back to the here and now. "Lilah was strictly on the executive side by then. Never in front of the camera. Dunno why—she's still got it. Had plenty of offers, she has."

"Is she still in the business? What about the husband?" Maybe they'd got together on the job. In all senses of the phrase.

"She is. Has her own company now."

I had to wait to find out what line of business the husband was in, because at that moment I got collared by the photographer for wedding-party shots, meaning everyone in either a penguin suit or a floofy dress. These were swiftly followed by family shots. Followed by group shots. By the time the mini blonde dictator in the trouser suit finally let us finish saying *ecclesiastical*, because apparently *cheese* wasn't godly enough, my face had permanently seized up into a manic grin and my eyes were watering from forcing myself not to blink at the wrong moment.

I was trying to dab at them discreetly—wouldn't want people to think I was the soppy sort who cried at weddings—when Cherry grabbed me into a hug that nearly knocked my top hat off, looking none too dry-eyed herself. "Oh, Tom, isn't it all lovely?"

Well, at least she seemed to have forgiven me for my phone ringing. I patted her back awkwardly, public hugging not really being a Paretski-family thing. Course, she wasn't a Paretski any longer, was she? The lady currently sniffling into my wing collar was henceforth to be known as Mrs. Cherry Titmus.

It felt weird, thinking about her that way. I wasn't sure I liked it, but was still trying to get my head round why it made a difference what she called herself, when she pulled back and fixed me in the eye. "Now, promise me you'll look after Mum and Dad at the reception. And Mike, obviously." Mike Novak that was, being my *actual* dad and Mum's dirty little secret from thirty years ago. Cherry left a significant pause. "But not together."

They'd invited Mike along to ease him into family gatherings in advance of my wedding, which we'd be celebrating in a worryingly few months' time. Did I say *worryingly*? I meant *excitingly*. Course I did. But anyway, the point was, this was the first social gathering Mum, Dad, and Mike had all been together for since, well, *ever*. Far as I knew, Dad and Mike had never even met before. And I wasn't, to be honest, all that keen for them to meet now. I mean, how exactly do you introduce the bloke who raised you to the man his wife cheated on him with?

God knew how we were going to manage the photos at Phil's and my do. Or the seating plan for the reception.

Gretna Green was looking tastier by the minute.

CHAPTER THREE

reg and Cherry's reception, like every other social event they hosted, was held at the Old Deanery, which was where Greg, and from henceforth until death do them part, Cherry, lived barely a stone's throw away from the cathedral. Not that Greg—or, presumably, the bloke upstairs—would look kindly on anyone throwing stones near those stained-glass windows. It was a buffet affair, with chairs only for the most decrepit, which solved the who-to-seat-where problem nicely but meant it was less of a formal do and more of a free-for-all.

I finally got a chance to talk to Phil over a Buck's Fizz and some homemade quiche. Made, I hasten to add, not by my sister's fair hands or even Greg's, but by one of his army of widows and spinsters of this parish. Plus a good few married ladies who'd got fed up with waiting for him indoors to pop his clogs and got on with doing what they wanted anyway. They could usually be relied on for a tasty, if not very imaginative, spread.

"Did Darren speak to you?" Phil asked before I could get a word in edgewise.

"You mean about the runaway bridegroom? Yeah."

"Husband, not bridegroom. They got married over a year ago. So are we doing it?"

"What, here and now? Don't think it's that kind of party."

Phil huffed a laugh. "The mate's missing husband. And you know it."

I supposed that meant he was all right with it, but it still felt dodgy to me. "You sure it's okay? Misleading the lady about how we find the bloke—assuming we do find him?"

"From what Darren says, she wants to be misled. What's it matter so long as we get results? She'll get her old man back, we'll get paid, and she'll get to brag to her mates how a psychic found him for her."

"Great. Just what I need—even more people knowing about my little party trick." I'd have to admit I felt a minor sting of betrayal. Time was, Phil was as keen as I was to keep it all low-key.

Phil shrugged. "That ship's sailed. All you can do now is take a running jump on board. Get what you can out of it."

He had a point. "Guess I'm game if you are. Long as you don't mind playing second fiddle to my thing."

Phil raised an eyebrow but, sensibly given we were out in public, decided to ignore the innuendo. "Anything's better than another cheating-partner case."

I had to sympathise. Besides being a sad reflection on society in general and the sanctity of the marriage vows in particular, infidelity cases had to bring up a few painful memories for Phil. You might be forgiven for wondering why he'd become a private investigator in the first place, seeing as tail-the-spouse jobs seem to be your basic bread and butter for people in his profession, but then you probably aren't as well acquainted as I am with the stubborn git who's my beloved.

"Fine. Tell Darren he can set up a meeting with the client. But, oi, you've gotta be there too. Not my area of expertise, this."

"Don't worry, I'll be there to hold your hand."

I could think of something I'd rather he'd be holding, but right then old Edie Penrose doddered up to say a quavery hello and I never got to tell him about it.

There were speeches—Dad mumbled something rambly and incomprehensible, then Greg said something touching and heartfelt that had Cherry blushing bright pink and the rest of us staring into our glasses, equal parts moved and embarrassed. And just when we were bracing ourselves for a speech from the best man, who was one of those tall, pale Church of England types I mentioned earlier and who looked like he could bore for England, the bishop stepped up. *His* speech was so polished he could have gone on the after-dinner circuit with it—actually, come to think of it, maybe that was where Greg and Cherry had found him. He had us all in fits with a short selection of hilarious but inoffensive ecclesiastical anecdotes and topped it off with a hearty toast, and an invitation for the happy couple to cut the cake.

There were two wedding cakes—a traditional fruit one, because you could get a shedload of little slices out of it, plus a croquembouche, one of those gravity-defying towers of profiteroles they like to make them do on *Bake Off*, for the photos and the favoured few. (And yes, since you ask, I was one of them.) Apparently Greg had been to a wedding in France at an impressionable age and never quite got over it. Not that I'm complaining. It was well tasty.

Soon after that it was time to say goodbye to the bride and groom, and we all trooped outside to wave them off in a taxi. Greg and Cherry had not only chosen a winter wedding, they'd decided for some incomprehensible reason to honeymoon in Scotland. In February. Hopefully they'd packed their skis. And their thermal undies, which had to be a bit of a mood-killer on honeymoon. I'd mentioned as much to Phil a while back, with a heavy hint I'd want us to be looking for somewhere a lot warmer for our own postwedding getaway.

"Somewhere you get blue sky more than once a summer. Where . . . where lemons grow on trees. I can't remember the last time I saw a lemon on a tree, instead of in a tray in the supermarket."

Phil had pointed out that the average honeymooning couple had other things on their minds than the ready availability of freshly picked citrus fruit, and outdoor temperature was unlikely to be an issue either.

He was probably right, I reflected with a last wave at the happy couple. I was pretty certain that Sis at least had been saving herself for her wedding night. Much as it pained me to think about it, all those decades' worth of pent-up passion wasn't likely to be deterred by anything short of a tungsten carbide chastity belt.

I shuddered. Enough of that, ta very much. Time to worry about more pressing concerns, like where the hell had Mike got to?

A lot of the guests toddled off after the hosts had gone. Fair dues, many of them were already out past their bedtime, it being well after teatime and them not exactly in the first flush of youth or even middle age. Close family, however, got to stay and help clear up the mess. And Mike was staying with me—I mean, with me and Phil—so I knew he hadn't gone anywhere.

Or rather, he *shouldn't* have gone anywhere. But he wasn't in the front room, the back room, the kitchen, or the loo. And neither was Dad.

I was starting to get a bad feeling about this.

CHAPTER FOUR

After poking my head around upstairs, a bit warily as if anyone would be rude enough to sneak into Greg's holy of holies for an illicit nap or heavy petting session (and bloody hell, I was never going to get the picture of Dad and Mike in the latter scenario out of my head), I looked in the study. Strictly speaking, it was supposed to be out of bounds for the duration, as most of Greg's "family" of taxidermied animals had been moved into there to prevent any smaller guests from getting too handsy or trying to feed them wedding cake.

So of course, that was where Dad and Mike turned out to be hiding out.

Together.

Nestled in with Buster the dog, Greg's surprisingly large badger, and sundry other woodland creatures who'd probably never imagined themselves ending up so far from home, Mike and Dad were comfortably settled on office chairs holding half-drunk mugs of tea. Talking about something that involved a lot of vigorous hand-waving on Dad's part.

Oh crap.

I was wondering whether I should break it up or steer well clear, but Dad spotted me and waved me over with his gesturing hand. It was the one holding a half-eaten custard cream, and a couple of crumbs fell off onto the carpet. I glanced automatically at Buster, being used to mates' dogs acting as impromptu hoovers, then remembered he was already stuffed. "There you are, Tom. We were just talking about you."

Oh double crap.

Mike nodded seriously. "Yes. Gerald tells me you don't plan to dress up for your own wedding."

They were on first-name terms already? I s'pose it wasn't like they didn't have anything in common . . . I shuddered internally and squashed that line of thought pronto. "I'll be wearing a suit."

"But not the top hat and the tail coat?" He waved at my current ensemble, in a gesture unsettlingly like Dad's.

"Uh, no?"

"But why not?" Dad demanded, and turned to Mike. "I haven't seen him look this smart since he was five years old—he was a page boy back then, at his cousin Robin's wedding. Or was it my cousin Hilary? Barbara would know. Tom, see if you can find Barbara, will you? No, wait, don't bother, I remember now. It was my godson George's wedding. You had a paisley waistcoat and bow tie. Quite the little gentleman, you were. I hardly recognised you. Until you ate too much cake and were sick all down yourself. So why not?"

"Why not what?" My head felt like someone had used it to smash open a bottle of champagne.

Dad rolled his eyes at Mike. "Morning coat. Top hat. Why not?"

"Uh . . . It's not a church wedding. Wouldn't be suitable. Gotta go."

I legged it.

I found Mum rearranging vol-au-vents with some of Greg's cathedral ladies, mixing in the chicken mayo ones with what was left of the more popular prawn cocktails ones. "Don't go in the study," I warned her. "Dad and Mike are in there. Conspiring."

Mum's face, which had been a rosy prawn-cocktail colour, paled to a chicken mayo hue. She swallowed. Then she straightened her back and pasted on a smile. "It's good that they're getting on together. It'll make things easier for the summer. I've been meaning to ask you, actually. I know neither of you is really the bride, but seeing as Phil's father is no longer with us, I assume you'll be the one who's given away?"

"What, like an unwanted Christmas present? Cheers, Mum. No. I'm pretty sure no one's getting given away."

"Oh. Well I suppose that does make it simpler. It's such a shame, though."

"It is?"

"Well, I suppose you won't have any bridesmaids either. The wedding party is going to look awfully funereal, all men in dark suits."

Great, Mum. Way to imbue my forthcoming nuptials with a sense of gloom and foreboding. "Yeah, but you'll brighten it up, won't you? I mean, you'll be wanting to wear this again, right?" I gestured down at her burgundy mother-of-the-bride outfit, which had probably accounted for a sizeable portion of the wedding budget all on its own.

"Oh, no. I couldn't wear this again. Besides, this was for a cathedral wedding."

Uh-huh. "So what, it's going to be jeans and a T-shirt for me and Phil's bash?"

"Don't be silly, Tom. I never wear jeans. Or T-shirts. I'll find a smart skirt and top."

The way she said it, I wondered where she'd be looking. The darkest recesses of her wardrobe? A car boot sale? "It'll be July, Mum. You should get yourself a posh summer frock."

Mum frowned at the vol-au-vents. "Are you sure? It's not like it's a . . ." She paused.

I bristled. "What, a *proper* wedding?"

"Church wedding, I was going to say. Do people dress up for civil ceremonies?"

"Are you telling me you've never been to one before? Haven't you got, like, mates who've divorced and remarried?"

"In my day, you got married for life."

Didn't stop you having a bit on the side, though. I didn't say it, because I'm only literally a bastard, but Mum turned as red as her outfit anyhow as if the thought had crossed her mind too. I coughed. "Mum, it's the twenty-first century. People wear what they want. And seriously, you and Dad need to have a chat about this. He seems to think we're going to be tarted up like the House of Lords. And he's got Mike agreeing with him."

"Oh." Mum looked faintly queasy, then rallied. "Well, it *would* be nice to have a new dress. And perhaps a hat."

Great. Apparently I was going to be shoehorned back into the penguin suit whether I liked it or not.

I broke the bad news to Phil over a last glass of bubbly (for me, not him, as he was the one driving today). He took it like a man who'd had Darren and Gary bending his ear about it already, which was rich seeing as how they'd worn normal clothes to their own do. "The idea's growing on me," he said, giving me an appreciative once-over, and if he kept that up, it wouldn't be the only thing that was growing. "So it's all happy families now, is it?" he went on. "Water under the bridge?"

"Dunno. I didn't dare ask." I glared at his expression. "Like you'd have been any braver."

He laughed. "Maybe not."

"Anyway, don't change the subject. Are you seriously okay with all of this?" I gestured up and down at my over-the-top attire, then frowned. "What did you wear first go around?"

"Just a suit." Phil's face cut off any further questions on that thorny subject. He never seemed keen to talk about his first husband, the Mysterious Mark, who'd cheated on him, hurt him, then as if that wasn't enough, died on him. Fair dues, it wasn't exactly my favourite subject either. Then he heaved a sigh. "Look, I'd better warn you, Mum's going to be comparing. So yeah, anything that makes our do different—better—it's got to be a good thing."

I wasn't so sure I liked the idea of what I wore on my wedding day being dictated by my fiancé's ex. Then again, it was being dictated by every other bugger, so maybe it was only fair to give the dead bloke a shout and all. "Right. Fine. Tell you what, how about we cut our losses and take Mike home?"

Mike seemed worn out by all the excitement. He didn't say a lot on the drive back to my house. Sorry, mine and Phil's. We'd been living together for a whole week now, me and Phil, and I still found myself forgetting.

Originally, the plan had been for him to move into mine in time for Christmas, but like a lot of plans, that one had ganged well agley. My fault more than his, and don't think *that* hadn't led to a few uncomfortable conversations.

It wasn't that I'd been getting cold feet, honest. We'd agreed he'd hold off giving notice at his flat until I'd got the house cleared out a bit, Phil's wardrobe being (a) substantial and (b) not exactly the sort that'd take kindly to being kept in suitcases long-term. And then, well,

I'd been busy—with Cherry's wedding preparations, with our own wedding preparations, and occasionally even with actual paid work. So we'd pushed the date back to January, and then of course it'd been tax-return season. For me, that was, seeing as Phil had naturally got his sent in back in September, the smug git. I gave up expecting sympathy while I faffed about with shoeboxes full of invoices and receipts, fielding increasingly frustrated calls from my accountant about badly described business expenses dated over eighteen months ago.

I finally got it all sorted a couple of days before the thirty-first January deadline, which was when Phil informed me that he'd given notice a month ago and would be moving in the following weekend whether the house—and me—were ready for him or not.

I might or might not have had a few choice words to say at this point on the subject of unilateral decision-making.

But the make-up sex was worth it. And, a week in, while I might have the odd moan about him beating me to the bathroom in the morning, I had no real complaints about the new living arrangements. He'd been staying at mine most nights anyhow, so to be honest the only real difference was the amount of stuff in the house.

For a bloke who'd been living in a small attic flat, my Phil had a *lot* of stuff. Maybe it'd seem less once we got it all out of the boxes, which were currently stacked in the living room (the ones we were definitely going to unpack any day now), the hallway (the ones we were thinking about taking upstairs and hadn't got round to yet) and our bedroom (the ones we didn't have a flippin' clue what to do with, like duplicated kitchen equipment and entertainment tech. They *had* been in the spare room, but it hadn't seemed polite to ask Mike to stay in a bed he couldn't actually get to without some serious mountaineering gear, whereas Phil was surprisingly un-put-out by having to climb all over me to get to his side of the bed). The cats were torn between appreciating the new sleeping and lurking places (mostly Arthur), and having a paddy over the unprecedented changes to their home environment (mostly, but not exclusively, Merlin).

Happy days.

Mike announced he was turning in soon after we got back from Greg's, probably worn out from all that ganging up on me with my dad. He'd travelled up the day before, and we'd spent the previous evening making polite conversation and passing round the family photo albums—or, as might be, Mike's phone and the new, turbo-charged laptop Phil had given me for Christmas, onto which I'd loaded a choice selection of pics of yours truly as a nipper, just on the off chance Mike might want copies. He had, as it happened, which . . . I dunno. I s'pose I still had mixed feelings about him having known from the word go that I existed, but never having got in touch. Maybe it was an older-generation thing—thinking a clean break was best for me and all that.

I mean, he was here now, wasn't he? So he definitely cared about me.

It made for a funny old weekend, having Mike there. His presence, welcome as it was, definitely put a dampener on anything bedroom related. And while I felt strange talking to him about his family—the legitimate son and all—it didn't seem right constantly interrogating him on the subject of my newly discovered Polish heritage.

Luckily I'm also half British, so was able to fall back on the weather, the England football team, and the state of the NHS as conversational topics.

We took him out for a Sunday roast at the Fighting Cocks, then put him on a train back west. Then it was time to start shifting all the boxes back into the spare room.

"When are we going to chuck out your old hi-fi?" Phil asked as, mission accomplished, we sat down on the sofa in front of the telly to enjoy a well-earned beer.

"What do you mean? There's nothing wrong with it."

"Apart from being ten years old? I got mine less than a year ago. And it's half the size. Doesn't make sense for it to be the one sitting in a box."

"Mine was here first." Okay, I do realise that wasn't the most mature argument I could have made.

"And it's your house, your rules?" Phil said it so mildly there was a moment when I actually didn't realise the big, deep pool of man-eating sharks I was hanging over by a thread that was fraying by the second.

"Course not!" I said—possibly a bit too heartily—once I'd clued in. "It's our house, now, innit?"

Phil laughed, the bastard. "Nice save. So I'll be getting my music system out of storage, then?"

I eyed my trusty old hi-fi sadly. It *was* looking a touch out-of-date these days, and at least this way I could stop feeling guilty about the dust piling up on top (and yes, I'm fully aware there was another potential solution, but trust me, it was never going to happen). "Fine," I said in an appropriately martyred voice. "But we're not chucking it out. What if, I dunno, your one breaks down?"

"Thought we'd make our own entertainment," Phil said with a smirk. "In fact, why don't we do that now?"

"Okay, you put the kettle on, and I'll get out the Scrabble."

Phil grabbed hold of me and started making his own entertainment there and then. And yes, there was a fair amount of knob-twiddling involved.

He'd known I wasn't serious about tea and Scrabble. For one thing, my lack of enthusiasm for the game has been pretty clear since that time I got thrashed by him, Gary, and Darren over at their place, mostly because they knew all the obscure, high-scoring words and I didn't. And for another thing, neither of us owns a set.

CHAPTER FIVE

Darren brought his old mate over to see us at my house a few evenings later.

Our house, I mean. Mine and Phil's.

Due to a failure in communication, me and Phil both went to answer the door, so when I opened it, we were side by side like we were practising for the receiving line at our wedding. Darren gave us a nod, clearly acknowledging the honour but disappointed at the lack of any red carpets being rolled out. "All right, lads?"

Standing next to Darren was a lady half a head shorter than him and about low-chest level on me, which I reckoned made her around four foot four. It was weird seeing Darren (a) without Gary in tow and (b) escorting someone smaller than he was. It made me feel all unnecessarily tall and loom-y, and trust me, that's not a feeling I get very often. Of course, with his confident swagger—which somehow he managed to pull off while standing still, don't ask me how—Darren always seemed a couple of feet taller than his actual height.

He turned to his companion. "Lilah, babe, this is Tom Paretski. And Phil Morrison," he added as an afterthought, which was a turn up for the books. Usually I was the afterthought where Darren was concerned.

"Charmed, I'm sure," she said with a cat-like smile.

I could see why Lilah Parrot had gone for a career in adult entertainment. Her plain V-necked T-shirt showed off her ample cleavage, and her skintight jeans hugged her full hips like they'd been made for her, which maybe they had—with her proportions, she'd struggle to get her kit on the high street. Tanned and with long, expertly bleached and straightened hair, she gave off sex appeal so strong even I could feel it—I mean, I've never fancied going to bed with a woman in my life, but meeting the luscious Lilah, I could suddenly imagine how, if I was single and she came onto me, I might be tempted to try switching sides for the duration.

It was unnerving, to be honest. Was this how married blokes in denial felt when they had a midlife crisis and realised they actually preferred blokes? I sneaked a glance at Phil, and was relieved to find he was still the one who revved my engine.

From what Darren had said about knowing her way back when, I'd assumed she'd be around his age, early forties maybe, but if she was, she was wearing it well. Her makeup, which was also expertly done, was eye-catching rather than subtle, and accentuated the vivid blue of her eyes, which were large and beautiful.

And staring straight at me with more than a hint of *Is he all there?*

Right. Words. Words would be good. "It's, uh, nice to meet you, Mrs. Parrot," I said, thrusting out a hand and narrowly missing whacking her on one well-rounded boob. "Come on in."

Her handshake was more of a squeeze. "Gawd, your mum brought you up proper, didn't she? Call me Lilah, love. We're all friends here, ain't we?" She gave her cowboy boots a good old scrub on the doormat, rather than the dainty shuffle a lot of women do, as if they'd be mortified if any grot actually came off their shoes.

"Lilah, then. And I'm Tom. Fancy a cup of tea?" I asked, because she wasn't wrong about my mum bringing me up proper.

"You're a lifesaver. I'm gasping, here. Just a dash of milk, please. No sugar." A woman after my own heart.

"Phil? Darren?" They both nodded. I let Phil show our guests to the living room and went out to the kitchen to flick the kettle on and get out some proper cups and saucers. Not because my mum brought me up to (although she did) but because according to Phil, you can tell a lot about a client from whether or not they rattle the cup in the saucer. Then I shook out some choccy biccies onto a plate, remembered Darren was with us and doubled the quantity, and was in the living room with the tray in a jiffy.

"Here you go, love," I said, handing Lilah her cup. Phil had got her and Darren settled on the sofa and was sitting back, fingers steepled in that *I'm about to listen intelligently, see me pointing at my brains with both hands* way.

She took the cup with nary a rattle. I doled out the rest of the cups, turfed a protesting Arthur out of the remaining armchair, and sat down.

Nobody took a choccy biccie, except Darren, who took the whole plate and sat back, munching happily. He obviously felt he'd done his bit by bringing her here and the rest was up to us.

Phil grabbed his notepad and flicked it open. "Right, Mrs. Parrot, in your own time, would you like to tell us what happened?"

Lilah arched a perfectly formed eyebrow. Any minute now she'd tell me she was here to see the organ grinder, not the monkey, and things really would go pear-shaped.

"Uh, Phil's best with all the routine stuff," I said quickly.

She took a delicate sip of tea. Still no rattle. "Like I told Darren, it's about my husband, Jonathan. He's buggered off."

"How long's he been gone?" Phil asked.

"Nine days." That was pretty precise, none of your waffling about whether it was last Tuesday or Wednesday, and for that matter, not a lot of hair-tearing, either. "I got home one day and he'd scarpered."

"Did he leave a note?"

She shook her head.

"Take much with him?"

Lilah paused, then let out a long breath. "He took a bag. Not a big one, mind. Only a few casual clothes. None of his nice suits." She seemed miffed about that. I deduced they'd been a present from her.

Heh. Maybe I was cut out for this detective business, after all.

"And what about his place of work?" Phil asked.

"Well, he wasn't going to carry on turning up there, was he? He worked at my sister's place," she explained at our blank looks. "It's an antiques showroom not far from where we live. The Old Smithy."

If I had a pound for every place around here called "The Old" something or other . . . I still couldn't afford to shop in them. At least it wasn't Ye Olde.

"And where's that?" Phil bored on. In the drilling sense, I mean. Not the can't-keep-my-eyes-open sense.

"Pluck's End." Lilah grinned. "The posh bit."

You had to warm to the way she said it. Like she was dead chuffed she'd made it far enough to buy a house somewhere upmarket.

If Phil was warming to her, he hid it well. "And have you spoken to your sister about it? Has she got any idea why he might have left home?"

"Oh, I know why he left." She humphed. "Got fed up with the straight life, didn't he?"

Phil's nose twitched at that one. "He'd been in trouble with the law before you knew him?"

"What, my Jonny?" She snorted. "He ain't *that* sort of bent."

My cup rattled loudly in its saucer. All of them turned to frown at me. "Sorry," I said, and flashed a smile that didn't seem to work on anyone.

Mind you, my Phil's got a great poker face. "He had same-sex relationships before you knew him?" He waited for her nod. "What makes you think he's gone looking for that kind of thing again?"

Her lips tightened. "There's been plenty of evidence, believe me."

"So why do you want him found?" I blurted out.

She turned her big, lovely eyes on me. "I miss him."

Poor girl. "How long have you two been married?"

"It'll be two years in August."

That was optimistic of her, in the circs. Then again, it'd be hard to divorce the bloke if she couldn't find him.

"And the kids want their dad back," she added.

"You've got kids?" I let out in unwary surprise.

Lilah's chin came up. "Yeah, I got kids. What you saying? You saying I can't be a good mum and work in porn?"

"Course not," I said quickly. "Just impressed how you've managed to keep your figure looking so good."

She cackled. "Oh, I like you."

Phil coughed. "So have you any idea where he might have gone? Old friends, lovers . . ."

She dismissed his question with an eye roll, and turned pointedly to me. "Oh, I know exactly where he is. I just need you to find him for me."

I blinked. "Come again?"

"Know where I met him? Camden Market, working one of the stalls. That's where he'll have run back to, if I know my Jonny-boy."

"So, uh, why don't you . . .?"

She sent me a withering look. "You ever been to Camden Market? Like the Mines of bleedin' Moria, that place is."

I blinked. Somehow, despite the background in film, she was the last person I'd expected to reference *Lord of the Rings*. Wasn't it a bit, uh, stereotypical about dwarves?

"*Pan's* effing *Labyrinth*," she went on. "You could hide a bloody elephant down there. If I set one foot in that place, he'll hear about it and he'll scarper. They're well tight, that lot, and look at me. Come on, look at me. Think I'm going to get away without being recognised? I can put on a wig, but I can't do nothing about my height, now can I? 'Sides, half of 'em know me from when me and Jonny was first going out. Or professionally." She gave another catlike smile.

Phil coughed. "So you want someone who'll be able to get close to your husband without arousing his suspicions. What then?"

Lilah flashed him a frown, as if she reckoned the monkey was getting above his station, and then switched the smile back on when she turned to me. "You give him a letter from me. Something physical. Something he can't press a button and delete."

Uh-*huh*. "Divorce papers, is it? Court summons?" *Threats of actual bodily harm?* I didn't say the last one out loud, obviously.

Her eyes went very wide. "Course not. Just a little note to tell him I miss him and want him to come home."

"You tried texting?"

"He ain't answering. He took his phone with him, but for all I know he dropped it down the toilet first chance he got." Again with the miffed expression, suggesting that'd been another token of her affection. I was surprised someone with all her personal charms felt the need to keep buying the bloke presents, but maybe she was the generous sort. I mentally added ten percent to the hourly rate I was planning to quote her.

Then I took it back off again, feeling bad about taking advantage of an abandoned wife.

"Email? Messenger?" Phil asked.

Lilah leaned forward in her chair, a move which made her cleavage even more prominent than it had been already.

Not that I noticed. Obviously.

"I've tried everything," she said, and added a pout I reckoned would have any straight or bi bloke adjusting himself in his trousers.

Was it me or was it getting flippin' hot in here? I'd have to have a look at that thermostat after she'd gone. I loosened my collar with a finger. "Right. Well. S'pose we'll see what we can do?" I glanced over at Phil for confirmation, and narrowed my eyes at his smirk.

"Did you bring the letter with you?" he asked.

She pulled a brown envelope out of her bag and handed it to me. It was the sort you could get an A4 sheet of paper in if you folded it double, and was fat enough there must have been at least a dozen sheets in there. Little note, my arse. It was sealed up with heavy-duty sticky tape, just in case me and Phil might have had any ideas about steaming it open.

"And photographs of your husband? To make sure Tom knows he's found the right bloke? Like you say, there could be any number of people hiding out in the market. Wouldn't want him to deliver the letter to the wrong man."

Another envelope, this one unsealed. I peeked inside, then spread the contents out on the coffee table. There were half a dozen photos, including one of what must have been the two of them on their wedding day. Lilah was radiant and anything but innocent in a tight white dress, carrying a bouquet of big, papery red flowers, while Jonny-boy stared at the camera with a shell-shocked expression on his mug.

Mind you, that could be in a good way, couldn't it? After all, he was . . . Well, all I could think of to say about him was that he looked like any other ordinary white bloke you might meet on the street or down the pub. In his late twenties or early thirties, not unattractive but not model standard either, and about my height, at a guess.

It was a bit of a mystery what Lilah had seen in him, to be honest. Still, they say love is blind.

I snuck another glance over at Phil, but he was busy studying the photos.

Darren shifted in his seat. He'd been uncharacteristically quiet up until now. I checked out the biccie plate. Yep, all gone. "What kind of stall was he working on when you met him, love?" he asked.

Huh. I'd have thought he'd have known already. If they were as close mates as all that.

"Old clothes." Lilah wrinkled her nose. "That's why I got him that job with my sister. Right up his street, wasn't it? Selling old junk."

The way she said it made me wonder how much say Jonny-boy had had in the matter. And how grateful he'd been. Something about her expression hinted that he hadn't been as grateful as she might have liked.

Or maybe it was his stock in trade she wasn't impressed by. Definitely one for the finer things in life, Lilah was, and I didn't reckon anything with a previous owner counted as *fine* in her view.

Darren was nodding. "Was he the trader?"

Lilah shrugged. "It wasn't his business, if that's what you mean. He was working it for this other bloke."

Phil pricked up his ears like a Rottweiler who'd just heard the sweet sound of a burglar climbing over the fence. "And his name?"

"Kelvin something." She said it impatiently and turned straight back to me. "Look, I brung a map so you can do your stuff."

"My stuff?"

"Yeah, you know. Hocus pocus, Avada Kedavra, what the bleedin' hell ever. Here you go."

Phil stood up and flashed me an evil grin. "I'll get your pendant for you."

Oh, bloody hell.

CHAPTER SIX

I had, actually, got a dowsing pendant, although not by choice. Cherry gave it to me, probably as an attempt to make up for years of lack of support of my *thing*, as she put it. It was a couple of inches tall and made up of slices of crystal in rainbow colours—allegedly to represent the chakras, but if you ask me, it was just her trying to kill two birds with one lump of brightly coloured stone when it came to gestures of sisterly solidarity.

Me and Phil had mostly been using it to play with the cats, not that they were any more impressed with its mystical properties than I'd been. When Phil brought it over, I noticed the purple stripe— amethyst, I think—had faded a bit. If I'd believed in all the chakra stuff, I might have been worried, but luckily I'd had the foresight to preserve my ignorance on matters spiritual.

Lilah pulled out a much-folded A4 sheet, clearly a computer printout, which had on it a sketchy map of the sprawling markets of Camden Town from some tourist website, and smoothed it flat on the coffee table. "Does it matter if it ain't to scale?" She sounded anxious.

Like she actually believed this ought to work, God help her.

I flashed Phil a dirty look as he handed me my pendant. If he was expecting me to put on a show and fake a communication with the spirit world, he was going to be in for a disappointment. I don't like deceiving people.

Still, there was always the off-chance this might be the one-in-a-million time my *thing* would decide to play along, so I angled my dangle, tried to clear my mind, and *listened*.

I got some strong vibes straightaway—but they were coming from that sealed envelope of Lilah's. Big surprise there. I did the psychic equivalent of shoving my fingers in my ears, and turned to Phil. "Can you shift that? It's interfering." I nodded to the offending article.

Lilah leaned forward, her mouth slightly open and her eyes dark and gleaming. "Does that mean it's working?"

"Uh, kind of. Just need to hang on a mo."

We all waited while Phil strode off. I heard the front door open, a car door slam, and then the front door closed again.

That's my Phil for you. You ask him to shift something, he shifts it. Right. Time to get on with the dog and pony show. I held the pendant over the centre of the map, which was trying to fold itself up again already. Great. Even printer paper knew this was a load of bollocks.

I *listened* some more, conscious of Phil tiptoeing back into the room. Well, not literally, but there was a definite air of trying not to break my concentration, assuming I had any to start with. Phil always reckoned I was sabotaging myself by not believing, like I subconsciously talked myself into half-arsing it, but this time I gave it my best shot. I focussed on the pics of Jonny-boy, still spread out next to the map, and tried to really feel it—guilty ran-out-on-the-missus vibes and all.

Nothing.

Out of the corner of my eye, I saw Merlin's ears prick up. Maybe I should ask him to have a go.

How long were they expecting me to keep on with the show? I shot Phil a worried glance, hoping he could somehow convey to me, maybe by eyebrow twitches, whether I should just pretend to find something.

And I'd probably better do it soon. Merlin, the little sod, had hunched down in his best imma-stalk-you-now posture, pupils blown and tail aquiver, clearly under the impression this was all a game and he was about to run off with the prize.

Phil coughed and broke the silence, thank God. "Have you got anything that belongs to him? Sometimes personal possessions can help Tom get a reading."

Lilah's face fell. "Sorry. Didn't think of that."

In the nick of time, I bunged the pendant in my pocket. Merlin expressed his feelings with his usual eloquence by settling down to lick his bum in my direction.

"I'll tell you what, then," I said. "Why don't we make another appointment, and you can bring something of his along then?"

She nodded earnestly. "What do you want me to bring?"

"Uh, clothes or jewellery are usually best. Personal stuff. Worn next to the skin if possible." This part was actually true, although don't ask me why.

"Got it. No problem." She got down from her seat and stretched out a hand to me. "I'll be in touch."

Just as she and Darren were about to go, I thought of something else. "Mind if I ask another question, love? Uh, it's not strictly related . . ."

"Ask away. Long as it'll bring my Jonny back."

"Uh . . . those papery flowers in your wedding pics, what are they?"

"Them? They're peonies."

"Yeah? I never knew you could get them in red. Ta."

She gave me a funny look and left, taking Darren with her.

After the door had closed behind them, Phil gave me an even funnier look. "Seriously? Flowers? Sure you don't want to ask her for makeup tips as well?"

"Oi, I was thinking about the wedding. Yours and mine. You were saying you hated pastel colours for the flowers."

"And you don't reckon it might be a bad omen, choosing the same flowers as a couple where the husband's gone missing?"

"So we're believing in omens now, are we?" I gave him a friendly dig in the ribs. "Better watch out Merlin never crosses your path, then. That's supposed to be well unlucky. Course, it could be difficult to avoid what with you and him living together and all."

Phil huffed a laugh. "Thought I was living with you, not the bloody cats."

"Nah, ain't you heard? Bestiality's best, boys."

"That explains the dirty looks Merlin's been giving you, then."

"That's 'cos I took his toy away. And no, I don't mean my dick." I shuddered. "With those claws? My balls are trying to climb back inside just thinking about it."

Phil smirked. "Want me to kiss them better?"

"Well, *technically* nothing's happened to them yet . . ." I leaned back against the wall and gave him a once-over with the old bedroom eyes.

Never one to be backward in coming forward, Phil said, "We'll have to see about that, then," and did.

Later, when certain portions of me had been thoroughly taken care of, I lay in Phil's arms on the sofa. "Why do you think Lilah came to us? Well, me, I suppose. I mean, all she really wants is a flippin' courier service."

Phil shrugged. As I was lying on top of him, it felt like a very small, localised earthquake. I suddenly sympathised with how the cats must feel when the nice warm lap they're sitting on shifts. Being better brought up than them, though, I didn't dig in any claws to complain. "All about the glamour, isn't she?" he said.

"You calling me glamorous? Seriously? Maybe I should stop wearing the heels and the feather boa to work."

He huffed. "Look it up in a dictionary sometime. It's not only used to describe drag queens."

"Oi, I know what the word means. I'm not a *Sun* reader."

"Just like the pictures, do you?"

"Yeah, right. Because topless Page 3 totty is so my thing."

"You seemed keen enough to ogle the client earlier." Phil gave me a hard stare.

"I didn't ogle Lilah. Although mind you, she is a very attractive woman—"

"I'll show you attractive."

Things degenerated a bit after that. Fun times.

I did look *glamour* up, later, when Phil wasn't watching. Only I did it on the internet, because who uses an actual dictionary anymore? And all right, I hadn't known it could mean *magic*, which is what ye olde peasant folk would probably have called my gift for finding things. If they weren't too busy ducking me in a pond and then burning me at the stake, presumably after a suitable interval to dry off first.

It made a sort of sense—after all, people get, well, bewitched, I suppose you'd say, by someone glamorous, don't they? Why else would all those celebrity gossip magazines get sold week in, week out?

And by the same token, anything with a whiff of magic about it was . . . enticing, I guess? Made me feel weird, thinking about it. I mean, I haven't got self-esteem issues or any of that guff, but I'm just your average bloke. Well, give or take a dodgy hip and an annoying extra sense.

Nah. It was all bollocks. Darren must have talked her into it, thinking he was doing us a favour.

I looked up peonies too, while the laptop had a full head of steam going. There was this website that had all the meanings of the flowers, and I felt totally vindicated when I saw what they had down for peonies: *happy marriage*, and—get this—*gay life*.

Also *shame*, but hey, two out of three ain't bad.

CHAPTER SEVEN

The only thing of note that happened over the next couple of days was Darren dropping off a copy of one of Lilah's old movies, back from when she'd still been acting. I thanked him politely and set it aside to go *What the hell?* about to Phil when he got home.

Oh, and a postcard from Scotland turned up. It was warped from where Cherry had posted it in the rain, and it didn't say a right lot apart from *having a lovely time* and other clichés. She didn't end it with *Wish you were here*, so I deduced the honeymoon was going okay.

The photo on the front was of a malt whisky distillery, so chances were, it was.

"Do you think Gary and Darren watch straight porn?" I asked as I bunged the DVD in the player late that evening.

Phil gave me a look. "You really want to know about their sex life?"

"Not as such, no. What's disturbing me now is that from the sound of things, you *do* know about it."

He smirked. "Darren's the sharing sort."

"Oi, I hope there's limits to what you go sharing with him." I *knew* him and Darren getting chummy was going to come back and bite me on the bum. And there was an image I could have done without.

"Don't you worry. Forsaking all others, remember?" Phil put his arm around me from behind and pulled me back onto the sofa.

I was about to go all mushy, when a thought occurred. "Yeah, but you haven't actually made that vow yet."

"No harm in practising. Are we going to watch this film?"

"Getting all eager, are you?" I hit Play.

The opening scenes were . . . not what I'd expected. For a start, there were two blokes in bed—in a hotel room, supposedly—getting it on with no Lilah in sight.

"You think he gave us the right DVD?" I asked, as one of the blokes went down on the other. "Not that I'm complaining, mind."

They weren't bad looking, and the sight of all that bare male flesh getting up close and personal was beginning to have predictable results. I adjusted myself in my jeans, not bothering to be subtle, in the hopes Phil might take it as a hint.

He just carried on watching, the git. There was another five minutes or so of guy-on-guy action, by which time even Phil was showing signs of feeling a little hot under the collar—and then the door flew open.

On screen, I mean. Not our actual door.

A younger, fresher Lilah stood there in the doorway, hip cocked. She was wearing what must literally have been the world's shortest French maid's outfit. "Room service," she called seductively, and closed the door behind her. The blokes on the bed stopped what they were doing and sent her a come-hither look.

I hit Stop. "Right, I can guess where it goes from here."

Phil smirked. "You can't catch being straight by watching it, you know."

"Yeah, but it's . . . I dunno. Disrespectful. She's a client."

"So if she was a singer, you wouldn't listen to her CDs?"

"That's different."

"Why?"

"She probably wouldn't be getting her kit off, for a start." I thought about it. "Not that you'd know from a CD. Maybe it's like newsreaders not bothering to wear trousers."

Great. Now I wasn't going to be able to listen to anything without picturing the artists letting it all hang out in the studio. Course, with some of them, that'd be a bonus . . .

"So you're saying anyone who gets naked for a living ought to be ashamed of it?" Phil asked. I could practically see his hackles rising, presumably on Darren's behalf.

Sod it. "No, I'm saying having a stiffie while watching our client in a porno is going to make it flippin' hard—pun *not* intended—to look her in the eye next time we see her, that's all."

Phil smirked. "There's ways round that."

"Oh yeah?"

"I could give you a hand. Get rid of the problem right now."

In the event, he gave me more than a hand. And we never did get around to watching the rest of that movie.

I needn't have worried about the whole looking-Lilah-in-the-eye thing, not in the short term at any rate. She never turned up for her next appointment, which seemed a strong argument in favour of her not having been quite as into all the mystic mumbo-jumbo as Phil had reckoned. Either that, or she'd loved the idea but been less than impressed by the reality, which I could hardly fault her for.

She still sent Jonny-boy's personal items along the Friday after we saw her, so she must have had some faith in me. They came courtesy of Darren, who I reckoned I must've seen more of over the last couple of days than his own husband had. Fortunately this was only a flying visit. The thought of Gary getting it into his head I was trying to poach on his property was as alarming as it was surreal. Although given the number of hints he'd dropped about a foursome . . . Nah, *alarming* was definitely winning here.

Darren reckoned Lilah was having problems with her kids or something. Maybe the babysitter had stood her up. You get a mix of feelings at a time like this. First off, I was relieved, seeing as it saved me from having to pretend all Phil's painstakingly researched information was wafting to me over the ether or being communicated by my nonexistent spirit guide. Then I felt bad about it, 'cos for all I knew the problems with the kids might be serious. Then again, they might not, so I also felt let down, like she'd had her fun and now she was bored with this particular trick pony. Except, it wasn't like I'd enjoyed all the jumping through hoops and whatnot, which brought me back to relief.

Then I decided it was time I got over it and got on with opening Lilah's package.

It was in one of those mailing boxes they sell you at the post office. I always wondered who bought those, when you could get perfectly good cardboard boxes free from any supermarket. I unwrapped it warily, a bit dubious over what Lilah might have seen fit to hand over. After all, I'd asked for stuff he'd worn next to his skin . . . I needn't have worried. She'd parcelled up a couple of worn T-shirts with faded logos, which were just about ideal for my purposes, with a note saying *Sorry I washed them.*

I wasn't, though. Sorry, that was. If they'd been hanging around in the laundry basket for a couple of weeks, they'd have been pretty rank by now, rather than wafting floral fabric conditioner up my nose to the extent I had to fight a sneeze. And it's not like it makes a difference to the vibes once whatever's been washed has dried out. Even your modern biological powders aren't proof against those stubborn psychic stains.

"Gonna give it a go?" Phil asked over my shoulder.

"What, with the map? You know that's all bollocks."

"Never hurts to try."

"Yeah, it does. I'm wounded you don't accept I know my own abilities better than you do."

Phil huffed. We had a long-standing argument going over my so-called talents, with me, on the whole, happy with the way things were right now (*happy* being a relative word, obviously), while he seemed to think I needed to exercise my psychic muscles as much as possible, presumably with a view to making them all big and manly.

He didn't say anything, which technically meant I'd won. Hah.

On the other hand . . . "Fine. Get the bloody map out, if it'll stop you looking at me like Arthur when I won't give him seconds."

Phil got the bloody map out, retrieved the pendant from where it'd been batted under the sofa by a furry paw, and smirked at me.

Once again, I gave it all I'd got.

Nothing.

Even Merlin had lost all interest in it by now. I glared at Phil and considerately didn't tell him *I told you so.*

He returned the favour by not asking if I'd really been trying. "Fine. So plan B it is. We go down to the market and do it the old-fashioned way."

"*A.* Plan A. Me getting a psychic hit? That was never plan A. *That* was plan B. Or more like plan Z. Or one of those letters that's not in the alphabet anymore."

"Plan A, then," he agreed easily.

I glared at him. "Git. You could at least pretend you're not humouring me."

He gave me a look as if to say *Where would be the fun in that?*

CHAPTER EIGHT

We decided to make the field trip to Camden Market that Sunday, which would normally have been my day of rest. So I wouldn't have to put off any plumbing jobs, Phil reminded me pointedly when I complained.

He'd done all the research soon after we'd seen Lilah the first time, getting a list of who ran what stalls, and gave me the edited highlights before we set off. "Luckily, there's not a lot of market stalls registered to a *K*. Somebody." *K* standing for Kelvin, obviously. At least, we were hoping she hadn't remembered that wrong. "If he'd been an *A*, a *J*, or a *T*, now, we'd have our work cut out."

Phil showed me a list of scrawled numbers, which presumably corresponded to market stalls. "So how do we find which stalls these are?" I asked. "I mean, it's not like pub tables. The stalls in St. Albans don't have handy bingo numbers on 'em."

"Which is why I got this." He waved a map under my nose—a fancier version of Lilah's printout. With numbers. "Right. You ready?"

I looked at him. "You going like that? Designer shirt and all? Don't you want to dress down?"

Phil shrugged. "They'll just think it's vintage or a knockoff." Then he smirked. "Don't worry. I'm taking you along to lower the tone."

"Oi, less of your cheek. These are my good jeans. And I paid five quid for this shirt from Primark." It was actually more like twenty-five, and it was from M&S, but hey, never let the truth get in the way of a good punchline.

You get to Camden Market by taking the Tube to Camden Town—trust me, it's not worth trying to bring a car—and walking up the high street towards Camden Lock. Did I say walking? I mean shuffling, side-stepping and excuse-me-ing. The place was heaving, mostly with tourists come to gawp at the shops, their storefronts decorated with massive . . . I wasn't even sure what you'd call them. Pop-art sculptures? Three-dimensional advertising hoardings? There was a brightly coloured Ganesh, a Chinese dragon, a twenty-times-life-size Converse trainer . . . It was like they'd taken the concept of pub signs and run with it. Probably to a crack den.

There was a clearer bit when we came to the bridge over the canal—Camden Lock itself, looking clean and pretty—then we reached the market and plunged into the crowds again. Savoury, spicy scents wafted over to us from the row of food stalls that went on as far as the eye could see, which to be honest wasn't all that far, and my stomach rumbled.

"Want to grab some lunch here?" I asked as we passed a particularly pungent noodle stall, with pork balls sizzling in a wok and colourful veg looking tasty on the side.

Phil huffed a laugh. "What, at eleven o'clock? Nice try."

"Oi, I didn't mean now. Later. Once we've finished up here." I was wounded by the implication I was a slave to my stomach, which promptly rumbled again to tell me it had a very different opinion on the matter.

"Maybe." He gave the stalls a side-eye.

"What, your mum tell you it was common to eat on the street or something?" Actually, I was fairly sure *my* mum had told me that, once upon a time, but apparently it hadn't taken. "Or are you just worried about getting sauce on your shirt?"

Phil glanced away. Heh. Guilty as charged. He cleared his throat. "We need to go down here."

"You sure? Those stalls are selling new stuff. Not vintage."

"Yeah, well unless your psychic talents have expanded to include teleportation, we've got to go through them first."

Gary would have loved this section of the market. Rainbow bright, with a T-shirt for every slogan you could think of, plus a few you'd have been as happy never to know. I wanted to stop and browse, but Phil gave me an impatient glare so I let him hurry me on past.

You could probably get them cheaper on the internet anyway. Like most things these days, short-term and negotiable companionship from the gender of your choosing not excepted.

We eventually reached an archway leading to a covered-over section of the market.

Phil nodded in its direction. "This is it. Stables Market."

I read the big brass letters beside the arch. "It says 'Horse Tunnel Market.' Not 'Stables.'"

Phil shrugged impatiently. "Who gives a monkey's what they call it? This is it."

The cobbles of the outdoor market gave way to wooden floorboards inside. A loose one shifted under my foot, and I stumbled, my hip protesting. I shrugged off Phil's support. "I'm fine. Which way now?"

Phil gave me a sharp look, but nodded to the left, where a narrow corridor meandered through stalls. Knots of tourists and shoppers clogged it entirely at some points. "First couple are down here."

I'd heard (from Darren, obviously) that Camden Market was prime real estate, the rent on stalls there costing you an arm, a leg, and enough internal organs to keep a modern-day Burke and Hare in clover. That hadn't stopped whoever had tarted the place up from bunging in whopping great brass statues of horses here and there, which of course you couldn't get near for tourists snapping selfies. I liked that they hadn't used all available space to make money, unlike a lot of new housing developments you see around my way where the houses all look like they're holding their stomachs in, crammed together so tight they have to spread up an extra floor to get all the rooms in. Still, all those stairs must keep you pretty fit.

I could think of more pleasant forms of exercise, though.

It turned out the stalls in the Stables Market *did* have handy bingo numbers on them, although a lot of them were obscured by what it'd be rude to call garish tourist tat, so I won't, but seriously, did anyone ever actually wake up thinking *Today I need to buy bread, milk, carrots—oh, and a half-size statue of Anubis and a lamp made out of a bong*?

The vintage-clothing stalls, now, I could see a point to that stuff. You could get your kit cheap *and* save the environment. We passed one with a rack of snazzy waistcoats Gary would be in raptures about, all for a tenner. And the leather-goods stalls grabbed you by the nose and pulled you in to gawp at an Aladdin's cave of . . . well, dead animal skin, I suppose, but the sheen on the belts, bags, and who-knew-what, plus the rich smell of leather you breathed in as you browsed, had you half thinking the animals wouldn't have minded all that much if they'd known where they'd end up.

"Oi, focus," Phil muttered in my ear as I reached out to stroke a thick leather belt that'd look great with my black jeans.

"Thought you wanted me to dress smarter," I muttered back, letting my hand fall. "So how are we doing this? Divide and conquer?" There weren't that many stalls on the list, so if we each took a few, we'd be finished in plenty of time for lunch.

Not that I was impatient to get back to that noodle stall or anything.

"We stick together, but talk to them separately. People get nervous and clam up if you go in mob-handed."

The first stall turned out to be a bust, *K* standing for Karol, not Kelvin, as Phil found out when he parked me like a troublesome toddler by a stall selling Hogwarts trunks and went off to investigate.

"Dunno why you even brought me," I complained as we headed off to the next. "I could be at home right now watching the footie."

"You can do the next one, all right? Christ, it's like having a kid." He said it fondly, so I didn't shove him into one of the trunks and slam the lid. It made me think, though. I knew he wanted kids, but we'd agreed, when we'd talked about it way back, we'd have them *one day*. Which to my mind, meant *not this year and not next year, either*. Him making a comment like that, did it mean it'd been on his mind? Like, seeing as we were getting married and all, did he want to start looking into adoption sooner rather than later? Kids . . . that was a big step. It'd mean a whole different way of life. I wasn't sure I was ready for that.

Maybe we should talk about it. Preferably some time we weren't in the middle of a job. I made an effort to shove all thoughts of sprogs out of my mind.

A lot of the stalls were set into mini tunnels leading out from the main hall, as if the place had originally been dug out by very large moles. They—the tunnels, not the moles, unless a shedload of genetic modification had been involved—had rounded, arched roofs and tiled walls. It felt a lot like being in a Tube station, although without the draughts, the reek of burnt diesel, and the constant warning to *Stand clear of the doors.*

Not that you could actually see very much of those tiled walls, as here, too, the stallholders were making the most of the limited space they had. Goods for sale were stacked up, pinned up, and stuck up *everywhere.* The clutter made the place seem even more cavelike, and I made a note to watch out for dodgy used-lamp salesmen.

Stall number two on our little list was a vintage-clothing store, selling mainly ex–military gear and used leather wear. Not the kinky stuff—come to think of it, if there was a market for used fetish wear, I wasn't sure I wanted to meet the sort of people who shopped there, seeing as you can't boil leather—but jackets, skirts, trousers, those big long coats people wear when they're going for dramatic effect. Or just want to look like a vampire, as may be. That kind of stuff.

We paused by a display of lavishly embroidered purses a few yards away to size up the target surreptitiously, but it wasn't a lot of use. The way the entrance was angled meant we couldn't see the stall holder.

"Right, in you go, then," Phil said, just as I started to have second thoughts.

"You sure? What if I do it wrong?"

"It's not rocket science. You go in, you check out the bloke on the stall, and if it's him, you give him this." He handed me Lilah's envelope, which I shoved unwillingly inside my jacket. "And if it's not him, you ask the bloke if his name's Kelvin and take it from there. I'm assuming if it's not a bloke, you can work it out for yourself." Phil smirked. "I'll have you tailing cheating husbands in no time."

"Oi. I got my own trade, ta very much. You can keep yours."

"I'll remember you said that, next time you go haring off to have tea with a murder suspect."

I didn't dignify that one with a response. "Any last-minute tips?"

Phil shrugged. "Just try to act natural."

That was a big help, immediately making me feel more self-conscious than any time since I'd been an awkward teenager with a massive crush on the school bully. Who was now my fiancé. Funny how things work out. I sidled up to the stall, half expecting a heavy hand to land on my collar at any moment and a loud voice start denouncing me to all and sundry. Which was daft, seeing as I was only there to pass on a message. To a bloke who probably wasn't even at this stall.

I picked up a waistcoat and pretended to be interested, then felt a complete muppet as I realised it was three sizes too large. I put it back on the rack. Luckily nobody seemed to have been watching. Right. Enough of the playacting. I went deeper into the store.

There was a bloke down there at the back who caught my eye. He had on one of those multipocketed aprons market traders use instead of tills, and he was engaging in some hard selling with a young goth girl. Oh, and he was dark haired, lean, and in his thirties, with a face I'd last seen on the photograph currently burning a hole in my pocket.

Jonny-boy was holding up a used leather jacket in front of little Ms. Gothette, presumably pointing out whatever features made it particularly desirable in her case. Its essential blackness, probably, as it was a tad short on death's-heads, studs, or anything else I'd have associated with gothdom. Still, what do I know?

I picked up a leather jacket of my own—checking the size this time—and hung around while he concluded the sale and the girl went off with a bag in her hand and a smile on her face that was all wrong with her general vibe of gloom and death.

One quarry dispatched and the next one in his sights, Jonny-boy ambled over in my direction.

He seemed younger in the flesh than he had in the photo. Younger, more ripped, and way better looking, with a cheeky glint in his eye and a swagger in his walk. Less formally dressed too—despite the season, he was wearing a black sleeveless hoodie that showed off a respectable pair of shoulders and some very adequate biceps, paired with faded blue jeans and that signature market-trader money belt. Even in that getup, though, he sparkled.

If I'd been Lilah, I'd have wanted him back too.

"All right, mate? What can I do you for? Present for the missus, is it?" I wasn't imagining the come-hither in that smile, or the wink he threw in with it. He hadn't bothered shaving today, and probably not yesterday either for that matter, and the roguish air was a definite bonus.

"Missus? What missus?" I matched his smile easily. "Nah, I'm after something for a bloke I know."

"Oh yeah? How well do you know this bloke?"

"Pretty well." I chucked in a wink of my own.

Jonny-boy wasn't fazed. "Around my size, is he?"

I gave him a slow once-over. It seemed only polite in the circs. "Bigger," I said in the end, with a grin.

"Ouch. Feel the burn. So what is it you're after? Jacket? Is he the biker type?"

No, he really, really wasn't. To be honest, I didn't reckon Phil'd be seen dead in anything from this bloke's stall. Not a huge fan of clothing that came secondhand—sorry, vintage, my Phil. Time to get down to business. "You're Jonathan Parrot, right? Late of Hertfordshire?"

The change was dramatic. JP's whole body tensed up, the smile did a runner, and his eyes looked like they were having a serious think about following suit.

Whoa. The last thing I wanted was him getting the wrong idea. "I'm here to deliver a message," I said, putting my hand in my jacket to get Lilah's letter.

The eyes made up their mind, and the legs got straight on board. Jonny-boy darted off down the narrow passage between the rails, vaulted over a display of shoes, and scarpered. All while I was standing there with my gob open and my hand in my jacket like a bust of Napoleon. And about as much use as one too.

Bloody *marvellous*.

CHAPTER NINE

I ran after him. What else could I do? If I lost him now, he'd go to ground properly, and not only would the client be asking me to do six impossible things before breakfast—or one, at any rate—but Jonny-boy would have burned his Camden Market bridges over a stupid misunderstanding.

Why the hell was he running anyway? God knew, but I didn't have time to think about it as we zigzagged around stalls and slow-moving shoppers. Christ, who'd laid this place out? A spider on meth? My hip was aching already.

And where the bloody hell was Phil? He should have caught me up by now, with those long legs of his.

Jonny-boy passed a leather-goods stall, sending bags swinging in his wake. Muggins here got there just in time to field a satchel in the face. Reeling back, I lost sight of my quarry and panted out a curse. He'd done that on purpose, the git. Besides the face-ache, my hip was hurting like a bastard and a stitch in my side was giving it a good run for its money.

I stepped on the gas, scanning the crowd as I dodged around knots of tourists, a constant mantra of *Sorry, sorry, coming through* on my now-bruised lips. There—he was about ten yards in front of me, dodging around a young Japanese couple in matching backpacks who were getting an earful from another trader about God knew what.

Just what had I said to spook the bloke? And where the effing, sodding, bleeding hell was Phil? Course, Phil's size left him a lot less nippy—score one for the short-arse.

Jonny-boy took a corner too quick past a stall selling knockoff mystic tat. A tray of blue glass evil eyes went flying, and they skittered across the floor in all directions. The stall holder jumped up from his chair and shouted abuse at our Mr. P., I swerved to avoid slamming into his broad, unfriendly back—and trod on an evil eye.

The eye rolled—sadly unironically—and my ankle turned. The wrong ankle. Pain shot through my bad hip, blindingly intense—and again when I landed heavily on the ground.

There might have been a certain amount of swearing involved.

The stall holder, a dark-haired guy with an even darker expression, turned to take his anger out on the sitting target presented by yours truly, but was forestalled by the Japanese couple. They crouched down beside me with matched worried looks to go with the backpacks.

"I'm fine," I told them, trying to force out a smile as I clambered to my feet.

Then promptly proved myself a liar by toppling against the girl. She caught me with a startled cry and staggered under my weight, her being a lot more on the sylphlike side than yours truly, and for a moment there I thought we were both going down like dominoes, possibly taking out evil-eye guy and his stall en route. Luckily for all concerned, her boyfriend was quick to grab hold, and I managed to stay roughly upright. It was clear I wasn't going to be doing any more steeplechasing in a hurry, though. Not surprisingly, Jonny-boy hadn't stuck around to check if I was okay.

Great. I was beginning to wonder why I'd bothered tagging along today. I limped slowly back to the Stables Market entrance, where I found my beloved hanging around like he had nothing better to do than glare at passersby like they'd insulted his mother. Or, by the depth of those frown lines, the concept of motherhood in general.

"You get him?" he demanded by way of fond greeting.

I wasn't feeling all that fond right then myself. "Didn't you? And, by the way, where the hell were you?"

"Tried to cut him off, didn't I?" Phil sounded as pissed off as I felt. "This part of the market goes round in a loop."

It did? I should have paid more attention to that map Phil had shown me.

"So where is he? If you've been watching the exit, and I came back the way we went in . . ."

We looked at each other. "He must still be in there," Phil said, his tone a lot more cheerful.

I frowned. "Yeah, but there's all these old stable doors in the walls leading who knows where. 'Spect if you work round here, you get to know about all kinds of rat-runs."

"What, and how to get through padlocks without leaving a trace? Besides, who says those doors lead anywhere? They're probably just lockups." He smirked. "I think it's time you earned your keep."

Oh, bloody hell. But if nothing else, it was more in the spirit of what the client was paying for. We'd even brought Mr. Parrot's T-shirts along in case the list of stalls had drawn a blank. Phil handed me the carrier bag. Feeling like a flippin' tracker dog, I cleared my mind, focussed on JP, and listened . . .

What do you know? There was a sharp, bright trail leading along the bit of the loop I hadn't covered. Not even all that far away. There was a hefty whiff of fear about it too.

Who did Jonny-boy think we were, the Hertfordshire Mafia?

"This way," I said grimly, and hobbled back down the loop.

Phil grabbed my arm. "What's with the limp? You were fine when we got here."

"I'm okay. Put a foot down wrong, that's all." The last thing I needed was Phil going off on a guilt trip about having inadvertently caused my long-ago pelvic fracture.

"Is your hip playing up? You should have told me. Sod it. I should've known he might try to run."

The implication being, if he'd thought about it, he'd have handled it all his big, butch self, not left it to the less-able half of the partnership. Great. "I'm *fine*. Do you want to find this guy or not?"

I stopped at another used-clothing stall, because that was where the trail went to ground. Was it some kind of brotherhood? The trader, a dark-skinned guy with a heavy accent I couldn't identify, didn't want to let us through to where I could feel Jonny-boy was hiding out, but Phil loomed at him while I nipped around the side and caught up with JP at the end of the tunnel, where he was doing a none-too-convincing impersonation of just another military greatcoat.

He had a trapped, defeated look on his face that would have made me feel guilty if my hip hadn't still been killing me. "For fuck's sake," I said as soon as I got within earshot. "All I want to do is give you a letter."

JP blinked. "What?"

"Here." I reached into my jacket again, didn't miss his flinch—seriously, did he think it was a hit or something?—and pulled out Lilah's envelope, a little damp around the edges from the sweat I'd worked up. "It's from the missus. She misses you. Pun not intended."

He took it, eyes wide. I wondered if I should get him to give me a receipt, or at the very least take a selfie, but sod it, if Lilah wanted proof of delivery, she should have asked for it.

As he stared at the envelope without opening it, I straightened up. "Right. You may now return to your regularly scheduled programming. Oh, and here's your laundry." I shoved the carrier bag at him. If he didn't want the T-shirts, he could flog 'em on his stall.

Then I limped off, cursing, to re-join Phil.

After all that, eating on the street didn't seem very appealing anymore. Luckily we found a pub with a decent menu and Sky Sports, so the day wasn't a total write-off. After a couple of beers, my hip was even talking to me again.

Me and Phil went on home, where Phil gave Lilah a bell to let her know the package had been delivered, and I put Jonny-boy Parrot out of my mind—well, not totally; I did wonder occasionally why he'd run, and what had been in the envelope, and whether he'd gone back to the missus, although from the way he'd been eying me up, the chances of that last one seemed pretty slim.

But then, of course, I switched on the telly Monday evening. And found myself a person of interest in a murder investigation.

CHAPTER TEN

I was so flippin' shell-shocked by the mock-up of my mug on the screen, I barely registered what I was doing when I picked up my phone. Luckily, it was Gary.

"Tommy, darling, have you been a naughty boy?"

"Not *that* naughty, I haven't." I gathered my scrambled wits together. "We're talking about the news on the telly, right? Because in case you're wondering, no, I didn't off the poor bastard."

"I should hope not. Darren's absolutely distraught on Lilah's behalf. He says if you *did* do it, you can kiss your nadgers goodbye. Although personally I have my doubts you're quite flexible enough. *And* he's going to tell her not to pay your finder's fee. After all, what use is a dead husband to man or beast? Or woman, of course," Gary added in an offhand voice.

"You can tell him indoors cheers for the vote of confidence," I muttered. God, what must Lilah be feeling? Finding her bloke only to lose him permanently the very next day?

"Anytime, mate. Anytime."

I blinked. That had been Darren's voice. "Oi, Gary, did you put me on speaker?"

"Naturally. Darren and I share *everything*."

"Including the low opinion of yours truly? No, wait, don't answer that. Either of you. Just tell me this—was it really so flippin' obvious that photofit was me?" I mean, *I'd* thought it was, but in the circs, surely a bit of paranoia was understandable.

"Well, I recognised you straightaway," Gary said thoughtfully. "Even though they underestimated your age by a good half decade."

"Half decade—they said late twenties. I'm thirty. That's, what, three years tops."

"If you say so, darling. Still, at least it's proof you don't look your age. To some people, anyway."

"That'll be such a comfort to me when I'm doing life for murder. Christ, I'll be at least forty-five when I come out. Middle-aged." Would Phil still love me when I was old and wrinkly and covered in prison tats? What were the chances of him staying faithful while I wasted away fifteen years at Her Majesty's pleasure?

More to the point, what were *my* chances of staying faithful, spending all those years locked up with a bunch of horny bastards without two morals to rub together?

I managed not to gulp audibly.

"Nah, forty's the new thirty," Darren threw in cheerfully. "You'll still have your best years ahead of you. Look at me."

"Bit hard, down the phone line." I'd always wondered how much older Darren was than Gary. I revised my estimate up a few years.

Christ, this was doing my head in. I couldn't even get my priorities straight. It was like my brain kept bouncing into the elephant in the room and careening off at a tangent.

"Oh, but he can't go to jail, sweetie pie," Gary was saying. "I've heard the food in there's dreadful. You'll have to flee, darling," he added in a louder tone. "Live the romantic life of a fugitive from justice on the Costa del Crime. It could be quite exciting—you'll be rubbing shoulders with famous villains like Ronnie Biggs—"

"Oi, Ronnie Biggs went to Brazil. And he's dead. If I end up rubbing shoulders with him, I'll really be in trouble."

"I said *like* Ronnie Biggs," Gary muttered sulkily.

"Anyway, it doesn't matter 'cos I'm not going on the run. I'm going to give Dave Southgate a ring." Dave being our friendly neighbourhood detective inspector, and fortunately, a good drinking mate.

"You wanna get your sister in," Darren put in helpfully. "Don't say nothing to the filth until you got yourself lawyered up."

"Cherry's on honeymoon, remember? Up in Scotland, cuddling up with the Loch Ness Monster."

"Ooh, is that what Greg calls it?" That was Gary. "He does have remarkably large hands. I always wondered if there was a correlation."

"Nah, it's the feet you gotta look at, pumpkin," Darren shot back.

"But then he has very large feet too. Oh, now you've got me wondering—"

Great. Here I was facing jail, or at least the third degree from Dave's fellow boys in blue, and all they could think about was Greg's penis size.

"Gotta go," I cut them off. "I need to call Dave before anyone else puts an oar in."

"Well, if you need any files baked in cakes, do call," Gary said, and we hung up, on my side not without a hefty dose of relief.

"Why is it Gary seems to reckon my life is some kind of soap opera put on for his entertainment?" I asked Phil.

He huffed and put his arms round me. "If it is, I'd fire whoever's writing the script. But yeah, you'd better call Dave before any helpful anonymous tips get made."

I frowned. "I know I said that, but . . . you really think anyone would call and shop me? If they know me, they'd know I wouldn't kill anyone, right?"

"If you want everyone to love you, you're in the wrong business."

"I'm in the plumbing business!"

"Tell that to the murderers you've helped put in jail over the last couple of years."

A chill ran through me, despite the body heat coming off Phil in waves. It was a bit worrying to think I might have enemies. Yeah, I'd had people try to kill me—but that was during an investigation. I supposed I'd sort of thought that once it was over, it was over. But then it wasn't, not for them, was it? Or their friends and family, who presumably still loved them despite them being killers.

It was unnerving to think about, so I dialled Dave straightaway so I wouldn't have to.

He picked up on the second ring, which wasn't ominous at all. Nor was the heavy sigh he greeted my "All right, Dave?" with.

I couldn't kid myself about what he actually said, though, which was, "*Please* tell me you're calling to ask me out for a pint and not about that bleedin' news story."

"Uh . . . Not sure you're meant to lie to an officer of the law."

"I knew it. I bloody knew it. Jen knew it. Even the bloody nipper knew it. We looked at that photofit, and she was all 'No, it can't be,' and I was 'Oh, yes it bleeding can.' What is it with you, Paretski? Got bored with the plumbing and decided to make your own entertainment?"

"Oi, all I did was find the bloke for a client. *And* he was still alive when I left him."

"And since when have you been a bloodhound for hire? Thought that was more in the boyfriend's line. 'Scuse me, fiancé. And don't tell me, I'm coming over. You're home, right?"

"Yeah."

"And I suppose the other half's there too? Or have you murdered him and all?"

"Phil's fine. And here, yeah. He lives here now."

"There's a surprise. I'll see you in ten." He hung up.

"Dave's coming round," I told Phil.

Phil huffed. "There's a surprise."

I blinked, because the thought of my lover channelling the very straight DI Southgate was all kinds of disturbing. Then again, Phil had been a copper too, back in the day . . . I shook my head. Not what I wanted to be thinking about at this precise moment in time. "So we're telling him everything, yeah?"

Phil nodded. "Yeah. Don't go trying to shield Lilah out of some misplaced notions of loyalty or chivalry or whatever."

"God, they're going to think she did it, aren't they?" I realised. "Got muggins here to find the poor sod so she could get rid of him once and for all." Even paying both of us by the hour, the bill we'd written up was a fair bit cheaper than your average divorce lawyer would charge.

"So? Maybe she did."

"What, her?" My flabber was seriously gasted.

"The bloke was running scared. With good reason, as it turns out. She's the most likely suspect."

"I know, I know, it's always the spouse what done it." It had to make you wonder why marriage is still so bloody popular, not that I was daft enough to say anything like that out loud to my fiancé. "But she's got to know we'd go straight to the police and tell them she hired us. She's not stupid."

"Maybe she doesn't think like that. Maybe she reckoned we'd keep our heads down, worried about being charged as accessories."

"No. No, that's . . . No, I don't believe it."

But I wished I knew what had been in that envelope I'd delivered.

Dave turned up in not much more than the ten minutes he'd quoted, with bleary eyes and a strong whiff of sour milk.

"How's the new hope?" I asked.

"Lucas? He's doing great. Proper little tiger. Got a pair of lungs on him that could put a drill sergeant to shame. Now, what's all this about you hounding market traders to their deaths?"

We filled Dave in over a cuppa, possibly underplaying the parts where we were essentially deceiving the client about services rendered. I'd *known* that was going to come back to haunt me.

"So all I did was hand over Lilah's love letter, and then we left him to it," I finished. "Haven't seen hide or hair of either of them since. Gave her a call to tell her 'job done', wrote out an invoice, and that was it."

He humphed. "Did she pay?"

"Haven't even had time to post it yet."

"Missed your chance there, then. Unless you're planning to bung it inside a card that reads *With Deepest Sympathy*."

I winced. Poor Lilah.

Dave allowed himself a brief chuckle at his own joke—or possibly my face on hearing it—then turned businesslike again. "Right. I'll have a word with whoever's heading up the investigation into your Mr. Parrot's untimely demise."

"Oi, he's not *my* Mr. Parrot."

"Oh? Your Mrs. Parrot's late other half, then. Happy now?"

Not really, no, but I wasn't going to say anything, seeing as he was doing me a favour. Or was he, come to think of it? Furthering the course of justice was pretty much in his job description, after all.

"They're going to want to talk to you—both of you—but they'll probably spare you the water-boarding and the fingernail pliers."

Dave's world-weary mug cracked into an evil grin. "I'm making no promises about the rubber hoses, mind."

"What, no telephone directories?" I asked.

"Don't be daft. It's all online these days. Think they're going to rough you up with an iPad? We're not made of bloody money."

Phil butted in, practical as ever. "What can you tell us about Parrot's death?"

"Bugger all. Been off for a week, haven't I? Jen reckoned she needed a break. All I know is what's on the bleedin' news, same as you. Found in the canal, suspicious death, suspect: one evil bastard by the name of Thomas Paretski."

"My name wasn't on the news—was it?" Bloody hell, that wasn't going to do the customer confidence any favours.

"No, only your ugly mug. Give 'em time." Dave stood up, stretched, and scratched his gut. He did a thorough job, so it took a while. "Right. We'll be in touch. And by 'we,' I mean my esteemed colleagues in the Hertfordshire Constabulary. Try not to piss them off too much."

"Cheers, Dave. I owe you."

"Too bloody right, you do. No, don't get up, I'll see myself out. Might have a nose round for the murder weapon on my way, you know how it is."

"If you think you're going to find a flippin' canal in my downstairs loo, good luck to you."

"Who says he drowned? Did I say he drowned? The body was found in the canal. Doesn't mean he was alive when he went in." Dave stomped off, whistling tunelessly.

The front door slammed behind him. Phil and me exchanged worried glances.

At least, I was betting I looked worried. Phil's face was giving away bugger all, as usual.

"S'pose it could have been an accident?" I suggested hopefully. "He definitely seemed stressed when we saw him. Maybe he'd had a drink or six to loosen up, went for a walk to clear his head, and missed his step? It happens."

"Maybe." Phil's tone said *In your dreams, sonny boy.* "Went a long way for that walk, though, didn't he?"

"Shit. Yeah. Uh . . . maybe he went to see Lilah, and *then* went for those drinks, etc., etc.?" I was clutching at straws, and I knew it. I sighed. "I'm bloody knackered after all that. Bed?"

"You go. I'll join you in a bit." He reached for his laptop.

Well, that hadn't been what I was hoping for. "Oi, you'd better not be watching porn on that. It's like the honeymoon's over and we're not even married yet."

Phil raised an eyebrow. "Thought you were knackered."

"I'm never *that* knackered." I winked.

He left the laptop where it lay.

Result.

CHAPTER ELEVEN

I had a downstairs loo refit scheduled for next day—not as big a job as it sounds, as Ms. T. wanted to redo the tiles herself, so I was only going to be plumbing in the loo and the washbasin. And fitting the fancy new smooth-headed taps that'd be a bugger to turn after a few months of limescale build-up from the water around here, which is so hard you risk giving yourself a concussion if you turn the shower on full blast. I'd warned her, but some people simply don't want to listen. So no skin off my nose, you'd think, but it goes against the grain, fitting something I know isn't going to last. Feels like I'm doing a botch job, even when I'm not.

So I wasn't in the best frame of mind, which might be why, when she cheerfully told me there had been a murderer on the telly last night who was the spitting image of me, I snapped out, "Look, I didn't kill him, all right? I just delivered a letter."

Ms. T.'s eyes went wide, and she left off the chat after that. She paid up promptly, mind—full payment in cash, and the correct money and everything—but I had a sinking feeling I wasn't likely to get a lot of repeat business from her direction. I cheered myself up with the thought that at least now she was unlikely to ask me to sort out the taps for free when they seized up.

I was heading back to Fleetville when Dave called. I thought it might be important, so I pulled the van into a side street and parked up, by which time of course he'd hung up, so I had to ring him back.

He answered with a fond, "Where the bleedin' hell are you, Paretski?"

"On my way home. Why?"

"I've got two detectives wasting our budget sitting on their arses outside your house, waiting for you to bother to put in an appearance, that's why."

"You know the thing about getting me to turn up on time for appointments? You've got to flippin' tell me about them, that's what." I frowned through the windscreen, startling a motorist coming towards me into swerving and almost mounting the kerb. Maybe he'd seen me on the telly too. "How come they're at my house anyhow? Usually it's me being told to shift my arse down to the station. What's with the softly, softly approach?"

"Yeah. Well." Dave paused. "I may just have gone off on one at them for slapping your face all over the telly like that."

"Dave, mate, I didn't know you cared."

"Bugger that. There's kids watching at that hour. Don't want them having nightmares from seeing your ugly mug before bedtime, do we?" He coughed. "Now are you going to get a shift on, or what?"

"I'm shifting right now, that quick enough for you?" I said, putting the van in gear.

"Well, put the bleedin' phone down, then. Christ. You trying to get yourself arrested?"

"Nah, I'll be fine. Got a mate on the force." And then I hung up, before he could tell me not to be so bloody sure about that one.

I wellied it home for a nice little chin-wag with the boys in blue, who turned out to be neither. Not in blue, that was, and not boys, plural—they were Detective Sergeant Gemma Cooper, who was wearing top-to-toe black like a wannabe ninja, which didn't do a lot for her British mouse colouring, and Detective Constable No-First-Name Patel, who was also wearing black and carrying it off far better.

I thought something was funny when the sarge introduced herself by her full name, instead of a curt bark of her rank and surname, and I was further thrown off-balance when she led with—get this—an apology. Not that the coppers I've been interviewed by in the past haven't been polite, except when they've been Dave, but usually it's a steely kind of politeness where calling you *Sir* is just how they bait their traps. This was more awkward and, if I wasn't mistaken, resentful.

Sergeant Cooper reminded me of nothing so much as a teenager who'd had a bollocking from mum and a threat of grounding.

Still, gift horses and all that. I—and Phil, when he got home half an hour after I did—answered a shedload of questions, not all of which seemed particularly relevant (what did Lilah's porn career have to do with anything, for example?). The whole lot was recorded by Constable Patel as his one contribution to the interviews.

We were promised statements to sign in a day or so, and Detectives Cooper and Patel finally took their leave. About flippin' time. My stomach reckoned my throat had been taken into custody. I glanced at the clock and groaned. I really didn't want to have to start cooking now.

"Takeaway?" Phil suggested, sitting heavily on the sofa after seeing the plod out.

"Developing psychic talents of your own, are you? Yeah, why not? Chinese?"

"I was thinking Indian."

We compromised on Thai. Phil volunteered to go pick up the food, so I rang Dave while I was waiting. "What exactly did you say to those two? Did you tell 'em I was royalty or something?"

There was a pause.

"Dave?"

"Ah. Well." Dave coughed. "It's not been officially announced, so don't you go shoving it on Facebook or telling all your mates down the pub, but . . . I got my promotion."

"Wait, what? You never even told me you were going for it. And congrats, mate. Seriously. So, what, you're a chief inspector now?"

"Will be. *Will* be. DCI Southgate. Ain't got a bad ring to it, has it? My Jen's dead chuffed."

With a bit of luck, it'd help stop her getting itchy feet this go around, although maybe I was getting cynical in my old age and she'd got over the midlife crisis, leaving-him-for-a-younger-fitter-model thing anyway. "Pleased for you, mate. I mean it. You've earned this."

"Up for a commendation too," Dave added in that trying-to-sound-modest voice people put on to excuse them blowing their own trumpet.

"Yeah? Congrats again. What's that for? Bravery in the face of late-night nappy changes?"

"Up yours." Then he laughed. "You're going to piss yourself when I tell you."

"Oi, I'm a plumber. We don't get leaks. Come on, out with it."

"LGBT relations."

I didn't actually piss myself, you'll be relieved to hear, but I barked out a laugh so loud that Merlin spooked and shot out of the room and even Arthur quirked up an ear. "Bloody hell, they've found you out at last. Dave 'Sensitivity Training' Southgate. We'll have you marching in Pride in no time."

"With my feet? You'll be lucky. But, oi, I'm a forward-thinking officer of the law, I am. Keen to take proactive measures to ensure that diversity in the force and the wider community is not only welcomed, but actively encouraged."

"Well, it's good to hear I've been rubbing off on you. Innuendo not intended."

"'Not intended' my newly promoted arse. And we'll have no dodgy comments about *that*, either."

"Perish the thought," I said politely. And very sincerely. "Mind you," I went on, "the force part I get"—he'd actually asked, and even taken, my advice on how to handle a couple of issues concerning LGBT officers recently—"but how exactly do you . . . what was it? 'Actively encourage diversity in the wider community'?"

"Buggered if I know, but that's what it said in the letter."

"Must be true, then. Well, good on you. Keep it up. Whatever it is."

Once Phil had got back with the food, me and him toasted Dave's promotion with a beer.

"Did you get anything out of the detectives before I got home? Cause of death, any leads?" Phil asked, nabbing half the satay chicken.

"Tried. No luck, though."

He nodded, like that was what he'd expected. "They teach you that in Hendon." Hendon being where baby police officers went to nursery school to learn their ABC, which I'm reliably informed these days no longer stands for *Arrest, Beating, Confession*. "Information is only supposed to flow one way."

"Yeah, the sarge must've got top marks in that class. What about you?" I challenged, scooping up some monks' veg in an attempt to convince myself this meal wasn't totally unhealthy. "Don't tell me you didn't spend half of today digging around for the dirt on our Mr. Parrot." I frowned at myself as I realised I'd echoed Dave's way of describing him.

"Busy," Phil said shortly. "Which is why I was planning to see what I could find out last night, until *someone* dragged me off to bed hours early."

"Yeah, right. Kicking and screaming." Well, to be fair, he had been by the end, not that I'm one to brag. "So what were you up to all day?"

"Client meetings all morning, and in court this afternoon."

"Oh, yeah? What did they do you for?"

"Funny. Domestic violence case. Victim was a former client. The husband didn't take too kindly to finding out she'd had him followed."

Uh-oh. "Bad?" Phil had a complicated relationship with that sort of offence.

He took a deep breath. "I've seen worse. A lot worse." The unspoken *but* hung in the air between us.

I put down my fork and gave his arm a squeeze. "Did they convict the bastard?"

"Yeah."

"And she's going to divorce him?"

"I bloody well hope so."

"You should have told me it was coming up." Because I *knew* he'd be feeling responsible for whatever that git had done to the wife.

Phil shrugged. "What were you going to do? Come and hold my hand?"

And all right, that stung, but sometimes you have to let these things go. "Might've made more of an effort to cook you dinner," I said, giving him another squeeze.

He half smiled, giving me a warm feeling in my belly. Which rapidly cooled when the smile turned into a smirk. "Who says I don't prefer takeaway?"

I glared at him and reminded myself that threatening to shove one of the discarded chicken skewers where the sun didn't shine would probably be in poor taste, coming straight on the heels of us talking about domestic abuse. "Well, if you want to do the cooking from now on, be my guest."

The smirk got broader. "Touchy sod. Your cooking's great. Why do you think I moved in?"

"And there were me and the cats thinking it was for the pleasure of our company."

"The cats weren't wrong."

I stuck up the appropriate finger in his general direction. "Any more of that and you'll be kipping down here with them tonight."

Phil slung an arm around my waist and pulled me close. "Did I say the cooking was your only talent?"

And that should have been that about poor old Jonny-boy.

Except . . . I felt bad about it—finding the bloke and handing over the message from the missus. He'd looked so much happier behind that market stall than he had in all his photos.

And yeah, all right, technically he was what the *Sun* would call a love rat, running out on the wife to go live with the lover and not even having the decency to keep her informed as to whether he was alive or dead, but . . . Actually, the more I thought about it, the more I was wondering why I felt so flippin' sorry for him, but sod it, if I hadn't been to see him, maybe he'd never have gone back to Pluck's End. And he'd still be alive today.

So later, after we'd cleared away the plates and the boxes from dinner, I might or might not have encouraged Phil to offer Lilah his services, professionally speaking. And maybe Phil had a bad taste in his mouth too from the way it had all gone down, because he didn't take all that much encouraging.

I edged round to it. "Should we offer our condolences to the grieving widow?"

Phil gave me a cynical look. "Want to check how deep that grief really runs?"

"Maybe. You telling me you're not a little bit curious yourself? After the way things panned out?"

"Maybe." He stared at the telly for a mo.

I waited. Then I got fed up waiting. "Think she might have done it? Played us for a couple of mugs and got us to find him so she could lure the poor sod up here to off him?"

He didn't answer my question. Well, technically speaking he didn't. What he did do was turn to face me with a firm set to his jaw, and say, "Couldn't hurt to pay a visit." Then he half smiled. "If nothing else, it'll save the cost of a stamp."

"You what?"

"Like you told Dave, we haven't sent her the invoice for finding the late Mr. Parrot yet, have we?"

Chapter Twelve

We took the drive out to Pluck's End to pay our respects to the grieving widow as soon as we could, which wasn't as soon as we'd have liked. It's a bugger, this having to pay the bills lark. I'd had a couple of customers booked in for the next day I hadn't wanted to let down, and Phil had had a case to wrap up. Ironically, it was another missing-person job—one of his meetings from the other day had been about a runaway teenager, who he'd managed to track down in a shelter in Manchester. Cue tearful reunions and promises of better understanding all round. Well, if by *all round* you mean *on the parents' side*. According to Phil, the teen herself had mostly looked pissed off at having been caught.

He reckoned, give it six weeks and she'd be off again. Still, as I reminded him, it's always good to get repeat business.

Anyhow, we finally set off for Lilah's house in Pluck's End on a bright, mild Thursday morning. It was too early for daffs, but crocuses were starting to poke their heads out of the ground and magnolias in front gardens were getting ready to strut their spring stuff.

We were counting on the lady in question not going into work so soon after JP's death, Phil not wanting to call ahead. Bit of a hangover from his police days, that, I suspected—never give the criminal a chance to make up a story and hide the body. As evidenced by the number of nippers out and about on the streets and playgrounds we passed on the way, it was school half-term holidays this week, which added to our chances of finding her at home with the kids. A calculated risk, but we wanted to take a nose at the crime scene too, so it wouldn't be a wasted journey whatever.

The canal was out at the far end of Pluck's End, one of those things you vaguely know are there but never pay much attention to.

Unless, I guess, you're in the market for a handy spot to commit murder. I seemed to remember Cherry saying they'd had a grant from the Lottery fund to tart it up a bit (not that she'd put it quite like that, obviously) but since I didn't spend a right lot of time in Pluck's End, I'd never actually seen it.

We parked in a newish-looking car park planted out with spindly trees in plastic tubes. Several other cars were already in occupation. Maybe we weren't the only ones who fancied a butcher's at a murder scene. Helpful signs pointed the way down to the canal, where we strolled along the path to the spot where JP had taken his terminal dip. Well, as near as we could get, at any rate. Around thirty feet of canal path each side of where, presumably, they'd dragged poor old Jonny-boy out of the water were still fenced off with police tape. They hadn't bothered to leave some poor bastard in uniform to guard it, though, unless he'd just nipped behind a tree for a call of nature or a crafty fag, so the forensic team must have already been and done their stuff.

As places to get yourself offed go, Jonny-boy hadn't chosen a bad one. The canal path had been made into a proper footpath, with benches every so often for the hard-of-standing and periodic notice boards either telling you which birds to look for flying over from the nature reserve on the other side, or reminding any medieval peasants that happened along that livestock could only be grazed on the common between Lammas and Candlemas.

"Candlemas I get—some kind of church candle fest, like the one with the oranges at Christmas—but what the hell's Lammas?" I wondered idly.

"It's when they used to slaughter all the spring lambs," Phil said confidently.

"Oh." Something about the way he said it made me send him a suspicious frown. "Oi, really?"

He laughed, the git. "God knows. Why don't you ask Greg, if you're that bothered?"

"Don't think Cherry would thank me for ringing him up about work stuff in the middle of their honeymoon. And hey, I knew he was up for promotion, but I didn't know he'd got the top job already." I gave Phil a hard stare. "Be good if he had. I might get more respect round here if I was brother-in-law to Him Upstairs."

"Yeah, but then you'd really have to mind your p's and q's when we go round for Sunday lunch."

"Me? Nothing wrong with my manners. I was brung up proper, thank Greg."

Phil gave me a look. "If you start screaming 'Oh Greg' in the middle of sex, we're going to have a problem."

I shuddered. "Cheers—way to give me a mental image of my sis doing just that. Can we change the subject?"

We walked on along the path. Everything was barren now, of course, and instead of grass and flowers, the predominant smell was damp earth with a whiff of diesel, but in a month or two's time it'd be a lovely place for a stroll. Come summer, with the wild flowers blooming in the meadows and the birds flapping about overhead . . . Yeah, pretty idyllic, I reckoned.

Well, as long as they didn't make a habit of finding dead bodies in the water, that was. I felt a momentary pang of regret that I'd turned down Cherry's offer of her house in Pluck's End at mates' rates, now she was shacking up with Greg in the holiest of matrimony, but hey, we could still come here anytime. It wasn't like it was a long drive out from St. Albans. Her daily commute from St. Leonards was going to be twice as far. Me and Phil had bets on as to how long she'd stick it out before chucking Ver Chambers for somewhere more local.

"Don't suppose it's worth asking you to give the place a once-over?" Phil asked in a low voice as we reached the tape barring our path.

I gave him a pitying look. "With a canal full of water rushing past?"

Phil raised an eyebrow. "'Rushing'?"

"All right, dawdling past, but it's still water. It won't just mess with the vibes, it'll *be* the vibes. At least, the only ones I'll be able to pick up. It'd be like trying to hear a pin drop at a heavy-metal festival." I shrugged. "Anyhow, if whoever killed him left some evidence here, chances are it was lost, not hidden. You know, dropped hairs, bits of fluff from his T-shirt, stray chunks of DNA. That sort of thing, though God knows how they find it." I was betting Phil knew how they did it too, but he didn't enlighten me.

"Forgetting the murder weapon, aren't you? You'd hide that."

"Yeah, but would you hide it here? Where you know they're going to be shipping in a vanload of lads and lasses in hazmat suits to comb over every inch of ground? What if it's something that'd give you away?"

"What, like a pet rock with your name on it?"

"Don't be daft. It wasn't a rock. Too . . . jagged. Could have been a . . . I dunno, a walking stick? Nah, that wouldn't fit, would it? Or would it?"

We'd discovered (from Dave, strictly on the QT) that Jonnyboy had suffered a blow to the head from that old classic, the blunt instrument, shortly before death. Trouble was, Dave couldn't tell us whether JP had been hit on the head, then chucked in the canal, or fallen into the water (with or without a helping hand from person or persons unknown) and *then* hit his head. The most likely suspects in that case were bridges and canal boats, of which there were a few on this stretch, mostly moored down by the town, no doubt with coppers on board taking notes.

The bang on the bonce hadn't killed our Mr. Parrot directly, but it had almost certainly contributed to his death by drowning—it being notoriously hard to swim whilst unconscious. And the water in the lungs had definitely come from the canal. I'd asked.

A woman strode by us, a matched pair of Westies straining at the lead like a couple of hyperactive cotton wool balls. "Gotta be popular with local dog owners, this place," I said, nodding at her. "You'd think it'd be a bit risky for a murder."

A bright-red dog-waste bin a few yards away bore witness to the fact I wasn't simply letting my imagination run wild, harassing hypothetical sheep and cocking its leg on notional trees. They probably had a bye-law about that sort of thing, round here.

Phil shrugged. In his posh wool coat and cashmere sweater, he'd have looked right at home walking something suitably classy yet macho—a golden retriever, say, or maybe a Great Dane. Me, I could probably just about get away with a Jack Russell. "Come down after dark, you'd be fine. Seen the state of the lighting here?"

I hadn't, because there wasn't any. Which, of course, was his point. "Okay, so you wouldn't get the lady walkers or the old codgers. And I s'pose runners wouldn't be too keen either—you'd want to know where you were putting your feet. Still, it's a risk."

"It's not overlooked, and the boats aren't likely to travel by night. Plus, if anyone came along, you'd hear them. Sound carries over water."

"Cuts both ways, that, though, doesn't it? Anyone walking along might have heard the splash when Jonny-boy went in, and come running to see if some poor sod had fallen in."

"Didn't, though, did they?"

I couldn't argue with that one. Or, at least, Dave's comrades in arms hadn't yet managed to find anyone willing to admit to it. Which probably meant they hadn't, but there was at least a faint chance they were keeping shtum from embarrassment at having witnessed a murder and failed to stop it—that, or they were worried about getting involved in a suspicious death. After all, if their own purposes for roaming lonely canal paths in the dead of night had been less than innocent . . .

No, in all likelihood, poor old Jonny-boy's swan song as he did a swan dive had been to an audience of one, i.e. his murderer. Or no one at all, if it had really been an accident, but I wasn't planning to stake my shirt on those odds. "Why would he even come down here after dark, though? I mean, obviously he must've been meeting someone— unless it was an accident—but he was scared of something, we know that, so why not stay somewhere well lit with a shedload of witnesses to discourage foul play?" I blinked. "He must have trusted whoever got him to come down here."

"Yeah. Or whoever he thought wanted him to come down here. Maybe he didn't meet up with who he expected."

"Well, if nothing else, we know Lilah couldn't have done it," I said. "Physically, I mean."

Phil snorted.

"What?" I asked, narked.

"Course she could have done it. She's not that small. And maybe she got him to sit down and then whacked him on the head. Wouldn't be that difficult—all she'd have to do was say she was getting a crick in her neck talking to him." He smirked. "You've got to be able to sympathise with her there."

"Up yours." I made the appropriate gesture, then shoved my hands in my pockets hurriedly when I realised there was an old dear coming our way with a Yorkie. I hoped she hadn't noticed, but the quavery "*Good* morning" she wished us as she passed was a bit on the pointed side.

Phil sniggered. Git.

We headed off after that, stopping again on the way to buy a bunch of flowers for the grieving widow. They had some peonies in the florist's, but Phil reckoned lilies were traditional. I pointed out the pollen stained like mad and was poisonous to cats, if she had any, not to mention the whole eau-de-death thing lilies have going on. Phil looked at me like I'd gone round the bend at that point, but trust me, I've been up close and personal with a dead body or two and it's not a smell you forget.

We compromised on white roses. I couldn't help thinking choosing flowers for the wedding was going to be a total bugger if we couldn't even agree what they smelled like.

Lilah's place turned out to be only a hop, skip, and a jump away from my sister's house. Funny to think of them being neighbours, although they wouldn't be for much longer. Cherry would be moving into the Old Deanery in St. Leonards with the Middle-Aged Canon as soon as they got back from honeymoon. If they hadn't fallen off a mountain or been eaten by a wild haggis, of course. Still, I couldn't see Lilah and Sis leaning over their respective garden gates to have a natter about recipes and/or the latest local scandal in any case. Sis liked to pretend she was above such things as gossip, and Lilah hadn't struck me as any more of the domestic-goddess type than Cherry was.

The house was big, but chalet style, with loads of floor space downstairs but the bedrooms all no doubt with low, sloping ceilings. Although I supposed that wouldn't be a problem for the lady of the house.

She opened the door to us herself, sporting a dark-grey wrap dress that hugged all her curves and managed to make her look both dignified and hot stuff. Objectively speaking, obviously. Her makeup was perfect—freshly applied to hide dark shadows and swollen eyes? I couldn't tell at a glance, and staring her in the face would have seemed rude.

Not that that stopped Lilah, who gave us a wide-eyed once-over that only ended when Phil held out the roses.

"We wanted to offer our condolences." He had the tone of voice just right: solemn, sincere and ever-so-slightly detached. It said *Sorry for your loss* with the merest hint of *Don't even think of blaming us for his untimely demise.*

She blinked and took the flowers with a sad smile. "Tom, Phil, that's so sweet of you. Come in."

We wiped our boots—that is, I wiped my boots, and Phil wiped his posh loafers—on her thick coir doormat. It was printed with the words, *Touch me, I want to be dirty,* and I wondered if it scared off the Jehovah's Witnesses. Then again, I was pretty sure Lilah could hold her own against all comers.

"I'm really sorry about what happened," I said guiltily.

"Oi, none of that. You only did what I asked you to. But come on, come in and have a cuppa."

She led us to a bright, airy kitchen, rather than her living room which I glimpsed through an open door. With some women I've had the dubious pleasure of calling on, this would be their none-too-subtle way of letting you know you're not good enough, clean enough, or important enough to risk wearing out and/or marking up the soft furnishings. Coming from someone like Lilah, though, an invite to the kitchen was probably a vote of confidence—her saying *We're all mates here, no standing on ceremony.*

Or, of course, she'd picked up some posh habits along with the posh house and lifestyle. But I wasn't betting on it, especially after seeing that doormat.

Me and Phil each pulled up a chair at a gleaming chrome-and-glass table set at one end of the kitchen while Lilah hopped onto a step stool by the sink to fill the kettle.

Glass doors opened onto the garden—or would, if it wasn't still a bit too nippy—which had a wide decking area up against the house and a built-in brick barbecue. The garden itself was well cared for. There were none of the tatty corners I had at mine, where I'd been meaning to do something about cutting stuff back but had then run out of summer. I wondered who looked after it. Lilah? Unlikely, given the pristine state of her manicure. Jonny-boy? More likely she paid someone to come round and see to it.

There were no playhouses, trampolines, or abandoned tricycles, despite what she'd said about her kids missing their stepdad. The fridge was free of brightly coloured modern artworks only a mum could love, too. How old were her kids? In their teens, maybe? That'd explain the lack of sight or sound of them—they'd be either out somewhere doing whatever young people did now that Pokémon was old hat again or holed up in their bedrooms with their headphones on, watching anime porn or moaning on about how unfair life was to their mates on Snapchat. At least, going by what I'd been told by the long-suffering Mrs. K. only yesterday as I fixed the kitchen tap her eldest had got a bit heavy-handed with.

Mind you, Lilah's kids actually had something to moan about.

"Tea?" Lilah asked, waving a posh earthenware mug in my face.

The kettle had boiled already? Time to start paying attention, Paretski. "Cheers, love. Milk, no sugar, ta."

"Phil?"

"Same, please."

She made herself one too—black today—and plonked a big biscuit tin on the table before climbing onto a free chair. "Help yourselves, go on. I ain't eaten a thing since I heard about my poor boy, but no need for anyone else to go hungry."

It'd been a few days, and she didn't look in any danger of keeling over, so I took that with a pinch of salt. Phil passed on the biscuits. I had a peek in the tin and snagged myself a bourbon cream.

"We're sorry for your loss, Mrs. Parrot," Phil said formally.

"Call me Lilah. Didn't I tell you to call me Lilah? *Mrs. Parrot* just makes me sad. Less than two years we was married, you know?" She sighed and took a sip of her tea.

I followed suit and scalded my mouth. And my tea had milk in it. Lilah must have lips of steel.

"It must be an added strain to have the police suspect foul play," Phil went on. "Have you got any idea who might have wanted to harm your husband?"

"Oh, I know who done it, all right. Like I told the coppers."

CHAPTER THIRTEEN

"**Y**ou know who killed your husband?" Phil asked while I was still working on closing my suddenly slack jaw.

Lilah nodded. "That bloke of his, he's the one. Couldn't stand the thought of my Jonny-boy coming back to me, could he?"

"He came back to you?" I blurted out, having finally got my mouth in gear.

Luckily, Lilah didn't seem miffed at my surprised tone. "Course he did. I mean, I hadn't seen him or nothing, but why else would he be around here? He was on his way home, bless him, and that bastard came running after him. Shoved my poor boy in the canal rather than give him up again."

Phil and me exchanged looks. Dave's brief report on the state of the investigation had conspicuously failed to include the words *It was the boyfriend what done it and we got him bang to rights*. Phil coughed. "Can you tell us about the man you suspect?"

"Already told you all I know, didn't I? If you found my Jonny, you must have found him and all."

I blinked. "Wait, do you mean Kelvin, uh . . ."

"Reid," Phil put in. "The stallholder?"

"That's him. Nasty piece of work." She shivered.

"What did the police think of your theory?" Phil went on.

For a moment I thought Lilah was actually going to spit. "Told me they'd *keep it in mind*. Bunch of useless tossers. Bet he slipped 'em a bung. They're all on the take. Always have been."

I could sense Phil holding himself in check after this slur on his former profession. Time I took the initiative. "What you want, love, is an impartial investigator. Someone who'll see justice done."

She looked up sharply. "Offering your services, are you? I can't say you didn't deliver on finding him for me, but you ain't gonna solve this one by angling your little dangle and communing with the spirits. No offence."

Ouch. She'd changed her tune on my so-called talents. But then I supposed it'd all been good fun before the killing started. Now, if I *could* commune with the spirits, that'd be a pretty surefire way of solving most murders, but since I couldn't, it didn't seem worth arguing the point. "Not my services. Phil's. He's a private investigator, isn't he? This sort of job's his bread and butter."

Well, to be honest, it was more like the posh crackers and whisky-laced marmalade they sell in John Lewis around Christmas as gifts for people who don't need anything. But the point was, it wasn't like he'd never done it before.

Lilah turned to face Phil and gave him a hard stare. "You telling me you can prove he done it?"

"*If* he did it. You want to make sure the right person gets punished, don't you?" Phil gave her a hard stare back. It was just as well they were sitting at opposite sides of a table. Anything that might have inadvertently strayed between them—like me, for instance—would have been fried in the laser beam of their combined glares.

"Course he done it." Lilah was wavering. Then she steeled herself. "What have you got that the coppers haven't, anyway?"

Phil didn't give an inch. "People will talk to a private investigator who won't talk to the police."

She wasn't buying it—or at least, not without checking its dental records. "You reckon."

"I know. I was on the force for six years. I've seen it from both sides."

I'd always thought, technically speaking, the police and Phil were on the *same* side, with the criminals on the other, but it didn't seem like a helpful thing to say right now.

Lilah fixed my beloved with a speculative eye. "Why did you leave?"

"Creative differences," I put in quickly. Phil could get touchy about that particular time in his life. Shame, though. Explaining how he'd been suspended for losing it with a wife-beating arse-wipe who'd intimidated his victim into dropping the charges might have given him some extra cred with Lilah. "Tell you what, you hire Phil to get the bastard who killed your husband, and I'll waive my fee for finding him, how about that?"

Lilah frowned, then nodded slowly. "You got a deal. But you dig stuff up, you tell me first, you got that?"

"Course, love." I darted a glance over at Phil in case I'd gone too far, but he was nodding.

Lilah flashed us a tiny smile. "Then we're good. So you're going to have words with Kelvin What's-his-arse now?"

Phil stood up. "It'll make sense to talk to people locally first, while we're here. Visit his place of work. And I'd like to have a look at his personal effects."

"His stuff? I can show you the things he left here, but anything that meant anything went back to Camden with him." For a moment she slumped, her face sad and tired, and I could believe Darren and her were the same age. "Didn't have much, did he? Travelled light, my boy did. Come on, then."

She got down from her chair. I cast a regretful glance back at the biscuit tin and followed her and Phil upstairs.

It was a lot roomier up there than I'd expected, and even Phil didn't have to watch his step so as not to bang his head. Lilah and Jonny-boy's bedroom resembled a film set, and I don't mean a low-budget porno. More like one of those not-very-historical (if you believe Cherry, anyhow) dramas about medieval kings and queens shagging their way through the court. There was the biggest four-poster bed I'd ever seen, and everything was draped in deep-red velvet. A proper old-fashioned fireplace on the opposite wall, which definitely hadn't started its life in this room, had a top-of-the-range electric fire installed, and what was probably a genuine bearskin hearthrug. Lilah's skimpy silk nightie lay draped across the unmade bed. I looked away quickly, feeling like a peeping Tom.

She opened up one end of a vast built-in wardrobe. "This is Jonny's end." Then she clammed up. Maybe it'd occurred to her too that should have been in past tense.

We poked our noses in. The rails were sagging in the middle under the weight of expensive, barely worn suits and crisply starched shirts, with a strong whiff of the dry-cleaners. It didn't seem like what you'd wear to sell antiques, but then again, most of what I knew about the trade came from dozing off in front of *Antiques Roadshow* when there was nothing else on the telly. There was a collection of soberly coloured ties hanging on the door, which I gave a quick once-over—and then peered at more closely. Huh. Not as boring as I'd thought: one had a moustache motif, another was covered in little airships, and yet another had discreet little Jolly Rogers.

"He loved his ties," Lilah put in sadly.

At the bottom of the wardrobe, next to half a dozen pairs of the sort of shoes that come in a little bag and with wooden feet in to keep them nice—amazing what I'd learned, peeking in Phil's side of our wardrobe back home—there was a crumpled stack of faded jeans and T-shirts.

I was starting to get a picture of our Mr. Parrot, and it didn't look at all like the image Lilah seemed to have of him. Or, probably more accurately, had tried to mould him into. I wondered why he'd let her. Money? Or had he really loved her and wanted to be the bloke she thought he could be?

Phil coughed, reminding me to get on with things. I did my best to block out everything else, focus whatever part of my mind was responsible for the old spidey-senses, and *listen*.

Nothing.

Or rather, there was plenty—but none of it was coming either from or to this little collection of orphaned clothes. There was a heavy background buzz that, as I concentrated, separated into different trails—

"What you looking for, then?" Lilah demanded, thrusting her head next to mine in the wardrobe and totally derailing my efforts.

I managed not to yelp in surprise, or swear as I straightened up. "Clues," I said shortly. Phil quirked an eyebrow at me, and I shook my head a fraction of an inch in reply.

"What about his other belongings?" Phil asked. "Did he have hobbies?"

"There's his golf clubs in the garage. But you might as well finish up in the house first, right?" Lilah didn't leave us for a second, and she didn't stop talking for more than a minute at a time, either. Mostly about how much she missed her Jonny-boy, she couldn't believe he was really gone, and *Oi, where do you think you're going now?*

That was when Phil tried to take a peek into a room near the end of the landing. He got as far as opening the door a crack and letting out a strong whiff of stale air and staler socks, before she stopped him. "That's Axel's room. You won't find nothing in there."

"Axel?"

"My little boy. He's been devastated by all this. You leave him in peace."

He'd been in the room? I sent Phil a questioning glance, and he nodded. I wondered what little Axel had been up to not to add his own protests about being barged in on. Sleeping, maybe? It wasn't noon yet, so it was still practically the middle of the night for your average teenager.

"How many kids have you got?" I asked to try to lighten the suddenly frosty mood.

"Just the two. That's Lola's room, so you don't need to go in there, neither." She nodded towards the next door along.

Lola? Christ, I hoped it wasn't short for Lolita, poor kid. "Is she very upset by her stepdad's death?"

I said it sympathetically, but Lilah still gave me a dark look. "Course she is. Just 'cos he wasn't her real dad don't mean she didn't love him."

Phil coughed. "I understand this is a difficult time for all of you, but it might help us to have a word with her and your son. Sometimes children pick up on things."

Lilah frowned, her mouth pinched. "I don't want 'em upset. Lola's not home, anyhow," she added, sounding pleased about it.

So, not so upset about Jonny-boy's death she hadn't nipped off out with her mates—or at least, presumably that was where she was.

"Perhaps we could start with Axel, then," Phil suggested.

"I suppose. But no upsetting him, right?" Lilah had a determined set to her jaw. "You go and sit in the living room, and I'll bring him down."

We went. "You don't reckon she's coaching him on what to say, do you?" I muttered as low as I could in Phil's shell-like once we'd reached the sofa.

"Who knows?" He glanced around the room with a suspicious gleam in his eye, although to be fair, that was pretty much a default expression for my beloved, especially when he was on a case.

"My guess is they're covering up for little Lola. She bashed Jonny-boy on the head to get back at her mum for the godawful name—I mean, seriously, Lilah and Lola? She might as well have called her Mini-Me." *And* now I had that Kinks song stuck in my head. Cheers, love.

Phil huffed. "You think? She's probably a foot taller than her mum, remember. Dwarf parents usually have kids of normal height."

"Yeah, but 'mini' doesn't have to mean height, does it?"

"Not unless you're going by the actual dictionary—"

He broke off at the sound of footsteps coming down the stairs.

CHAPTER FOURTEEN

Seconds later, Axel slouched his way into the living room, his hands in the pockets of his hoodie and his gaze skittering away from anything close to eye contact. Lilah's little boy towered over his mum and looked to my inexpert eye to be in his mid to late teens, with dark eyebrows and five-o'clock shadow that proved he was at least old enough to shave. He slumped into an armchair and stared fixedly at his knobbly knees, both clearly visible through the rips in his jeans.

"Axel," Lilah said sharply, perching her own bum neatly on the other chair. "Hood *off*." She made a brusque gesture with both hands.

Her son sent her a sullen glower, but did as she'd told him, revealing fashionably cut dark hair and a pair of top-brand headphones that must have cost Lilah almost as much as one of Jonny-boy's suits.

That explained Axel's lack of reaction to Phil bursting into his room. Lilah made another angry gesture, obviously used to having to communicate via sign language, and the kid took the headphones off and hung them around his neck.

He had that translucent clear skin some teenagers get, presumably to make the less-fortunate majority feel even worse about sprouting a galaxy of zits, and he'd be pretty good looking if he straightened those shoulders, kept his chin up, and stopped glaring at the world like it'd just kicked his puppy.

Christ, I was getting old. Next thing you knew I'd be banging on about wanting my country back and getting excited about new slow-cooker recipes.

"Axel." Phil stood up to hold out his hand across the fluffy fake-fur rug. "I'm Phil Morrison, and this is my partner Tom Paretski. We're investigating your stepfather's death."

The kid stared for a moment, then pulled his hand out of his pocket and gripped Phil's hesitantly, as if he wasn't sure he was doing it right. He straightened up in his seat afterwards, though. Nice one, Phil.

"Axel," Lilah butted in. "Say hello. Be polite."

Great. Axel slumped back down again with a mutter that could, conceivably, have been "'Lo."

Phil showed great restraint in *not* sending Lilah a death glare, and leaned forward to talk to the kid. "Were you surprised when your stepfather left?"

"Course he was," Lilah snapped. "Weren't you, baby?"

Baby? Just what a lad needs on the cusp of manhood. Axel's face turned a not-very-manly shade of blotchy pink, and even I felt hot and embarrassed on the poor kid's behalf.

Phil humphed and turned to Lilah. Everyone has their limit. "Mrs. Parrot, if you wouldn't mind letting Axel answer for himself?"

"'Scuse *me*. Well, go on then. Answer him."

Axel's shoulders hunched so far his headphones half-covered his mouth. "Didn't know he was going, did I?"

"Had he shown any signs of feeling under threat?"

"Why would he?" Lilah burst out. "He wasn't in any danger here, was he? He was fine until he went back to that bastard."

Technically, according to Lilah, Jonny-boy had been fine until he'd decided to come back to *her*, but she probably wouldn't thank me for pointing that out.

"Mrs. Parrot, please?" Phil's patient-with-the-client tone was starting to wear thin. "Perhaps this would be easier for Axel if you weren't here?"

From the ferrety look Axel shot her, I wasn't sure he agreed. Interesting. I'd have thought he'd be only too keen to undo the old apron strings.

Lilah pursed her lips. "He's only fifteen, you know. Ought to have an appropriate adult with him."

An appropriate adult. Funny how easily that phrase tripped off her tongue. Had young Axel found himself on the wrong end of a police investigation in his past? Course, I shouldn't be sexist about it. Maybe it was his sister who'd come to the attention of the Old Bill. Or Lilah herself—I certainly wouldn't put it past her to have had a misspent youth.

"Are we done yet?" Axel whined, hands on his headphones.

"*No*," Lilah snapped. She watched him until the hands flopped back to his knees. Axel didn't *actually* roll his eyes, but I could tell he really, really wanted to.

"We're not the police, and this isn't an official interview," Phil told her in his best you-can-trust-me tones. "Just a chat. And kids often worry about disappointing their parents, even if those fears are groundless. Wouldn't it be better for him to feel he can speak freely?"

"Well . . ." She was clearly wavering.

Axel stood up in an explosive, uncoordinated motion. I had to duck so as not to get hit by flailing limbs. "This is stupid. I don't know anything, and if I did, it's not going to bring him back, is it?"

"Axel, baby—" Lilah reached out to her son, but he shook her off.

"And it's *Axe*, all right? Just Axe. I'm not a little kid, Mum." He stomped off, his face tight with misery.

Lilah gazed after him helplessly for a moment, then turned back to us with a defiant, "It ain't his fault. He's been that cut up about it all."

I felt like a git for doubting her word about it earlier.

"Not to worry," Phil said. "Perhaps you could show us the garage, now?"

She led the way, and we duly inspected the golf clubs. They were suspiciously shiny and free from stray bits of mud and grass, but it was possible he'd been the sort of bloke who liked to look after his kit. After that she showed us the pool room, which was a room with a pool table in it, rather than somewhere you could have a dip and a splash about. The balls were stacked on the table in a neat triangle, and cues stood ready by the wall.

"This was my Jonny's birthday present back in September," Lilah said sadly. "Him and Axel used to be in here every night after dinner."

We probably ought to take that with a pinch of the proverbial— how many teenage lads would want to spend all their evenings with their real dad, let alone the new(ish) stepdad?—but then again, the blue cubes of chalk sitting on the edge of the table showed deep hollows.

We poked around a few other nooks and crannies after that, but for a bloke who'd been living here over a year, old Jonny-boy had left an unusually light footprint on the place. Maybe he really had spent all his time bonding with his stepson over pool? After all, you didn't have to be blood to be family. My own dad—the one who'd raised me as his own, despite me being a permanent reminder of Mum's little indiscretion—was proof of that.

I'd been feeling bad enough about JP's untimely demise. Now I felt even worse for the young lad who'd lost his father figure, unlikely as it had seemed.

We got a few more details from Lilah—addresses for Jonny-boy's family, apparently estranged, and his former place of work—then took our leave. Not before time, if Lilah's increasing tetchiness was anything to go by. Maybe *her* stomach was reminding her it had been a long time since breakfast too.

"Did you see those golf clubs?" I asked Phil as we walked down Lilah's weed-free red-brick drive. "Looked like they were barely out of the wrapper. What do you bet he slung 'em in the car, told her he'd be on the course all day, and sloped off down the pub?"

Phil grunted. "Make a good cover for other things too."

"You reckon he was cheating on her? Nipping off down to Camden to see the ex?" I frowned. "S'pose he doesn't really count as an ex if Jonny was still seeing him, does he? But oi, you sure it's not just all your other cases making you cynical in your old age?"

"Maybe," Phil said in a tone that meant *Yes, I'm sure.*

We reached the car and got in. "She didn't seem all that enthusiastic about us investigating Jonny-boy's death. Although, mind you, I s'pose if you're a brand-new widow, it's hard to scrape up enthusiasm for anything much. You went for the hard sell a bit," I added, buckling up my seat belt.

Phil humphed. "Like you didn't? There's something dodgy about this case. That package she got us to deliver, the way he ran . . . That story about the boyfriend doesn't fit. And I don't like the timing."

"You mean, him getting offed right after we found him?"

"Yes." Phil stared straight ahead through the windscreen as he started the engine, a haunted look in his eye.

Huh. Seemed I wasn't the only one worried we'd basically delivered a death sentence to the poor bastard.

"Did you get anything at all?" he asked after we'd pulled out onto the road.

I screwed up my face, thinking. "Nah. Not really. There was stuff, lots of it—but I'm pretty sure most of it was Lilah. I s'pose if you work in porn, you're bound to have a few secrets. It didn't feel like she had the murder weapon stashed somewhere in the house," I added, because I knew Phil was about to ask.

"Most of it," he said thoughtfully, turning onto the main road.

I blinked. "What?"

"You said, 'most of it.' So was some of it our Mr. Parrot?"

"I dunno . . ." I shook my head. "It was flippin' hard to tell, but I don't think so? It was more . . . maybe one of the kids? What did you make of Axel, sorry, *Axe*, anyhow? Seemed genuine, him being all cut up about his stepdad."

Phil didn't answer for a moment. "Seemed to be," he said at last.

"You didn't buy it?"

"Could've been guilt."

"What, you reckon he done it? Huh. Lilah's going to be pissed off if she ends up paying you to get her kid banged up."

"Did I say he'd done it? Maybe Axel and his stepdad didn't get on as well she reckons they did, and the kid blames himself for Jonathan walking out and going back to the ex."

"You mean all those evenings in the pool room weren't as cosy as she painted them?" I thought about it. "Yeah, I could buy Axe being a little shit to try and drive his stepdad away better than I could buy him actually killing the bloke. Shame we didn't get to talk to him properly, though."

Phil hummed something noncommittal. "I'd like to have a word with his sister."

"Yeah. How old do you think she is? Must be teens at least, or Lilah wouldn't have let her out the house on her own."

"We don't know that. Some mums are more protective of their sons than their daughters. *And* we don't know she's out on her own."

"Yeah, guess not. S'pose we should have asked Lilah about her."

"No. I'd rather do a bit of digging first."

"Fair enough." I was silent a mo, watching the countryside fly past. "How's your sister doing these days?"

"Leanne's fine." He gave me a sharp look. "Since when do you worry about my sister?"

"She's family now. Or going to be. You know, when we, uh . . ."

"The phrase is 'get married,'" Phil said drily. "If you can manage to get the words out, that is."

"Oi, are you suggesting I'm getting cold feet?"

There was an ear-splitting silence. "I *wasn't*," Phil said in the end.

Oops. He didn't sound amused. "'Cos, well, I'm not. Obviously. Been thinking about flowers and everything, haven't I?"

There was another silence, this one slightly less wince inducing.

But only slightly.

"So, uh, where are we off to now?" I asked with the sort of fake brightness you use with terminally confused old folk and loved ones you've just mortally pissed off.

"Lunch. Then the Old Smithy," Phil said, changing gear with unnecessary force.

"Right. Good." I clammed up.

Phil was an ex-copper, remember? Anything I said could and would be taken down and used in evidence against me.

CHAPTER FIFTEEN

I was worried the conversation over our pub grub would be stilted, but as I ought to have guessed, Phil treated it as a working lunch. We'd picked a likely looking local establishment, the Brewer's Droop—all right, Phil had picked it, using criteria not vouchsafed to yours truly—and he grilled the bar staff about Jonny-boy while the kitchen staff grilled our Aberdeen Angus steak burgers.

Given how much they were planning to charge us for the food, I hoped they were doing a bloody good job of it. And yeah, I'd already got an inkling from the prices, not to mention the poncy microbrews on offer, that this might not have been old JP's home from home in any case, but you never knew. And I was flippin' starving.

I sat back with my Diet Coke and checked my phone for messages—one from Gary with a link to the box set of *Prison Break*, which I deleted without a qualm, and another from a customer with a leak which I felt a bit bad about leaving for later—until Phil came back with our meals.

"Any joy?" I asked, just about managing not to snatch the plate he passed me from his unwary hands. "And you do know they have people to bring the food over, right?"

Phil shrugged. "Not like I wasn't coming this way. And no. They said our Mr. Parrot had been in here once or twice, but it wasn't his local. They suggested we try down the road at the Spanish Inquisition."

"Oh? I wasn't expecting that," I said idly, picking up a fry—it was way too skinny to qualify as a chip—with my fingers and bunging it in my gob.

He winced, which, fair dues, was all that feeble Monty Python joke deserved. "Word of advice, Paretski. Don't give up the day job."

I laughed, because his face was a picture. "Which one? The plumbing, or the nosy-parker business? Don't answer that. So it's a pub crawl, then, is it? Cheers." I raised my Coke in an ironic salute, then tucked in to my burger. It wasn't bad. The meat still had a bit of life in it, so to speak, and the bun was decent quality, with a generous amount of homemade pickle.

"You wish. No, we're sticking to the plan. It's the Old Smithy next. Makes more sense to do the pub in the evening."

"A whole day out in Pluck's End? Blimey, it's like we're on honeymoon already." I hesitated, then decided to go for it on the basis it might help persuade Phil I wasn't having second thoughts about the wedding. "While we're on the subject, we probably ought to get something booked—"

"Let's keep our minds on the case for now," Phil cut me off almost literally, with a wave of his steak knife. "We can talk about that when we're off the clock."

"What, we don't even get a lunch hour? I'm guessing there's no such thing as a trade union in the private-eye business, then."

"Smart-arse." He smiled, though, so I reckoned I was back in his good books. "Just think we should focus on the case while we're out here and it's all fresh in our minds."

"Fair enough." I scoffed down some more of my burger, and a thought struck. "Oi, we need to interview Darren, don't we? Him being a mate of Lilah's. And by we, I mean you. Tell you what, we'll make a night of it. I'll distract Gary with martinis and you can have a word with Darren."

"They're not joined at the hip. I can catch him on a Monday night." Monday nights were when Gary went out to tug repeatedly on something long and sausage-shaped and make a lot of noise in the company of other like-minded individuals—in other words, he had bellringing practice.

I shrugged. "Fine." I could catch up with Gary another time. Although despite what Phil said, catching Gary on his own hadn't got any easier since him and Darren had tied the metaphorical. What with Dave being stuck indoors changing nappies, I was feeling the lack of someone to have a drink and a moan about my bloke with.

Not that I'd actually got a lot to moan about, with Phil. Obviously. But it'd be nice to think the opportunity was there if I needed it.

It was like the ex-Mrs. Z. had been saying to me when I went round to fix her loo—once all your mates get coupled up and/or sprogged up, any poor sod left single finds their social life's completely gone down the pan. Maybe it's just part of getting older. Maturing.

I blinked as fingers snapped in front of my face. "What?"

"Still in there?" Phil asked with a smirk.

"Oi, I was focussing on the case," I lied, and took a large bite of my burger to cover up any tells.

"Right." I'm sure I imagined the scepticism in the voice of my beloved. "So you've come up with a strategy for dealing with our Mr. Parrot's colleagues at the Old Smithy?" he went on.

"I didn't say I was focussing *productively*. Anyhow, thought I'd leave all that to you. Wouldn't want you to think I was after your job." I chewed on a fry thoughtfully. It was edible, even borderline tasty, but give me proper chip-shop chips any day. "Wonder what Lilah's sister's like? The antiques business is a bit different from, well, porn."

"Find out soon enough, won't you?"

I hesitated, then said it anyway. "Sure we shouldn't be heading off down to Camden to have a word with Kelvin Reid? I mean, I know we reckoned it didn't sound right . . ."

Phil shook his head decisively. "No. The police will be covering that angle—remember Lilah said she told them it was him?"

"Doesn't mean they believed her any more than we did."

"They don't have to believe her. They do have to check out any leads provided by the public, even if they're probably bollocks." He gave a grim smile. "Tends not to go down too well with superior officers, ignoring that kind of thing. Especially if it turns out the lead was on track all along."

"Voice of experience?"

"Not personally. Thank God. Anyway, we'll stick to the plan—talk to the colleagues this afternoon, and visit the pub in the evening. We can pay a visit to Mr. Reid in a day or so. Give him time to get over the official interviews."

I frowned. "That's very considerate of you, seeing as he's a murder suspect."

Phil huffed a laugh. "Not as such. Sorry to shatter your illusions. It just means they'll either have found something on him and arrested him, or he'll have let his guard back down."

"And there's the ruthless bastard I've come to know and love. Right, are we done here?" I gave up on the fries and placed my cutlery neatly at twenty past four.

It got me a raised eyebrow from Phil, who'd left his own plate so clean you could eat your dinner off it. So to speak. "You, leaving food? Are you feeling all right?"

"Hey, I don't want to be bursting out of my wedding dress, do I? Hand your plate over."

Phil knocked back the last of his mineral water, and I took the plates over to the bar, which earned me a smile and a "Bless you, love" from the barmaid. Then we headed off out to the Smithy.

CHAPTER SIXTEEN

The postal address of the Old Smithy might have claimed it was in Pluck's End, but the place itself was so far out in the wilds I half expected to turn a corner and find Bear Grylls doing naked push-ups to stave off hypothermia.

Okay, so there might have been a certain amount of wishful thinking there.

After a couple of false starts (because hey, this was our neck of the woods, more or less, so we weren't going to cop out and use the satnav), we reached our destination down a winding narrow lane with only a few houses for company, of the big, posh persuasion that had names like "Hunter's Lodge" and "Water End House" instead of numbers. Just in case plebs like me hadn't got the message *They ain't for the likes of you, mate.* It was a sturdy, rambling building, painted gleaming white and no doubt with a discreet plaque somewhere proclaiming its listed-building status, topped off with a neatly maintained thatched roof.

There was a car park set off to one side in what I guessed had once been a paddock—a sort of waiting room for the horses coming to get shod, maybe? Only without the posters telling you more about various health issues than you really wanted to know, and with no dog-eared, germ-ridden copies of *Reader's Digest* to thumb through, either. Or hoof through, as might be. Phil pulled his Golf in there, tutting under his breath as a muddy puddle splashed its pristine silver sides.

"We're working for Lilah now," I comforted him. "You can claim for the car wash on expenses." Then I thought about it and brightened up. "Hey, that means our lunch was on expenses too, right?"

Phil huffed a laugh. "I suppose you'd have gone for dessert too if you'd thought about it."

"I wouldn't dream of taking advantage of the client like that." Although I might've had a side salad. Hey, vitamins are important.

Once out of the paddock, we were walking on deep, crunchy gravel. The near end of the building was set up as a tiny café with its own entrance flanked by big stone urns planted up with colourful winter pansies, and a tastefully chalked-up blackboard advertising fair-trade coffee and gluten-free cakes. I felt like going in and asking for a mug of PG Tips and a choccie biccie on principle, but it was a bit soon after lunch. Maybe later.

"You'd have thought a thatched roof would be a health and safety risk back in days of yore when the forge was lit and sparks were flying," I said idly as we walked up to the main entrance.

"Maybe that's why they built the place so far from town," Phil suggested.

"Yeah? Seems rough on the horses, having to hobble miles to get their shoes fixed."

"It'd be rougher if the whole village went up in flames." Phil's face was grim, and I wondered if he was remembering the fire at the Dyke, which me and him had had front-row tickets for. And great, now *I* was picturing it in all its terrifying glory. We could have lost each other that day. I shuddered and pushed open the door.

The theme of arsonist's delight carried on inside the Smithy, with bare wooden floorboards scattered with the odd flammable rustic rag rug, firewood furniture and fittings, and a large, open wooden staircase leading up to the first floor, presumably to allow airflow to fan the flames. Not that I'm paranoid or anything. The centrepiece of the ground floor was a massive anvil, nearly three feet long, displayed on a cast iron stand. It looked just like the ones in cartoons, with one pointy end and one square, although it didn't have the brand name *Acme* written on the side, and there were definitely no flattened coyotes underneath. When I ran a hand over its surface, it wasn't as cold as I'd been expecting, and the metal, although pitted by hammer blows, felt smooth.

Having worked with cast iron pipes, which were what half the plumbing in this place likely consisted of, I did a rough-and-ready guesstimate in my head. "Blimey, this must weigh three or four hundred pounds. And that's without the stand."

Phil raised an eyebrow. "You'd know about that if it fell on your toe."

"Or if it got dropped on you from a height. Actually, hang about, no, you probably wouldn't, in that case. You'd be too busy doing pancake impersonations." I grinned. "Think anyone's ever been murdered by anvil?"

"You want to murder someone, you'd be better off using something from that little lot." Phil nodded towards the back wall, which was hung with a wicked selection of aggressively large hammers, long-handled pliers and other implements of medieval torture and the farrier's trade.

"Point. Think they're for sale? Or just there for decoration? Or, you know, defence against burglars?"

"Place like this? They don't defend against burglars. All they do is put in a hefty insurance claim once the stuff's gone walkabout."

So much for Lilah reckoning this place to be a home away from home for a bloke from Camden Market. The Old Smithy bore about the same relation to a market stall selling vintage goods as I do to the Queen. Oh, they had old stuff for sale, but that was about the only similarity. In fact, when I examined it all more closely, I saw that half the goods on offer weren't proper antiques, just crafty stuff in vintage style, like hats and mittens your granny's granny would have turned her nose up at as too old-fashioned and knickknacks made out of leather or felt that didn't seem to have any purpose apart from looking vintage. It didn't even *smell* old in here—more like potpourri and furniture polish.

Then there was a whole section labelled *Vintage, Retro, and Reclaimed Lighting*, which mostly seemed to consist of perfectly good, if battered, pieces of equipment like phones with actual dials, tripod cameras, and old electrical meters—which some git had then desecrated by shoving a light bulb in the top.

I felt like taking them home and giving them a decent burial—until I saw the prices. "Bloody hell, who buys these things?"

Phil cast an appraising eye over the poor bastardised gadgets. "Steampunks?"

"Do what?"

"You know. Dress up like Charles Dickens gone postal in a clock factory. Say 'Splendid' a lot and go on about tea. Read a lot of Victorian science fiction. Jules Verne, H.G. Wells, and all that."

"Oh. Right." I squinted at the, for want of a better word, lamps. "I don't get it. Where's the steam? Where's the flippin' punk, even?"

Phil shrugged. "It's an aesthetic."

"Don't reckon it'd send me to sleep. Give me nightmares, maybe."

"Funny. And seriously, a bunch of lamps?" Phil actually took a step away, all the better to give me the side-eye.

I hunched my shoulders. "It's . . . I dunno. Making things be something they're not. I don't like it."

His eyes narrowed. "It's not a—"

"Nope. It's not."

We both knew he'd been about to ask if it was in any way, shape, or form related to my so-called gift.

We also both knew I hadn't exactly given the matter due consideration but trust me, when I'm already on edge *and* we're about to talk to someone about the murder of a family member isn't the best time in the world for indulging in spiritual self-examination.

"Can I help you, or are you just browsing?" We both spun round at the sound of that nicely-brought-up voice. Giving us a polite smile was a young man—early twenties, I'd guess—who set my gaydar pinging off the scale. So going by past results, he was probably happily married to his second wife and with a baby or six on the way. He had fashionably—but not *too* fashionably—cut dark hair and the figure of someone who watched what he ate. Good-looking, but in an abstract way, not in an I'd-tap-that way.

Phil cleared his throat. "Are you the manager here?"

"Me? No. Merely a humble minion. Would you like to speak to Ms. Lovett? She's the owner." He didn't bother waiting for our yay or nay, and took a couple of paces away from us before twirling like a dancer to ask, "What can I say it's about?"

"Jonathan Parrot," Phil said quietly, but with emphasis. "We're investigating his murder."

That stopped the bloke. He retraced his steps and stretched out a hand, which Phil grasped for a short, businesslike handshake. "Oh, how thrilling to meet you. I'm Oliver. Oliver Proudfoot."

"Phil Morrison. And my partner, Tom Paretski." My turn to shake hands. Oliver gave my palm an extra squeeze, which got me wondering if I'd pinged *his* gaydar, and then Phil went on, "Before we see Miss Lovett, you must have known Mr. Parrot pretty well." It was half a question and half not.

Did Oliver freeze for an instant there? Or had I imagined it? Almost immediately, his face turned sad. "We're quite a tight-knit team here. We're going to miss him terribly."

Phil put on a puzzled expression. "From what I heard, he stopped working here several weeks ago. Had you seen him since then?"

Okay, I definitely hadn't imagined it, because there it was again. That tiny pause before Oliver answered. "No. I'm afraid not. Shall we go on up? It's *Mzz* Lovett, by the way. She's very particular about that. And no jokes about pies, if you want to stay on her good side."

Phil smiled, but it seemed forced to me. "Let me guess, she's heard them all before?"

"Uh?" was my intelligent contribution to the discussion.

I got a pitying look from Oliver. "*Sweeney Todd*? The musical?"

"He killed 'em; Mrs. Lovett baked 'em," Phil explained.

"'Worst pies in England,'" Oliver singsonged helpfully if tunelessly. "Or was it London?"

"London," Phil told him, at the same moment as I said, "Right. I knew that." We'd watched the film round at Gary and Darren's a while back, though it hadn't really been my cup of gin.

"And no," Oliver went on as he gestured up the open staircase. "Ms. Lovett tends not to have a sense of humour about her name."

I got the sense he was itching to add, *Or at all*, but that could just have been me. And after all, this was Lilah's sister we were talking about. Mzz Tallulah Lovett was likely to be as down-to-earth and unpretentious as the original.

We trooped up the stairs, me in the lead and Oliver politely following us, probably so he could get a good view of Phil's arse.

"Ms. Lovett?" he called out as we reached the top. "There are some gentlemen to see you."

A pair of denim-clad female ankles appeared in my field of vision, swiftly followed by another pair, these ones in sheer tights and flashily expensive shoes. I looked up and blinked.

"All right, Tom?" Lilah said loudly.

CHAPTER SEVENTEEN

Lilah beamed at us from the top of the stairs with a smile like a shark's. "I thought I'd better give Loos here a heads-up you might be coming round. Didn't want you to catch her on the hop, did I?"

Bloody hell. So much for the element of surprise. That'd teach us to stop for lunch en route. "Lilah, good to see you again so soon," I said cautiously as I reached the landing. I was having real trouble working our esteemed client out. Did she want us on the job or not?

I shot Phil a glance as he joined me, but he had that stony expression he always wears when he wants to hide the fact someone's just bogged up his best-laid plans.

Standing next to each other, Lilah and Loos—*Loos?*—looked exactly like before-and-after pictures of some poor woman who'd been stretched on the rack. It was well weird. The sister was, I realised once we were on the same level, no more than a couple of inches shorter than me, but in all other respects she was eerily like Lilah. Even down to clothes size, in anything that didn't come with long sleeves or legs. Except . . . somehow the figure that was so voluptuous on Lilah seemed average and nondescript on the sister.

Phil recovered before I did, and stepped forward to offer his hand. "Phil Morrison. And this is my partner, Tom Paretski. We're investigating Jonathan Parrot's death."

"Where are my manners? This is my little sister, Tallulah Lovett." Lilah smiled. Mzz Lovett didn't, although she did shake Phil's hand while giving him a thorough examination. Apparently big, built, and blond was her thing too.

But ye gods, Lilah, Tallulah, and Lola? I was struggling to see what Axel thought he had to complain about, name-wise. And while Lilah was every inch Sampson's temptress (hey, I paid attention in Sunday School. Until they kicked me out), Tallulah's name didn't seem to fit her, as if she'd borrowed it from her sister.

If I'd had to guess, I'd have put Tallulah as the elder, and not because she was taller. There were hard lines around her mouth, and the cords in her neck stood out, ropy and taut above the designer scarf she was wearing in a failed attempt to make her jeans-and-blazer outfit less boring. I also got the distinct impression she wasn't half as fond of her big sis as Lilah seemed to think she was, although fair dues, it could have been down to the godawful nickname. Oh, Loos smiled to Lilah's face all right, but her expression soured as soon as Lilah turned away. She noticed me noticing that, and sent me a glare of my very own that seemed to say *Keep your nose out of my family business if you know what's good for you.*

Or maybe she just didn't like me. Actually, come to think of it, I was fairly sure there was something personal about it. I say personal, but maybe it was men in general she didn't like. Or gay men. Or plumbers, come to that—you get a few who've been ripped off once by some cowboy, and think we're all like that.

I wondered what the word for it would be, if there was one. Plombist? Mariophobic?

"Lilah told me about you," Mzz Tallulah said, proving me right with a curl of her thin, imperfectly bleached upper lip. "I told her it was all a big con."

Okay, maybe she simply had a natural aversion to anything that smacked of mystical bollocks, which was fair enough. Her accent was a weird mix—her consonants were all present and correct, but the vowels kept wandering off to somewhere less reputable when she wasn't paying attention. She and Lilah might have left the East End behind, but it hadn't left either of them, and whereas Lilah was happy to display her origins in her front window, in Tallulah's case they might as well be a nasty smell coming out of the cellar. I flashed her a smile I wasn't feeling and put on a chipper tone. "Found him, though, didn't we?"

"You gotta admit, Loos, he's got a point." Lilah turned to us with a rueful smile that tugged on the old guilt strings. "I'll be buggering off now. You must be getting sick of the sight of me."

"Course not, love," I assured her. "What bloke would ever get tired of looking at you?"

And yeah, I was laying it on with a shovel, but Lilah's eyes sparkled at the compliment, so clearly she wasn't complaining. "Watch out for this one, Loos, he's a right charmer."

Phil coughed. "We'll need to ask you a few questions, Ms. Lovett, but we hope not to take up too much of your time."

Tallulah gave a tight little smile. "Of course, I'll be happy to give you any help I can in finding out what happened to poor Jonathan." Her face called her a liar. "Although I don't see—"

"Laters, Loos," Lilah cut her off. "And don't forget you're taking Axel out on Sunday, yeah?" She gave my arm a squeeze as she went past, heading for the stairs.

"*I* won't forget." Tallulah watched her sister leave with narrowed eyes and not a word of farewell. I hoped she was nicer to her nephew. "You'd better come on through," she told us snippily. "I'm not doing this here."

Tallulah strode off briskly in her sensible heels to a small office set right at one end of the building. With me and Phil in it as well as Mzz Lovett, it threatened to burst at the seams, particularly as she didn't bother to go sit behind the surprisingly modern desk. It could have been politeness, seeing as that was the only chair in the room, or it could simply have been a natural desire not to get loomed over.

I mean, I could relate.

"Well?" she asked, folding her arms in an *I'm far too busy to bother with minor matters like the murder of a brother-in-law* way.

"What can you tell us about Jonathan Parrot?" was Phil's opening salvo.

She parried it with a snapped, "What do you want to know?"

The adversarial approach wasn't working. Phil, ever adaptable, put on his sympathetic face. "Do you think he was happy in his marriage?"

"Course he bloody wasn't. If he had been, he wouldn't have left her, would he?" Tallulah's accent was rapidly losing its middle-class polish. "I thought you were working for Lilah, anyhow?"

"We are, but that doesn't mean—"

"So what does the state of their marriage have to do with his death? Unless you think my sister killed him?"

She was sharp, you had to give her that. Phil was sharper, mind. "I'm trying to establish if there could have been another reason for him leaving his job and his wife," he went on calmly. "Something—or someone—he was scared of, maybe?"

Tallulah's face went an unattractive shade of pink that really didn't go with her lipstick. "I don't know no—anything about that."

Phil changed tack. "What happened the day he left?"

"Nothing. He came to work as usual, left as usual, and didn't turn up next day. It was a ri—it was very inconvenient. I had to get Hazel to come in full-time after that."

"How many people work here apart from you?"

"Why?"

Bloody hell, it was like pulling teeth. "So we can be sure we've spoken to everyone," Phil told her patiently.

"Oliver and Hazel. That's it. And Brian, I suppose, but he doesn't deal with the day-to-day running of the business."

"Brian?"

"Brian Tarbox. My business partner."

Phil nodded. Either he'd come across the name before or he was taking a mental note of it. "Everyone here get on all right with Jonathan?"

"Of course." She was lying. I could tell. Not by any sixth sense, or seventh, or whatever number I'm up to these days. I just had a feeling in my water that her and Jonny-boy would have hated each other's guts.

Or would they? Maybe she wasn't a lot like Lilah, personality-wise, who our Mr. Parrot had presumably been at least a little bit fond of or he wouldn't have married her, but thinking back to how he'd been when I'd met him . . . I couldn't see him being bothered about Tallulah enough to hate her.

Which would have made her hate him all the more, if I was any judge. And let's face it, she was easily tall enough to have knocked old Jonny on the head and shoved him in the water.

"Was he good at his work?"

She hesitated. "Obviously there was something of a learning curve, but he was a reasonably good salesman." Speaking well of the bloke clearly didn't come naturally to her.

"And he was happy here?"

"As far as I knew. I was his employer, not his friend."

"Yeah, but he was family," I couldn't help butting in.

"He was married to my sister. That's not quite the same thing."

Phil changed tack. "Did your sister's first husband also work with you?"

Tallulah made an impatient gesture. "I already told you about Brian."

"Wait, Brian?" I blurted out. "Your business partner is your sister's ex?"

Her mouth went tight. "And?"

"And he was okay with employing her current husband?"

"Lilah and Brian split up years ago," Tallulah said dismissively.

That must make for some interesting family get-togethers. Then again, glass houses, stones, don't throw.

Maybe I should ask her for tips.

"So they've stayed friends?" Phil asked.

"Of course. They have the children to think about." Her lip curled so slightly she probably didn't even realise she was doing it.

"Some men find it hard to see an ex-partner moving on," Phil commented.

From the way her face darkened, Tallulah clearly wasn't deaf to the subtext. "You don't know what you're talking about. There was no strong feeling there."

Presumably she meant Brian and Jonny. Or did she mean Brian and Lilah? And if so, did she mean *ever*?

"Not the jealous sort, then?" Phil said mildly.

She snorted. "With Lilah's 'profession'?"

Ouch. You could hear the quotes around *profession*. Maybe that was the cause of the sisterly ill-feeling I'd picked up on.

Tallulah unfolded her arms. "Are we done? Because I've got work to do."

"One last question: is there anything else you can tell us that might be relevant to Mr. Parrot's death?"

"No."

"Then do you mind if we have a word with your employees?"

I could tell she was itching to say yes, actually, she did mind, but controlled herself womanfully. "I suppose you can. But please remember I have a business to run here."

Phil nodded. "Thank you for your time."

"Yeah, cheers, love," I smiled, but could have saved myself the effort. She barely waited for us to shift out of her way before barging out of that tiny office and back onto the shop floor.

"Well, she loved us and left us," I muttered. "Except without the *loving us* part. Or anyone else, for that matter. Didn't sound like she'd be crying at old Jonny-boy's funeral, did it?"

Phil shrugged. "Families. Never easy when money gets involved."

"Money?"

"I'd hope she was paying him. Maybe she resented getting him foisted on her by her sister."

"Nah, he was a good salesman. She said it herself. I'd reckon the bottom line's what it's all about, with her." I grinned. "She definitely got the short straw when it came to nicknames, didn't she?"

"What would you shorten Tallulah to, then? *Tall*? That'd look like she was taking the piss. Come on, then. Work to do." Phil led the way out onto the shop floor.

CHAPTER EIGHTEEN

"**W**ho are we tackling first?" I scanned the shop. Oliver wasn't visible, but now we were out of that shoebox of an office I could hear his smooth tones somewhere downstairs, extolling the virtues of some unidentified item of old tat that'd be *perfect* for his unseen listener's conservatory. "Better make it Hazel," I said, because if we lost Tallulah a sale, she'd probably drop that anvil on us. Phil nodded, and we set off at an easy pace, browsing the shop for someone who looked like they worked here.

We found Hazel busy tidying knickknacks over at the far end of the top floor. A well-rounded sort of girl, not what you'd call fat but definitely not thin, she was wearing a big goggly pair of glasses that made her face appear even rounder. I guessed she was in her early twenties—certainly not older, despite the fuddy-duddy outfit of officey trousers and blouse that could have been picked out of a catalogue for fashion-unconscious over-fifties. Her long, dark hair was pulled back in a limp ponytail. The quirky Star Trek insignia she'd pinned to her top to give it some geek cred seemed embarrassed to be there.

"This one's yours," Phil murmured in my ear.

"What? Why?"

"Look at her. Give her a bit of the old Paretski charm and she'll be putty in your hands."

I looked. She glanced round, caught me staring and averted her eyes, blushing.

I had to agree she'd probably find me less intimidating than my beloved. "Fine. But no moaning if I forget to ask something vital."

"You must know the drill by now. How well did she know him, when did she last see him, was there anything odd about him, all that sort of stuff. And no leading questions."

"Would I?" I girded the metaphoricals, pasted on a friendly smile, and ambled over to Hazel. Phil followed, keeping back and to one side of her, where he wouldn't be right in her face but could still hear what was going on, and picked up a brass box with a cuff link stuck to the top. I made a mental note of it, because he's a bugger to buy gifts for and I had no clue what to get him for a wedding present. Did couples buy each other wedding presents, anyway? I mean, he'd be getting me, which some might say was quite enough to be getting on with.

Hazel looked up at my approach and took a breath, presumably steeling herself to ask if there was anything she could do me for.

I beat her to the punch. "Hi, I'm Tom Paretski. Me and my partner are investigating Jon—uh, Mr. Parrot's death. You heard we were coming?"

"Oh." Her smile, already strained, gave up the ghost completely. You'd think I was the grim reaper here to make up the soul quota. "Yes. Oliver said."

"You're Hazel, right?" I tried to keep the smile going as I waited for her nod. "You must have known Jonathan Parrot pretty well?"

Hazel sniffed. Close up, I could see her eyes were red and swollen. "Yeah. I can't believe he's g-gone."

Hugging the witness would probably be unprofessional, so I patted her arm gently. "I know it's hard to think about it, but have you got any idea who might have had it in for him?"

"I'm not sure I ought to . . ." Her eyes darted around and behind me.

"Don't worry. I had a word with your boss. She's fine with us having a quiet chat."

"Oh."

"So, any ideas about who might have taken exception to Mr. Parrot?" I prompted her when she clammed up.

She shook her head jerkily, and a lock of hair escaped from her ponytail to hang forlornly in front of her ear, as if it had no idea what to do with its newfound freedom. "No one. I mean, he was lovely.

It must have been an accident, mustn't it? He slipped and hit his head on something in the water?" She seemed desperate to believe it.

"We're not ruling anything out at this stage." I was pretty sure I'd heard Phil use that phrase. Or some copper on the telly. "He worked here up until a few weeks ago, didn't he? Did he seem worried, last time you saw him? Did he mention he was leaving?" Whoops. That was probably too many questions all at once.

Hazel shook her head once more, this time a tiny, rabbitty motion. The stray lock jiggled, and she tucked it behind her ear. "No. He didn't say a word. But he always . . . I mean, he wouldn't have."

"He didn't talk to you?"

She gave me a twisted smile. "All the time. But not about stuff that mattered." She sniffed again.

Lucky I had a clean hanky. I got it out and offered it to her. "Go on. Have a good blow."

She eyed it as if it might bite. "Oh, no. I couldn't possibly."

"Course you can. That's what it's there for."

With a hesitant hand she took the hanky, gave a dainty little toot, crumpled it up, and dithered for a moment. Then she handed it back to me with a "Sorry."

"No problems." I shoved my no-longer-clean hanky back in my pocket. "I'm a plumber by trade. Trust me, love, I've dealt with far worse than a bit of snot."

Hazel giggled, then looked appalled at herself.

"Now, I know he didn't say anything directly, but— Well, you're pretty intelligent, aren't you?" I tried not to cringe at myself. It came out sounding so flippin' fake, which was ironic seeing as I reckoned it was probably true. Although maybe I was letting the glasses influence me? "I bet you noticed there was something going on with him, even if he didn't come out and say it, am I right?"

She stared down at her fingers, which were going through the motions of cat's cradle without any string. "I—I think he was worried about . . . about something."

Finally. "Any idea what it might have been? Health? Money? His marriage?"

Hazel glanced up with a jump. "I couldn't tell you anything about that. It was fine, anyway. Everything was fine."

She'd closed her shutters so fast I could still hear echoes of the slam. Was she worried she'd get in trouble for gossiping about the boss's big sis? "You know, whatever you tell me will be in strictest confidence," I encouraged her, then spoiled it with a conscience-prodded caveat: "Unless the police need to know about it."

"No. They don't. I mean, if there was something. But there isn't."

"Maybe he'd been getting calls from his ex? Threats, even?" I couldn't see it—why would the bloke have gone back to him if so? But Hazel grabbed hold with both hands like it was the last lifebelt on the *Titanic*.

"Yes. That was probably it."

"That might have caused a few domestics. If Mrs. Parrot got wind of the calls, I mean, and jumped to the conclusion the bloke wasn't as ex as he ought to be." I tried to make it sound sympathetic, and also open, sort of like a question but not. It was flippin' hard work, this digging for information lark.

Hazel turned wide eyes on me. What with the glasses, she looked alarmingly bug-like. "Oh, no. They didn't argue. They were happy together," she finished with, but I got the impression she was trying to convince herself.

"Did you see them together much?"

"Well, yeah. Course I did." She gave me a strange look. "You know, don't you?"

"Know what?"

"I still live at home."

Where else was she supposed to hang her hat? Then it hit me. "Wait a minute—you mean at Lilah's place? *You're* her daughter? Lola?" I couldn't keep the disbelief out of my voice. She wasn't anything like Lilah. Not in appearance, not in the way she spoke— not in *anything*.

She'd turned a shade of pink that would have really suited her mum. Hazel just looked hot and uncomfortable. "Only Mum ever calls me that."

"Sorry. Should've realised it was a pet name." I did the self-deprecating eye roll, what-am-I-like thing, and gave a little laugh for good measure. "Lilah and Lola—get real."

"It's short for Lorelei."

Oops.

"But I've always preferred Hazel. It's my middle name."

"Uh, yeah. Nice name. Suits you," I said quickly, trying to get back some ground.

She hunched in on herself, which was totally the opposite of what I was going for. So much for the old Paretski charm. "My brother says it's boring."

"Yeah, but what does he know?" I coughed. "I, uh, met him earlier. Round at your mum's. He seems really cut up about his stepdad."

"We all are," she said, giving me the bug-eyed stare again. "You don't know—everyone thinks we ought to hate him, but he was lovely, and he made Mum happy."

Until he left her, I didn't say.

"I still can't believe he's gone. It doesn't seem fair. Just . . . One wrong step, and now he's . . . It shouldn't be like that."

Christ, I felt old next to her. What age had I stopped thinking of me and mine as invulnerable and realised how bloody fragile life is? I mean, seriously. People pop their clogs all the time, and for the daftest of reasons—nipping over the road to get a pint of milk right when some half-blind old codger tootles along; plugging in the Christmas tree lights without checking the wiring; rushing headlong into danger to save their significant other from some murdering bastard . . .

Okay. It has to be said, my appreciation of the fragility of human existence has definitely increased since I got together with Phil. But I wouldn't have it any other way.

Most days.

I realised Hazel was looking at me expectantly, so I tried to dredge up a suitably comforting platitude. "So you still reckon it was an accident?" was what I actually blurted out.

"It must have been," she said, doing the phantom cat's cradle routine again. "No one would've *wanted* to hurt him."

"Do you know why he left your mum?"

"He didn't leave her. He just . . . went away for a bit. He was going to come back."

"Did he say that?"

"No, but . . . he didn't even take all his things."

Not a lot of use for a set of golf clubs in Camden, unless he was planning to flog 'em in the market. I didn't say it, obviously. "When was the last time you saw him?"

"You know when he left, don't you? Didn't Mum tell you, when she asked you to find him?"

"Yeah, but—" I took a deep breath; this was the sixty-four-dollar question "—did you see him at all after that?"

"Excuse me, sorry to interrupt your chat." The gentleman—and you can take that as a euphemism for *git*—who'd interrupted us was the sort you get knocking on your door around polling time, trying to browbeat you into voting Conservative. He had that weird, excessively straight posture you get with blokes not overly gifted in the height department who're nonetheless bloody well determined to sneer down their noses at the world even if it knackers their backs. "I was looking for some of your hand-knitted gloves for my wife, but you don't seem to have any in purple."

"Oh—I think we've got some out the back. That is, I know we have. I'll get them for you." Hazel flashed me a guilty glance. "Sorry. Um. We were finished anyway, weren't we?"

She scuttled off without waiting for an answer.

As I watched her go, I noticed Tallulah giving me the evil eye from behind the till.

Metaphorically, that is, which my hip for one was glad to see. It still hadn't forgiven me for that tumble in Camden.

"What's the betting she sent that customer over?" I muttered to Phil, who'd come out of lurk mode and joined me by the knickknacks. "Reckon she was trying to stop Hazel spilling too much?"

"More likely just pissed off about us stopping Hazel from doing her job. She couldn't have heard what the girl was telling you from there, and they're not exactly overstaffed. Doesn't matter. We can follow up with Hazel later."

"Yeah, I s'pose. Course, it'd mean going back to Lilah's. You heard all that, right?"

Phil nodded.

"Talk about your apples falling far from the tree. That one rolled across half of Europe. And then bounced on board a slow boat to China. What do you think about her banging on about it being an accident?"

"Interesting."

"Bloody hell, and you accuse *me* of being reluctant to commit." I winced. "Uh, forget I said that. Oliver?"

"Oliver."

We headed down to the ground floor.

Oliver was *still* charming the pants—or at least, the contents of their pockets—off the customers. Or possibly he'd moved on to some different customers. They all looked the same to me: white, middle class, middle-aged. But whatever Tallulah was paying young Ollie, he was definitely doing his best to earn it. Me and Phil hung around for a while, pretending to consider a case full of tiny stuffed birds. Then we hung around a bit longer, *actually* considering it—would Greg and Cherry like it as a back-from-honeymoon present? Did Greg like dead animals in general, or only ones he'd taxidermied himself? Would he see it as an inspiration, or as us saying we didn't reckon he could do anything as good? After all, they were a lot more delicate than any of his morbid little "family."

By the time we'd decided the price tag wasn't worth the risk, Oliver had moved on to *another* lot of customers. Bugger it. "Want to grab a coffee and try again later?" I suggested.

Phil nodded, and we made our way outside.

I took in a deep lungful of earth-scented air as the door of the shop closed behind us. Funny how you don't realise how claustrophobic some places are until you get out of them. "Fair-trade coffee, here we come. Think they'll let us bring it outside?"

There were a few wooden picnic tables set up between the café and the car park, but they were damp and forlorn right now. Phil gave them a dubious look, probably worried about marking his posh trousers if he sat down on one of those benches. "Tell you what. You wait out here. I'll grab the coffees and have a word with the staff while I'm at it. See if they can tell me anything about our Mr. Parrot."

"Yeah, okay." I was happy not to be the one doing the grilling.

Of course, that was before he'd been in there fifteen minutes chatting up the staff, with no sign of him coming out again anytime soon and no sign of my flippin' coffee either.

It's times like these when a nicotine habit would come in handy. I paced up and down, kicking at the gravel and feeling like a spare part.

Thought about playing with my phone, but I'd forgotten to charge it last night and didn't want to run it down completely. If I'd had a key to Phil's car, I could have sat and listened to the radio while I waited for my beloved, but we hadn't quite got to that stage of entwining our lives just yet. On Phil's side, I wasn't sure if it was down to him being possessive about his sleek, shiny Golf; complete disinterest in driving my van and/or Fiesta; or if he'd just, like me, forgotten what he'd done with his spare keys.

Sod it. I was sick of hanging around. I turned my steps towards the café—

And slammed straight into a wrecking ball of fury that knocked me off my feet.

CHAPTER NINETEEN

Bloody *hell*. I gasped for air, but fuck it, there was nothing there. My ears were ringing, mostly with shouts of *You fucking bastard*.

Jesus Christ. I scrabbled in the gravel, failed utterly to get back on my feet and gawped up—and then up some more—at the bloody man mountain who'd just punched me in the gut.

"You bastard!" he yelled again, and took a step forwards. He was a big—very big—white bloke with an earring that glinted evilly in a stray shaft of sunlight. Although possibly I was biased about that last bit.

I was certain I'd never seen him before, so Christ knew why he was so bloody keen to rub in uncomfortable truths while pummelling me into the dirt. Anxious to avoid any further pummelling, I scuttled back like a crab with six wooden legs and a terminal case of dry rot. "Wha—" I managed to gasp out.

Doors were opening; people sticking their heads out and shouting. Not one of them did anything useful like get between me and Tyson Fury's angrier little brother. Or deck him with that anvil. Inching back further, I hit one of the stone flower pots and used it to lever myself up onto my feet, so at least the git would have to hit me again before he'd be able to put the boot in.

Then Phil burst through the café door like a human cannonball and launched himself at my attacker. Tyson junior swung another pile driver punch, but Phil dodged it and grabbed hold as it went past him. There swiftly followed a twisting manoeuvre he'd taught me a while back. Why for God's sake hadn't I remembered that when it counted? It all ended with one angry git face down in the gravel, an arm wrenched up behind his back and my beloved's not inconsiderable weight pinning him to the ground.

"Wha—" I coughed painfully, and finally got enough air in my lungs to make a whole sentence. "What the bleeding hell did you do that for?" The initial shock was wearing off, and my stomach was hurting like buggery. On the plus side, I'd somehow managed to fall without knackering my hip this time. Go me.

"You *shit*. You killed him!" Well, it was an answer, although it made bugger all sense.

It ended in a wordless cry when Phil yanked harder on that twisted-up arm and bent closer to snarl in the guy's ear. "You mind your fucking language."

I sent him a sharp look. "Oi, not in the police anymore, all right? Might want to ease off on the brutality." I gave a nervous laugh. It wasn't funny.

Phil's face went stony, which was in fact an improvement, and he eased up on the heavyweight wannabe. Very, very slightly. "Name," he ground out.

"Kelvin Reid. That *shit* killed my man."

"What? You got that wrong." Although at least now the attack made some sort of sense. "All I did was deliver a package." It sounded defensive even as I said it. Then again, I had a bloody good excuse to be on the defensive right now.

"Shouldn't believe everything you see on the telly," Phil growled, but he sounded a little less like he was planning to enact Viking-style vengeance out here. "We need to have a chat. Me and Tom aren't the enemy here. If I let you up, will you sit down at that table and not do anything stupid?"

"Fine," the bloke spat out.

And yeah, right, like he was actually going to say *No, please manhandle me some more instead*. I bit back an instinctive cry of *Don't do it* as Phil gave the bloke his arm back and let him haul himself to his feet.

Standing, Reid was a weird study in contrasts. His tall, hefty frame—easily as broad across the shoulders as my Phil, and Reid had a couple of inches on him in the height department—screamed that here was a guy who could do serious damage if he put his mind to it. His face, on the other hand, was soft around the edges, now that it wasn't twisted in rage, with big, sad eyes that seemed on the verge of tearing up.

If you only looked at his face—and ignored the growing ache in my gut—you could be fooled into thinking that if he hadn't been in mourning for his lover, he'd have been off rescuing baby birds and helping little old ladies cross the road. After all, he could scoop 'em both up in those brawny arms of his with equal ease, which is far from a foregone conclusion. I've had experience with elderly neighbours who've taken a tumble, and little old ladies can be surprisingly heavy. Maybe it's all the bionic hip and knee joints weighing them down.

Okay, I was possibly starting to get a bit light-headed.

"Sit," Phil barked out, and I nearly dropped bum-first into the pansies.

Then I realised he'd been talking to Reid, who glared at him for form's sake and then parked his bulk on one of the picnic benches. His shoulders slumped, which hopefully meant the fight had gone out of him.

"Tom, are you all right?" Phil asked, turning to me with a tight expression.

"Yeah. Yeah, I'm good," I lied.

"Let me have a look at your stomach."

"What, now?"

"Yes. Now."

"He hit me. He didn't bloody knife me." Clearly I was still woozy, though, as I found myself unbuttoning my shirt and pulling up the T-shirt underneath. "Happy?"

As far as I could tell, there wasn't a right lot to see, but Phil gave it a good long examination. Then he nodded. "Sit down," he suggested much more gently this time.

I wasn't all that happy about anything that brought me into closer proximity with Reid, but on the other hand, collapsing where I stood would be painful as well as embarrassing. I sat down at the furthest corner of the picnic table from Reid, and only then realised I had grazes on both palms that were bleeding slightly. Bloody gravel.

Phil took hold of my hands. "We'll need to wash those out."

"It can wait." I was pretty sure Reid wouldn't be hanging around while Phil stuck a plaster on and kissed me better.

"Sure?"

"Bloody hell, just get on with it before he does a runner," I muttered under my breath. Phil gave me a grim smile and turned to loom over Reid.

"Kelvin. What are you even doing here?"

He sniffed. "I came to see that *bitch* of an ex-wife of his. No one answered at the house, so I came to see if she was here."

"She was. You missed her."

I wondered where Lilah was now. For someone who'd recently lost the love of her life, she seemed to do an awful lot of gallivanting around.

"What did you want to see her about?"

"Why do you think? I want her to admit what she did. I want her to look me in the eye and tell me she didn't have Jonathan killed."

I wanted Kelvin to make his flippin' mind up. "Thought you thought I killed him?"

"You're working for her. Aren't you?"

"Well, yeah." Admitting it made me feel weirdly guilty. "But she hired us to find out who killed Jon—Mr. Parrot. And before he died, to deliver a package. And that's all we did."

"You said *ex*-wife. Did he tell you they were divorced?" I thought Phil's tone was a bit on the sharp side, until I remembered that Kelvin was supposed to be answering our questions and not the other way around.

Kelvin pouted. "Wife, then. But it was nothing, their marriage. She's all glamour, that one. She's a witch. She sucked him in and made him believe a whole load of crap, but when he came to his senses, he came back to me. For good."

"Jonathan told you that?"

"You think I'd have taken him back if he hadn't? I've got my pride." Then his shoulders sagged. Was he thinking that was all he had left now?

"So you kept in touch with him during his marriage?"

Kelvin looked at the table. "Not at first. I didn't see him for a whole year. But he came by the market about six months ago. He said it was like he was in a dream, and now he'd woken up. And he was sorry." Our man Reid could be surprisingly soft-spoken when he wasn't hurling abuse and trying to kill me.

"And you carried on seeing him after that? As a lover? A lot of people might have moved on by then."

"Jonathan and me, it was the real thing."

"Did you have other lovers while you and Jonathan were apart? No one would blame you."

"Yeah, of course I did. I'm a man, aren't I? But they didn't mean anything."

"So there was no significance in him going to see you at the market rather than at home?"

"No." Kelvin relaxed visibly from one moment to the next. Like, say, he'd that minute thought of an answer. "He wasn't sure I hadn't moved. And he couldn't get away in the evenings, could he? That bitch kept him on a tight rein."

If he wanted to be convincing, he really needed to learn to stick to the one excuse and work on the poker face.

Phil didn't go in for the kill and challenge it directly, just went for slight bruising with a mild suggestion. "Maybe he was trying to keep both sides happy. In case he decided to stay with the wife after all."

"It was all over between them already." Kelvin snapped it out. A touch of conscience there? Or maybe he'd realised it made him sound like every bloke's bit on the side in the history of the world. "He hadn't slept with her for months."

Yeah, right. And guess what? She didn't understand him, either.

Blimey, I was getting cynical in my old age.

Meanwhile, Phil's brain was still remorselessly on track. "Did he ever say or do anything that made you suspect he was worried about something? Frightened, even?"

"He was scared she'd send someone after him. And she *did*." Uh-oh. Sad-eyed Kelvin was gone, and Tyson junior was back with a vengeance. I made sure I hadn't got my feet tangled round the legs of the picnic bench. Just in case I had to get out of the firing range, sharpish.

"He told you that, did he?" Phil went on, clearly oblivious to my discomfort.

"He didn't have to. I could tell he was on his guard—always jumping when there was a knock at the door."

"Could it have been someone else he was worried about?"

"Who?"

"That's what we're trying to find out. Did he—" Phil broke off as sirens filled the air, lingered for half a minute or so, then stopped.

Kelvin had tensed and half risen, a look of betrayal on his face. "You called the police?"

"*I* called them." It was Tallulah's voice—her poshest one—and I turned to see her standing by the entrance to the café with her arms folded and the café staff peering anxiously over her shoulders. "I want you all off my property, and don't come back. And yes, that includes you two," she added, glaring at Phil and me.

Victim-blaming, much?

There was a moment's stillness—and then Kelvin jumped up from the bench with a grace that belied his bulk, and scarpered in the direction of the car park.

Phil swore, but I couldn't bring myself to be that upset about the bloke running *away* from me. Interestingly, Phil didn't make any attempt to give chase.

"Not going after him?"

"What, and have the police turn up as I tackle him to the ground a second time? They'd arrest both of us and sort it out at the station."

"I s'pose you'd know. As an ex-copper, I mean, not as an habitual brawler. Unless that's what you and Darren get up to when me and Gary go for a drink?"

"Tag-team wrestling," Phil said, straight-faced. "We're getting quite a following."

A car door slammed. An engine revved, and we were treated to a front-row view of Kelvin's van screeching through the car park, taking out the wing mirror of a Ford Mondeo en route. Followed by a godalmighty slam as he drove straight into the police car just turning in.

I winced. "That's not going to do him any favours."

CHAPTER TWENTY

After that, it was simply a matter of making sure we got our side of the story over to some not-very-gruntled boys in blue, who took our names, ranks, and serial numbers and then escorted Mr. Reid off the premises in handcuffs. Tallulah looked disappointed to see that me and Phil hadn't been given the same treatment, so we decided it wasn't the best time to stick around in the hopes of finally catching Oliver for a chat.

Then we had domestics over whether or not I should see a doctor. You can guess which side of the argument I was on. I'd made the mistake of admitting I was glad I hadn't had that dessert at lunchtime, which my overprotective fiancé apparently chose to interpret as a symptom of possible internal bleeding, massive organ failure, and impending death.

"I'm fine," I told him as we drove off from the Old Smithy, getting more narked about it by the minute. "It was just a punch. *A* punch."

"That's all it can take. We're going to A&E."

"For fuck's sake, it's not like I haven't had worse." For starters, I'd been shot, poisoned, bashed on the head, nearly strangled . . . Okay, reminiscing about all that really wasn't helping me feel any better. But the point was, all that was serious stuff. Not a single punch in the gut.

"I don't care if you've had worse. You're getting checked out."

"Jesus, would you stop treating me like I'm some delicate bloody flower?"

"Nausea's a possible sign of internal bleeding."

"You always have to know best, don't you?"

"People have *died* from being punched in the gut, you stubborn bastard."

"Name *one*."

"Harry Houdini, heard of him?"

Not only that, I'd known how he died. But at this point in the argument, with my pride hurting almost as much as my stomach, I wasn't exactly thinking straight.

"Fine. Do whatever you want. You always bloody do, anyhow." I folded my arms and stared out of the side window. I was going to feel a right muppet when the nurses laughed me out of A&E for coming in after the equivalent of a sodding playground fight.

Phil didn't answer. It was probably just as well.

As it happened, the hospital staff didn't laugh, but I still felt like it was a waste of their time and mine as they checked my blood pressure (fine) and gave me a scan (ditto). On the plus side, they gave me some painkillers, which were a godsend. Never mind the blunt-force trauma to the gut; after several hours on those waiting room chairs, my bum wasn't talking to me anymore.

I'll say this for my beloved: all through the whole sorry business, there was no trace of anything other than concern in his manner. Not even a smirk and a muttered *I told you so* as they gave me the works instead of telling me to piss off and stop being a crybaby. As the drugs kicked in and the pain receded, the guilt started to creep in, and I began to feel I'd been a bit of a git to Phil. After all, he'd only been worried about me.

It was just . . . It was humiliating, all right? Like I wasn't man enough to stand up for myself. Like I needed Phil to rush in and save me, and then coddle me afterwards. The fact that if he hadn't been there, I'd probably have needed a lot more than a few painkillers to get over Kelvin Reid's attack only made it all the harder to swallow.

Most of the time it's fine being a short-arse. No worries about banging heads on doors, and in my profession, the ability to squeeze into kitchen cupboards and under baths can come in pretty handy. But sometimes, I could wish I'd been more gifted in the physically imposing department. Like, say, a certain pigheaded private investigator.

The upshot was, when we got home—not, you'll note, out to that pub where we'd been planning to go digging for info on our Mr. Parrot—I was in a foul mood.

"I'll cook," Phil announced as we walked in the door. "What do you fancy?"

"Not being treated like a sodding invalid?" I asked without a lot of hope.

"Not on the menu." And yep, there was that smirk I'd come to know and . . . Oh, fuck it. Yeah, all right, love. But that didn't mean I had to *like* it. "Pork chops do?" he went on.

"Great, if we had any." I didn't stomp into the living room, because that would have been childish. Merlin taking one look at me and shooting out of the room like he'd been turbocharged meant bugger all, the nervy so-and-so.

"We have. I went shopping."

Huh. This was another thing that was taking a bit of getting used to. It felt weird, not knowing the contents of my own fridge. "Fine, then," I said, and sat down on the sofa, which was something of a painful process. Funny how you don't notice how much you use your stomach muscles until some great git with iron fists tries to punch your guts out through your spine.

Not that I was laughing. It would've hurt too much anyway.

"While you're waiting, have a read of this." Phil's voice right behind me made me jump but, give him his due, he didn't laugh, just handed me his tablet. There was a document open, and at the top of it a picture that was etched into my recent memory, although without the rabid snarl I remembered. Kelvin Reid. "It's what I dug up on him so far." He paused. "You might want to scroll down to the part about hobbies and interests."

"What, are you writing his CV for him?" I scrolled and read. It was, as it happened, a lot like a CV, although more warts-and-all than I'd have been happy sending off to potential employers. When I'd finished, I put the tablet down. I didn't turn round, because my stomach would not have been a happy bunny. "You're still there, aren't you?"

"Yep," came a gruff voice from behind my left lughole.

"You know, you could have *told* me he was an amateur boxer. I might not have argued with you about going to A&E so much."

"You, not argue? That'll be the day. Besides . . ." Something about his tone as he trailed off made me twist around to face him after all, despite what my gut thought about it. "I forgot you didn't know. Forgot I hadn't showed you the file."

I could feel the grin spreading over my face. "What, the great Phil Morrison admitting a mistake? Bloody hell, is the world coming to an end?"

"Shut up. I was rattled, wasn't I? Don't like seeing you hurt."

The warm and fuzzies still had a bitter edge to them. "Yeah, well, I s'pose it serves me right for not watching where I was bloody well going."

Phil leaned over the sofa back to put his arms around me. "He hit you with a sucker punch. It happens."

"Ever happen to you?" I was betting it hadn't. There's a world of difference between five foot eight and six foot one when it comes to picking victims for your next mugging. And that's leaving aside the fact that my fiancé tends to make your proverbial brick outhouse experience a sudden urge to go on a high-protein diet and get down the gym.

Phil surprised me. "Yes. Early days on the job. I was chasing down a shoplifter; he hid round a corner and waited for me to catch up."

I cricked my neck giving him a sidelong look. "Ow. Did you feel a right muppet too?" I rubbed the skin over the pinched nerve.

Phil laughed, kissed it better, and nodded. "Took me months to live it down too. He was shorter than you. Or possibly she was."

"You got decked by a little girl? A big strong bloke like you?"

"Did I say that? Our thief was assigned male at birth, but wearing a dress at the time. We never did clear up if that was a gender-identity thing, a fetish, or a disguise for when they fancied a bit of bargain hunting." He let go of me and straightened up, which wasn't a bad move. His back had to be killing him, leaning over like that, and the last thing we needed was both of us crocked. "Right. Food."

I sat watching the telly and contemplating my own mortality until Phil brought a couple of loaded plates in. Pork chops and beans on toast. Plus half a grilled tomato each wobbling self-consciously on the side of the plate. Suddenly I was ravenous. Okay, it wasn't what I'd have cooked, but it was good, solid comfort food. Just what the doctor ordered. "Brown sauce?" I asked hopefully, taking my plate.

Phil rolled his eyes and went to fetch it.

For once the gods smiled on us, and Dave Southgate didn't turn up until after we'd finished eating and were kicking back with a beer in front of the telly. And yeah, I know, pills and alcohol. But it was one beer, and they weren't the really good drugs. Even Phil had given in after a token moan.

"Thought we might be seeing you," I said as Phil showed Dave in. Arthur gave him a hard stare and then slunk off to the kitchen. He's not daft, my cat, and Dave didn't look like he was in a cuddly mood.

"We're all hooked up to computers now, aren't we? Every time your name comes up in a report, I get an email alerting me and a bloody big klaxon goes off. Happens so bloomin' often I'm going deaf in one ear."

"Nah, that's just the excuse you give to the wife when she asks why you didn't get up for the nipper in the night. How is he, by the way?"

Dave's face softened for an instant—then solidified to granite. "Don't you change the subject. He's fine. What's this I hear about you kicking off with a murder suspect?"

"Oi, he hit me, not the other way around. And, I might add, because of that flippin' mugshot your lot put out on the telly. I ought to sue. Defamation of character, adding injury to insult—"

"Don't push it, Paretski." Dave dropped heavily into an armchair with an *oof*. Good thing Arthur wasn't still sitting there. "You all right, then? Seen a doctor?"

"Don't you start," I muttered as Phil came out with a suspiciously smug "Yes, he has."

Dave gave him a dark look. "Christ, any more of that and I'll start thinking you're a good influence. So he's been checked out?"

"Yes, he has," I said pointedly. "And what's this about Kelvin Reid being a suspect? You got anything on him?"

"Only statistics." Dave must have caught my blank stare. "He's the lover, isn't he?"

"Yeah, but he hit me because he thought I'd done it. So it can't have been him."

Dave turned to Phil. "And you let him out on his own?"

"Oi!"

"Hate to break it to you, mate, but sometimes, murderers aren't honest." You could have used Dave's sarcasm to lag a pipe.

"Git. I know that, but . . . he seemed really upset."

"You'd be bloody upset if you were facing a life sentence." He didn't ask what Reid had been doing up there in the first place, so I presumed Big Kelv had told the arresting officers the same story he gave us.

"Any news on the cause of death?" Phil put in.

"He died of thirst," Dave said flatly. "No, wait, that was me. Newly minted DCI, cut down tragically in his prime by a fatal lack of hospitality."

Whoops. My mum brought me up better than this. "Sorry, mate. Beer? Phil'll get it," I added, flashing a smile in the appropriate direction.

Phil muttered something I didn't catch, but disappeared into the kitchen.

"You've got him well trained," Dave said with a smirk.

"Too right. Want to see him come when I call?" I winked in case he hadn't got the innuendo.

Dave's shudder probably had seismologists miles away wetting themselves in glee. "You can leave your sex life out of it when I'm around. Oh, cheers, mate." He took the beer Phil handed him.

"That was pretty nippy," I told Phil approvingly as he sat back down beside me. "Worried you were going to miss all the good stuff?"

Dave snorted. "Chance'd be a bloody fine thing. It ain't like on the bleedin' telly, you know, with all their tame lab coats working through the night. Our lot clock off at 5 p.m. sharp, and half past three on Fridays. *And* they've got a backlog that makes NHS waiting lists look like the queue for the gents at a bleedin' Women's Institute jam-making workshop. No, we have not got any news on the cause of death. Forensics are working on it. Allegedly. So what the bloody hell did you say to Kelvin Reid that made him go postal on you?"

"Nothing. Literally, nothing. I didn't even see the bastard before he hit me." I frowned. "Which is what I told your flippin' minions."

Dave shrugged. "Yeah, but you can tell me the real story."

"I told them the real story! Seriously, he recognised me off the telly. That's all."

"And where were you when all this was going on?" He turned to Phil with a suspicious air.

"Café."

"Yeah, I never did get my coffee."

"Right. You two just happened to stop in at Jonathan Parrot's old workplace to get a cup of coffee and a muffin."

"Well, no." I glanced at Phil. "We're investigating the murder. I mean, Phil is. Obviously. 'Cos that's his job. I'm a plumber. Pure and simple."

"Simple, maybe. But pure? Pull the other one, mate, it plays 'God Save the Queen.' Right. Who's hired you?"

"Mrs. Parrot," Phil told him before I could get a word in.

Dave gave him an assessing look. "Think she did it?"

"We're keeping an open mind at the moment." Phil's face would make a professional poker player hang up his cards for good. *You can take the lad out of the police force . . .*

"Up yours." Dave clearly wasn't impressed with this reminder of my beloved's gamekeeper-turned-poacher status.

"Nah," I answered Dave's question. "She might have had some serious delusions about the state of their marriage, but she wouldn't have killed him." An unpleasant thought hit me. "S'pose you're going to say statistics are against her and all. Going to have to pick one and stick with it, aren't you? Or do you reckon they were in it together, Lilah and Reid?"

Dave wasn't fazed. "Stranger things, Paretski. Stranger things. So you interviewed the staff at the Smithy?"

"Kind of," I said, as Phil gave a curt, "Yes."

We exchanged glances. "Well, we didn't get to talk to the Hobbit properly," I explained.

"Who?" Dave's look said he was starting to wonder if I'd been hit in the head, not the gut.

"Proudfoot. Young Oliver. He was busy with customers all the time. Popular lad. Had a natter with Lilah's daughter, Hazel, though. She seemed genuinely cut up about it all."

"Yeah, that's what our boys and girls thought. Not that I'm discussing the case with you lot in any way, shape, or form."

"Perish the thought. Did they happen to mention what they thought of Tallulah?"

Dave cackled. "Hoping we'll do your job for you? Not a chance. You can form your own conclusions. Although strictly off the record . . ." He paused dramatically.

"Yeah?"

"Begins with *B* and rhymes with 'snitch.' But quote me on that, and we're having words." He glugged down the last of his beer and stood up. "Right. Some of us have got nippers to see to. Try not to piss off anyone else, won't you?"

"Cheers, mate. We on for a pint next week?"

"Christ, yes. Jen donated all my beer to a bloody food bank. I told her, they don't even want alcohol, but did she listen? Just dumped it all in the box with the cans of soup and instant noodles. She doesn't like me drinking around the lad. Says it's a bad influence. I ask you, how's he supposed to know what's in the bottle? He still thinks that's what food comes in. No, don't get up. I'll see myself out. Again."

He stomped off. I turned to Phil with a grin. "Think it's his age, or has this second go at fatherhood finally mellowed him?"

Dave's dulcet tones sounded from the hall. "Oi, I heard that, Paretski. You go round getting yourself half killed by any more murder suspects, and you'll find out how much I've bloody mellowed." The front door closed behind him. Quietly.

Phil smirked. "Definitely the kid."

CHAPTER Twenty-One

I woke up stiff next morning, in more ways than one. Phil took care of one problem, although I had my suspicions it was just an excuse to check my belly over for signs of internal haemorrhaging while he was down there. I had a couple of paracetamol with my breakfast to deal with the other, feeling a wuss even as I gulped them down. I'd had a gander at the relevant area myself, and to be honest, the bruising was less than impressive, visually speaking. Also, a few crunches now and then wouldn't go amiss.

"Working today?" Phil asked as I munched on my toast.

I swallowed. "Seeing as how it's that or make a choice between eating and paying the mortgage this month, yeah."

He gave me a look over the top of his coffee mug. "There's two of us paying the bills now. You can take a day off if you need to."

"Took one yesterday, didn't I? Anyhow, I don't want to disappoint the customers." Start getting a reputation as unreliable in my line of work and you can flush your business down the toilet. "What are you up to today? Jonny-boy's case? Or have you got other stuff you need to do?"

"Paperwork. And a meeting that's not going to come to anything."

"Why not blow them off, then?"

"Same reason as you. *She* might not end up employing me, but she's got plenty of friends with money to spare. And husbands who like a bit on the side."

"Fair enough." I hesitated. "Could take a trip up to Pluck's End tonight, though, if you still fancy checking out that pub."

Phil frowned. "We're shooting tonight."

"Oh. Right. Forgot." It was a barefaced lie. "We could miss one night. For the sake of the case."

His frown deepened. "You sure you're okay to work today?" It was clear he reckoned I was feeling the effects of yesterday's assault and battery worse than I'd let on.

Which left me in a quandary. On the one hand, I didn't want to give him any more reasons to wrap me in metaphorical cotton wool. On the other . . . here was an excuse to miss shooting tonight, handed to me on a silver platter.

It was taking all I'd got not to grab it with both hands.

Joining the shooting club had been Gary's idea, and I'd thought it was a pretty naff one at the time, but it'd grown on me to the point I actually did a quick search on the internet for local clubs and mentioned it to Phil as something to get us out of the house.

More fool me. He'd been all for it. Apparently he'd been on the waiting list for firearms training when he left the force sooner than planned. I couldn't say I'd been sorry—at least this way, we'd be novices together.

"You know they do stag do's too?" I'd told Phil on the way to our introductory session, just before Christmas. "Take you up to Scotland or Budapest for a weekend with all your mates and let you blast away at anything that doesn't move. The website's full of bollocks like 'Do you want to be James Bond?' and 'Time to be a real man.'" I flashed him a lewd grin. "They *literally* go on about your testosterone rising when you're holding your weapon. Makes you wonder about straight blokes, if they go for that kind of marketing."

Phil kept his eyes on the road, but his mouth quirked up in amusement. "If you want that sort of thing for the stag do, you'll have to talk to Darren and Gary."

Our respective best men. We'd left all plans for the stag do in their so-called capable hands, and I for one was beginning to have second thoughts. "Might just do that. I've been having nightmares we're going to end up with a bondage night at a local dungeon."

Phil smirked outright. "Or a Morris dancing evening."

"Better watch out Darren doesn't catch you taking the piss out of his favourite pastime or he'll shove his stick—sorry, *staff*—where the sun don't shine."

"I wasn't laughing at the thought of *him* doing it."

"I could jingle my bells with the best of 'em." I gave him a sidelong look. "Bet my staff would be bigger than yours and all."

"Promises, promises."

The gun club was down in the basement of a community centre in an area of St. Albans that was even dodgier than the estate Phil had grown up on. I wondered if any of the members ever got mugged for their guns. Possibly in a bid to stave off the robberies with violence, it was completely unmarked both outside and in the building—no helpful signs to tell us *Lethal Weapons This Way*. We had to ask at the desk.

Maybe it was simply to preserve the polite fiction that Brits don't have anything to do with those nasty firearm things. Well, not unless they're the type who live out in the country on their own estates and have a surname as double-barrelled as their shotguns.

Given that I'd had a gun pulled on me twice in the last couple of years, I wasn't buying it.

We met up with a guy from the gun club and a group of other gun virgins, some of them alarmingly young (seriously, one little lad looked around five; I'd known older kids who weren't even allowed to play with *toy* guns). The gun club guy, who was your average late-middle-age white bloke and introduced himself as Trevor, showed us around and told us the rules of the range, most of which boiled down to *Don't kill anyone, including yourself.* Then we got to the fun part, which was where we got to try out the hardware.

This being Britain, which (according to Trevor at any rate) has the strictest firearms laws in the world, there weren't any submachine guns, antitank missiles, or James Bond–style handguns. We were left with rifles of a couple of different calibres and degrees of banginess, and antique muzzle-loading pistols last fired in anger at the O.K. Corral.

While any visiting American gun enthusiasts would have been totally underwhelmed, and Trevor certainly seemed to mourn the good old, pre-Dunblane days of handguns for all, it was bloody good fun. Particularly the antique pistols, which had a decent kick and, more importantly, were prone to shooting actual flame out the sides as they filled the whole range with gun smoke to the extent that you could barely see the targets by the time we were done shooting.

So why wouldn't I want to go on this particular Friday night? Well, for starters, once the initial fun and frolics were over, probationary members were restricted to .22 rifles. Compared to more serious weapons, these make a noise slightly less impressive than your average slammed door, and have a kick like a one-legged gnat that's not trying too hard.

For another thing, and here was where it got hard to admit it . . . Phil was better than me. A lot. We'd only been going a couple of months, and already the established club members were looking at his retrieved targets with approval and mentioning competitions. Mine, they grimaced at and gave helpful advice over. The *same* advice. Every bloody week, because my shooting wasn't getting any sharper. No matter which gun I tried or how much I worked to make my grip more relaxed and stop jerking the trigger, the results were the same—a pretty splatter pattern of widely spaced holes in the target, as opposed to the neat, tight grouping exhibited by my beloved.

It was embarrassing. Okay, I'd always known I'd never be able to beat him in a fist fight, not that I ever intended to find out for certain. But for Christ's sake, here we were competing on a level playing field for once, and I was still failing to make the cut.

So, yeah, not that bothered about missing a week, as it happened. Not that I was planning on telling Phil that. "I'm fine," I said shortly. "We can talk about this evening later, okay? Don't want to be late for my first job."

The first job was an emergency kitchen sink. If the customer— *"It's Miss M., not Mrs., but call me Joy,"* a lovely lady in her thirties who had a generous hand with the choccy biccies—had called me in to start with, it wouldn't have been an emergency, but apparently the new boyfriend had offered to change the tap himself, presumably to impress her with his handyman skills.

I was definitely impressed. "Got to say, I don't often see a sink so bloody knackered." It was one of the old Victorian-style ceramic ones, and it was literally in pieces. "I mean, when you consider how most of those sinks have survived through two world wars . . ."

Joy sipped sadly on her mug of tea. "That's the last time I listen when a *man* says he can do something. No offence."

"None taken." It's a sad fact that most of the DIY bodge jobs I've been called upon to fix in my career have had the whiff of testosterone about them, although the bloke himself is rarely in evidence when I show up. Funny, that. "Just lock up your tool kit next time he comes round."

She snorted into her mug, and I had a feeling the relationship might be showing a few cracks and all. I snagged another biccie and got down to work. It was a fiddly job, with the new sink I'd managed to find her not quite the same size as the old one, so I had to play about with the worktop to get it to fit. Looked a treat when it was done, though.

Joy did a much better job of living up to her name when she saw the finished article, and paid up without a whimper. "I'd offer you another biscuit for the road, but I get the impression you've had a couple too many already," she said as she handed me the cheque.

I gave her a sidelong look. "Oi, I'll have you know I'm still wearing the same size jeans as when I was twenty."

She cracked up. "Oh, God, sorry. I wasn't calling you fat. I just meant, you keep rubbing your tummy. And you winced when you had to get under the sink."

Oh. I had? I'd caught myself once or twice, but hadn't realised it'd become a habit. "Yeah, I, uh, walked into something yesterday. Got a bit of a bruise."

"Ooh, poor you. Let's see." She gave me a flirty smile. Apparently the possibly-now-ex boyfriend had been right about household maintenance being the way to get into her good books. And other things.

"Sorry, love. My fiancé doesn't like me getting my kit off for anyone else." I smiled to show no hard feelings. And took a step back to show I meant it.

She sighed and took another choccy biccie. "The best ones are always taken. Hope you have a lovely wedding."

After that, it was getting on for lunchtime and I wasn't far from Brock's Hollow, so I gave Gary a bell. "Pub lunch?" I suggested.

"Ooh, why not? If only to celebrate you still being at liberty. Four Candles?"

"Sounds good." I'd be happier, though, when the Devil's Dyke was back up and running. The Four Candles is all right, but it hasn't got a lot of character. Personally I prefer the Duck and Grouse further up the high street, but Gary's not a fan, probably because they have Sky Sports and he almost choked on the olive in his martini one time when England scored a goal and the place erupted into cheers.

I keep telling him, it's not like there's much danger of it being repeated, but he never seems all that convinced.

I got to the Four Candles to find Gary already perched happily on a barstool, martini in hand, and his great big Saint Bernard, Julian, slobbering all over a petite barmaid who didn't look old enough to drink. Apparently she'd come out from behind the bar for the express purpose of getting drenched in doggy drool, not that I was complaining. Usually it was me who ended up doing the human-sponge act.

"Tommy darling!" Gary threw open his arms for the obligatory hug. I was just congratulating myself on getting through it without any more betraying winces when Julian decided to get in on the affection and nuzzled me right in the tender part of my stomach.

I hissed and backed off before I could stop myself, nearly falling over the barmaid, who giggled and retreated behind the bar. Julian whined and put his head down on his paws.

"Was that necessary?" Gary pouted, clearly taking my rejection of his canine companion personally. Then his eyes narrowed. "Are you *injured*? I hope that man of yours hasn't been getting rough with you. Unless you've decided you like that sort of thing, of course?"

There was a gleam in his eye that said if so, he wanted full details, probably with accompanying diagrams and an invitation to come and film a sex tape next time. I shuddered. "No. And no."

"Hmm. I asked you three questions. At *least*. Which one aren't you answering, I wonder? Oh, and Tom will have a Diet Coke, please, and another of your excellent martinis for me while we peruse the bar menu," he added to the barmaid, who'd been hanging around expectantly and meanwhile listening in to every word. "Now, tell me about this war wound of yours."

"Ice?" she asked brightly, and for a moment I thought she was talking about my bruised stomach as well.

"Uh, yeah. Cheers. And it's just a bruise, all right?" I told Gary. "Not even an impressive one."

He sniffed. "I think *I* should be the judge of that. And how exactly did you acquire said bruise?"

I dropped my voice. "Walked into a sucker punch. And no, not from anyone you know. Far as I'm aware, anyhow. Jonathan Parrot's ex-bloke. Seemed to be under the impression I was some kind of hit man."

"Ooh, how thrilling. But you, murder for money? You don't even stretch the truth on your VAT returns. I can't see you cold-bloodedly setting up a sniper rifle and taking someone out." Gary smiled at the barmaid, who'd returned with our drinks, and handed over a twenty-pound note. "While we're on the subject, how's the shooting going? I was so pleased you took my little suggestion. It's so important for a couple to have interests in common. Besides dead people, obviously."

"Oi, I'm not *interested* in dead people." It came out a bit loud, and great, now I sounded like a necrophiliac who was protesting too much.

"No? You seem to spend an inordinate amount of time around them. Anyway, no changing the subject. What did the nasty man do to you? Show Uncle Gary where it hurts. Go on, shirt up."

Bugger. I thought he'd forgotten about that. Why was everyone so keen to see the damage done to yours truly anyway? "What, in the middle of the pub?"

"Well, I suppose we could repair to the gents."

"Yeah, like I'm walking into the gents with you to get my kit off after having a drink together. That's how rumours get started. Not to mention getting barred from the pub."

"Hmm. Perhaps not, then. Although it would spice village life up a little." Gary looked worryingly like he was considering starting his own rumours for fun. "It must be so much easier being a lesbian, mustn't it? After all, women are notorious for going to the ladies together."

I frowned. "You think girls get up to stuff in toilets too, then?"

"Why not?"

"I dunno. It just seems . . . I thought girls were more into romance and stuff. Not a quickie in the bogs."

Gary raised an eyebrow. "You've always had some strange misconceptions about women, haven't you? Which is odd, seeing as you always seem to get on well with them. Or maybe that's *why*?" He cocked his head thoughtfully.

"Yeah, anyway. I wanted to ask, did you ever meet any of Lilah's family? What with her and Darren being mates."

"Darling, I've never even met *her*." He beamed. "I think Darren's trying to preserve my essential innocence. He's such a sweetie."

"Gary, you haven't been innocent since the day you were born."

"You wound me. I was an adorable baby. Positively cherubic. No, it's Darren you need to talk to. He's Lorelei's godfather, you know."

Ye—appropriately—gods. I couldn't think of anyone less suitable to oversee a nipper's spiritual growth, although to be fair, she seemed to have turned out all right. "Hands-on sort, is he? Or is it just cards at Christmas?"

"Did you want to order food?" the barmaid butted in at that point, which was probably all to the good. Any implied criticism of Darren tended to go down like the *Titanic* as far as Gary was concerned. We ordered—ham ploughman's for me, and scampi for Gary—and bagged a table over in the corner. I slumped gratefully into the chair.

"You seem troubled," Gary said with a pointed look. Julian turned mournful eyes on me in solidarity.

I took a sip of my Diet Coke and wished I could have asked the barmaid to bung a shot of something in there to keep the bubbles company. But (a) I was driving and (b) I was working this afternoon, and who wants a tradesman who turns up with booze on his breath? "Do you ever feel . . . I dunno." I grimaced.

"Come on, you know it's better out than in. With certain exceptions, obviously. Tell Uncle Gary every sordid detail."

Sod it. "Do you ever wish you were, well, more butch?"

Gary gave me a blank look. "Why on earth would I want to be *more* butch?" Then his face changed. "Oh. Oh! You mean, *you've* been feeling lacking in the manliness department? Don't worry." He patted my knee, prompting Julian to get in on the act and plonk his massive head down on my leg. "If Phil hasn't noticed by now, it's highly likely he's not going to. Love is, as they say, ocularly challenged."

"Oi, I'm not worried about what Phil thinks." At least, I hadn't *thought* I was. "It's just . . . he's a lot more, well, physical than I am."

"Mm. He does tend to give off a rather rugged, Neanderthal vibe. But what's brought all this on? Has he been casting aspersions on our little Tommy's masculinity?"

"Nah . . . the thing is, I can't compete, you know?"

"But why would you want to compete with him? True soul mates, like my sweetie pie and me, should complement each other. They're not supposed to be locking horns at the drop of a hat. Unless that's what you're into, obviously. You're the yin to his yang; the Robin to his Batman; the socket to his plug—"

"Oi, we switch it about. Sometimes."

"I was talking metaphysically. But do tell."

The food arrived at that point, which was a good thing too, and I managed to get Gary talking about wedding stuff instead.

I couldn't help bringing it up again as we were about to go our separate ways. "So you don't think it's an issue if one of us maybe isn't pulling his weight in certain areas?"

"Of course not," Gary said reassuringly. Then he ruined it by adding, "It's hardly your fault that your weight is so much less than his."

CHAPTER TWENTY-TWO

The afternoon's job went like clockwork, for once: all it took was replacing a section of copper pipe and job done. Great for the customer; not so great for yours truly, as it left me with time on my hands, but not enough to make it worth ringing round the customers I had booked in for next week to see if I could pop in early.

And yeah, I could have knocked off, gone home, and put my feet up—even filled out one of those scrupulously honest VAT returns Gary had been not-quite having a dig about—but, well. None of my paperwork was urgent, and I had an itchy feeling at the back of my brain. I wanted to be doing something.

So I took a tootle out to Pluck's End in the van to see if I could catch Oliver Proudfoot in a free moment.

Look, I know what you're thinking. Not my area; I ought to leave it to Phil. Shouldn't take any risks, particularly after what happened with Kelvin sodding Reid. But Phil would be busy with his meeting—probably—and if we left it to the weekend, there was no chance we'd find Oliver without a customer to charm into buying some old tat, sorry, antique-stroke-retro whatsits. And, well, I didn't need a babysitter, did I? I could take care of myself. So I parked my van in the paddock and strode confidently towards the Old Smithy.

Okay, so maybe I snuck the odd wary glance behind me as I trod over the gravel Kelvin Reid had flattened me onto yesterday. I was just being cautious, all right? Once bitten, and all that. I was maintaining my whatchamacallit. Situational awareness. That was all.

Once I was safely across the danger zone, I poked my nose into the Old Smithy, hoping I'd find the Young Hobbit before Tallulah found me and ordered me off the premises again. I found Hazel, as it happened, which was the next best thing. I tipped her a wink and jerked my head in the direction of the door. She blushed, but caught on, and after an anxious shufti around followed me out to the courtyard. It was a chilly day, but the buildings sheltered us from the wind.

Hazel hugged herself as we crept guiltily away from the Smithy's door. "Have you found something out?" she asked immediately, which caught me on the hop.

"Uh, it's early days yet," I hedged. "Is Oliver in today? I was hoping for a quiet word."

Her face fell, and I felt like a git. "Oh. He's . . . Um. I'll get him."

She scurried back inside before I could ask her how she was doing, what with the dead stepdad and all, which I should have done to start with. It was a good thing Phil wasn't here. His faith in the so-called Paretski charm would've been well and truly shaken.

On the other hand, I'd got results. Oliver sidled through the door in under five minutes and gave me an assessing look. "All alone today? I'd have thought you'd have that big watchdog of yours firmly at heel, after what happened last time."

Great. Someone else who thought I wasn't safe out on my own. "We're not joined at the hip," I said shortly, then remembered I needed to stay on his good side if I wanted to get anything out of him. "Got time for a cuppa?"

He nodded. "I told Ms. Lovett I was taking my tea break. But you'd better hope she doesn't come anywhere near the café while you're around."

"If it's going to cause issues for you, we could go and sit in my van."

Oliver smiled. "I'll be fine."

There was something about the way he said it that got my suspicions up. Seemed smug, maybe? As if he knew he wouldn't be fired whatever. I started wondering what he had on Tallulah.

Then I started wondering when I'd got so paranoid. "You worked here long?" I asked, keeping it conversational.

"A couple of years. I like it."

"The antiques or the customers?"

"Both. I worked in a high-street store before, and believe me, we get a *much* better class of clientele here."

I probably should have been offended on behalf of my fellow plebs, but I'd read an online article recently on what retail workers had to put up with, and I could see where he was coming from. I mean, the Old Smithy didn't even *have* any changing rooms for people to poop in.

"And you've always got on all right with the people you work with?" I'd timed that question badly—we'd reached the café. I pushed open the door and waved him ahead of me. The place was only half-full, with a few couples on the elderly side sipping well-stewed tea and a trio of thin women with designer handbags and matching nails, nursing cappuccinos that were presumably equally skinny.

The lady behind the counter, a comfortably middle-aged, motherly sort, smiled and asked Oliver if he wanted the usual, which he admitted he did. Then she did a double take at yours truly. "Aren't you the poor boy who was assaulted?"

The cappuccino three pricked up their ears. I might have reddened a touch. "Er, yeah." Boy? *Seriously?*

"That was dreadful, that was. I haven't felt safe since that happened. I had my husband bring me to work this morning, and he's picking me up tonight. You can't be too careful, can you? I'm glad to see you up on your feet today. They said it was something to do with poor Jonathan?"

I was still trying to work out what to say when Oliver butted in. "Now, now, Sarah. You know he can't talk about an ongoing investigation. Why don't you make us a couple of fair-trade teas, and we'll both have a slice of your lovely carrot cake?"

Great. First Gary and now Oliver. Apparently I couldn't even be trusted to make my own drinks order anymore. Still, at least he'd got her off the subject of my losing encounter with Kelvin Reid's fist. "We'll sit over by the window," I said to prove I could come to *some* decisions on my own, and marched off to the table furthest from the counter.

The weight of the designer trio's eyes was upon me every step of the way. I made sure to take a seat at an angle where I wouldn't be facing them, but I wouldn't have to suffer their gaze boring into the back of my neck either. Yep, here was the paranoia, back in force.

Or maybe not, as I realised with a shock that one of them had actually snapped a picture of me with her mobile.

Bloody hell. I was strongly tempted to walk over and offer her my card—if she was going to be so flippin' nosy, I might as well get some free advertising out of it—but common sense prevailed. Oliver probably only had a fifteen-minute break, and we'd used up five already.

I waited until he'd sat down opposite me before I hit him with another question. "So, uh, yeah, you and Jonathan—get on all right?"

"Of course." He looked me straight in the eye, his voice low but distinct. "It was nice to have someone I could talk to. Hazel . . . She's family, isn't she? As in, the family business. I couldn't exactly use her to vent about my employer being a bitch."

"Don't mince words, do you?" About Tallulah or her niece—seriously, *use* her? "But hang on a mo, Jonathan was family too."

"Say that to Mzz Lovett and she'll scratch your eyes out."

"She didn't like him?" I wondered if he'd mentioned that to the police. "Why employ him, then?"

"Because while she likes to think she rules the roost here, it's Brian who really holds the purse strings. And he's always been a little . . . short-sighted when it comes to Dinky Delilah."

Interesting, the way he spoke about her. Using her porn name and all. And by interesting, I mean I got the impression he didn't have too high an opinion of our Lilah. "You mean Brian Tarbox? Lilah's ex? He's still hung up on her?" There was a motive for the bloke to take out old Jonny-boy if ever I heard one.

"You'll have to ask him about that." Oliver leaned back, which I thought meant he'd decided he wasn't feeling talkative after all until I realised our teas had arrived.

"Cheers, love," I said with a smile as Sarah bunged cups and plates on the table between us. "How much do I owe you?" I asked, in case the reason Oliver hadn't mentioned money up at the counter was that he'd expected me to fork out.

"Oh, don't worry about it. I don't charge people who work here, and you're doing your bit, aren't you? I hope you catch him."

"'Him'?" I asked, because, well, you would, wouldn't you? I mean, chances were she was just assuming our murderer was male as most of 'em are, but on the other hand, if she had her suspicions as to who it was, then me and Phil needed to know about them.

"Whoever did for our poor Jonathan. He was a lovely boy, he was. Such a charmer. Not a bad bone in his body. I feel so sorry for his poor wife."

I happened, not very accidentally, to cast a glance over in young Oliver's direction as she spoke. He caught me looking almost immediately, and chimed in quick with "Yes, we all miss him" and an appropriately sad expression.

Maybe I was imagining it, but I could have sworn he'd had a sneer on his face a moment ago. Had that been for Lilah, or for old Jonny-boy? If they'd been best mates, there was a fair chance that young Oliver knew a lot more about Jonathan than, say, Sarah did. Shame the hasty cover-up suggested he wasn't planning on spilling any beans, fair trade or otherwise.

On the plus side, though, *boy* was clearly what Sarah called all men under forty, so I wasn't feeling quite so bad about it now.

I forked up a mouthful of carrot cake while I considered my next question. Not that I was being overly dainty; it just looked too gooey to manage with fingers. It was surprisingly good—not as sickly sweet as you'd think, and plenty of nuts added to the mix.

"Yummy, isn't it?" Oliver said, taking up a forkful of his own.

Even the tea was all right, I discovered when I took a sip to wash down the cake. "Not bad. But we probably ought to get down to business. So . . . the last time you saw Jonathan was the day he left work here?"

There was a pause before Oliver answered, but it could have been due to cake. "Mm. Although he didn't *tell* us it was his last day. He left a note for Ms. Lovett. The rest of us didn't find out until the following day."

"You must've been miffed, right? You and him being mates and all."

"We weren't *mates*. Just colleagues who were friendly." Oliver carefully stirred half a little packet of sugar into his tea.

"And you didn't have any contact with him afterwards?"

Another pause. Bloody cake. "There might have been a phone call or two."

"What about?"

"He felt bad about going off without saying anything to me. As you said."

"And did he explain himself?"

"He told me he couldn't go on living with Lilah." Oliver shrugged. "Well, obviously it would have been awkward for him to carry on working here, and he could hardly give Ms. Lovett notice and expect her not to tell her sister."

"So you don't think it was a spur-of-the-moment thing? Like, he decides one day he can't hack it anymore, dashes off his resignation letter on a spare piece of paper and chucks it on the desk on his way out, then goes home to shove some stuff in a bag?"

A longer pause, and seeing as how Oliver had scoffed his cake already, he couldn't put it down to having his mouth full. "Are you going to finish that? I didn't have time for lunch today."

"What— Oh." I blinked down at my plate, which had all of my slice of carrot cake on it bar one forkful, and then slid it over to him, not without a pang. I know there's a long and honourable tradition of investigators bribing witnesses to talk, but I hadn't realised it'd call for this kind of sacrifice.

"You're a darling. And I'm afraid I can't tell you about Jonathan's thought processes, but he did have a bag with him that day. He said he was going to the gym after work."

"Oh? Was he a regular gym bunny, then? Lilah never mentioned that."

Oliver grinned. It was slightly unsettling. "He used to tell the little woman"—and there was a sarcastic emphasis on those last two words which didn't endear him to me—"he was going to the golf course. She was never all that keen about the thought of him getting hot and sweaty with a lot of pumped-up men. I can't imagine why."

Yeah, right. Young Oliver had a smirk on his face that told me he was only too happy to imagine why, most likely in HD and surround sound. Hah. Seemed my gaydar had got it right for once. "You ever go with him?"

"I'm not really the gym sort. How about you? I could tell by looking at him that your . . . partner likes to work out." He'd clearly enjoyed making that observation and all. Just as well Phil wasn't here.

I mean, *confident* is attractive in a bloke. Smug? Not so much. "Uh, yeah. He does." Although not as much as you'd think from the size of him, unlike me, where the reverse is probably true. Genes can be bastards. "But, uh, Jonathan?"

"What about him?"

"Did you see him again after his last day at work? Go pay him a visit, or did he pop back up here for anything?"

"No. Why would I?"

Was he maybe a bit on the defensive side? "I dunno. Thought you might have, that's all. So what did you think about him and Lilah? Were you surprised when he told you it'd ended?"

His nostrils flared. It wasn't attractive. "I was more surprised it ever started."

Me-*ow*. "You knew him before they got hitched?"

"No. What makes you think that?"

"Just asking. Uh—"

I broke off as Oliver stood up. "Break's over, so it's back to the grind for me. But it's been lovely. Do come again." He swept off, leaving me sitting there like a lemon with my cooling cuppa.

Great. I downed the tea, bunged a couple of pound coins on the saucer, and made for the door.

Then I spun on my heel and went back to carry my crockery over to the counter, because my mum brought me up better than that. "Cheers, love. That was smashing."

Trade had slowed to a stop, and Sarah was wiping down the coffee machine. She paused to dimple in my direction. "Thank you, dear. Was Oliver able to help you— Oh, of course, I shouldn't ask that, should I? I do hope you get him locked up."

Or her, I didn't say. "I expect you saw a lot of Jonathan. And Oliver, of course. Did they take their breaks together?"

"Oh, no, Ms. Lovett's very strict about that. Can't have the shop understaffed. But I know they were good friends. Oliver's been so brave about it all." She shook out a paper napkin. "Now, I saw you letting him have your cake, bless your heart. Let me wrap you up a piece and you can take it with you."

"I couldn't—"

"Shush. No arguments." She cut two generous slices and made a parcel of them. "You take care. No getting yourself attacked again, you hear me?"

"Wouldn't dream of it, love," I said with a smile, because if you're going to give in, you might as well do it gracefully.

CHAPTER TWENTY-THREE

Phil was home when I got in. I might or might not have done a double take when I walked into the kitchen and found him making a cup of tea.

"Forgot I live here now, did you?"

Oops. He'd noticed. "Didn't think you'd be back so early. Uh, busy day? Mine was quiet, had a job go quicker than expected. Still, tomorrow's booked up, so I can't grumble." I crouched down to have a poke around in the fridge.

"I dug up a few things about Lilah's ex, Tarbox," Phil said after a mo. He didn't *sound* pissed off, although there was definitely a lacklustre tone to his voice.

I'd make it up to him. "Yeah? Anything good?"

"Maybe. They used to work for the same porn studio, although we're talking some years ago now. There were a couple of incidents."

I paused, leek in hand, from where I'd been rummaging in the veggie drawer. "Incidents?"

"There were complaints about coercion. Specifically, female models who'd been made to film stuff they weren't comfortable with. One of them alleged he'd assaulted her, but the charges were later dropped."

Well, that wasn't good. I bunged the leek on the counter top. "What happened to the girl? Didn't take a swim in any handy canals, did she?"

Phil huffed. "Nope. She's now a divorced mother of three and working as a hairdresser. The coppers on the case reckoned he'd paid her off. There was another case where they heard he'd got a little more aggressive—this time it was with a distributor, a few years later when

Tarbox was getting into the production side. Apparently he wasn't happy with the deal he was getting. Again, all charges were dropped—and the alleged victim got out of the business so quick he left scorch marks."

"Not a payoff this time?"

"Not unless you count Tarbox *not* breaking both his arms."

"Ouch." I straightened up, a packet of sausages in my hand. "You all right with plain stuff tonight? I'm not feeling like anything fancy."

"Fine by me."

I took the sausages to the grill and started unwrapping them. "I, uh, popped over to Pluck's End this afternoon. Spoke to Oliver." I braced myself for a furious barrage of *Personal safety just an abstract concept for you, is it?* Or at the very least, a sarcastic *If you're trying to get out of marrying me, there's easier ways than offering yourself up to murder suspects on a plate.*

"What did he tell you?" Phil said mildly.

Huh. That was it? I waited a beat, but apparently it was.

Okay, so what had he told me? "Well, I'm not sure I trust the bloke as far as I could throw him, but if anything, I reckon it's Jonny-boy's secrets he's keeping. Apparently they were like that." I held up two slightly greasy fingers in an illustrative and nonprofane fashion. "Oh, and our Mr. Parrot used to bunk off golf to go to the gym instead of the pub, like we thought. So he definitely lied to Lilah."

Of course, we already knew Jonny-boy had been carrying on with Kelvin behind her back. *If* we could believe a bloke who said hello with his fists.

"According to a bloke you don't trust."

"Well, yeah." I frowned. "I dunno, though. I think Oliver was telling the truth about that. He was too pleased about it for it not to be true. Not a big fan of our Lilah, young Ollie."

"Wouldn't be, would he? Not if him and Jonathan had a thing going."

"Uh, what? I never said that." I finished laying out the sausages and went over to the sink to give my hands a wash.

"No. I did." Phil looked grim. "Just a theory."

"Based on what?"

"Based on my extensive knowledge of cheating bastards."

Both professional and personal, he didn't add, and I couldn't argue with that one. "So, what, does that mean Oliver's a suspect too? Surprised you didn't go off on one at me for paying him a visit on my tod."

Phil's gaze took on a flinty quality. "*Were* you on your own with him?"

"Well, no. We had a quick natter in the café, that was all. If he'd tried anything funny, I'm sure the lady behind the counter would've saved me. Oh, that reminds me." I pulled an only slightly squashy parcel out from my jacket pocket. "I brought pudding. And no, it's not poisoned. Unless it was Sarah what done it. Maybe Jonny-boy criticised her cakes."

Phil huffed. "You know you can leave the investigating to me, right? It's not actually your job."

"You say that now, but next thing I know, you'll be dragging me off somewhere to switch on the old spidey-senses. Again." I slung my jacket over a chair and glared at him. "I'm beginning to think you only love me for my brain."

"And the cats," Phil reminded me, as Merlin slunk through the cat flap with perfect timing and wound himself around my fiancé's legs, totally ignoring the hand that fed him, i.e. mine. Well, most of the time.

All right, it was about half and half between me and Phil these days. But still.

"Beans with those?" he asked.

I frowned at the cake, then realised he meant the sausages. "Nah, I was going to do a leek-and-tomato sauce. And grilled polenta."

Phil laughed, carefully stepped over Merlin, and grabbed me round the waist, pulling me close and planting a kiss on my somewhat surprised lips.

"What was that for?"

"You, and your *plain food, nothing fancy*."

And I hadn't even mentioned the fresh basil and parmesan. I snogged him back for a bit, then pushed him away. "Later. Or it'll be beans on toast after all."

"Later? I thought we were shooting later. Or are you not feeling up to it?"

Oops. "Hey, who said anything about not feeling up to it? If you'd rather get up close and personal with a small bore rifle than with your own fiancé, who am I to judge?" I reached out to grab a handful of arse just to drive the point home.

Phil gave me a look, but kept shtum as he let me draw him in close.

We never did make it to shooting. And luckily I remembered to turn the grill off before the sausages burned to a crisp.

CHAPTER Twenty-Four

We hadn't planned any more visits on Saturday—for a start, I was working all morning, sorting out a cesspit out in the wilds of Redbourn. Don't ask, and don't take any deep breaths, either. I ended up having a late lunch, mostly because there was no way I was eating anything I'd touched before having a shower.

First job on the list for the afternoon was disinfecting the van—I'd done my best with a dust sheet over the driver's seat, but I'd have needed a whole different set of psychic powers to drive home without touching the controls. I'd just about finished that when Phil popped his head around the van door. "Fancy a trip up to Pluck's End?"

"What for?"

"I want another word with Axel. Half-term's over, so he'll be back at school next week."

"What about tomorrow? We're not due anywhere for Sunday lunch, are we?" My big brother, Richard, and his wife, Agatha, had been threatening to invite us, but fortunately hadn't got round to it yet. I was kind of hoping they never would.

Phil gave a brief headshake. "Axel's going out with his aunt, remember?"

"Uh, *no*." Actually it did ring a faint bell.

"Lilah mentioned it Thursday," he reminded me. "So it's now or never."

"Do they know we're coming?"

Phil looked shifty. "I rang Lilah, told her I wanted to have another go through Jonathan's things. She said not to come on Saturday as she'd be working."

"So you're planning to catch Axel home alone? Sneaky. Unless he goes out, of course."

He huffed. "Did he strike you as the sort who's keen on fresh air? Anyway, if he's not in, we can drop in on Leanne."

"At the salon? Sorry to disappoint you, but if I ever decide to go for some professional manscaping, it's not going to be by my future sister-in-law."

"Nothing like that." He looked even shiftier. "We were spotted on Thursday. Mum reckons Leanne's got the hump because we were in Pluck's End and didn't walk in the shop and say hello."

"Oh. Right. We can do that, then. Maybe we could take her out for dinner?" I felt a bit guilty. So she wasn't my favourite person in the whole world—I hadn't forgiven her for embarrassing Phil by casually dropping a very personal piece of information about his first marriage into the conversation when we'd gone round to his mum's for Sunday lunch a while back—but she meant well. Mostly. "She's not still on the diet, is she?"

"She's always on a flippin' diet. No. We'll go in and say hello. That's it."

I nodded. "Going there first, so we've got an excuse to dash off?"

Phil paused, clearly tempted, then shook his head. "No. Let's do Axel first. It's late enough already, and who knows when Lilah's going to come home."

As I locked the front door behind us, Phil pulled out his car keys. It was getting to be a habit, taking his car.

"How about we take the Fiesta?" I suggested. "It could do with a good run."

He shrugged. "Fine."

When I turned the keys in the ignition, the Fiesta sputtered into life like it'd been having a snooze and wasn't too chuffed to be woken.

Phil huffed. "When was the last time you drove your car?"

"Uh . . . I refuse to answer on the grounds it may cause you to make a suggestion that'll hurt her feelings."

"Her?"

"Well, yeah. All cars are female, aren't they? Like ships."

"I think Lightning McQueen would have something to say about that."

"*Who?*"

"Disney character. In the *Cars* film. Male, in case you were wondering."

"I'm mostly wondering how come you know the names of Disney characters." Was this the kids thing coming up again?

He gave me a look. I could feel it burning into the side of my face. "Remember shopping for a present for your mate Dave's kid? You dragged me into the Disney store and we didn't get out for half an hour."

Oh. That. Time to change the subject. "Right. Uh, there was something that came up when I was in the pub with Gary. Pun not intended. Our honeymoon. About time we booked that, innit?" I braced myself for another argument—sorry, spirited discussion—on the topic of idyllic Caribbean beaches and why they were no substitute for holiday destinations involving activities that were more, well, active both physically and, god forbid, intellectually.

Phil shrugged, staring straight ahead through the car windscreen. "Plenty of time for that."

I frowned. "You sure? It's the second week of July, remember. Isn't that around when the school holidays start? If we leave it too late, everywhere'll be booked up."

"Don't worry about it," Phil said, and then we got stuck behind some idiot blatantly talking on his mobile and driving like he was on the M25—all variable speed limits. So I didn't.

It was getting on for four o'clock by the time we finally got to Lilah's house. We knocked and waited. Too late, I realised the flaw in the plan. "Hang on, if Axel's up in his room with his headphones on, he's not gonna hear the door, is he?"

Phil cursed—just as the door opened after all.

The man who stood there giving us an unimpressed once-over had clearly heard the phrase *go large* at an impressionable age and had decided then and there to adopt it as a personal mantra. I don't mean he was obese, although he had a definite look of prosperity around the middle. He was easily as tall—and as broad shouldered—as Phil, and had for some unknown reason decided to add a few unnecessary inches with heeled cowboy boots and an honest-to-God bowler hat. He was wearing a waistcoat too, but there any resemblance to your stereotypical English civil servant ended. A splash of colour of the eye-watering variety was added by an exuberant purple paisley cravat.

Some blokes would've come across as camp in that little lot. This guy somehow managed to give the whole ensemble a rakish, macho air. I wasn't surprised when he tipped the hat to us, then folded his arms to stand there, feet hip-width apart, with a smug, self-satisfied smile. As if to say *My balls are so big my legs won't close.*

Even if I'd been inclined to trust him as far as I could throw him, which I hadn't been, that stance would've done it for me.

"Gentlemen?" He stroked his neatly trimmed goatee with one powerful hand. "What can I do you for?"

"We're working for Mrs. Parrot," Phil said with more than a hint of a challenge as he squared up to fix the bloke in the eye. I don't think he could help himself. Testosterone breeding testosterone, and all that. "Is she in?"

"Nope. Girl's got a business to run, ain't she? What're you here about, then?"

"Her husband." Phil's voice was getting curter and curter. He'd be down to words of one syllable and incoherent grunting soon.

"You're not police," the bloke guarding the door said with a lot more certainty than he could legitimately have felt, although to be fair he had his eye on me at the time.

Then I started wondering what it was about me that screamed, *Not a copper*, and if it was something I should worry about. "Sorry, mate," I butted in cheerily. "Didn't get your name."

"Tarbox. Brian. Lilah's other husband. The one what lived. And you are?"

"Private investigators, looking into Jonathan Parrot's death. I'm Phil Morrison." He said it grudgingly and didn't mention my name, which meant he was either playing his cards close to his chest or getting annoyingly overprotective. I knew which one my money was on.

Tarbox grunted. "Might have known. No other bugger cares that useless tosser's dead."

CHAPTER Twenty-Five

Frowning, I drew in a breath to call him on it, but Phil beat me to the punch.

"You didn't approve of the marriage?"

"That wasn't a bloody marriage. That was Lilah with a bee in her bonnet and a bloke with just enough smarts to know when he was onto an earner."

"Why do you say that?" Phil's tone was a lot milder now he was getting something from our man.

Tarbox narrowed his eyes. "Bleedin' obvious, innit? Talk about your life imitating art. Load of bollocks. Being a woofter might not be a sodding lifestyle choice, but marrying Lilah bloody well was. She's got her head in the clouds, that one."

I gave him a suspicious look. Casual homophobia about the bloke his ex had married, I could put down to jealousy, but digs at the lady herself? "Are you taking the piss?"

"What?" I wasn't sure who said it—could have been both of them—as Phil and Tarbox turned identical blank expressions at me.

"You know. A dwarf, with her head in the clouds? That some kind of short joke?" It was possible I'd been spending too much time around Darren lately, and it was making me paranoid.

Tarbox stared at me—and then his face cleared and he laughed out loud. "Hah. That's a good one. I gotta tell her that when she gets home."

I could see why she'd divorced him. Although to be fair, he had to know her better than I did. Maybe Lilah would actually get a kick out of it. I mean, it takes all sorts. Maybe off-colour jokes about their respective appearances were what had passed for foreplay in the Tarbox-Lovett marriage.

"Can we come in?" Phil asked, striking while the iron had thawed.

"What for? I told you, she's working. Won't be back until tonight." Tarbox didn't move to close the door, though.

"You're here to look after the kids?" I asked, keeping it light.

Tarbox shrugged. "Kid. Lorelei's working and all. Got a good work ethic, that girl. Least she got one bleedin' thing from her mum."

Poor Hazel. Not exactly what you'd hope to hear from a fond and doting father.

"Axel's taken it hard, hasn't he?" I said sympathetically. "Losing his stepdad and all. I heard they were pretty close."

Okay, so I was being a git, too, but this bloke rubbed me right up the wrong way. And it got results. Of a sort.

Tarbox laughed again, and if I hadn't heard him before, I might've thought it was genuine. "Bollocks. You've been listening to Lilah, ain't you? Axel put up with him. He's a good lad. But that bloody Parrot was a total waste of space."

I had a sudden urge to remind him that seeing as old Jonny-boy was an ex-Parrot and had ceased to be, maybe he should give the bloke a little respect.

"Mr. Tarbox, we've got a few questions for you too," Phil said, stony-faced. "I'm sure you don't want to carry on this conversation on your ex-wife's doorstep."

"Who says I want to carry it on any-bleedin'-where?" He threw up his hands in an overdramatic gesture. "Fine. Last thing I want is Lilah getting her tits in a tizzy 'cos I won't talk to her pet detectives. Come on in, but make sure you wipe your bloody feet. Christ knows what you lot go walking around in."

Did he reckon we'd been knee-deep in gory corpses before we came over? Tarbox had a seriously inflated idea of Hertfordshire crime statistics. Either that or he'd found out what I'd been up to in Redbourn.

We duly gave the door mat a good time, then followed his cowboy boots as they swaggered down the hall. To the kitchen again, so clearly him and Lilah had a few things in common. Unlike Lilah, Tarbox didn't offer us a cuppa, although he did invite us to sit at the table. Me and Phil took chairs next to each other, facing down the enemy.

Tarbox leaned forward in his chair, planted one beefy forearm on the table, and tipped his hat back with his other hand, the better to stare us out from under its brim. I couldn't help wondering why he was wearing it indoors. Bald spot, maybe? "Go on then. Ask your bloody questions."

Phil went straight in for the kill. "Where were you the night Jonathan Parrot died?"

The bastard actually laughed at him. "Why don't you ask the filth? Been through all this with them, ain't I?"

"I'll do that," Phil said mildly. "How about you tell me how you came to be employing a man you obviously didn't think much of?"

Tarbox shrugged. "Did I need Lilah bending my ear about it all day at work? No, I bloody didn't."

"At work?" Phil frowned.

"'S what I said. Lickett & Lovett Productions Limited. Adult entertainment."

Lovett being, of course, Lilah's, ahem, maiden name. I bet Tallulah was thrilled about them using it in the name of a porno company. "So you'd be, uh, Mr. Lickett?" I had to ask.

"Hah. You're funny, ain't you? No. Just a name." Tarbox shrugged. "We could've gone for Tarbox & Lovett, but it would've sounded like we were doing all that specialist stuff, know what I mean?"

No, and I was pretty sure I didn't want to.

Phil cleared his throat and wrested the conversation back under his control. "So you're in partnership with Mrs. Parrot as well as with her sister?"

Funny how it didn't surprise me one bit to find Mr. Tarbox was the sort who liked to have his fingers in all kinds of pies, innuendo not intended.

"Christ's sake, less of the *Mrs. Parrot*. Call her Lilah. God knows everyone else does. And yeah, we run the film business together. That's how we met, innit? Her and me, back in the day. Other side of the cameras then, of course. Mind, I still play the odd role if the script calls for it. Like to keep my hand in, know what I mean?" He winked, and yeah, this time I knew exactly what he meant, and I didn't think it was his *hand* he wanted to keep in. Or at least, not *only* his hand.

"So you and her, you had all the chemistry on set and off?"

"Strictly business at first. You've got to be professional about these things. Nah, back in them days, it was me and Tallulah."

I blinked. "Really?"

"Oh yeah. She's a good girl, she is. Always had a crap-load more class than her sister."

I was liking this bloke less and less. "So what changed?"

He smiled fondly. "Lilah's got her ways, the daft tart. Sometimes class don't pop your cork, does it?"

Did I say he'd smiled? It had degraded into a leer now.

Phil coughed. "So did you have much contact with Mr. Parrot?"

"No more than I could help. And no, I can't tell you who'd hate the little shit enough to kill him, but I'd take a gander at the boyfriend if I were you." He made a weird snorting noise, half amused and half in contempt. "Either of 'em."

I frowned. So did Phil, but it was him who asked. "Meaning?"

"If you reckon he wasn't getting it from some bloke on the side all the time he was with Lilah, you're dafter than she is."

I swear I could hear a bristling sound as Phil's hackles stood up. "Got someone in mind?"

"I wouldn't say that. But you might want to have a word with that nance in the Smithy."

Bloody hell. So Phil had been right about Jonny-boy and Oliver. Allegedly. I made a point of not glancing over to see the smug expression he was no doubt wearing right now.

Tarbox stood up. "We done, then? 'Cos I wouldn't mind seeing something of my son while I'm here."

Phil stood too, and I scrambled to join them so as not to get terminally loomed over. "We were actually hoping to have another word with Axel."

"Were you now?" Tarbox folded his arms. "See, what you don't seem to realise is, my boy's just a kid. He don't need all this hassle for some little poof no one misses. And you, like it or not, are not the police. So I'm thinking no."

No? Somehow I hadn't expected an outright refusal. I mean, we'd asked nicely and everything.

Phil rallied first. "As my partner said earlier, Axel seemed quite upset about Mr. Parrot's death. I'm sure he'd like to feel he's—"

"He'll get over it," Tarbox cut Phil off with a touch of menace.

"Don't you think Lilah would want us to—" I didn't get much further.

"Yeah, see, what *I* want right now is for you two to kindly fuck off. *If* you wouldn't mind. Or I could call the filth and see what they think about you two sticking your noses where they ain't wanted. Your choice."

We fucked off. Well, what can you do? Dave wouldn't thank us for wasting police time getting arrested for trespassing or harassment or whatever you charge people with who've overstayed their welcome.

"What do you reckon about that?" I asked Phil as I pulled the Fiesta out onto the road. "All a bit incestuous, innit? Tarbox swapping sisters, then trying to keep in with both of 'em. *Actually* keeping in with both of 'em, which can't have been easy. I mean, seriously, say you dumped me for Cherry, you needn't think *we'd* be mates anymore."

Phil huffed. "Who says he's still friends with them? Some people can separate business from their personal lives."

"S'pose it's a handy skill to have in the porn industry." I hesitated, but credit where it's due and all that. "Sounds like you hit the thingy on the whatsit about old JP and Oliver—sorry, 'that nance in the Smithy'—doesn't it? Weird, though. Oliver just talked like they were mates."

"People have been known to shag their mates." Phil paused, looking thoughtful. "If he didn't tell you yesterday, he's probably not planning on admitting it at all."

"Well, it's fair enough, innit? He'd be daft to let on he's got a motive for murder. I mean, Jonny-boy ran out on him as well as Lilah, didn't he? *If* they really were having a fling. We need to talk to Hazel again," I said decisively. "Get her away from that shop, somewhere she feels more comfortable talking. And I *don't* mean her mum's house."

There was a silence.

I glanced over at Phil. "What?"

"For someone who keeps saying he's only a plumber, you're getting pretty sharp at this game."

"Like I've had a choice?" I grinned. "You ought to be flattered. Me taking such an interest in your career and all. It's not like you ever return the favour."

"Go on, then. Tell me the best thing you've found blocking up someone's bog."

"Oi, it's not all about the grotty stuff, plumbing isn't. I was fitting gold-plated taps up in West Common only the other week. Mingling with the nobs and all that." The name *Common* being anything but a clue as to the sort of people who lived round that way. "Okay, I only actually met the cleaner, but the biscuits she gave me with my cuppa were dead posh. Proper Belgian chocolate." I glanced at my watch. "I dunno what time this place your sister works at closes, but it can't be too far off. Time to pay a flying visit?"

Phil nodded, not looking too cheerful. "Seeing as apparently we have to."

I could see where he was coming from—seriously, it was a daft thing for her to have got worked up about—but, well, while I couldn't say I really *liked* Leanne, in the sense of choosing to spend any more time with her than was inevitable, I definitely felt sorry for her. It couldn't have been easy, growing up overweight and shy with three strapping brothers who easily qualified for most people's definition of *fit*. Not to mention a mum who, it didn't take a lot of reading between the lines to see, had way more time for her sons than for her daughter.

Leanne's salon was on Pluck's End High Street, sandwiched between an estate agent selling local properties for silly money and a florist with a window full of equally overpriced pink and white Mother's Day stuff. You get mixed feelings about seeing a display like that a good month before the date in question. On the one hand, it's a cynical bid to cash in on the guilty feelings most of us have towards our mums—we never call, we never write, etc., etc. On the other hand, you could argue it's a public service giving us all a handy reminder well in advance. Saves a lot of potential wear and tear on family ties.

I made a mental note of the date, which was on the window in big pink letters, although it was anyone's guess whether I'd still remember by March.

The salon door jangled as I pushed it open and walked in. It was quite a big place, and there were three other girls all dressed identically to Leanne in those Chinese-style tunics beauticians always seem to wear, and with their hair scraped back and subdued into a bun on top of their heads. They all looked up when we walked in, perfectly arched eyebrows rising in unison.

It was like walking into some creepy movie where the women had been replaced by robot dolls. I had to work to dredge up a smile, not to mention dart a glance round to make sure I was talking to the right girl. "All right, Leanne?"

She smiled so widely I was worried something would crack. "Tom! And Phil. I wasn't expecting you."

Now the clients, a mixed bag of ladies at least twenty years older than the salon staff, turned to stare at us.

"Remember I was telling you about my brother, Mrs. Edgeworth?" Leanne twittered to the lady in her chair she'd been attacking with something resembling a length of dental floss. "This is him, and his partner, Tom. He's the psychic one," she added in the sort of hushed, gleeful voice I could imagine her using to talk about the latest celebrity scandal.

Mrs. Edgeworth's eyes gleamed under mismatched brows: one neat but reddened, and the other doing a modest caterpillar impersonation. "You don't think one of *us* is the murderer, do you?" She seemed to quite fancy the idea.

It was bleeding obvious why Leanne had wanted us to drop in: to bolster her cred with her colleagues and clients.

Marvellous. I could feel Phil starting to bristle behind me, and cranked up my smile in desperation. "Well, I hope you've got an alibi for the night of the murder."

There were giggles.

"Can you, like, actually read minds?" one of Leanne's colleagues asked. "Do you know what we're all thinking?"

There was another cascade of giggles, some of them sounding a lot more nervous than before, and a "God, I hope not!" from a girl with a dainty nose stud.

"Just 'cos you've got a dirty mind, Simone!" one of the other girls cackled.

The ladies in the chairs were all looking at me and Phil like we were a couple of long, tall, skinny lattes and they hadn't had a coffee since Christmas. I had to fight the urge to back away slowly. "Nah, not that kind of psychic."

"Do you do readings?" a lady getting her nails blinged up asked.

"Uh, no." I'd thought I'd covered that with *not that kind of psychic*, but apparently not. "All I do is find stuff."

"Did you find the body?" someone else asked.

"Uh, no."

"And do you know who tried to frame you?"

"'Frame me'?" *Definitely* wanting to back away now.

"That picture of you on the telly," Leanne put in helpfully. "We all saw it."

"Although I thought he'd be taller." Eyebrow lady sounded like I'd personally let her down.

"Do you think it was the wife who did it?"

"Uh . . ."

"We can't comment on an ongoing investigation," Phil's voice rumbled out from behind me. "It's been good seeing you, Leanne. We'll talk later."

Give the girl her due: she only quailed slightly at his tone. But then, that's sisters for you. I don't get any respect from mine, either.

I gave them all a cheery wave and a wink, and then legged it with my bloke.

"Pub?" I asked, suddenly desperate for a pint.

He nodded. "Pub."

CHAPTER TWENTY-SIX

It was around five o'clock, on the early side to start drinking—or at any rate, round here it was. If we'd been in the city centre at this time on a Saturday and stuck our heads round the door of a Wetherspoons, we'd no doubt have found the place heaving with lads and lasses who'd been on the piss all day shouting at the telly, but in a place like Pluck's End, they at least try to pretend they only have a tiny glass of Chateau Posh with a meal until later in the day. There were a few people in small groups in the corners, so quiet it wasn't easy to tell if they were early starters or stragglers from lunch, but on the whole the Spanish Inquisition was pretty empty. It probably wouldn't warm up until the dinnertime lot got here in a couple of hours.

True to form, Phil spent a lot more time chatting up the bar staff than was actually necessary to get our drinks.

"Decided to ask about old JP after all?" I asked when he finally returned. "And, oi, what's this?" He'd handed me a bottle of pale ale.

"Trixie's recommendation," he said, putting down his mineral water on a beer mat. "I asked her for something to impress this bloke I'm with."

"I can think of better ways you can impress me than with a bottle of gnat's piss."

He smirked. "Oh, yeah?"

"Yeah. You can tell me you got something useful from her about old Jonny-boy."

"As it happens, I did." He paused, and took a swig of his water. Over-dramatic git. "He came in a few times. With a dark-haired young man who was a bit on the swishy side—sound familiar?"

Oliver. "Well, he did say they were mates . . ."

"Trixie reckoned they were more than that. You could have knocked her over with a feather when she saw on the news about Mr. Parrot's murder and realised he was a married man."

I snorted. "Touching faith in human nature, there."

Phil looked bleak for a moment, and I kicked myself. Metaphorically speaking, as there wasn't a lot of legroom under the table and if I'd swung my size nine into Phil's shin by accident, I'd have felt even guiltier than I did already.

"It's not like I think everyone cheats," I said quickly. "Just, well, it's not like it's a shock when people do, is it?" Christ, Paretski, put down the spade and walk away before that hole gets big enough to swallow you whole.

Sod it.

"Not actually on my bucket list, in case you were wondering. Infidelity and all that," I explained awkwardly.

Phil rolled his eyes, but at least he was smiling. "Shut up, you daft bastard."

"You say the sweetest things. Cheers." Crisis averted, I took a cautious sip of my beer. "Hey, this is all right." I raised my bottle in the direction of the bar, and Trixie beamed back at me.

"Wonder how Cherry and Greg are getting on in the Highlands?" I said, more to change the subject than anything else. "You know, I can see him fitting right in there. Plenty of wild haggis to stuff, and I bet he'd be good at tossing the caber."

"Maybe." Phil grinned. "But on the other hand, do you honestly want to see him in a kilt?"

I shuddered. "Cheers, mate. That image is going to haunt me in my dreams tonight. Not that I make a habit of dreaming about my sister's husband, mind." Although there had been one or two times, after he'd spent a night in my bed—entirely platonically, I hasten to add, but I still shuddered again in memory.

"Do I want to know what's going through your head right now?"

"No. You really, really don't." I took a hefty swig of beer and turned the conversation to the football.

Phil smirked but played along anyway. I knew there was a reason I was marrying him.

"Want another?" I asked when I'd finished my beer. "If we head off home now, we'll get caught up in traffic." Plus I was finally feeling nicely mellow, and in no rush to leave the cosy atmosphere of the Spanish Inquisition.

And I bet that's a sentence they didn't hear a lot back in the day.

"You're driving, remember?"

Bugger. I'd forgotten that. Sitting here swigging a soft drink didn't hold the same appeal. "Home, then, and hope we get lucky on the roads?"

"Thought we'd have another word with Mr. Proudfoot before we leave. See what he's got to say in the light of Tarbox's insinuations."

"Is he here, then?" I looked around warily.

"No, but I've got his home address."

"He's going to think I'm stalking him."

Phil smirked. "Then he'll be on the defensive. Ups the chance he'll give himself away."

We had a brief discussion about whether to go straight to Oliver's, seeing as it was after six now and he'd presumably clocked off for the day, or stay at the pub and grab a meal first. I was all for heading straight over, the late lunch meaning I wasn't on the brink of starvation, but Phil talked me out of it on the grounds that (a) chances were the shop staff stayed later than the place's hours of business to close up, or popped into the shops for something to cook on the way home, and (b) he reckoned I'd be more on my game with a full stomach. He was probably right about that, although obviously I didn't do anything daft like actually admit it.

So we grabbed a couple of menus and ordered fish and chips with fresh minted peas, mushy peas being presumably far too common for a place like Pluck's End. Although when I mentioned that theory to Phil, he claimed to have been surprised they weren't serving them "ironically."

I wondered about that. "How do you even serve peas ironically? For dessert? Raw and still in their pods?"

"Don't be daft," Trixie the barmaid told me with a smile. She seemed to have taken quite a shine to me and Phil, her new regulars, despite the fact that Phil had been on the mineral water since we'd got here and I'd reluctantly switched to Diet Coke now. "Mushy peas don't come in pods. They come in cans. And we're not allowed to serve anything ironically. It's against hygiene regulations."

I was taking quite a shine to her and all.

The fish was good, fresh tasting and in light, crispy batter. The chips were less so, being of the chunky variety and served in a stack like that game with the wooden blocks where you're supposed to pull one out and try not to make the whole lot collapse. I didn't feel guilty about leaving most of them. The minted peas came in their own little ramekin, which was just as well, given the meal was served up on a flat wooden board instead of a plate and they'd have rolled off the edge like little green lemmings.

"It's meals like this that give gastro pubs a bad name," I said, keeping my voice low so Trixie wouldn't hear. "I ask you—what's wrong with a flippin' plate? Or normal-size chips that actually stay crispy?"

"This is more authentic," Phil said. "It said so on the menu."

"I reckon they need a dictionary. They meant to write 'pretentious.'"

He grinned. "Shut up and eat your Jenga."

Trust him to know what it was called.

The sky was fully dark when we left the pub, which always makes me do a double take. I mean, I know the sun doesn't rise and set for my benefit alone and is quite happy to get on with it even when I'm not outside to oversee the process, but somehow I still expected it to be half-light, like it had been when we'd gone inside . . . I glanced at my watch. Huh. Over two hours ago. It's a hard grind, this detecting lark.

The address Phil gave me was only a short drive away, aided by the GPS on his phone as this wasn't a part of Pluck's End I was familiar with. The town might be upmarket, but it still had its good areas and bad areas, and Oliver's postcode was definitely nothing to shout about. I supposed there was a limit to how much anyone got paid for working in retail, no matter how good they might be at charming the customers. The houses in his Victorian terrace backed straight onto the railway tracks, with a postage-stamp-sized front garden most of the residents seemed to use for cultivating weeds and discarded takeaway boxes. As we got out of the Fiesta outside Oliver's front door, a train thundered past unseen, and I swear the cheap windows rattled in their frames.

It was probably just as well we'd left Phil's Golf at home.

"He'd have been better off getting a flat in St. Albans or Berko and driving in," I said, keeping my voice low although it was far too nippy out for Oliver to have any windows open. "Even a room in a place like this must cost a fortune round here."

Phil shrugged. "Maybe he wants to save the planet."

"Or he lost his licence?"

"No. No previous—not so much as a speeding fine. Few parking tickets, mind."

We knocked on the door and waited.

Another train went past.

"Maybe he nipped into the shops on his way home?" I suggested. "After staying late, like you said he might. I mean, it doesn't take two hours to get round Tesco's, so he must have done both."

Phil gave me a look. "It'd be less passive-aggressive if you just came out and said, 'I told you we should've come straight here.'"

"Me? Passive-aggressive? I don't even know how to spell the word. Or does it count as two words? I'm never sure, when you bung a hyphen in it. Nah, I'm sure you were right. It's not like anyone ever goes out on a Saturday night, is it?"

Phil banged on the door again, harder this time. I chose to take that as a sign he wanted to get Oliver's attention, not that he was working out any frustration caused by our recent conversation.

Still nothing.

"I told you—" I began, then broke off as a light went on inside. "Hang on, someone's coming."

Phil barely had time for a smirk before *finally*, the door was opened.

By a duvet with a face. I blinked at it. It was olive toned, with a bit of a sallow cast, and it needed a shave—the face, not the duvet, although on closer inspection the cheap polycotton cover had gone bobbly. It didn't look any too happy.

"You're not Oliver," I told it.

"*That's* what you woke me up to tell me? Cheers, mate. Really fucking appreciate it."

"Bit early for bed, innit?" Okay, it was a weak comeback, but I was still reeling from all that sarcasm slapping me in the face.

"I work nights. *Duh*."

"Oh. Sorry. So is Oliver around?"

Not-Oliver made a show of peering in all directions. "Well, *I* can't see him."

"He's not in the house, then?" Phil was clearly getting fed up with all this.

Not-Oliver half turned to yell over his shoulder, "*Oliver*?" He must have noticed my beloved's general lack of gruntlement, and decided to save the attitude for a less intimidating target, i.e. me.

We all waited.

Not-Oliver turned back. "No. He's not."

"What time does he normally get home?" I tried.

"I don't know. Because I'm usually fucking *asleep*."

"Are you his bloke?" I had to ask, because seriously, how would their sex life even *work*?

He gave me a withering stare. "Get bent."

I guessed from that, Not-Oliver was either straight or into big beefy leather daddies rather than skinny camp shop assistants. Or, you know, wanted us to think he was.

"Do you mind if we come in and wait for him?" Phil asked.

Not-Oliver closed his eyes for a long moment, then gathered the duvet even more snugly around his frame. "Whatever. Make yourselves at home. Feel free to make as much noise as you want," he added pissily as he stomped off down the hall, his bare feet slapping on the lino.

Phil and me exchanged an eloquent glance, mostly on the subject of gift horses, mouths, don't look, and followed him in.

CHAPTER Twenty-Seven

I felt a bit guilty when the bloke flung himself on the sofa and switched on the telly, obviously having given up on sleep for the foreseeable. I wondered if I should offer to make him a coffee, but it seemed rude in his own house. Although come to that, for all I knew he might have been some bloke off the street Oliver let kip on his sofa.

Whoever he was, he was in his early twenties or thereabouts, with unstyled afro hair and prominent cheekbones. His skin was on the pale side for his African features, so I was guessing he was mixed race. Or maybe it was just that he didn't get to see much daylight with his hours. He wasn't bad looking in a lanky, scruffy, bed-head sort of way, in stripy PJ bottoms that hung low on skinny hips and a T-shirt from some sci-fi show I only vaguely recognised. I wondered if him and Hazel were mates, and if not, whether I should introduce them.

Course, he hadn't told us what the night job actually was. If it was shelf-stacking at the local Tesco, Lilah might not thank me for introducing him to her darling Lola.

Besides the sofa, there were only a couple of hard wooden chairs in the room, but it was them or sit on our reluctant host's feet. Well, at least it'd warm them up—his toes must've been frozen, walking barefoot on that lino. We could, of course, stay standing, but again it seemed rude to loom menacingly over the bloke.

We sat on the chairs. And waited. Several trains went past, reminding me it was rush hour and the traffic was going to be a mare going home. Thank God we'd eaten at the pub.

Which, come to think of it, was probably what Oliver was doing right now. I could picture him sitting in some warm, cosily lit restaurant, glass of wine in hand. Maybe with a hot date, maybe with his mates, casting a leisurely eye over the menu before deciding to go for something with lean meat and steamed vegetables. Or would he go for fish? Yeah, I could see that. As long as it didn't come in batter. A nice light hollandaise sauce, maybe. Served on the side, because calories.

Christ, I was bored.

Phil stuck it out another five minutes, then caved. "Maybe we could give him a call and see where he's got to?"

Not-Oliver slapped his forehead. "Now why didn't I think of that? Oh, right, *I* didn't barge in here for the sole purpose of seeing him, did I?"

"Uh, yeah, see, we haven't got his number," I said apologetically. "Think you could do the honours?"

I got a foul glare instead of an answer, but he did heave himself and his duvet off the sofa and stomp off upstairs, stomping back down shortly afterwards without the duvet and with his phone in one hand.

He did a few swipes and stabs at it, then held it up with a weary flourish so we could hear it ringing. Except . . . was that an echo?

"Is that it ringing upstairs?" I asked.

Not-Oliver was frowning. "He never leaves his phone when he goes out. It's like they're surgically attached."

"I'll go and see," Phil offered, jumping up from his seat and legging it out of the room before Not-Oliver had time to unfurrow his brow.

Phil was back, minutes later, with a ringing phone. "Does he charge it every night?"

"I don't know, do I? Probably."

It was an iPhone so yeah, he probably did. Which meant . . . "Was it charging?" I asked.

Phil shook his head. "No. Just slung on the chest of drawers. So my guess is he's been home this evening already, and gone out again. Without his phone." His tone was even, but somehow sounded ominous nonetheless.

"Why would he do that?" I asked. "You think he's trying to stop the police tracking him or something? Isn't it a bit late for that?" The murder was already done and dusted, after all.

Not-Oliver had ended the call and was staring at us.

"Mind if we take a look around?" Phil asked briskly in what I liked to think of as his copper voice.

"Uh, why? Who are you anyhow?"

"We're investigating Jonathan Parrot's death." Phil tossed Oliver's phone down on the sofa.

Not-Oliver shivered, but fair dues, him and Oliver could stand to turn the heating up a few degrees and he didn't have his duvet on him anymore. "I guess it's okay."

It didn't take long to search the house. Not only was it on the small side, Oliver and his mate didn't have a huge amount of stuff, or at least, not the sort of stuff you could hide a person in. The usual stack of games consoles, controllers, and associated discs, plus an intriguingly respectable collection of music on your actual vinyl. I looked around and yes, there in the corner of the living room was an antique record player, if by *antique* you meant *from the 1980s*. I wondered who it belonged to.

Several rooms had marks on the carpet where larger items of furniture, now departed, had stood for years, and Not-Oliver's bedroom, which was the biggest one at the front of the house, was a weird mix of middle-aged fittings covered in adolescent male trappings. Maybe the bloke was younger than I'd thought.

"You picking anything up?" Phil muttered to me as we established that no, Oliver wasn't doing a Harry Potter impersonation and hiding in the cupboard under the stairs.

"Uh . . . Thought we'd try it the low-tech way first, right? I mean, he could've forgotten his phone when he nipped down the pub, and there's no chance I'd pick up on that. Or like I said, maybe he didn't want anyone knowing where he'd gone. Any good old-fashioned cruising areas around here?"

It was daft. I knew it was daft. Just 'cos I was worried what I might find if I listened for it, didn't mean it wouldn't still be there if I didn't. I knew that.

But . . . the last time I'd used my spidey-senses to try to find someone, he'd ended up dead. Okay, not when I'd found him, exactly, but . . .

Didn't I say I knew it was daft?

Phil gave me a long look. "Cruising? No. Dogging, maybe. But let's check out the back."

The way to the back garden was through the kitchen, which was surprisingly well set up for what I'd assumed was a rental property occupied by two young, single men. It was the sort of kitchen you'd expect to see in a family home, although on the cheap and cheerful side. I was beginning to wonder about this place. Not-Oliver's childhood home? I wondered what had happened to his parents. Hopefully they'd retired somewhere sunny, rather than any less pleasant alternative.

The door was locked, but the key was in the lock so we didn't have to get Not-Oliver to come and let us out. I'd thought it was cold in the house, but once we got outside I realised I hadn't known when I was well-off. The stiff breeze blew right through me, and the chances were my hip wasn't going to be talking to me tomorrow.

Not without a guilty twinge about Oliver's heating bill, not to mention the planet, I left the door wide open to let as much light as possible spill into the garden.

Which was more of a yard, really, as it happened. It was concreted over, with a few token shrubby things in large tubs looking sorry for themselves. After stubbing my toe on one of them in the dark, I wasn't too happy either. At the far end—which wasn't all that far; only around thirty feet, max—I could make out a hip-high brick wall beyond which, I guessed, were the railway tracks.

As if to prove me right, at that moment there was an ear-watering low whistle and a thunderous rattle that got louder and louder until my ribs shook with it, and then just as suddenly, died away again.

At no point whatsoever did I see hide or hair of a train. I mean, yeah, it was dark, but what with streetlamps and all, it wasn't *that* dark. And the train should've been lit up inside, shouldn't it?

"Has Herts Rail invested in stealth technology, or what?"

"We're by a cutting, here," Phil informed me from the shadows. "The line's twenty feet down."

"Huh." I wandered over to the wall to have a butcher's. It was actually slightly lower than my hip level, which didn't seem the sort of thing modern building regulations would allow, although fair dues, there were signs it'd used to have a wooden fence built up on top. Maybe it'd rotted, or they'd taken it down for a better view of the tall trees beyond. "They ought to get that fixed. Wouldn't want to live here with nippers, would you? I'd be worried sick they'd take a tumble onto the tracks."

There was a silence.

I looked at Phil, his face ghostly in the secondhand streetlight. "Oh, *bloody* hell."

CHAPTER TWENTY-EIGHT

Taking a deep breath, I steeled myself, thought hard about Oliver Proudfoot, and *listened*.

Christ. It was all I could do not to throw up. The trail was thick and foul, and we were right on top of what it led to. Literally, almost. There was a fetid reek of death surrounding us, a buzzing aura of violence with an undertone of satisfaction that was worse than all the rest. I *knew*, as if I'd seen it happen, that there was a body on the other side of that wall. Twenty feet down. On the train tracks. For a moment, I felt dizzy and faint, as if I was tumbling over to join it.

"What is it?" Phil's tone was sharp over his footsteps as he joined me by the wall and slung his arm around me. I'd turned away, and sensed more than saw him peering over the edge. Another wash of vertigo hit me.

"How many trains do you reckon have gone past since we got here?" I asked shakily.

Phil pulled me close, and it was only then I realised that it wasn't just my voice. I was shaking all over. "Four or five. Maybe six." He said it softly, into my hair.

"Hope whoever comes out likes jigsaw puzzles, then," I said, and may have giggled although it really, really wasn't funny. So much for saving the planet.

Oliver hadn't even been able to save himself.

It's times like this that a mate on the force is worth his weight in whatever he bloody well chooses. Beer, probably, knowing Dave.

Ringing up the boys in blue to report a body on the railway line—when you haven't actually visually located said body—tends to lead to questions of the *And how exactly did you know he was there, sir?* variety. Shortly followed by invitations to try on a pair of handcuffs for size and come along to inspect the inside of a cell.

I suppose I *could* have claimed I'd shone a torch onto the tracks and seen a body part—if I'd managed to get the words out without gagging—but it made for a lot less emotional wear and tear, not to mention suspension of disbelief, to ring up our friendly neighbourhood DCI and say *Sorry, mate, I think I've found another one.*

There were the usual groans, but otherwise he took it fairly well, all things considered. I relaxed into Phil's embrace. We'd come back into the shadow of the house, where the breeze was slightly less icy and my voice wouldn't carry the news of murder most foul halfway down the street. Not that anyone was likely to be out in their garden to hear me, in the pitch-black chill of a February evening, but it didn't hurt to be cautious.

"You all right, mate?" I asked. "You've hardly sworn at all."

Dave muttered something under his breath. Probably making up for the deficit. "Home with the nipper, aren't I?" he said more audibly. "Jen says if his first word's a four-letter one, she'll divorce me after all."

Ouch. Considering how close they'd come a year or so back, that was a bit near to the bone. "Better hope he doesn't start with 'Mama' then. Or 'Dada,' come to that," I pointed out. "Course, if he did, you'd get to find out who's more important to him."

"That'll be a toss-up between his bottle and his bloody bunny rabbit. Oh, for—" There was further muttering, plus a distant sound of what I was pretty sure was Jen laughing her head off, then Dave's voice came back full force. "Right. I'll get the wheels in motion. Despite actually being off duty and enjoying some well-deserved family time. You sit tight and wait for reinforcements. And, for God's sake, don't get it into your head to go prancing about on those flippin' tracks looking for evidence. The other half's with you, I assume?"

"Yeah, Phil's here." His arm tightened around me, and I sent him a grateful glance, not that I could see him that well.

"Thank God for small mercies."

Huh. I hadn't thought Dave liked Phil all that much.

"At least he'll stop you doing anything terminally daft," Dave went on.

"Oi, I'm not an idiot," I protested, but Dave had already hung up. After that, there was nothing else for it but to go back inside to fill Not-Oliver in on the grisly not-quite-discovery. It wasn't like he wasn't going to find out anyway when Dave sent the boys round to see if it was all in my head, which, believe me, would've been my preferred outcome.

Not-Oliver had wrapped himself back up in his duvet and wasn't looking any less haggard than before. He shot us an anxious glance when we trooped back into his living room.

I tried to find a way to break it to him gently. "Uh, it's about your mate. Oliver," I started.

"No. Really? You don't say." He'd livened up now: the sarcasm was back.

Sod the gentleness. I was about to give him both barrels, but Phil beat me to it. "We think he's had an accident."

No, we bloody well didn't.

"What do you mean?" Not-Oliver was wide-awake now.

"We think he's gone over the garden wall"—Phil made it sound as if Oliver had simply decided to take a stroll and nipped over the wall as a shortcut—"and onto the railway line."

Now the bloke looked like he was having a nightmare. "You . . . saw him?"

I could tell by his tone he had a fair idea of what the passage of a rush hour's worth of trains could do to a body, and it wasn't an image I enjoyed having in my head, either. "Listen mate— Oi, you got a name?"

"Pete."

"Right. Okay, Pete, I'm Tom and this is Phil, and we're not certain that's what's happened"—fuck me, I'd never been more certain in my life—"but the police are coming over to check it out. So we're gonna sit tight here and wait for them to do their stuff. You want me to make you a cuppa?"

"Uh. Yeah?"

I popped into the kitchen, located the kettle without recourse to any psychic abilities, gave it a good rinse (nasty scale problem, not that Oliver would be worrying about crunchy bits in his cuppa anymore), filled it, and switched it on. The tea was a box of fair-trade stuff Oliver had probably liberated from the café at the Smithy and the biscuits, which I tentatively put down to Pete, were Asda own-brand chocolate digestives. I shoved the packet under my arm so I could carry them in with all three mugs at once.

I'd made Pete's tea white, no sugar, which was apparently how he usually drank it, if his lack of reaction on taking a sip was any guide. Course, it could have been shock. Perhaps I should've added sugar after all. I gave him a biccie to make up the lack.

Phil let him get halfway through before turning on the pressure. "Can you think of anyone who might have wanted to harm Oliver?"

Pete swallowed too quick and choked on a crumb. My beloved expressed his sympathy by tapping his foot until the coughing fit subsided. "No?" Pete managed in the end, his face bright red.

"Was he involved with anyone?"

"Uh, no?"

The bloke *really* needed to work on that habit of making his answers sound like questions.

"Anyone at work, maybe?" Phil persisted.

Pete roused himself. "Are you trying to imply something?"

"Just trying to get at the facts. Did he talk to you about his work colleagues?"

"No. We hardly see each other. When he's home, I'm asleep, and when I get back from work, he's on his way out."

Phil didn't correct him on the tense. Fair enough, we didn't know for *sure* Oliver was dead, although I knew what my money would be on. "What time do you start work?"

"Ten o'clock. Shit. I'm going to be late, aren't I?"

Not as late as Oliver.

"And you usually sleep until . . .?"

"Nine."

"Not great for the social life, that, is it?" I put in. "Wouldn't it be better to sleep early and have your evenings with everyone else?"

Pete turned to glare at me. "What, and see literally zero hours of daylight at this time of year? That'd be fucking fantastic, that would."

Phil leaned forward. "You must have talked to Oliver sometimes. Before he went to work, days off, whatever. So how did he seem, lately?"

"I don't know. The same as he always was."

"He didn't seem troubled?" Phil's tone was steady, almost mesmerising.

"No."

"Did he talk to you about Mr. Parrot?"

"I can't remember." Pete was bright red again, and the coughing fit had been over ages ago. I snuck a glance over at Phil, but there was nothing on his face to say he reckoned Pete was telling porkies.

"Did you ever see them together?"

"Dunno. Look, why are you asking me all this? We don't even know for sure if he's—" Pete swallowed.

I huffed. "Jonathan Parrot certainly is."

"Well, I didn't kill him." Pete took an angry gulp of tea.

"I'm not suggesting you had anything to do with either death," Phil said smoothly. "Just trying to build a picture."

It didn't help. Pete's answers got shorter and shorter, and then dried up completely. We sat there in moody silence.

After a while, I realised I hadn't heard a train go by for ages. I thought about having a sneaky listen to see if the vibes had gone, meaning they'd found him. But I bottled it. I'd know soon enough, right?

And in fact it wasn't long after that there was a knock on the door. Phil got up to answer it. He came back in with a bloke in a hi-vis jacket over his British Transport Police uniform. "Tom, this is Sergeant Kapoor."

"Mr. Paretski?" Kapoor was a youngish lad, early twenties at a guess, with light-tan skin and black hair cut aggressively short, probably to make him look less like a teenage heartthrob and more like a rough, tough officer of the law. With eyelashes like that, he was onto a definite loser there, though. "I understand you're the person who reported the fatality?"

"You found him?" I blurted out. The sombre expressions had been a clue, but well, Phil had always had a bit of a resting-grim-face thing going on, and for all I knew the sarge had had other plans for his Saturday night than traipsing up and down train tracks combing them for hamburger.

Okay, so I'd been clutching at straws.

"We've confirmed there's been a fatality. It'll take some time before we'll be able to positively identify the victim."

Meaning, they were still picking up the pieces and working out which one went where. My stomach lurched. Phil swallowed.

Our host Pete was nursing his mug of tea in a clear state of shock and, if he had any sense, anxiety for his own potential treatment by the coppers. After all, he had to have been here when it happened, even if he had been dead—pun very definitely not intended—to the world. Had he heard a noise? Half woken up, then rolled over and gone back to sleep?

Was he torturing himself now with knowledge that if he'd only done things a little bit differently, he could've saved Oliver's life?

He wasn't the only one.

"Sir?"

I realised I must have missed a question or something. "Sorry, mate. Uh, say again?"

Kapoor was staring at me like I'd sprouted an extra head. Great. Another copper who'd refuse to believe in anything he couldn't see for himself. "I understand you had a . . . premonition about the incident?"

I grimaced. "Sort of. You, uh, you want to check with DCI Dave Southgate. I've worked with him before."

The bloke was nodding, but still seemed uncertain. "Yeah, I got the memo. I was just wondering . . . What's it like?"

"What?"

"See, my great-gran, she always used to know when people in the family were going to die—is it like that for you? Did you see it happen in, like, a vision?"

Even worse. Not a sceptic. An *enthusiast*. "No. I don't get visions. I get . . ." Christ, I wasn't sure how to describe it. "It was really bright. And, uh, thick." The worst thing was, there had been a sense of *smugness* about it. Like, *That's you disposed of.* "Unpleasant."

Kapoor was rapt. "My great-gran, she used to see them wrapped in a white cloth, like a shroud, a few days before they died."

Lucky her. "I didn't know in advance." Christ, if only. That might actually have been useful. "I just knew where he was, once I'd started looking."

He frowned. "You were looking for remains on the track?"

"No, I was looking for Oliver. Well, not exactly looking. More sort of listening. For the vibes." Shit. I'd only been speaking to him yesterday. He'd shared—all right, scoffed—my carrot cake.

I was never going to eat carrot cake again.

"I thought you'd been briefed," Phil put in impatiently. "What's with the twenty questions? If you've got an issue with Tom, take it up with DCI Southgate."

"Oh. Sorry." Kapoor's face fell. "Yes, that's all—"

"Is it like a Hindu-tradition thing? Your gran's visions, I mean?" I blurted out, both because I'd started to feel bad for the bloke and because Christ knew it'd be nice to think I wasn't the only one with a so-called gift he'd like to return.

"What? Nah, Great-gran was Scottish Presbyterian. From Aberdeenshire. She met my great-grandad when—" He broke off at a glare from Phil. "Sorry. I understand DCI Southgate knows how to get in touch with you?"

"Yeah." I wouldn't have minded hearing a bit more about Great-gran, actually, but Phil was probably right. It wasn't the time.

"Then you're free to go." Kapoor turned to Pete, who'd been busy staring at me like I had *three* heads, and one of them was David bloody Blaine's. "Mr. Steadman? We're going to need to ask you some questions."

Pete looked like he wished he'd never come out from under his duvet.

CHAPTER TWENTY-NINE

I was glad it was me who was driving us home. There's something about being a passenger in a car, especially when it's dark, that always gets my brain working on overdrive. Maybe it's the lack of visible scenery, coupled with the lack of anything to bloody well do. It's not the same when I'm at the wheel, thank God, but even so, by the time we got back to St. Albans, my thoughts were coming thick and fast. And I didn't like the direction they were coming from.

"We should've gone straight there," I muttered to Phil as we finally staggered through our front door sometime after midnight. "Soon as the shop shut. Sod it, we should've waited for him outside the Smithy."

"We didn't know what was going to happen," Phil reminded me.

"Yeah, it's not like murderers ever kill more than once, now is it? Christ, how can you be so calm about this? We practically threw him to the fucking wolves. There we were in the pub having a laugh about peas and eating our fish and sodding chips, and he was here getting murdered."

Phil spun and slapped the wall, openhanded. "I know, all right? Christ, I *know*."

He looked wrecked.

Shit. All my frustration, my anger, fizzled and died. "It wasn't . . . I'm not blaming you," I said weakly.

"No? Because I sodding well am."

There wasn't a lot I could say to him. Not and have him believe me, anyway. I pulled him in for a hug. "Call it a joint effort, shall we?"

Because okay, he'd talked me into going round to Oliver's later rather than sooner. But it wasn't like I'd put up much of a fight.

"Do you think it's a coincidence—the timing, that is?" I asked later, when we were sitting on the sofa with a couple of beers, exhausted but too wired to sleep yet. "We talk to Brian, he drops his heavy hints about Oliver, and a few hours later, the bloke turns up in pieces?"

"Has to be. How would anyone else know what Tarbox told us?" Phil was silent a moment. "For all we know, he's been telling everyone about Parrot and Oliver since day one."

"I s'pose Axel could've overheard us talking . . . Nah, it doesn't make sense. That kid, go round to Oliver's and shove him over a wall?"

"They were pretty evenly matched for weight, I'd say. And he wouldn't have needed much force. Not with the height of that wall. If he hit the bloke just right, gravity would do most of the work for him."

"That's not what I mean. Axel's just a kid, yeah? But if he killed Oliver, that means he must've killed Jonathan as well, doesn't it? A bit cold-blooded for a fifteen-year-old." I frowned. "Unless . . . he killed Oliver because he found out *Oliver* killed Jonathan? Wouldn't he go to the police, though, instead of doing the whole vigilante-vengeance thing?"

"Kelvin Reid didn't."

I stared at him. "Fuck. What happened to him, anyway? They charged him with assault, didn't they?"

"Out on police bail."

Merlin poked his head into the room, decided he didn't like the atmosphere, and sodded off again. Arthur, made of sterner stuff, padded in and jumped up on Phil's lap. Phil stroked his head absently.

"And we already know he knows his way around Pluck's End." My aching abs reminded me Reid would be easily capable of tipping Oliver over a hip-high brick wall. Hell, he could probably chuck him over one twice as high.

Phil was frowning. "Why would Oliver let Reid into his house, though? Especially if he had a guilty conscience?"

I gave him the old eye roll, because seriously? "Like Reid couldn't have barged in anywhere he wanted?"

"Without waking the flatmate?" Phil pointed out.

"Shit. S'pose not."

"Whoever killed Oliver, it was someone he trusted. Or at least knew well enough to let in when they knocked on the door." Phil's face was grim.

"Think whoever killed him knew there was a bloke asleep upstairs?" I thought about it. "I mean, that'd be the first thing you'd say, right? 'Keep your voice down, the roomie's on nights.' It'd make it bloody risky, though. All Pete would've had to do would be to take a look out the window, and it'd all be over."

"First, you're forgetting it was dark. And second, the back bedroom was Oliver's. Pete had the one that overlooked the street." Phil huffed. "Could've used that as an excuse to take it outside, out the back."

That made a nasty kind of sense. "You don't reckon he was in on it, do you? Pete? Or did it himself, even?"

Phil shook his head decisively. "Nobody's that good an actor. And it doesn't make sense. If it was him, he'd want to make it look like an accident, so why deny all knowledge?"

"I dunno. Maybe he thought it'd be less suspicious if he claimed he'd slept through the whole thing and Oliver was out there on his own? Like people would think he'd, I dunno, leaned over the wall too far while trainspotting?" I grimaced, because even I could tell how daft that sounded. "Pete was hiding stuff. Uh, information. I don't mean actual physical stuff."

"Trying to protect Oliver. Not that it matters now."

"Do you think whoever did it went there planning to kill him?" I took a hefty swig of beer. My head was aching from all the crap going round and round in it. "They must have, mustn't they? Or why bother going out in the back garden in the dark? Come to that, why would Oliver go with them?"

"Could have been to avoid waking Pete up. Or maybe Oliver was killed first, or incapacitated somehow, and then dragged out the back."

"That'll show up when the forensics team do their stuff on the body, won't it?"

Phil gave me a look. "You reckon?" His tone was grim.

I swallowed. "Right. Jigsaw puzzle. Christ, I need my bed."

"Agreed." Phil stood up, much to Arthur's yowled disgust as he was tipped onto the floor.

We stumbled upstairs and into bed, leaving our clothes scattered on the floor, both way too tired for any life-affirming hanky-panky.

You can probably guess how well I slept, and what I dreamed about.

CHAPTER THIRTY

Sunday morning being traditionally a day of rest, we were of course woken up at eight by the phone ringing. Given the night I'd had, I wasn't too pleased about having to roll out of bed and root around in the heap of clothes on the floor until I finally located my phone in my jeans pocket.

It was Lilah. "All right, love?" I greeted her, trying not to let my lack of enthusiasm show in my voice.

"What the bleedin' hell's going on?"

I held the phone further from my ear, her voice being a little louder and more piercing than I was feeling up to at that hour of the morning. "What?" Was she calling to complain about our abortive attempt to corner her beloved son without her to act as chaperone?

"That lad from the Smithy. Oliver. He's brown bread!"

Dead, my knowledge of little-used cockney rhyming slang provided, the fact I'd been the one to discover the body adding a helpful hint my sleep-fogged brain sorely needed. "Uh. Yeah. How do you know?"

"Pete called my little girl and told her about it this morning. She's in a right state."

Huh, so Hazel and Pete *were* friends. And it sounded like Pete hadn't slept any better than I had.

"She said you found him. With your whatsit." There was a touch of awe underlying her *The world's gone mad* tone.

"Yeah..." I glanced over at Phil, who was sitting up in bed looking unfairly with-it, not to mention gorgeous. "Hang on a mo." I covered the bit you speak into with my thumb. "It's Lilah. She's heard about Oliver."

"Tell her we'll be over in an hour."

I relayed the message and hung up. Then I slumped back onto the bed. "An hour? Great. Just time to bung some clothes on and shove down a slice of toast."

"Shower first."

"Have we got time?" I asked wearily, staring up at the ceiling.

"If we do it together." Phil's face appeared in my field of vision wearing a hint of a smirk, and although thirty seconds ago I'd have said I hadn't got the energy for anything like that, suddenly all I wanted was to forget about this bloody case for five minutes.

"You're on." I held out my hand.

Phil pulled me up and kept on pulling so I landed smack against his hard, naked body. It wasn't the only thing that was hard, either. I shivered, either from the chill of the room or from the feel of his skin on mine, and he grabbed hold of a buttock and squeezed.

"Shower," he reminded me, and kissed me roughly, sending a jolt of desire straight down to my groin.

It's not exactly huge, my shower. Well, not when you've got a bloke in there with you with shoulders the size of my Phil's. We had to get *really* close. Not that I was complaining. I buried my head in Phil's neck as he jerked us off, both our dicks together in one big hand. "Christ, that's good," I moaned. "Want me to—"

I didn't get to finish offering to blow him, much less go through with the act, because he stopped my mouth with a kiss. It was forceful and hungry like his grip on my dick, just the right side of pain. His other hand was on the back of my head, stopping me breaking the kiss—not that I wanted to.

Maybe I wasn't the only one who'd had bad dreams last night. With the water cascading down on us, it was difficult to breathe and our chests were heaving.

Light-headed, I dug my fingers into the slippery mounds of his arse, not bothering to worry about leaving marks. I *wanted* to leave marks. I wanted everything. I ran my hand down his crack, my fingers teasing his hole, letting him know what I intended in case he had a problem with that.

Phil grunted into my mouth as he shoved his arse back against my touch. Nope, no problems there. I circled his hole once with my middle finger and then pushed it deep inside him, owning him. I felt it in my dick as his inner muscles gripped me tight, pulling me inside—and then spasmed as he came, shooting hot jets of spunk up between us.

He'd barely stopped shuddering before he pushed me away—and dropped to his knees.

Christ. I nearly came from the sight. His blond hair was soaked several shades darker, and water was beaded on his muscular shoulders where they were outside the spray. The streaks of his spunk on my belly were disappearing as the water washed them away. I backed up about an inch to lean against the tiles. They chilled my shoulders to the bone, but I didn't care. The rest of me was feverish with want.

Both hands on my hips, he bent his head—but not to my dick, as I'd expected. Instead, he gently kissed my belly, right where Reid had punched me. Christ. Even after all the time we'd been together, his tenderness still blew me away. My heart melted—then he dipped his head further, and suddenly it wasn't my heart that was uppermost in my mind.

My knees trembled as Phil's mouth enveloped me. Bloody hell, he was good at this. My world narrowed to the heat and pressure on my dick. God, I never wanted this to end. Phil's head bobbed up and down as he rolled my balls in his hand, and I groaned wordlessly.

Then he looked up, straight at me, still sucking on my cock, and that was all it took. Pleasure and release ripped through me. Possibly I shouted something. It was fucking glorious.

And then the water went cold, my knees gave out, and I collapsed onto Phil. We were both laughing like a couple of sex-drunk hyenas as we staggered out of the shower to grab our towels.

"Feeling better now?" Phil asked, rubbing his hair dry with a lot more than a hint of a smirk. *His* towel was an Egyptian cotton bath sheet personally hand-woven by Nefertiti and fluffed up by the breath of baby angels, while mine was the washed-out, cardboard-textured dishrag I'd got in a bargain-price bundle from Tesco. The bath sheet had moved in with my beloved, along with a load of other top-notch linens currently giving my airing cupboard ideas above its station.

I might just possibly have developed a touch of towel envy. "Git." It was the wittiest thing I could think of after that brain-shattering orgasm.

"Your git," he reminded me. "Coffee and toast?"

"You're a lifesaver." I gave up trying to dry myself off with my sorry excuse for a towel, and nodded at Phil's not-so-little bit of luxury. The towel, I meant, although obviously the description also applied to something else of his. "You finished with that?"

Phil laughed and chucked it at me. "Why didn't you grab one of these for yourself in the first place? It's not like we've only got the one."

"Yeah, but they're yours," I said awkwardly, wrapping myself up in what felt like a very posh cloud that somehow managed to smell subtly of Phil even though he'd just showered.

He gave me a look. "We're getting married, remember? That means joint custody of the household linens. 'With my worldly goods I thee endow.' Sound familiar?"

"Nope. Don't remember that part at all. I never got past 'With my body I thee honour.'" And don't think it hadn't been traumatic hearing Greg vow that to my sister in a packed-out cathedral. Trust him and Cherry to have the most archaic service possible that didn't actually call for her to promise to obey him.

"We've done that bit. Now do me a favour and take the towels. That one of yours isn't fit for lining the cats' baskets."

"They never sleep in their baskets. I've had the flippin' things under the bed in the spare room for the last five years."

"That's exactly what I mean. That towel isn't fit to be a cat's reject."

"Harsh, mate. Harsh."

Phil wrapped his arm around my be-towelled self and gave me a squeeze. "But fair."

CHAPTER THIRTY-ONE

We were later than we'd said, getting to Lilah's house, but she didn't call us on it. She opened the door looking less put-together and more like her actual age than I'd ever seen her, in jeans and a faded T-shirt with her hair scraped back and no makeup. The T-shirt had writing on it: *Though she be but little, she is fierce.* I had a vague idea that it was a quote from something, and I'd have asked her about it, but it wasn't really that sort of visit. Phil would probably know, anyhow.

"Come on in," she told us, and led us straight to the kitchen again.

Axel was sitting at the table with his hood up and his hands clamped around a mug of something steaming. He took one look at us and bolted, presumably for the womb-like security of his room.

I hoped he didn't spill his drink on the way. Those carpets weren't cheap.

Lilah made a sad face. "My poor baby. It's brung it all back for him, this happening. Thank God his auntie's coming round for him in an hour."

"Yeah? They going somewhere nice?"

"Some gaming-exhibition oojamawotsit. Tallulah's always been better with all that geek stuff than I have. I ain't got the patience. Never did have."

"She spends a lot of time with him, does she?" Phil asked.

"Oh, yeah. Since he was a baby. Well, I had the business to run, didn't I? She was glad enough to have me pay her to mind him. I always say she brung him up more than I did, so any bad habits he's got, they're on her, not me." Lilah cackled. "Coffee?"

"Uh, yeah, ta."

We sat down at the table, me in the seat still warm from Axel's bum and Phil on the opposite side, while Lilah bustled about with the kettle and stuff. Axel's mug had left a ring of what looked like hot chocolate on the glass surface of the table, and I had to keep reminding myself not to put my elbows in it.

Lilah didn't ask how we took our coffee, just plonked a couple of mugs in front of us with plenty of milk and no sugar, which was what she was having. She didn't bring out the biscuits this time either, but then it was a bit soon after breakfast.

"So what the bloody hell's it all about, then?" she asked, hopping onto the chair next to mine. "Are the filth all sitting around with their fingers up their bums? Why haven't they locked that nutter up and chucked away the key?"

Me and Phil exchanged glances.

"There's not a lot we can tell you," Phil said, his tone sympathetic. "We haven't even heard if the body's been positively identified."

Lilah rolled her eyes. "What, and it's all some big coincidence how Oliver went and disappeared last night? Pull the other one." She turned to me. "No, what I want to know is, how was it you were the one to find him? What gave you the idea to go round there in the first place? Did you have, like, a premonition?"

"It wasn't like that." I stopped, not sure how much I should tell her.

"We actually went round to talk to Oliver about another matter," Phil said cautiously.

"You mean, about my Jonny?"

"Yes." Phil gave me a nudge.

Great, so I got to be the bearer of bad tidings. Although on the other hand, telling her this might make her feel better about Mr. Proudfoot's unfortunate demise. "Uh . . . I know this isn't going to be easy for you to hear, but . . . there's been a suggestion that your husband was, um, having an affair with Oliver."

I braced for an emotional outburst, but Lilah simply looked baffled. "Well, yeah. I knew all about that. Wasn't an affair, though. They were just shagging."

I stared, gobsmacked.

Phil leaned forward. "He told you about it?"

"First off, it was that nosy cow at the café—couldn't *wait* to tell me how she'd seen them around together, and wasn't it *nice* how they were such good friends? Bloody shit-stirring, that's what it was." Lilah made a disgusted face.

Sarah, I'd thought better of you. Although maybe she'd meant well.

"Then my Axel came to me about it, bless him. Got himself all worked up and all. Spent weeks worrying how he was going to tell his mum, poor baby. I told him, 'When you're an adult, you'll understand.'"

He would? I was an adult, and I bloody well didn't. Still, takes all sorts.

Then I frowned. "How did Axel find out?"

"Saw them in the stockroom at the Smithy. He was helping out on a Saturday when his sister had the flu." Lilah cackled. "Gawd, if Tallulah had caught 'em at it, there'd have been hell to pay. She's always had a stick right up her arse, ever since we was kids.

"So I had a word with my Jonny," Lilah went on. "I told him, if he wants to have his bit on the side, it's no skin off my nose. Blokes have got their needs, ain't they? You're not going to stop them getting their end away, so why worry? Long as he still came home to me, that was the main thing." She shrugged, a gesture almost as big as she was. Then she sighed. I guessed she was thinking about that time he hadn't made it.

Or maybe she was thinking about poor old Oliver. Who knew? It was like she was speaking a different language, except that the words made sense all right. It was just the sentences that didn't. At least, not to me. I couldn't imagine me having that attitude, if I found out Phil was screwing around. I *certainly* couldn't imagine him being okay if it was me. It's like Marmite, I s'pose. Lilah might find an open relationship tasty and good luck to her, but there's no way it'd ever pass my lips.

So to speak.

Maybe it was the porn career? Like, she was used to separating sex from emotions? Or was it a fetish in itself? Like, she got off on hearing about him shagging other men? I swallowed.

Lilah scrubbed her face with her hands. "And now they're both gone. You know what? I'm scared. I told my girl she's not going back to work, not while that bastard's running around loose. That git's *mental*. If Loos has any sense, she'll shut the shop down for a week or two, not just today. It ain't safe. I got my ex coming round later."

Phil leaned forward. "You still think Kelvin Reid is the killer?"

"Who the bleedin' hell else? He killed my poor Jonny 'cos he left him, and now he's killed that lad because of them shagging. I rang them up, you know. After I spoke to you. I rang them up and said, 'Why ain't he in jail?' But all they did was fob me off. 'Can't give out information about an ongoing investigation.' Ongoing load of bollocks, more like. I told them that and all."

I guessed *they* were Hertfordshire constabulary. And I wouldn't mind betting our Mr. Reid of the big fists was even now helping them with their enquiries. I wondered if he had an alibi for last night. Then again, I still couldn't see how he could've got Oliver to let him in. Not without waking Pete up.

That made me think of something else. "Your daughter"—calling her Hazel to Lilah's face seemed rude, somehow, but no way on earth was I calling her Lola—"are her and Pete good mates?"

"Oh, yeah. More than, I reckon. On her side, anyhow, though she always says not." Lilah made a face. "Like she's going to tell her mum anything, right?"

"Did she meet him through Oliver?"

"Other way round. They were in sixth form together, Pete and my girl. She used to go round his house and play these Dungeons & Dragons games and whatnot. I ask you, what happened to teenagers going out on the piss? That lot just sat around drinking tea and playing flippin' board games. Not even video games, they weren't. Unnatural, I call it. That was when his mum and dad were still alive, of course. He was living there on his tod after they had that accident, until Oliver's landlord kicked him out 'cos he wanted to sell the place. So my Lola says, 'Why don't you move in with Pete?' And he's been there ever since. Lived there and died there, Gawd rest his soul if you believe in all that bollocks." She drew in a deep breath, and Christ knew she must've needed one after all that. "He's a good lad, that Pete. Bit of a weirdo, but who ain't? Living on your own, it's bad for a boy that age. 'Specially working nights. He never had a right lot of friends, and now he's gone and lost another one."

I hoped for Pete's sake she wasn't planning on repeating this to the police. Then again, even I was starting to wonder if maybe young Mr. Steadman was a better actor than we'd given him credit for.

"Is your daughter at home now?" I asked, expecting a *Gawd, yes, I'm not letting her out of my sight till she's thirty.*

"Lola? She's gone round to see Pete, bless her heart."

"What, at the—" I stopped myself just in time from saying, *murder house* "—house by the railway?"

"Nah. Crime scene, innit? They made him put up in a hotel, and what bloody use is that when you're working nights? I told her to bring him back here, poor lad."

"Is that a good idea?"

"More the bloody merrier if you ask me. Safety in numbers, innit? Tell you what, you two'd be welcome and all if you want to kip here tonight." She gave Phil's broad, muscular shoulders an approving look. "'Specially you."

Hands off, love. This one's taken. "Uh, sorry, but we've got to be home to feed the cats."

"Was it just me, or was Lilah giving out seriously mixed messages about Pete Steadman?" I muttered after the front door had closed behind us. "There she is inviting him round to make himself at home, and in the next breath she's one step away from saying 'He was always a quiet one, kept himself to himself.' That's practically the dictionary definition of *serial killer*."

Phil huffed. "Don't reckon she realised she was doing it."

"Think we should tell her?"

"What, not to trust him? Or to watch her mouth when she's talking about him?"

I shrugged. "Either. Both."

"I can't see the lad trying anything at Lilah's house. Likes to get his victims out on their own, doesn't he, our murderer? Dark canal path, dark railway . . ."

"Yeah. Think he's got a thing about transportation?"

We reached Phil's car, which was parked a little way down the street, and he zapped the central locking. "Don't know. But for the meantime, you might want to steer clear of motorway overpasses. At least at night."

"Or footbridges. Or cycle paths," I added as I opened the passenger door, since even murderers probably like to be environmentally friendly and keep in shape every now and then.

Phil gave me a look over the top of the car. "Cycle paths? Worried you'd get stabbed with a spoke?"

"Oi, he could throttle a bloke with a lock and chain. Or bash him over the head with a bicycle pump."

Phil was shaking his head. "Doesn't fit the MO. Our murderer's not the hands-on sort."

"Yeah, I s'pose they've got that whole *out of sight, out of mind* thing going on."

"You think that's why you were able to find Proudfoot's remains? I've been thinking about that. They weren't exactly hidden."

His tone was sharp, and I felt intimidated by the focus of my beloved's gaze, despite the fact there was a metric tonne and change of metal between us. Neither of us made any move to get in the car. "I dunno. I mean, I know they were just, well, lying there, but would anyone have found them if they hadn't been looking? You'd get foxes and stuff taking them away and eating them, wouldn't you? And eventually they'd rot and stuff." I was getting queasy thinking about it. "Maybe it's, uh, the intentions? Like, I don't get vibes from stuff that's lost, so it was all to do with how the murderer was feeling? Like they reckoned that was Oliver out of the way, body disposed of, job done?"

Phil nodded slowly. "That could explain it."

Great. "Cheers, mate. Good to know you're willing to believe there's an explanation other than I put him there myself."

He audibly *tsk*ed. "Christ, you know I know *you* didn't kill him." Then he grinned. "Haven't been away from my side long enough, have you? No, I was wondering if . . . whatever it is that lets you find things, if it's getting stronger."

"Why would it do that?" I'm not going to pretend I wasn't alarmed at the prospect.

"Been using it more, haven't you? Getting better at tapping into it, from what I've seen. I keep telling you, it's like a muscle."

"What, and working these cases with you has been like the psychic equivalent of a few hours in the gym and a five-mile run?"

"Could be."

"Great. On top of everything else, now I get to worry about my brain bulging out of my ears." I got in the car and Phil followed suit.

"Anyhow, if you're so curious about it all," I asked as I buckled my seat belt, "why'd you shut down that transport copper when he was telling us about his gran?"

"Because it was all family legend, and chances are it was a load of bollocks. And he was treating you like a bloody freak show instead of getting on with investigating the murder. Next thing you knew he'd have been asking for a demonstration."

Phil switched on the engine, put the car in gear—and froze.

Chapter Thirty-Two

I frowned at Phil—then looked up. There were a couple of cop cars, one of them in plain clothes but with a spinner on the top, coming down the road towards us. No sirens, just the lights.

"You don't think . . ." I said slowly as they passed us.

We twisted round in our seats, and yep, you guessed it. The cars came to a halt in front of Lilah's place.

The plod piled out. Phil switched off the engine.

"They're going to make an arrest, aren't they?" I said, getting out of the car.

"Must be." Phil's tone was grimmer than ever as he joined me on the street.

It's awkward at a time like this. You feel you ought to do something, but there's not a lot you can do, is there? Help the client resist arrest? That was assuming it was Lilah they were here for, of course. Christ, if it was one of the kids . . . Well, she'd definitely be in need of support. I started walking towards her house.

Phil grabbed my arm. "Don't be in too much of a hurry. They won't thank you for getting in the way."

No, but Lilah might. But like I said—what could we do except stand there like a couple of gawkers at a sideshow, as much use as a chocolate teapot at a coffee drinkers' convention?

It was horrible. Lilah was led out in handcuffs, her face defiant. Axel, his hoodie down and headphones off for once, ran out after her and threw a wobbly on the doorstep. He had to be restrained by a couple of uniformed coppers, while his mum screeched at them to leave him alone, she'd have 'em for police brutality, the effing bastards. She didn't seem to notice me and Phil, which was probably just as well given how she yelled at her neighbour, a pleasant-looking middle-aged lady who'd poked her head out of her front door to see what the fuss was all about to "Go on, have a good gawp, I bet you're loving this, you stuck-up cow."

Once Lilah had been driven away and Axel shepherded back indoors by a stony-faced copper, me and Phil knocked on the door. The copper showed no signs of softening up when she answered it. Axel was still in the hallway, leaning against the wall, his hoodie now up and his head down.

"We're friends of the family," Phil said.

The copper didn't look convinced.

Axel looked even less convinced. "You let them take her away! It's not fair. She didn't do anything." He jerked himself away from the wall, which made the policewoman tense up, but instead of doing a runner, he sat down on the stairs and hugged his knees.

Phil coughed and casually planted one of his size elevens just inside the door. "What's she been arrested for?"

The copper glared at my beloved's foot like she was strongly tempted to slam the door on it. "I'm afraid I can't—"

"Murder," Axel broke in wildly.

"They think she killed Oliver?" I asked.

"What? No. Jonathan." Axel buried his head once more.

Me and Phil exchanged glances. There must have been some kind of breakthrough, some piece of evidence found. We needed to talk to Dave, pronto.

"Uh, you're going to get the boy's dad round to keep an eye on him, right?" I said to the policewoman.

"I'm not a bloody kid! I don't need—" Axel broke off with a sob. "I want my mum back."

"Don't worry, sir. I'll make sure he's taken care of." She said it firmly, in a *please go away now and stop upsetting him before I lose it and arrest you too* sort of way.

So we went.

I rang Dave as soon as we got back to the car, which was totally because we needed information and not at all because I was avoiding the "Do you think she done it?" conversation with Phil. Dave answered on the first ring, with a tired, "Why am I not surprised it's you?"

"Are you working today?" I asked, remembering it was Sunday morning.

"When am I ever not?"

"Oi, don't give me that. You can't have it both ways. Last time I rang, you were complaining about me interrupting your time off. Which, while we're on the subject, you've been taking plenty of since the New Hope came along."

"Maybe, but no other bugger's going to get my paperwork done for me, are they now?"

"You sure you're not just getting out of the house for some peace and quiet?"

"You tell the wife that and you can kiss goodbye to any more favours from this direction. So to what do I owe the very dubious pleasure? As if I couldn't guess."

"You're aware they arrested our client five minutes ago, then?"

"Got you on speed dial, has she? Or did she send up the bat signal the minute they knocked on her door? What is it in your case—a pair of crossed pipe wrenches? Or a bloody crystal ball?"

I decided to ignore the digs at my profession(s). "We were there. We practically tag-teamed your lot on the doormat. So come on, what have they got on her?"

"You do realise informing members of the public about police investigations is not, actually, part of my job? To the extent of being specifically frowned upon? A DCI has to think about these things. Can't go setting a bad example."

"Yeah, but . . . Come on, Dave. We're mates. And you know I wouldn't do anything to, uh, pervert the course of justice or whatever you call it."

There was a heavy sigh down the phone that nearly blew out my eardrums. "You know what the really tragic part is? You and Morrison would owe me so bloody many nights babysitting, if only I could believe either of you knows which end of a nipper is up."

"The noisy end goes up, the smelly end goes down. Easy. Book us in for Friday night." I fought the urge to cross my fingers he wouldn't. "So what have they got on Lilah?"

"They found his phone. Which you did *not* hear from me."

"Whose?"

"Whose do you bloody think? Parrot's. It'd been chucked in the water, or fell in when he got bashed on the head"—and yeah, I noticed that was apparently now an established fact—"but they managed to dry it out and get the records off it. Message from one Lilah Parrot, nee Lovett, shortly before her husband went for an unseasonal swim: *Meet me down by the canal.*"

"What?" My gob was thoroughly smacked. "But that's . . . Didn't she have an alibi for when he got offed?"

"Haven't you heard, Paretski? Only the guilty bother getting themselves an alibi." Dave sighed. "Got to hand it to you. I always thought you had bleeding tragic taste in men, but your choice of clients tops that, easy."

"But . . . why? I mean, why would she kill him?"

"Is that a serious question? Bloody hell, he ran out on her; he was probably cheating on her; if she asked for a divorce, he'd probably take her for every penny . . . What more do you want?"

She didn't mind the cheating. She told us so, I didn't say, because even as I thought it, I realised how bloody stupid it'd sound. "So Kelvin Reid is in the clear?" I asked instead.

"For the Parrot murder, yeah. And don't quote me on this, but they'll be trying to pin the Proudfoot one on your girlfriend and all."

"Lilah? She's well under five foot, for Christ's sake. How's she supposed to have shoved a strapping lad like Oliver over his own garden wall?" Okay, so *strapping* was pushing it, but the idea was still pretty far-fetched.

"No room for ableist attitudes in your modern constabulary. And I never said she was acting alone, now did I?"

"Who else have your lot got their eye on, then?"

There was another heavy sigh. "The DI's playing it close to his chest, but her and Tarbox are each other's alibis for when Parrot took that dive. Claimed they were working at the office until eight, by which time Parrot was already very literally sleeping with the fishes.

So if she goes down, Tarbox is going with her. Whether he helped her out on the job or just after the fact for old times' sake, I don't know."

"What about Oliver?"

"What about him?"

"Uh, why would they want to kill him?"

"Word is, him and Parrot were having it away, so there's Lilah's motive for you."

"Yeah, we heard about that," I said incautiously.

Phil was prodding at me. I frowned at him, tried to make out the words he was mouthing at me over the sound of Dave's swearing, and swiftly gave up. "Hang on a mo, Dave." I covered the bit you speak into with a finger. "What?"

"Ask him about Lilah's package. Did they find it?"

I uncovered the phone. "Dave?"

"Still here. Waiting to see if there's any other minor little details you've been holding out on us, like a signed bloody confession from the murderer, maybe?"

"What? Nah, that was . . . We didn't know for sure about Jonny-boy and Oliver until this morning. Listen, I wanted to ask: did you find Lilah's package? The one she had me and Phil deliver."

"Have I mentioned this isn't my case?"

"Not in the last thirty seconds or so."

Dave sighed. "Hold your horses." There was the muffled sound of computer keys being pressed and expletives being uttered. It went on so flippin' long I was practically climbing out of my car seat in frustration.

"No," was Dave's final reply. "It's on the action list. Priority low."

"Cheers, Dave. I owe you." I hung up and reported what he'd said to Phil, whose expression suggested he had a similar view to mine of that priority level. Because what I reckoned, now I'd had a chance to think about it, was that if Lilah *had* killed her Jonny-boy, that package was key.

And okay, maybe I also wanted to be reassured I hadn't delivered a death warrant.

"Camden?" I asked.

"Camden," Phil said grimly, and pulled the car out onto the road.

"He's got to be on the stall today, right?" I asked as we drove down to Hampstead, where we could hop on the Tube. "I mean, Sunday's got to be a busy day, with all your tourists and whatnot, and it's not like he's got Jonathan to run it for him now."

"Doesn't matter. If he's not there, we can catch him at home. It's still early for anyone who's not working to be out."

"Have we got his address?"

Phil nodded. "Electoral register."

I grinned. "It's like I've always said: just because the politicians are all useless tossers doesn't mean there's no benefit to living in a democracy."

CHAPTER Thirty-Three

We got off the Northern line smelling not-so-faintly of burnt diesel. I've never been sure how that works, seeing as the trains are electric, but it's probably best not to ask. Probably best not to think too hard about the black smuts on your hanky when you blow your nose afterwards, either.

There was a chill wind blowing down Camden High Street when we got above ground again, and I hunkered down into my jacket, missing the warm air gusting through the tunnels. We had a brief disagreement on where to try first—all right, Kelvin was more likely to be working the stall than slobbing at home, but on the other hand, his flat was nearer.

"Might as well try the flat, first," I said. "Save us walking all the way down to the market."

Phil gave me a look. "Is your hip giving you gyp again?"

"Course not," I lied. "I'm just, you know. Being efficient. Time is money and all that bollocks."

I wasn't sure I'd convinced him, but instead of walking directly down the high street to the market, do not pass Go, do not collect £200, we veered off halfway. The flat was only a couple of streets off, above an Indian takeaway down a not-very-kempt side street. The noise on a Saturday night, as everyone spilled out of the rough-and-ready pub on the corner and staggered into the takeaway for a curry, had to be phenomenal. An unpleasant patch of ground not six feet from Kelvin's front door was vivid proof that for at least one person last night, either the alcohol or the spicy food had been a very bad move. Suddenly Jonny-boy's decision to give all this up and run off to Pluck's End with Lilah was a lot more understandable.

As luck would have it, we'd backed a winner, and Kelvin Reid was at home to gentlemen callers this fine Sunday morning. He looked shifty when he opened the door and saw us, as well he might.

"Congratulations," I greeted him with. "You're off the hook for Jonathan's murder. They've arrested Lilah."

We'd discussed it in the car en route, and agreed that the way to play it was as we're all mates now, no hard feelings about the commission of actual bodily harm upon my person. Phil had expressed his doubts as to whether my acting ability was up to this. I'd expressed my considered opinion that he could shove it up his arse.

It didn't matter anyway, as we'd both agreed any attempt to intimidate the bloke could turn ugly fast.

I'd expected Kelvin would react with vindictive triumph, but in fact he drew in a long, shaky breath and sagged against the doorframe. "It's true, then?"

"Like you said all along," I reminded him.

"Yeah, but . . ." He shook his head, like he still couldn't quite believe it.

I knew how he felt.

"Can we come in?" Phil asked.

"Oh, right. Of course." Kelvin stood back to let us into the flat. The door opened directly onto the living room, which was of the cosy variety, with a squashy sofa that looked way too small for anyone Kelvin's size in front of a large-screen telly. Actually, the whole flat looked too small for Kelvin, throwing his sheer bulk into stark relief. If Phil hadn't been here with me, this was the point I'd be backing away slowly and apologising for bothering the bloke. It wasn't a pleasant feeling.

Maybe he read my mind, as Kelvin hunched over and turned to me. "I want to apologise. For, you know."

"Trying to punch my intestines out through my spine?"

"Uh. Yeah. That. I wasn't thinking straight. Like, it did my head in, what happened to Jonathan, and seeing you, I just lost it. I never knew you didn't have nothing to do with it. I was hoping, maybe you could, uh, talk to the police? Tell them you don't want to press charges?"

From what I'd heard, charges were going to be pressed whatever, but they also reckoned I'd need to do a victim statement to be read out in court, so I didn't feel too dishonest pasting on a smile and saying, "Yeah, sure. I'll have a word."

Because like the man said, he'd been in mourning. I shouldn't bear a grudge, and I probably wouldn't—once the bruising had gone down.

Kelvin visibly relaxed. "That's brilliant. Well decent of you. I owe you."

And while we were on the subject: "We were wondering if you still had that package we delivered to Jonathan."

"Why?"

Good question. Luckily, Phil had an answer. "Professional reasons."

"Yeah, we don't like to think we passed on any death threats." I gave an unconvincing laugh.

"Oh. Oh, right. I don't know what he did with it. Like I told the police."

"Did he show you what was in it?" Not that we'd necessarily believe what Kelvin said.

"No. I never saw it. Didn't know nothing about it until after . . . you know."

"Have you searched for it?"

"You mean, here?" Reid looked around the flat as if expecting it to jump out at him and wave a Pride flag in his face. "Well, yeah. I had to sort out all Jonathan's stuff. I didn't see nothing like that with his things."

"You sent his things back to his family?" Phil asked.

Kelvin shook his head. "To her? *No.* Charity shop. And some of it went on the stall. It's what he would've wanted," he added defiantly.

Seemed a bit heartless to me, but then again, I hadn't known the bloke. Maybe old Jonny-boy would have been dead chuffed with the idea of living on through recycled consumer goods.

"Speaking of which," Phil put in, "is there a reason you're not working right now?"

"Chelsea's minding the stall today. My mate. It's been really stressful, all this happening." It sounded defensive, as if we'd accused him of malingering.

Phil nodded. "Do you mind if we have a look around? Just to see if we can find the package?"

Kelvin hesitated, but I could see the cogs whirring as he worked out that me putting in a word for him ought to trump any natural disinclination to let us rummage through his underwear drawer. "Go ahead," he said finally. "I've got nothing to hide."

Yeah, right. Everyone's got *something* to hide. And I know my cue when I hear it. So as not to make a spectacle of myself, I wandered over to the bookshelf, which was stacked high with DVDs, CDs, action figures still in their boxes, and even the odd actual book, and wished fervently but hopelessly that Kelvin would bugger off so I could concentrate.

"Any chance of a cuppa?" Phil asked. I could've kissed him.

With Kelvin in the kitchen boiling the kettle, I was able to relax. I took a deep breath, focussed my mind on Jonny-boy in general and thickly stuffed brown envelopes, not to mention the contents thereof, in particular, and *listened*.

Nothing.

Nothing?

CHAPTER Thirty-Four

I tried again. The place was so free of vibes that I picked up on the stale, flat murmur of the water in his toilet cistern. And that was just *wrong*. Not so much as a dirty mag or two stuffed in a bedside drawer in case the coppers (or his mum, as might be, seeing as even big bastards like Kelvin had to come from somewhere) came round? Well, maybe Kelvin was out and proud about his porn—looking more closely at the DVDs on the shelves tended to support that view, and hang on, wasn't that one of Darren's old movies?—but he had to have *something* to hide.

I was beginning to think it wasn't only Jonathan's worldly goods and chattels our Kelvin had cleared out. "You know what?" I said out loud. "I don't think we've got time for a cuppa. Remember we've got to . . ."

I flashed my beloved a significant look.

Phil coughed. "Right. Should've remembered. Never mind the tea," he called out to Kelvin. "We'll see ourselves out."

The flat door closed behind us, and Phil narrowed his eyes. "Don't tell me you picked up on another dead body in there."

"What? No. About as far from that as you can get. Seriously. There's nothing hidden in that place. And I mean *nothing*. He's cleared it all out. Cleaner than a nun's whatsit."

He gave me the side-eye. "Since when have you been thinking about nuns' whatsits?"

"*Cell.* I meant cell. And, oi, stop getting distracted. I reckon we need to get down to that stall again, sharpish. Before he clears that out and all, if he hasn't already."

Phil frowned. "Can't see it. Traders don't leave their stock out overnight. Anything he had with him at the stall would've had to go at the end of the day."

"Yeah, but maybe he hid it *in* the stock? Some of those military greatcoats have got flippin' big pockets."

"What, and risk some punter buying it?"

Okay, maybe I hadn't thought that one through. "Still . . . it can't hurt to have a butcher's, now we're down here, can it?"

"Might as well. Could be worth a chat with this Chelsea, anyhow."

A not-brief-enough blast of that chill wind again later, we were back underground in the Stables Market, heading for Reid's stall. It was weird, thinking how it'd only been a week since we were last here, and two men had died since then. And by weird, I mean deeply unpleasant. My hip twinged in memory. Or maybe it just hadn't warmed up yet.

"Think anyone'll recognise me?" I muttered to Phil, trying to avoid the eyes of any stallholders who glanced our way. "I don't fancy getting lynched by a mob of market traders. There aren't any leftover pitchforks in these stables, are there?"

"Stop worrying. You were last week's wonder. No one's even going to remember you now."

From the general lack of interest people were showing in yours truly, he was probably right. I was still glad when we reached Reid's stall, though.

From the name Chelsea, I'd been expecting a leggy blonde girl with hair extensions and fake nails. Well, I wasn't wrong about the hair colour, although it was more dishwater than peroxide. She was a washed-out thirtysomething with deep dark circles under her eyes and no makeup, wearing grimy jeans and a padded jacket with a rip in one sleeve that couldn't exactly be helping her sell the merchandise.

Phil greeted her with a professional smile. "Chelsea? I'm Phil Morrison. We've come from Kelvin Reid's place. He said he didn't mind us having a look for something Jonathan Parrot might've left lying around."

Nice. All, strictly speaking, true, but adding up to implied permission to poke our noses around the stall that very definitely hadn't been granted.

She frowned. "Maybe I should give him a ring?"

"We can wait," Phil said confidently, which was fair enough. After all, Kelvin was still in the business of keeping us happy, wasn't he? And even if he did tell her to tell us to piss off, that'd just show us we were on the right track.

Chelsea didn't move to pull out her phone. Actually, chances were she didn't have any reception down here, which would explain her reluctance to check our story out. After all, asking us to mind the stall while she went outside to call Kelvin would sort of defeat the object. "I s'pose it's all right."

Result. I made my way to the back of the stall, as far from Chelsea as I could get, and *listened*. The vibes were strong and unmistakeable. Guilt and defiance led me down a slimy, unpleasant trail directly to . . . Chelsea's back pocket, currently hidden under her thick winter anorak.

I stood there staring at her well-padded bum for a moment. Maybe she felt the weight of my gaze, as she spun round and demanded, "What?"

"You're skimming, aren't you?" Which was a polite way of saying she was robbing Kelvin blind.

She flushed an angry red. "Fuck off. You don't know shit."

"Yeah, I do. Pocket of your jeans, love. No, not that one. Back pocket. On your right."

"That's my money." She was definitely worried now. "You can't prove nothing."

"Uh-huh. So you won't mind us mentioning it to Kelvin?"

"You *bastard*. I need this money. I got a kid, ain't I?"

"Course, I might forget all about it. If, say, I had a reason to get distracted." I glanced around. "Where does Kelvin keep his stock? You know, the off-season lines, surplus stuff, all that?"

She glared at me for a moment before she spoke. "He's got a lockup in Cutter Street."

Phil stepped up. "And would you have a key to that?"

"Maybe."

"You scratch our backs, love," I suggested.

Chelsea threw me a glare that seemed to imply she'd be quite happy to do that, if we wouldn't mind waiting while she got hold of some barbed wire dipped in battery acid. "You won't say nothing to Kelvin?"

"Our lips are sealed."

"Fine." She dug around in the pockets of her money belt-cum-apron, and pulled out a bunch of keys, from which she selected one with a grubby lilac plastic cover. "This one. It's number thirteen."

Our lucky number? "Cutter Street, yeah?"

"And you gotta bring the keys back. I'll need them when I close up."

"Course, love." I flashed her a fake smile. "We'll see you later."

I probably imagined the sound of her growling as we headed off.

The lockup turned out to be far enough away from the market that I was having to concentrate on not limping by the time we got there. Cold weather's always a bugger, and the punishment my hip had taken over the last week or so hadn't exactly helped. Cutter Street wasn't so much a street, more a line of lockup garages with white-painted doors in various states of disrepair, bang smack in the middle of a housing estate. There was hard standing out the front so you could park your van to load up, and a pleasant view of the blank brick sides of adjacent houses. One of the garages had a *Police Aware* notice on it.

"Think they're aware of anything in particular?" I wondered. "Or just generally keeping their eyes peeled and their ears to the ground?"

Phil huffed a laugh. "You wouldn't want to put your ear on this ground." He nodded to a discarded condom and, not far from it, another Technicolor memento of a night out with the lads. Or lasses, as might be.

"Yeah, I'm thinking we don't want to hang around here one minute longer than we have to." I got the keys out, found the lilac one, and opened the garage door, sliding it up with a creak and a clatter loud enough to wake the dead, should there be any deceased persons taking a nap inside.

I was really, really hoping there weren't.

It was surprisingly un-damp inside the garage. I suppose I'd subconsciously expected it to look like the stall inside, but of course all the off-season clothes were packed away in boxes, not invitingly displayed on racks. There was a moveable clothes rail to one side, but it was empty of everything but hangers.

There were a *lot* of boxes—the big, heavy-duty plastic sort. If we'd been planning to search them all by hand, it'd have taken us till Christmas.

"Come on, do your stuff," Phil said.

"Oi, what did your last slave die of? When are *you* going to pull your psychic weight around here?"

"When the pope comes out as a gay trans woman and converts to Buddhism. I'm about as psychic as that used condom out there, and you know it."

Feeling oddly cheerful about it, I did my stuff.

Whoa. It wasn't just vibes, it was *all* the vibes. "You remember I said Kelvin had cleared out all his dirty little secrets? This is where he cleared them to. It's going to take a mo to puzzle it all out." And by *a mo*, I meant *a good long while.* My stomach rumbled, reminding me it was getting on for lunchtime and I'd had an early breakfast, for a Sunday.

I gritted my teeth and got on with trying to untangle Spaghetti Junction. At least it was all petty stuff, by which I mean there were definitely no meatballs in the form of actual dead bodies in here, or as far as I could tell, anything related to the provision of dead bodies to parts unknown. But there was a slimy, dishonest feel to most of the trails, which didn't make the job any more pleasant.

I soon realised most of the trails had what I could only describe as a sort of Kelvin-ness about them. A sort of . . . softness, somehow, with a bitter, sly aftertaste. Which I at first thought was going to be no help whatsoever—it being his lockup, after all—but then I noticed a thin strand of something else. It had a whiff of sadness about it, and what was almost certainly indecision, although ironically I couldn't be sure.

At any rate, it was different from the others. So that was the one I followed. Because while it was entirely possible that dear old Kelvin had been lying through his teeth when he said he didn't know where

Lilah's package was, it was equally possible he'd been telling us the truth, and it'd been Jonathan who'd stashed it—maybe in here. If Chelsea had access to the keys, then so must old JP have had. And I was counting on him not having been living in the area long enough—this go around—to have too many other options locally for stashing stuff at short notice he didn't want Kelvin's beady eyes on. Which begged the question, why *hadn't* he wanted Kelvin to see it?

The quickest way to answer that little Countdown Conundrum was to stop faffing about and get on with finding the thing. So I did.

It took me ten minutes or so, but I eventually tracked it down in a far corner of the lockup. Me and Phil had to shift a fair few boxes to get to it, and it was buried halfway down a box full of flowery shirts.

"Well, this is it," I said, holding up the still-bulging envelope. I opened it up and a stack of glossy photos slid out. Moment of truth.

CHAPTER THIRTY-FIVE

Not blackmail material, as it turned out. In fact, it was all kind of sweet. Glamour stuff, yeah, and by *glamour* I mean *page 3 of the Sun, get your tits out, love* soft porn. But to be honest, they were, well, sweet.

Lilah was in all of them. Just her, posing in a variety of skimpy outfits. They'd been taken at different times and in different places, and one at least was probably a wedding night shot—she had the full bridal lingerie on, with everything in ivory lace and a saucy little blue-ribboned garter around one thigh. And a veil, which was the clincher.

She really had wanted him back, and she'd gone for it the best way she knew how—with her body. And from the vibes I'd felt earlier, old Jonny-boy had been anything but unaffected.

It was weird, though. It hadn't read like lust. It'd been too tender for that. Which was weird, as I said, because . . . he'd cheated on her, hadn't he? With more than one bloke, by all accounts. Well, by a couple of accounts, anyway. Lilah might view their marriage as an open relationship, but to my mind, the underhanded way he'd gone about his affairs had been anything but open. How could you cheat on someone you . . . if not actually loved, then cared about, anyhow?

Did that mean Phil's ex had still cared about him, even though he'd screwed around? It made me uncomfortable to think about, but . . . Phil had still cared about *him*, hadn't he? Enough to be screwed up when the bastard popped his clogs although they'd already separated.

Was it better or worse if the Mysterious Mark had still loved him too?

It was doing my head in.

"What do you reckon it means?" I asked when we were back on the Tube heading north, having returned the keys to an ungrateful Chelsea. Granted, it was a bit of a public place to be discussing the case, but the bloke next to me was nodding in time with whatever music was playing through his headphones and ignoring the rest of the world, while on the other side of Phil a gaggle of teenage girls was chatting excitedly in Italian. What with that and the clatter of the train, I was pretty sure nobody would be able to hear a word.

Phil stared at the map of the Northern line above the heads of the passengers opposite for a mo. "It ties in with the phone message. Maybe she was set on getting him back, but when he met her by the canal, he said it was never going to happen, and she lost it?"

I didn't like it. "How do we know she actually met him there?"

"Why send the text if she wasn't planning to show up?"

"Maybe she didn't send it?" Okay, there might have been a certain amount of straw-clutching going on.

"Who did, then? They'd have needed access to her phone. Axel? Hazel?"

I didn't like that idea much, either. "She's pretty tight with the ex-husband," I reminded him.

Phil looked doubtful. "So tight he'd want to frame her for murder?"

"Maybe. If he was really pissed off about her being with Jonny-boy."

"Except she split up with Tarbox years ago and has worked with him ever since. And if Tarbox wanted her back, why wait so long? And if he just didn't like seeing her with anyone else, why not kill Parrot anytime over the year and change he and Lilah were together, instead of waiting until he'd left her to do it?" He paused. "More likely they were in on it together."

"But what about Oliver, then? Why would he let them into his house?" I had a light bulb moment. "Hang on. Hazel's chummy with the flatmate, isn't she? Maybe she's got a key."

Phil huffed a grim laugh. "So they were all in on it? Family-bonding activity, was it?"

"I don't bloody know, do I? But yeah, I could see Tarbox as our killer. Don't reckon he'd lose any sleep over Jonny-boy's death or Oliver's either for that matter. 'That nance at the Smithy,' remember?"

"Most killers aren't that free with the negative opinions about their victims."

"So it's a whatsit, a double bluff, all right? Or he's, I dunno, sociopathic or whatever they call it. Thinks they deserved to die and that any reasonable person would be on his side about it." I sighed and closed my eyes. Then I opened them again because the motion of the train was making me queasy. Or maybe it was just the smell. "So have we got any idea what our next move is?"

"And by 'we' you mean me?"

"Well, yeah. This ain't *my* area of expertise."

"Pub."

I grinned. "Serious? The great Phil Morrison, driven to drink by the insoluble mystery?"

"No, the great Phil Morrison fancies a pint with his mates. Darren reckoned him and Gary would be heading to the Four Candles for lunch today. We should be able to catch them."

We were late for lunch, it being well after two, but luckily the Four Candles serves food all day so we were able to bung in a quick order for the Sunday roast before I keeled over with hunger. We pulled up a couple of spare chairs to Gary and Darren's cosy table for two by the window (Julian had obviously had a prior engagement) while we waited.

Gary greeted us with a "Tommy darling! How lovely to see you. And Phil."

Darren, who was tucking into rhubarb crumble and custard, paused with his spoon halfway to his mouth. "All right, lads? What's all this, then?"

"We need to talk," Phil said bluntly.

"Ooh, that sounds ominous." Gary's eyes were wide and greedy, but that could have been down to the chocolate cheesecake he was eating.

I was too hungry to go pussyfooting around it, so I gave it to them straight. "You know your mate Lilah? They've arrested her for Jonny-boy's murder."

Darren's spoon dropped with a dramatic clatter, bounced off his plate, and fell to the floor. "They never! The effing bastards. She wouldn't hurt a fly, Lilah wouldn't. Why the bleedin' 'ell would they think she'd done it?"

"Yeah, well, it turns out old Jonny-boy was having it away with a bloke he worked with. Who, by the way, also had an unscheduled meeting with his maker last night. Oh, and the London ex claims him and Jonny were also back on more than friendly terms even before he left Lilah. So the police reckon she's got a motive."

Darren picked up his fork to gesture angrily. "Bollocks. He could've slept with half of Hertfordshire and she wouldn't have given a toss. Lilah ain't the jealous sort."

Gary pursed his lips. "So young Jonathan was not only married to the lovely Lilah, he was indulging in one illicit affair at work and had another for weekends? If nothing else, I have to say I admire his stamina."

"Allegedly," Phil reminded us all. "We've only got Reid's word for it they were back together before Parrot left his wife."

"And that's another thing," Darren butted in. "Why the bleeding hell did he leave her in the first place? Christ, she's got money, she's a proper looker, and she didn't give a monkey's about him shagging around. This ain't just having your cake and eating it. This is all the bloody buns you can eat and a fruit tart for afters."

"Maybe he came down with a case of emotional diabetes?" I shrugged.

Phil cleared his throat. "We're forgetting: he was scared of something. Maybe he didn't want to leave, but he was too scared to stay?"

"Yeah, but scared of what?" I asked.

"Your menacing visage?" Gary blew me a kiss.

"I'll menace you in a minute." I screwed up my eyes. "It doesn't make sense. Unless . . . Do you reckon Axel told Jonny-boy he was going to spill the beans about him and Oliver to his mum? Blackmailed him, even?"

"For what?" Phil asked.

"I dunno. Money?"

Phil was already shaking his head. "No. So Parrot refuses to pay—what's the worst that can happen? His marriage breaks up. So why break it up preemptively?"

I peeped over at Gary and Darren, who were glancing from one to the other of us like they were watching the Wimbledon final.

I glared at them. "So what do you think happened?"

"Buggered if I know." Darren shrugged. "Tell you what, though, that's Lilah all over. She wouldn't give a toss where her bloke stuck his dick. And even if she did, she wouldn't let on. Not to anyone, and definitely not to some prick trying it on with blackmail. Even if he was her son."

So in his considered opinion as an old friend of hers, Lilah was either (a) telling the truth or (b) a good liar. Cheers, mate. That was well helpful, that was.

"He must have had a dark secret." Gary had definitely perked up at the thought.

"Like what?"

"Ooh . . . perhaps he had his hands in his employer's till?"

Darren cackled. "Or his other bits in something else of hers?"

"Have you ever met Tallulah Lovett?" I asked in amazement.

He shrugged. "Nope. Not in all the years I've known Lilah. She a stunner and all?"

"Not next to Lilah, she isn't. And seriously, no. No way. She didn't even like him."

"Who says that's a perquisite?" Darren demanded.

"I think you mean a prerequisite, sweetie pie," Gary cooed. "A 'perquisite' is a perk."

"Pumpkin, when I look at you, all I can think of is the perks." They swapped soppy smiles.

I rolled my eyes. "Oi, enough of the mushy stuff. Some of us haven't had our lunch yet and we don't want to lose our appetites."

"What's the lad like?" Darren asked suddenly. "I never met him, neither."

"He's . . ." I shrugged. "He's a teenager. Good-looking, I s'pose," I added, remembering that clear skin.

"Oi, no funny ideas about Lilah's boy or you'll be running scared and all." Darren jabbed his fork in my direction.

I stared. "He's fifteen!"

"And just you remember it. Bloody hell. Poor Lilah. It's a bleedin' travesty, that's what it is. Still, if I know her, she'll have a good lawyer. She ought to sue 'em for all they got." Darren dug his fork viciously into his rhubarb crumble.

Luckily at that point Phil and me were called back to our own table for food.

"So did that actually help?" I asked, digging into my roast beef and Yorkshire pud. Sometimes all you want is a hearty, traditional dinner.

"Not sure." Phil speared a carrot, considered its crimes for a mo and then dunked it in his gravy before eating it.

"Didn't sound like Darren reckoned Lilah could've done it. Course, we never mentioned that phone call, did we? Text message. Whatever. You know what? It's a shame we can't ask her about it."

Phil gave a grim laugh. "Don't worry. They'll be asking her plenty of questions about it down at the station."

"Yeah, but I bet she'd rather be talking to us. Ah, sod it. It doesn't make *sense*."

By the time Gary and Darren re-joined us, we were onto dessert. Well, one of us was. The *other* one of us was clearly trying to make everyone else feel bad with his *Just an Americano, thank you*. I didn't care. The rhubarb crumble was seriously tasty.

"Have you solved the case yet?" Gary asked optimistically, eying my pud like a shark checking out a shoal of baby seals. Or whatever the collective noun for baby seals was. I had a feeling it wasn't *a club*. I bowed to the inevitable, shoved my dish a few inches closer to him, and handed over my fork.

"No." Phil didn't exactly bark it, but there was the definite suspicion of a growl.

Darren nodded sagely. "You'll get there, mate. You'll get there. So how's the wedding preparations going, then? Got it all sorted yet?"

Bloody hell. I'd almost forgotten about the wedding in the last couple of days. Luckily I had my mouth full of crumble so I didn't just blurt that out. "Uh, it's going okay," I said instead after I'd swallowed. "Still need to book the honeymoon, mind."

Darren flashed Phil a sly look. "Yeah, you don't want to forget about that. Best fourteen nights of my life, our honeymoon was. And that ain't counting the days."

"Oh, the pleasure was all mine, sweetie pie," Gary trilled, then turned back to me. "Still, there's plenty of time to worry about that."

I stared at him. "Hang about, aren't you the one who's always been on at me to 'Don't leave it too late, everything gets booked up, you'll end up with a reception at McDonald's and a honeymoon in Torquay'?"

"Oh, pish." Gary waved his fork airily. "There's always lastminute.com."

He laughed. Darren cackled.

I shook my head and grabbed a gulp of Phil's coffee.

On the way back home, I suggested, seeing as we weren't busy on the case right at that minute, that we call in at a travel agent's—there had to be at least a couple of them open today in St. Albans—but Phil reckoned he had too much paperwork to do. Nice to know his priorities in life.

I didn't sulk, honest. I was just feeling quiet on the way back.

It was a relief to get home and slump in front of the telly. I switched on the sport and stared at Formula One for a while.

"Where are they this week?" Phil asked, coming into the room with his laptop.

"Uh..." I peered at the screen. "Germany? Somewhere in Europe? Bugger it. I've got no clue."

"Real hard-core motorsports fan, aren't you?"

"Oi, it's not my fault. All these tracks look the same. Except Monaco, obviously. Hey, you ever fancied going to Monaco? We could do the whole James Bond thing—get togged up, bet our shirts on red in a casino..."

Phil had opened up his laptop and was ignoring me.

Great. "Guess I might as well get on with my invoices," I muttered.

CHAPTER THIRTY-SIX

I'd cheered up a bit by teatime, mainly because I'd found a mistake in my figures that meant I was a couple of hundred quid better off than I'd thought. And then Phil had announced he'd found a few local bands to choose from for the wedding—I avoided making any pointed comments about all the paperwork he'd supposedly been doing—and we spent the rest of the evening watching YouTube vids and arguing about musical integrity versus broad appeal. The one we decided to go for, and even managed to book with a swift phone call, had a dodgy name but they were willing to play just about anything you asked for, which is pretty handy when your guest list skews heavily towards the older demographic.

And no, I didn't include me and Phil in that.

We were getting cosy on the sofa, and I for one was debating the merits of an early bedtime when the phone rang.

"Is that Mr. Paretski?"

The nervous, breathy female voice was familiar, somehow, but I couldn't quite place it. I scrabbled around for my work diary. "Yeah, that's me. Paretski Plumbing. What can I do you for?"

"It's Hazel. Hazel Lovett."

Oh. Not that I didn't feel bad for the girl, but couldn't she give us our Sunday night off? It wasn't like there was anything we could do for her at this precise instant. "All right, love?"

"It's— I don't know what to do. Everything's so . . . Oh God." There was a loud snuffling sound, and when she spoke again, her voice was stretched to breaking point. "I don't know if you've heard—"

"About your mum being arrested?" I finished for her, because God knows she sounded like she needed the help. "Yeah, I know. Me and Phil are working on—"

"No! It's not— I mean, yes, but it's . . . Oh God." There was an actual sob this time, and then silence.

"Hazel?" I was getting worried now.

"It's Axel. He tried to k-kill himself."

Bloody hell. Christ, I felt like a bastard for wanting to give her the brush-off a minute ago. "Is he okay?"

"He's gone to hospital. The ambulance just left."

"Where are you? Are you on your own? Is Pete with you?"

"I'm at home. He had to go to work."

On a Sunday night? That was unsociable hours and then some. Or did it count as Monday, if half his shift was after midnight?

And why the bleedin' hell was I wasting time thinking about that right now? "What about your dad?"

"He's not here. I . . . I really need to talk to you. Can you come over?"

"Course, love. We'll be straight there."

I hung up and turned to give Phil the good news.

There was a bit of déjà vu when we got over to Pluck's End to find another uniformed copper answering the door. Actually, I thought it was the same one for a mo, until I remembered the morning one had had shorter hair.

She had an identical scowl on her face, mind. Maybe they teach that at Hendon too: advanced glowering, intimidation of pesky members of the public for the use of. "Can I help you, sir?" There wasn't a hint in her tone that she desperately wanted to add *into a nice, comfy cell* but the eyes gave her away. What on earth had we done to her? Failed to correctly perform the secret knock?

"Tom Paretski and Phil Morrison."

The copper-cum-gatekeeper nodded, which solved that little conundrum. She'd heard of us.

"Hazel asked us to come round," I went on quickly, speaking loudly in the hopes the young lady in question would hear me, and sure enough, a pale face appeared over PC Pleasant's shoulder.

"Thank God you're here," Hazel said shakily, and after that her police escort had no option but to let us in.

Hazel was wearing baggy leggings and a massively oversized hoodie with saggy pockets. Comfy clothes, for lounging around on a Sunday night. Inside them, she was a ball of tension and misery. "Come on through," she said, hugging herself.

We followed her into Lilah's living room, which looked like it'd been yarn-bombed. There were balls of wool everywhere, in all different colours—on the sofa, on both chairs, and on the floor. Arthur and Merlin would've thought they'd died nine times and gone to heaven. Laid out on the arms of the sofa and chairs were hand-knitted mittens in varying stages of completion.

"Hey, you make all these? For the Smithy, right?" I asked to distract Hazel.

"Oh. Yes. Sorry. I should've . . ." She gazed hopelessly around at the muddle, obviously feeling she should tidy but not knowing where to start.

"How about we go in the kitchen and have a cuppa?" I suggested.

Hazel's lip trembled, but she held it together. "Okay."

I felt the urge to put an arm around her as she led us to the kitchen, but wasn't sure if she'd welcome it. It wasn't entirely clear why she'd called us over, but it seemed more likely it was for professional reasons than because the sudden crisis gave her an irresistible urge to see yours truly.

Once we were in the kitchen she seemed lost, so I gave Phil a nod to see to the kettle and shepherded her over to the table, where I sat down beside her.

PC Pleasant hadn't followed us in, and the door to the hallway was shut. I made a mental note not to forget she was probably earwigging, mind.

"How do you take your tea, love? Or would you rather have hot chocolate?" I suggested, thinking of Axel. Also of the time, which was after eleven. Hazel was going to have enough trouble sleeping tonight without added caffeine.

Hazel sniffed and nodded. Phil seemed to be doing a sterling job of searching through cupboards, so I left him to it. "How are you doing?" I asked her.

"It's all so h-horrible. First Mum and now—" She choked.

"Do you want to tell me what happened?"

Hazel took a couple of deep breaths and tucked a strand of lank hair behind one ear. "He . . . he took some pills. From Mum's cabinet. I don't know what they were, but I heard him being . . . being sick, and thought he'd just drunk too much—he had a bottle of Mum's gin— but then I saw the pill bottle and . . ."

"You called the ambulance?" I finished for her, as she seemed to have run out of words.

Hazel nodded again, tight-lipped. "Why didn't he *talk* to me? I could have helped . . ."

"Have you got any idea why he did it?"

"I— No. That is, he left a note. But it didn't make sense."

"Can I have a look?"

"The police took it. They wouldn't say w-why. Why would they do that?" The lip quivered again, and this time I did give her a hug. She snuffled briefly into my shoulder, then pulled back as Phil put a couple of steaming mugs on the table. "I'll . . . I'll get some biscuits."

"I'll do it," Phil said, and fetched the tin.

Hazel snagged a Rich Tea and dunked it in her hot chocolate before taking a dainty bite. It seemed to calm her down.

"Can you remember what the note said?" I asked gently, taking a bourbon cream to show willing.

"I took a picture. On my phone." She fumbled in her hoodie pocket, dropped her phone on the floor, picked it up—thankfully intact—and handed it over.

It wasn't easy, as, understandably, the focus wasn't great, but through zooming in and swiping from side to side, I managed to make out what it said:

I'm sorry. It's all my fault. I never meant anything bad to happen.

It was signed, *Axe.*

CHAPTER THIRTY-SEVEN

Bloody. Hell. No wonder the police had wanted a closer look. Phil leaned forward. "Have you got any idea what it means?"

"No." Hazel cradled her mug in hands that had retreated into the sleeves of her hoodie. I realised with a jolt that it was probably Axel's.

Unless it was Pete's, of course. "You don't know what he might be feeling guilty about?"

She shook her head. "He's been so . . . I mean, he's always like that, but ever since Jonathan left, he's been *more*."

I struggled to unravel that. "More . . . withdrawn? Unhappy?" It seemed a fair guess, based on what I'd seen of Axel.

"Yes." She nodded eagerly. "We always used to . . . to talk, even if it wasn't about anything much. But the last few weeks he's been different."

"Different in what way?" Phil asked.

I thought we'd covered that already, but Hazel scrunched up her face like she was thinking about it. "Um. It sounds horrible, but—but they said he's going to be all right. He will be all right, won't he?"

"If that's what they said," Phil told her in his comforting-the-clients voice. I was impressed. I'd still been trying to work out what she'd been on about.

"Well . . . and you mustn't tell anyone, but . . . he's been really nasty, sometimes. Spiteful." Hazel went bright red and ducked her head to stare into her hot chocolate.

I was getting a bad feeling about this.

"How close was your brother to Jonathan?" Phil went on, his tone giving nothing away.

"Very close. Axe was devastated when he left. And then when he . . ." She hugged herself again. "It's all so horrible."

"Do you think he might have confided in anyone else?"

She shrugged. "I don't know. Not Mum. Dad, maybe? Or Aunty Loos? He will get well again, won't he?"

There was a sharp knock on the kitchen door, and then PC Pleasant strode in without waiting for an answer. "I've heard from the hospital. Your brother's in a stable condition, and he should make a full recovery."

Me and Phil exchanged glances. It was so bloody well timed she *had* to have been listening at the door.

"Will you be all right if I leave you now?" she went on. "I've been told to get back to the station if you're okay."

More like she wanted to get home and get some kip, but you could hardly blame her.

"Yes. I'm fine." Hunched in on herself and avoiding PC Pleasant's eye, Hazel didn't look fine. She waited until the kitchen was a copper-free zone and then grabbed my arm. "You'll stay, won't you? At least until Pete gets back?"

"Uh, yeah. If you want. Sure you wouldn't rather have your dad, though?"

"He'll want to stay at the hospital."

"He's there now?" I guess it made sense. If it was my kid in the hospital, I'd want to be there. It still felt weird, him leaving Hazel all on her own to worry.

"I think so. They said they'd call him. And I left a voice mail."

"He hasn't got back to you?" Not even to tell the poor girl her brother was out of danger?

Hazel shook her head.

"Right. No problem. When's Pete coming back?"

"Um. His shift doesn't finish until 6 a.m." She bit her lip. "You should go. I'll be fine."

No, she wouldn't be. "You sure you don't want to give your dad another call?"

"He won't come." She stared at the wall for a moment, while I swapped worried glances with Phil. Then she went on, "He's not really my dad, you know. Just Axel's."

Oh. That . . . explained a couple of things.

Poor Hazel. Here was me getting my knickers in a twist over having two dads, and by the sound of it, she didn't even have one.

I was suddenly deeply pissed off with the police for carting off her mum and leaving the poor kid in a situation where she was begging a couple of virtual strangers to keep her company. Okay, so she was legally an adult, but that didn't change anything. Christ knows I wasn't exactly independent at nineteen.

"Any other family around here?" I asked. "What about your auntie?"

"She's probably at the hospital with Dad. I don't want to bother her."

"What about mates? Pete can't be your only old school friend around here."

Please, God.

"The others all went to uni."

Well, crap. "How come you didn't? A smart girl like you."

"Mum reckoned it was a waste of money. And I didn't want to leave Pete. His mum and dad had just died. But you don't have to stay. I'll be fine, really."

"We're staying," I said firmly. "You've got Pete in your spare room, right? Chuck us a spare blanket or two, and me and Phil can fight over who gets the sofa."

"I'm sure Pete wouldn't mind you borrowing his room for the night. He doesn't go straight to bed when he gets back from work anyway."

"Yeah? That'll be perfect for us, then."

"But there's only one bed— Oh." She turned pink. "I'll go and change the sheets."

"Oops," I said wryly after she'd scarpered upstairs. "I think I just outed us as a couple."

Phil huffed. "If she's got a problem with any kind of relationship at all, she's not her mother's daughter."

We waited. I yawned. "Think she needs a hand?"

"Wouldn't hurt to check."

One weary trudge up the stairs later, we found Hazel sitting on Axel's bed, hugging a well-loved stuffed hippo with a desolate air. Hazel, that is, not the hippo, which only looked moderately distressed.

"All right, love?" I asked gently.

She jumped and got up, putting the hippo down carefully on Axel's pillow. "Sorry. I've done the bed. I should've . . ."

"Nah, no worries. Are you going to be able to get some sleep if we all turn in now?"

"It was sleeping pills he took," she said suddenly. "Mum got prescribed them after Jonathan left."

"Temazepam?" Phil asked. "That's the most common prescription. They're not as deadly as a lot of people think."

"Oh."

"He'll be fine," I said, because the hospital had said he would be, and really, what else could I say?

We all turned in. The spare room bed was one of those nonstandard ones that's bigger than a single but not quite a double. It must've been a bugger to buy sheets for, but at least it meant me and Phil's shoulders could both fit in at the same time without too much aggro.

I'd like to say I lay awake for hours, pondering on the pressures of life and family murders that could lead a young lad to try to do himself in, but it'd been a bloody busy day and I was knackered. I went out like a light. It barely seemed like five minutes later when I was woken up by voices outside our door.

I waited until they'd faded away into the distance before getting up for a much-needed pee.

Phil had woken up too by then. "Pete back?"

"Sounds like it." I pulled on my clothes from last night, just in case it turned out to be Hazel's dad instead— okay, so it was early, but 6:30 a.m. wasn't *that* unfeasible for a house call in the circs. "Gotta go see a man about a dog."

I made it to the bathroom without bumping into anyone, then wandered downstairs to put the kettle on and say *Good morning, sorry we nicked your room* to Pete. I was only fifty percent successful—the kettle being present and correct, but Pete, not so much—so I wandered back upstairs again. "Think Pete's holed up in Hazel's room. Pun not intended. I guess we're on our own for breakfast."

It was well weird, making ourselves breakfast in Lilah's kitchen without the lady herself present or even aware we were there. Then again, she *had* said we'd be welcome—Christ, had that really been only yesterday morning?

She had a well-stocked fridge, so I made bacon and eggs, which I reckoned we were owed for the overnight stay, not to mention the early wake-up call. Hazel and Pete put in an appearance just as the bacon started to crisp up, so I made them a couple of butties. She needed a bit of good old comfort food. Pete needed the calories.

They sat down next to each other at the kitchen table, so me and Phil took the chairs opposite.

Phil waited until Pete had had his first mouthful before clearing his throat. "While we're here, I've got a couple of questions for you."

"What about?" Pete asked, looking trapped.

"There's no point you covering for Oliver now. So if there's something you didn't tell us the other night that might have a bearing on things, now's the time to say. *Did* you know Jonathan and Oliver were having an affair?"

Pete froze and stared at his bacon butty as if he was worried it was about to bite him back. "I don't know anything about that."

I didn't believe him this time, either.

Phil let it slide. "Have you got any idea what Axel's note might have been about?"

"Who, me? I hardly know him. Think I spend all my time hanging round fifteen-year-olds?"

Said with all the lofty maturity of a bloke who hadn't even finished his second decade yet.

"Maybe he was just upset about his mum getting arrested," Pete went on, with another shifty glance at Hazel.

"So Oliver hadn't mentioned anything that might have upset the boy?" Phil asked. "Something that happened at the Smithy, maybe?"

"He never said nothing." Pete took a savage bite from his butty, having presumably got over his earlier fear of reprisals.

We didn't get to grill him any further, as the doorbell rang. We all looked at each other. Let's face it, if whoever it was had to ring the doorbell, they weren't likely to be bringing good news.

"I'll go," said Phil, getting up.

I followed him out to the hall, in case moral or any other kind of support was needed, just in time to see him crack a smile and throw the door open wide.

Bloody hell. It was Gary and Darren.

"Surprise!" trilled Gary.

He wasn't wrong there. They trooped on in, Darren having a good cackle about the doormat on the way.

Hazel came out of the kitchen to see what was going on, Pete close behind her. I wondered what she'd think of her mum's old mate, and if we could somehow stop Darren regaling her with stories from his old porno days.

Duct tape might do it, but I wouldn't be betting my shirt on it.

"All right there, babe?" Darren flashed his gold tooth in a grin.

Hazel stared for a moment. Then her face broke into a big, sunny smile for the first time since . . . well, since I'd met her. "I know you! Uncle Darren."

Uncle Darren?

Darren held out his arms. "Little Lola. I knew you'd remember me. Didn't I say she'd remember me, sugar muffin? Blimey, girl, you got big. What's your mum been feeding you on, then? Raw steaks and protein shakes?"

Hazel bent down to give him a hug that went on longer than the prescribed three seconds, and even looked teary-eyed when she finally broke free. "You used to take me to buy sweeties and make me laugh. Why did you stop coming to see us?"

"You want to ask your stepdad about that, princess. But none of that now. I want to introduce you to the love of my life. Babe, this is Gary."

Gary stepped forward and kissed her on both cheeks. "Delighted to meet you. Darren tells me you used to be a positive cherub."

"And she ain't changed a bit," Darren put in, blithely contradicting himself. "This your bloke, then, babe?"

Pete, who'd been hovering warily in the background, startled and then stepped forward. "Yeah. I'm Pete."

Darren looked him up and down. Well, mostly up, given Pete had almost two feet on him. "What do you do for a living, then?"

Pete's Adam's apple bobbed. "Uh, I'm working in a warehouse right now."

"He's got his own house," Hazel put in defensively.

Darren's eyes had narrowed. "So why ain't he in it, this time of the morning?"

"Someone died there," I explained.

Gary's eyes lit up. "Tommy! You didn't tell us there'd been another murder. Was it very grisly?" he asked with audible relish.

Pete turned ashen. Hazel went more of a greenish hue.

I winced. "Uh, Gary? Bit of consideration? It was their mate."

"He was my lodger." Pete clearly wanted to distance himself from Oliver now he'd proved to be such an unsatisfactory tenant as to get himself murdered.

"I just worked with him," Hazel said, jumping on that bandwagon with both feet. Then she blushed. "I mean, it's awful what's happened, but ..."

But your brother's in the hospital and your mum's in the nick. Fair enough.

"What are you doing here?" Phil asked.

"Not that we want to seem unwelcoming," I added hastily.

"Couldn't leave my little Lola all on her tod without her mum, now could I?" Darren said easily. "Not with all this murder bollocks that's been going around. So I'm taking the day off."

Gary beamed. "And I've brought my laptop, so all I'll need is your wi-fi key and I'll be about my business. Although a coffee would be nice. And a chocolate croissant, if you happen to have one lying around just gagging to be eaten."

I rolled my eyes.

"I think there's some in the freezer," Hazel said, still smiling at Darren. "Come into the kitchen."

Me and Phil exchanged glances. Clearly surplus to present requirements, we left them to it.

"Oi, you don't reckon she's ..." I muttered to Phil as we walked back to his car.

"She's what?"

"You know. *Darren's.* All that business about him knowing her when she was little, and Tarbox telling him to piss off when him and Lilah got together."

Phil stopped dead in his tracks, and I don't reckon it was because he was trying to work out who all those *hims* were referring to. He turned to look back at the house.

Then he shook his head. "Can't be."

"What, because no dad would off and leave his kid with another bloke like that?" Okay, there might have been a fair bit of bitterness in my tone.

"Darren doesn't go for women."

"What about when he was getting paid for it?"

"He said she was the other side of the camera when they made films together."

"No, what he actually said was that she was the other side of the camera when they made *great* films together. Maybe they made some crappy ones before that."

Phil winced. "For God's sake, don't go saying that where Hazel can hear you."

"Oi, what do you think I am?"

After all, the most enlightened of us would probably not exactly be chuffed to discover we'd been conceived in a porno by two people getting paid to shag each other. It'd have to be even worse to know it'd been a *bad* porno.

CHAPTER Thirty-Eight

"So what's on the agenda for today?" I asked as we drove off back to St. Albans. "Assuming we survive feeding the cats a late breakfast."

"I thought you'd have work booked."

"Yeah. I was kind of hoping not to have to cancel on anyone." I looked at the clock on the dashboard. As it was, I should probably give Mrs. W. a ring and tell her I'd be late, but at least she'd be reasonable about it. Later on this morning I was booked to sort out a slow leak at the house of an elderly couple in St. Albans, and the lady of the house was likely to get right on my case if I tried to put them off. Still, that's mothers for you. "How about you?"

"I'll be working on the Oliver Proudfoot angle. See if I can find out some more about the bloke."

I nodded. "Yeah, his death's got to be related to Jonny-boy's, hasn't it? What are the odds of it being a coincidence, him popping his clogs barely a week after the bloke he worked with *and* shagged?"

"Allegedly," Phil said.

"Come on, how many people have to tell us they were at it before you're going to take it as fact?"

Phil shook his head. "Someone's lying to us. I just wish I knew who."

"Pete," I said suddenly. "Him and Hazel—he wouldn't want to drop her mum in it, would he? So maybe he did know about Oliver and Jonathan all along, and didn't want to admit it as that'd make it look like Lilah was the murderer?"

Phil was nodding, like he was way ahead of me. Again. "Doesn't help us, though, does it?"

"S'pose not. Bugger. So what are you up to today, then?"

"Need to get my head round it all. I can't help thinking we're missing something."

"Uh, like, a clue what we're doing? Don't answer that."

As it turned out, even after I'd placated the cats, showered, and changed my clothes, I was still on time for Mrs. W. So I suppose there was something to be said for that early wake-up call courtesy of Pete Steadman. Sod's law, though, the job overran, so I was still late for Mum and Dad.

"We were beginning to think you weren't coming," was Mum's friendly greeting when she opened the door to me. "And you have got a key, you know. You don't have to ring the doorbell."

I hefted my tool kit over the threshold, wiped my feet, and kicked off my shoes. "Yeah, but it seems rude barging in without warning. Who knows what you and Dad might be up to?"

"Very funny," Mum said, in the tone that humour forgot. Dad, who'd just wandered into the hall to say hello, coughed to hide a smirk.

I got the leak fixed in a jiffy, but it didn't save me from an earbashing. Not about my plumbing skills and general lack of punctuality this time. This one was about the wedding.

"I've made a list of people you have to invite," Mum said as I was packing away my kit, having left them with a shiny new section of copper pipe I wasn't going to be seeing a penny for. "Have you had the invitations printed yet? You shouldn't leave it too late."

Bloody hell, not that again. I frowned. "Hold on. What do you mean, people we *have* to invite?"

"Family, *obviously.*"

"Yeah, well, I was kind of assuming you and Dad would be coming. And Cherry and Greg, and I guess Richard and Agatha." I didn't mention the Novaks, because I'm not a git.

"There are the aunts and uncles you need to consider too. And your cousins."

Most of them were a decade or several older than me, and I wouldn't recognise them if they ran me over on the street. "What, like Aunty Sandra, who got all snotty when she saw me and Phil at Cherry's do and said she'd hoped I'd grow out of it?"

"You can't just ignore her. If you don't invite Sandra, your Aunty Marion won't come either."

"And the downside is?"

Mum tutted. "Aunty Marion used to send you presents when you were little."

"Yeah, but she doesn't even send me back a Christmas card now I've got big. I want people at the wedding who actually mean something to me and Phil."

"You can't turn your back on your family. Blood's thicker than water." Then she went red, as well she might. Aunty Marion was from Dad's side of the family. "Oh, you know what I mean."

"Look, I don't want the place filled out with people who couldn't care less about us."

"Just because they never see you doesn't mean they don't care. And has it occurred to you that your father and I might want to see them?"

I was getting fed up with this. "So hop in the car and go and see them, then."

"You know your father doesn't like to drive too far these days. And I think you're being very self-centred about this."

And so on, and so on.

The icing on the cake was when Dad caught me as I was trying to sneak out the front door, Mum having finally let me go. He shuffled his feet, asked how the work was going, asked how Phil was, said "Good, good," to my replies, and then coughed and asked if I realised how important the upcoming occasion was to my mother.

I bit back a sarcastic question as to whose bloody wedding it was anyway, and left.

To cheer myself up, I gave Phil a bell and asked if he was (a) anywhere in the vicinity and (b) fancied meeting up for lunch.

There was an amused huff down the phone. "I'm home, as it happens. Just about to do beans on toast. Want me to put a couple of extra slices on?"

Finally, things were looking up. "Yeah, why not? Tell you what, why don't you bung those sausages I bought under the grill and all. Let's really push the boat out." I grinned, feeling better already.

My way back took me through town, which jogged a memory. I managed to find a parking space not too far from the travel agent's—all right, it maybe wasn't technically a *legal* parking space—and more or less ran in, grabbed a bunch of brochures, and ran out again.

I was feeling pretty pleased with myself when I got back home. I was less pleased when I noticed the lack of a certain aroma filling the house.

"Oi, what happened to the sausages?"

Phil, starting to serve the food, didn't quite meet my eye. "Oh. Didn't think you were serious about that."

"Do I ever joke about meat? Fine, dish out the beans and toast, then." I managed not to sigh too loudly, which wasn't easy. I'd been looking forward to those sausages. They were Tesco's Finest and everything.

"How are your mum and dad?" Phil asked.

"You know. Banging on about how we've got to invite Uncle Tom Cobley and all to the wedding even if they don't hold with two blokes getting hitched. How was your morning?"

"Unproductive." He finished tipping the beans onto the toast and handed me a plate. "Let her invite who she wants. Family's important."

"Oi, don't you start and all."

He raised an eyebrow. "You sound like you could do with an early night tonight."

"I'm fine," I snapped, then ruined it with a yawn. "Maybe," I conceded grudgingly, and carried the plate into the living room to get on with replenishing my energy stores.

When I took the plates out to the kitchen, I saw the travel brochures, which I'd tossed on a counter when I came in, and brought them back into the living room. "I picked these up on my way home. Thought we could have a read of 'em and sort something out."

"Oh."

"Oh what?"

"Nothing." He didn't meet my eye.

I gave him a suspicious look, but soldiered on anyhow in fake-hearty tones. "Okay, you mark up what you fancy, and I'll do the same, and we can—"

Phil huffed. "It's already booked, all right?"

I stared at him. I couldn't believe it.

Wait a minute. Coming on top of him forcing the issue over moving in, yeah, I could totally believe it. The git. I narrowed my eyes. "And I s'pose I missed the part where we sat down and discussed what we both wanted?"

He had the grace to look shifty. "It was a spur-of-the-moment thing. I was walking past the travel agent's, and I saw they had the new brochures in."

"And what, they turned on the tractor beam and sucked you in? Hoovered the credit card straight out of your wallet? Tied you to your chair until you'd signed on the dotted line? When exactly were you planning on mentioning this?"

"I just did, didn't I?" He threw up a hand. "Christ, I knew you'd be like this."

"Like what? A bit pissed off you went ahead and made all the decisions without consulting me? What next—planning on selling the house out from under my feet? Adopting a couple of Romanian orphans? Getting the cats rehomed and buying a Rottweiler?"

"I thought you'd be happy."

"Happy? What, that I apparently don't get any say in my own life anymore?"

"This is about me moving in, isn't it?"

"No, it's about the bloody honeymoon."

"We talked about moving in together. We agreed a timetable. But if I'd left it to you, you'd still be dragging your heels and coming up with excuses."

"Christ, are you even listening to me? It's not about you moving in. I just don't like you making all the decisions, all right? You know what? You were so bloody keen to live in this house, why don't I get out and let you enjoy it?"

I slammed the door on my way out. And immediately regretted it—the glass rattled and the next-door neighbour looked at me funny—but what the hell. It was done now.

Chapter Thirty-Nine

The phone rang a couple of hours later when I was halfway to Brock's Hollow in the van—for a job, not to go and cry on Gary's amply-padded shoulder, in case you were wondering. I was about to ignore it, but then I thought, maybe it was Phil, with an apology? If I didn't answer, I'd have to ring him back. And, well, what if he *hadn't* rung to apologise?

If I called him back, it'd seem like I was desperate for his attention. Which I wasn't.

I pulled over at the next available spot and had a butcher's. The call, as it happened, was from Darren. I managed to catch it before it went to voice mail. "Darren?"

He didn't beat around the bush. "Oi, you heard from your other half lately? 'Cos he ain't answering his phone."

Great. Now I was reduced to being my fiancé's answerphone. Please leave a message after the expletive. "We had lunch together," I said shortly. "We may have had words."

"Oi, what you gone and done now?"

"Me? I haven't done a bloody thing! He's the one who—" I cut myself off before it got nasty, and also because a sneaking suspicion had raised its ugly head. "Did you know about the honeymoon?"

"He told you? Daft git. Supposed to be a surprise, that was. He was worried how you'd take it, but I told him you'd be dead chuffed."

"Never mind that," I said quickly, starting to wonder if I might, just possibly, have been a bit hasty with the whole storming-out thing. "He's probably busy."

"That's what I'm worried about. See, me and Lola are on our way to visit Axel. Poor girl's worried about her baby brother, ain't she?

Which, by the by, cheers for not mentioning that little incident before pissing off this morning."

"Uh . . . we didn't want to ruin the mood. Joyful reunion, and all that? So, uh, you're going to the hospital, yeah?"

"Yeah. We're going to meet Lilah there and all—you know they let her out this morning?"

"No, as it happens."

"They haven't charged her—not yet, anyhow—so they had to let her go. It's your scabious corpus, innit?"

"What about that phone message?"

"She told them she didn't send it."

And they'd believed her? There had to be more to it than that.

"Anyhow, that ain't what's important here. I reckon Phil's gonna want to be in on this, and it ain't like they'd let him in to see the lad without family. So if you manage to get hold of him, tell him we're at the Alban Croft Hospital. We're on our way now."

"Got it. Alban Croft." It was a private hospital out near Pluck's End. "That's got to be costing Lilah a few bob."

"Yeah, so? It's family, innit? Right. Gotta go."

We hung up. There was no point me calling Phil, as Darren had just tried that, but I did it anyway, on the grounds that the more people trying to get in touch, the more likely he'd be to actually bother calling one of us back. There was no answer, of course, so I left a message for him to give me a bell. I drummed my fingers on the steering wheel for a mo. Might as well head on over to the hospital myself. It'd mean putting off a job for a couple of hours, but the customer would understand if she knew it was about a young lad who'd tried to top himself. Not that I was planning to tell her, mind. The catch-all phrase *family emergency* is a wonderful thing.

One thing I've noticed about hospitals, private or NHS, is that there is never enough parking. It's like it never occurs to whoever plans these things that people might actually want to visit their loved ones. Trying to find a space to wedge the van in the tiny car park was impossible. I finally had to leave it on the side of the road a hundred yards down from the entrance, where with my luck it'd be taken out by the next passing tractor.

I hurried into the hospital reception. The girl behind the desk, who looked eerily like one of Leanne's colleagues at the salon—seriously, was there something in the water around here?—flashed me a perfect smile. "Can I help you?"

"Uh, I'm here to see Axel L-Tarbox." I only just remembered in time he probably wasn't a Lovett.

"Are you family?"

"Yes," I lied. "Supposed to be meeting the rest of them here, but I got caught in traffic. His sister and her uncle? Tall girl, little bloke?" I held my hand out at approximately Darren's height, and hoped she wouldn't notice I hadn't said Darren was *Axel's* uncle.

My luck was in. "Down that corridor, turn right, through the doors and it's room 153."

"Cheers, love." I headed down the corridor.

Private hospitals never seem quite . . . hospitally enough. There's too much carpet, which you wouldn't think would be hygienic, although I suppose they know best. And they don't even smell like they ought to—more like a hotel room after the maid's been than the usual bouquet of disinfectant and bodily fluids. Don't get me wrong, I'm not saying it isn't an improvement, but it's disconcerting. Gives you the constant nagging feeling you've come to the wrong place.

Still, it must be nice, having the money for it. Axel had his own room, rather than a bed in a ward, and I found Hazel sitting by his bed and Darren hovering nearby. "No Lilah?" I asked, instead of saying hello like a normal person.

Darren gave me a considering once-over. "She'll be along in a mo. Wanted to make herself look decent for her boy. Did you get hold of Phil?"

"Uh, no. Thought I'd come along instead." I turned to Axel, who as the main attraction probably felt he was being unfairly ignored. "You all right, mate?"

Okay, so it wasn't the most inspired question to come out with to a teenager who'd, however briefly, decided death was preferable to his current reality. Axel looked younger, lying in bed, his hair mussed up and his face even paler than usual. He'd have made a great anime character—he had that vulnerable, big-eyed beauty down pat. I hadn't realised Hazel had been holding his hand until he wrenched it from her grasp, obviously embarrassed.

He darted a glance at me and then away again, and didn't say anything.

"I've been trying to tell him it wasn't his fault," Hazel said.

Axel stared out of the window.

I sat down on the bed. "Listen, mate, I know everyone always says this, but things often seem worse than they are when you're in your teens."

He snorted, in a *What the bleedin' hell would you know about it?* kind of way.

I swallowed. Because, as it happened, I did know something about it. "You're not the only one, mate. I nearly did what you did, back when I was at school."

Axel jerked his head round to stare at me, so I carried on.

"See, I had this crush on a bloke, and everyone knew about it. Him too." Christ, even with all that'd happened since, this felt like ripping duct tape off an open wound. And then chucking in a shedload of salt. "And, well, he wasn't interested. Which, you know, was putting it mildly. So I had a lot of problems with bullying, as well as the whole the-bloke-I-love-hates-me thing. And yeah, I, uh, got pretty close to doing what you did. Made all the preparations. Even wrote the flippin' note." I found I was rubbing my hip, and pulled my hand away quick. "But you know what? It turned out it wasn't the end of the world. I got through it." And ended up engaged to the bastard, but mentioning that now would just confuse the poor kid.

Axel was staring at me. Then he gave a choked-off sob. "I thought he liked me," he said, so quiet and broken it tore my heart.

"Who? Oliver?"

He made a sound that could have been a laugh if it hadn't been so despairing. "No. Jonathan."

Bloody hell. "Uh . . . you don't mean like a son?"

"No. He—he was always so nice to me."

I nodded, my mind racing. "Teaching you pool and stuff?"

"Yeah. And one night . . ." He stopped.

Hazel and Darren were silent. I could feel the whole bloody room holding its breath. Any nurses barging in now to take Axel's temperature would probably get lynched.

"We . . . you know." Axel's face was bright red.

I wasn't sure I did know. And bloody hell. He was *fifteen*, for God's sake. What the hell had old Jonny-boy been thinking of? "You . . . kissed?"

Axel nodded.

"Any, uh, any other stuff?" God, I hoped he wouldn't ask me to spell it out. I wasn't sure what I'd meant myself. A quick grope? Hands going where they shouldn't? Whose hands, come to that? I couldn't believe it'd been all that serious—but then, was I reading too much into one brief meeting with the bloke and the vibes I'd got at Kelvin Reid's lockup? Surely that only proved that *Jonathan* hadn't reckoned he had anything to feel guilty about?

"I wanted to . . . but he wouldn't let me. Then the next day, he said he only kissed me because he was drunk." A tear rolled down Axel's cheek. "He said it couldn't happen again."

"Was he drunk?" I blurted out, because clearly that was the most important thing here.

Axel looked shifty. "Maybe. I don't know."

Yes, you bloody did. And I wasn't sure what to think about old JP. If a drunk person can't consent, can they commit sexual assault, if you can call a kiss that, on a willing—if underage—victim? Could anyone actually consent to anything, and would anyone really be guilty? It was doing my head in.

I tried to focus on what was key. "Did you tell anyone?"

He started to cry in earnest then, bringing up his knees and hugging them to himself as he sobbed.

I don't know about anyone else, but I jumped a bloody mile when I heard Lilah's voice. "Oh, my baby boy."

We all spun to see her standing in the doorway, her face under the makeup almost as pale as her son's.

Lilah marched in and gave the kid a hug, kissing the top of his head, then backed off to arm's length and looked at him. "You told your dad, didn't you, babe? And he got up in my Jonny-boy's face about it, 'cos ain't that just bleedin' like your dad, and that's why Jonny left home. I *knew* he wouldn't have left me without a bloody good reason." She didn't wait for Axel to confirm or deny it. "You done nothing wrong, you hear me? What's a kiss when it's at home? And I'm going to have *words* with your father. Lola, you take care of your brother until your auntie gets here."

She turned on her heel and marched straight out of there, while we all sat there frozen like a bunch of flippin' waxworks.

CHAPTER FORTY

Darren was the first to recover. "Blimey, talk about your cat among the pigeons."

I shook myself. "Axel," I said urgently. "*Did* you tell your dad about it?"

He was crying silently with his head on his drawn-up knees.

"Axe," I repeated. "Did you? Did you want him punished for, you know, turning you down?"

Axel looked up at that. "I never wanted him hurt! I wouldn't have . . . It was a threat, that's all, so he'd give me another chance. All I wanted was a chance with him. M-Mum didn't need him. She could have anyone."

"So you didn't tell your dad anything?"

"I just wanted to talk to Jonathan. He never let me catch him on his own anymore at home. So I had to go to the Smithy. I didn't know . . . h-he was there." Axel buried his head in his knees again.

I struggled to make it out. "What? Your dad was there? What, when you were talking to Jonathan?"

Axel didn't answer and didn't look at me, either.

I patted his arm. "Your mum's right, you got that? You didn't do anything wrong. You weren't to know he was going to fly off the handle about a drunken snog."

"That all it was?" Darren's voice broke in, making me jump. I'd almost forgotten him and Hazel were in the room with us. "See, I know Brian Tarbox of old, and he ain't the sort to blow something like this out of proportion. Kill a bloke for kissing his son? Seems a bit excessive to me. Break his legs? Yeah, I can see that. Tell the poor sod if he don't sling his hook, there'll be worse coming. But murder?

That's taking a risk, and he ain't daft, old Tarbox ain't. So I'm thinking maybe he got the idea somehow there was more to it than that. Would I be right there, Axe?"

Hazel drew in a sharp breath, then sat on Axel's bed and put her arm around him. "Axe? You can tell us. Did anything else happen?"

Axel choked out a no.

"When you were talking to Jonathan about it, though," she went on, then took another deep breath. "Did you say you were going to tell Dad he'd done more than that?"

He broke down completely into racking sobs that shook them both. Christ. I was taking that as a yes. So Tarbox had taken the threat at face value and killed Jonny-boy for messing around with his kid.

And Lilah had just gone to confront him about it. I turned to Darren. "You look after them. I'm going after Lilah." I mean, bloody hell, she was half his size. Less than. A quarter his size.

"Oi, hang about." Darren grabbed my arm. "You even know where you're going?"

Shit. No, I didn't. "Okay, where would Tarbox be, right now?"

"Who knows? Got fingers in a lot of pies, that one." Darren said it with an air of satisfaction I didn't quite understand.

"He said he was going to the office," Axel said, his voice hoarse.

"So where's that?"

Darren folded his arms, then sighed. "Studley Bottom. But, oi, you don't want to go down there and get yourself caught up in any aggro."

"What?" I shook my head, trying to clear it. "But what about Lilah? She'll be on her own with him, won't she?"

"See, it's like this. Lilah's a mate. But she's made her bed, ain't she? And Phil's a mate and all, and he won't thank me for sending his fiancé off to get flattened by a bloody bellend like Tarbox. Sorry, Axe, but that's the truth. Your dad ain't the kind of person you want to mess with." Darren turned back to me. "I'll have another go getting hold of the man with the muscles, and you just sit tight, yeah?"

What, and leave it for the big boy to sort out? Sod that. I grabbed my phone. Fortunately the company name, Lickett & Lovett, wasn't one I was going to forget in a hurry. I bunged it in the search bar, added Studley Bottom—was that seriously a real place?—and waited impatiently for the 4G I was paying for to kick in.

There. Found them. "See you later," I said, and legged it.

It all made sense. I drove as fast as I could without risking an accident. That's why Jonny-boy had been running scared back in Camden—he'd known Tarbox was gunning for him. Bloody hell, he must have been crapping himself when he'd found out Tarbox had heard him and Axe talking.

The only thing that surprised me was that Tarbox hadn't done him in there and then, given what he thought old JP had been up to. Natural caution? Darren seemed to think he was generally risk averse. Or was he just a revenge-served-cold sort of bloke? Did that mean Lilah was safe, even if she laid into him with righteous indignation after having only heard half the story? I couldn't take that chance.

Studley Bottom was almost due north of Pluck's End as the crow flies. The B road network not having been laid out by crows, Lilah's drive to work wouldn't be quite as quick and easy as you might think, and meant doing a fair bit of wiggling and winding around narrow country lanes. I'd have done better to bring the Fiesta instead of the van, but it was too late now.

I was beginning to wish I'd been around in the 1930s, when murders were civilised and took place on posh trains, cruise ships, or in snowed-in country houses, and your suspects didn't keep sodding off to who knew where. Hercule Poirot never had to worry about his GPS letting him down.

Then again, if him and Captain Hastings had wanted to sail off into the sunset together, they'd have found themselves on the wrong side of the law sharpish, so maybe things were better these days after all.

I clenched my hand on the steering wheel to stop myself beeping at a couple of old dears tootling along at thirty miles an hour. As soon as the road got more or less wide enough to get two vehicles abreast, I zipped past them, the hedge on the wrong side of the road knocking my wing mirror wonky. Ah, sod it. Roads like this, no other bugger was going to be daft enough to try overtaking.

Tarbox wouldn't hurt Lilah—would he? They'd been married for . . . Actually, I wasn't sure how long they'd been married, but long enough to produce Axel. And they'd worked together for a couple of decades, presumably amicably. That had to count for something, right?

Damn it, where was this bloody place?

I pulled over, had another butcher's at the GPS and realised I'd taken a wrong turning, damn it. I heaved the van into a three-point turn—not easy in these narrow lanes—waved an apology at the line of cars I'd been holding up (although it was their own fault for appearing from nowhere) and set off again.

At this rate, I might just make it in time for Lilah's funeral.

I eventually screeched into the car park outside Lilah's office building, parked the van in a space marked "Holborn & Co, Accts," and ran to the door.

I dunno what I was expecting "the office" to be like—wall-to-wall naked people, the inside of a BDSM dungeon, whatever—but in reality it was just, well, an office. In a building with a bunch of other offices. Christ alone knew what the accountants thought about sharing an address with a porn company. Maybe it was good for business?

The further I got inside the tastefully carpeted, magnolia-painted building, the more certain I was that I'd been wildly wrong about Lilah being in danger. It wasn't the sort of place you could imagine anything violent happening. What was Tarbox going to do to her, anyhow? Bash her over the head with a hole punch? Even the windows were sealed to keep the air-con in and the unfortunate fatalities out.

It wasn't big enough to have a receptionist, so I followed the signs up to the first floor and walked straight into Lickett & Lovett. At least here, it was more obviously something to do with the entertainment industry, with shelves full of DVDs and a big telly on the wall.

And Lilah, sitting at a desk and making a phone call without a care in the flippin' world.

She raised her eyes, smiled at me, and held up a finger, presumably to let me know she'd only be a mo, seeing as it wasn't her middle finger. Then she got on with her conversation while I stood there like

St. George togged up in full armour and battle regalia to face down a dragon, only to be confronted with a kitten in a bow.

Lilah hung up. "Sorry, love, I was booking in a private shoot." She gave me a flirty smile. "They're getting really popular with couples, you know. Get your own sex tape, but professional production values and all. I could do you and your other half a discount if you want."

"Uh . . . Thanks. I'll, um, let you know." What the bleedin' hell had happened to all the mortal peril I'd been expecting?

"If you want to hire some models to play along, I can let you have a flick through." She brandished a Lever Arch file at me.

"Where's Tarbox?" I asked desperately.

"Little boys' room. Why, did you want him?" The light of speculation was in her eye.

"I . . ." I sank into the visitor chair opposite her, across the desk. "Bloody hell, Lilah. I thought he was going to kill you!"

"What? Why would he want to do that?" She seemed honestly baffled.

"But—" I broke off as the door opened, and Tarbox swaggered in. I jumped up instinctively.

His eyebrows almost disappeared under the brim of his bowler hat. "What's all this, then? Come to audition for us, have you?" He ran an assessing eye up and down my body that somehow made me feel extra naked under my clothes.

"You killed Jonathan," I blurted out.

Lilah and Tarbox stared at me. "No, he didn't," she said after a pause. "He was with me that night."

Shit. I'd forgotten that, hadn't I? Her and Tarbox were each other's alibi for the night Jonny-boy died.

Tarbox pushed back his hat. One of these days he was going to do that a time too many and it'd fall right off, but apparently today was not that day. "Like I told Lilah, I never touched the bloke. Think I'm stupid? I know when my own son's telling porkies. Cry for attention, wasn't it? I told him, if he wants to make up stories, he wants to do it proper and sell 'em to the papers."

I stared at him in disbelief. "What, so you hear Axel talking about Jonathan and him . . . you know, and you just told him to pull the other one?"

"That's right." He folded his arms. "Because it's a load of bollocks."

"Course it bleedin' is," Lilah put in. "My Jonny wouldn't do nothing like that. Everyone kisses family. It don't mean nothing."

"See? And that's why I never told you about it at the time. All a load of bollocks." He rolled his eyes at me in a *Women, eh?* sort of way.

I was so weirded out by this surreal, anticlimactic calm I actually laid a hand on Tarbox's arm. "So it wasn't you Jonathan was scared of? Because when I met him in Camden, he was jumpier than a bloody bunny-rabbit who's just heard foxhunting's been banned."

Tarbox sent me a glare that said *Move your hand, chum, unless you want to be taking your fingers home in a bag.*

I moved it.

Lilah *tsk*ed loudly. "We've been through all that. You tell him, Bri."

"I may have made one or two comments on what anyone who messed around with my boy might expect from the rest of his short, miserable life." Tarbox sounded like he'd enjoyed doing it too. "But I never laid a finger on him. Not my fault if he ain't got the courage of his convictions, now is it?"

Lilah squared up to him across the desk, hands on her hips. "Oi, don't you say nothing about my Jonny. I loved that man."

"He wasn't good enough for you, babe."

"Not good enough for your precious bloody son and heir, you mean."

"So? What of it? Wasn't wrong, was I? Snogging an underage boy like that. Disgusting, I call it."

Lilah's eyes narrowed. "He was drunk, wasn't he? Made a mistake. Like we ain't all done that. And you know as well as I do you wouldn't have given a toss if it'd been a woman Axel had been messing about with. All them stories you used to tell me about bunking off school to have it off with your best mate's mum . . . You'd have patted the boy on the back and given him a bleedin' cigar for being a chip off the old block."

"So?"

"So what's the difference, just 'cos it's a bloke, eh?" Lilah was leaning over the desk so far her boobs were almost popping out of her dress. Tarbox had his eye on them, presumably so he could offer a hand to help keep them in line if necessary.

I couldn't help thinking they were both missing the point. Surely underage was underage, whatever the gender and/or orientation involved?

"Lilah," I interrupted, because *somebody* had to keep his mind on the actual murder case. "That message that was sent luring Jonathan up from London, did you send that?"

"Course I bleedin' didn't." She sighed. "Wish I had, mind. 'Cos then I'd have been there. And he'd be okay, and we could've got this mess with Axel sorted out proper. I know just 'cos he came up to meet me don't mean he wanted to come back for good. I ain't daft. But maybe he wanted to tell me to my face? That it was over? That'd still have been better than what happened."

I swallowed. Should I say something about the vibes I'd felt from the package? But I was still only guessing about Jonathan's state of mind. And anyway, that wasn't what was important right now. "Have you got any idea who might have used your phone to send it?"

"It's like I told the police. We all went out for lunch at the Brewer's Droop—me, the kids, their dad here, and their Aunty Loos—and I must have dropped my phone. I didn't even realise it was missing till I got home. Had to go back to the pub to look for it, and when I got there, they had it behind the bar. The girl found it on the floor when she was clearing tables. So it could've been anyone."

And wasn't that convenient? Maybe my thoughts showed on my face, as Lilah gave me a sharp look. "You can ask 'em at the pub if you want, they'll tell you."

Tarbox was nodding. "She rang me up bitching about it and all."

For a couple—sorry, *ex*-couple—who'd just been having a shouting match, they were pretty quick to get back to the united front. Well, he would back her up if he'd been the one to borrow the phone, wouldn't he? "Whose idea was this meal, anyhow? Was it like a birthday or something?"

Lilah turned to Tarbox. "It was you what suggested it, wasn't it?"

"Me? Nah. Least, I don't think so."

"Maybe it was Hazel, then. She's a good kid, and she knew her mum needed cheering up. Or maybe it was—"

"Now I think about it," Tarbox interrupted, "it could have been me after all. It ain't like we never go out normally. Family's important."

I stopped listening. Because there was one person nobody had mentioned—although my guess was that Lilah had been just about to—who could quite as easily have made the suggestion. Who else spent a lot of time at the Smithy—more than Tarbox, in fact—and might have overheard Axel making his threats? Tallulah. His Aunty Loos, who was closer to the lad than his mum, in some ways. Close enough to take him for days out; one of 'em on the very day he'd tried to kill himself. What if she'd heard Axel's bluff too, and unlike Tarbox, had believed the tales he'd been threatening to tell were true?

What if she'd decided to sort Jonathan out herself?

Had she told Axel what she'd done, on that Sunday outing? Or had he worked it out for himself? I'd thought the kid tried to off himself because he reckoned his dad had killed Jonathan. Was it possible that he was trying to pull the wool over our eyes and damn his dad to shield his aunt?

"Did anyone else know about Axel's claims?" I demanded, fixing Tarbox in the eye.

He shrugged. "Not from me, they didn't."

"Where's your sister now?" I asked Lilah.

She stared at me for a mo. "Why?"

"Uh, she wasn't at the hospital. I just want a word."

Lilah shrugged. "S'pose she'll be at the Smithy, this time of day."

"Even if it's closed? Or was she planning to open up today?" I frowned. "Wouldn't she have called Hazel in for that?"

"She wouldn't have bloody got her. I told my girl she's either with me or with her Uncle Darren today." Her lips tightened, and she looked suddenly older. "My poor baby would never have hurt himself if I'd been with him."

"Could you give her a call? Your sister, I mean. Not your daughter."

Lilah rolled her eyes but pulled out her phone and dialled.

"No answer."

Bloody hell, it was turning into a full-scale epidemic.

"What do you want to go bothering Tallulah for, anyhow?" Tarbox was looming right in my face. "Girl's got a business to run, and having her staff keep dying on her ain't helping."

I bet Jonny-boy and Oliver would be feeling horribly guilty about that. If they weren't, you know, *dead*.

"Yeah, you leave my sister alone," Lilah butted in. "She ain't got nothing to do with all this."

"Yeah? How do you know? Really? She's close to Axel, isn't she? Close enough she might come over all protective?"

"Yeah, but . . ." Lilah made a face. "She ain't got the balls to kill anyone. Him, now"—she jerked her head at Tarbox—"I could see *him* bumping someone off. No offence," she added with a smile in his direction.

He smirked. "None taken, love."

"But Loos?" Lilah went on. "She ain't got it in her."

"No? Any idea where she was on the nights of the murders?"

"She wouldn't," Lilah repeated, but I reckoned she was wavering.

I fixed her straight in the eye. "Somebody did. And you might want to ask yourself if Axel's in any danger from her too. Now he's started telling people what happened. What if she panics?"

"But . . . he's with his sister. And Darren."

Tarbox snorted.

Lilah paled. "Oh, bloody hell. I'm going back to see my boy."

"I'm coming with you," Tarbox said, his face stony.

They reached for their coats, and I realised I'd better get out of the office sharpish, unless I wanted to be locked in for the night. Two minutes later, I was standing in the car park watching them drive off, Lilah in a racy and presumably specially adapted little Honda and Tarbox in an honest-to-God Rolls-Royce, the poser.

Great. I was on my own.

And where the bloody hell was Phil? I hated to say it, but he was usually quicker at working things out than I was. And even if he hadn't, wouldn't going to talk to Tallulah be an obvious step, seeing as how Axel had spent the day of his suicide attempt with her?

If he was with Tallulah . . . There had to be a reason he wasn't answering his phone. And I didn't like to think what it might be.

CHAPTER FORTY-ONE

Fighting a sudden rush of nausea, I scrambled back into the van, made a last futile attempt to get Phil on his phone, and headed for the Smithy.

I know what you're thinking. I should have called Dave, got some police backup. But the trouble was, all I had was guesswork. There wasn't one shred of evidence against Tallulah, and if there's one thing coppers don't like, it's going in mob-handed without at least some sort of evidence. In America, based on what I've seen on the telly, they'd call it *probable cause*. In this country, they'd call it *Stop wasting our time, sonny-boy, or we'll pull you in for looking at us funny. Oh, and while you're there, do something useful and fix that bog in the station that's been a no-go area since last week's curry night.*

While I was expanding my knowledge of the B-road network in Hertfordshire, I ran my theory through my head, desperately trying to convince myself I was wrong. But it all fit. The only reason me and Phil hadn't taken more interest in Tallulah was that she hadn't seemed to have a motive, but with Axel's confession, everything made sense. She loved that lad. The thought of old Jonny-boy doing stuff he shouldn't with the kid would've made her see red.

I wondered why she hadn't talked to Tarbox about it, if they'd both been there. But maybe they weren't that close anymore. Or maybe she had, and finding out the boy's own dad hadn't taken him seriously had only fuelled the outrage? The details didn't matter, though. What mattered was making sure no one else got hurt.

The only thing I wasn't sure about was what I'd do if I got to the Smithy to find Phil was nowhere to be seen. As it happened, though, I never had to make that decision. When I got there, Phil's Golf was parked in the car park. There was only one other car there, which seemed like a pretty big clue the place wasn't open. If, you know, the big Closed sign in the entrance hadn't given it away.

I climbed out of the van and shut the door as quietly as I could. I was getting a bad feeling about this.

Okay, that's a lie. I was getting a *worse* feeling about this. Because okay, Phil was twice Tallulah's size—but Jonathan had been bigger than her too, and he'd still ended up floating facedown in the canal. What if Phil hadn't fingered her for the killer yet? All she'd have to do was catch him in a moment of distraction and then . . . well, God knew what she'd do then, given the lack of any handy combined murder-weapon-slash-body-disposal transport networks. Unless she planned on tying him up and leaving him lying in the road like Penelope flippin' Pitstop on a train track, and waiting for him to be flattened by a passing combine harvester or vintage steam roller.

My mind helpfully reminded me that another name for those traffic-calming speed bumps was *sleeping policemen*, and Phil was an ex-copper. I broke into a run.

Skidding to a halt just short of the door to the Smithy, I frantically tried to come up with a plan. Would it spook Tallulah into making a—possibly fatal—move if I went in all guns blazing? Figuratively speaking, obviously. I didn't have a gun. Bloody hell, I hadn't even thought to bring my pipe wrench. Christ, where was my brain when I needed it?

At any rate, it was killing me not knowing what was going on in there. For all I knew, it was killing Phil too. I wrenched open the door.

There was no one in sight. Were they upstairs? Was Phil about to take a faster-than-anticipated trip *down* the stairs? Would that be fatal?

Did I want to find out?

I stuck my head all around downstairs, but still no one. So I headed for the wooden staircase. I didn't want to take off my work boots, in case anything violent kicked off, so I gave up on stealth and just trotted on up, my size nines hitting the steps with a clatter.

Phil was up there. So was Tallulah.

My blood turned to ice.

Phil was leaning over a laptop that was open on the counter. And, behind him, Tallulah was hefting one of those hammers we'd joked about the first time we visited the place, her arm raised like she was about to bring it down on Phil's head.

They'd both turned to face me. It was like a snapshot, or a frozen TV screen. Murder, interrupted.

I didn't even think—just grabbed the closest thing to hand and chucked it at her. It was a china teapot, and it hit her on the shoulder, bounced off, and shattered on the floor.

She screamed. Phil jolted back, then stared at me. "Tom? What the hell are you doing?"

"Saving your flippin' life?"

He looked from me to Tallulah, and his eyes widened when he clocked the hammer now dangling from the end of her arm. "Jesus!"

"Guess you just came to talk to her about Axel's day out, then?" I tried not to sound smug. "And, uh, Ms. Lovett? You mind putting the hammer down?"

Tallulah did her best to shrivel me with the force of her glare. "I don't know what you're talking about. You attacked *me*."

"What, and you were only planning to swat a fly with that hammer?"

She drew in a breath—and then her face closed off, and she didn't speak.

Phil's eyes widened. "Tom—"

"What's going on here, then?" a voice cut him off right in my ear, and I wrenched my head round to see Brian Tarbox looming inches behind me. For a big bloke, he'd been scarily light on his feet coming up those stairs.

I was too glad to see him to moan about it out loud, though. "She was about to kill Phil!" It might have come out a bit high-pitched.

Tarbox shook his head. "Tallulah, Tallulah, Tallulah. What the bleedin' hell do you think you're doing?"

He strode past me, up to where Tallulah was standing, hammer still in her hand. As if he thought depressed skull fractures were something that only happened to other people. I wanted to yell at him to be careful, but the words stuck in my throat. Phil was there, though—he'd stop her killing Tarbox if it came down to it, right?

Right?

Tarbox raised a hand—and just as I was trying to work out what looked odd about it, he swung round faster than I could've believed possible. I don't remember seeing the blow land, or hearing it, even. All I remember is Phil crumpling at the knees and dropping slowly to the floor.

Tarbox watched him fall, then gave a heavy sigh. "How many times do I have to tell you, babe? We don't shit where we eat." Then he looked straight at yours truly, standing there petrified like a rabbit in the headlights. "Your turn now, chum."

Then he came towards me.

Weirdly, I wasn't scared. I was fucking *furious*. Some of my anger was directed at Phil, both for coming here alone and for going down from a single punch to the jaw—for fuck's sake, did he think he was *me*? But that paled into insignificance beside the incandescent fury I felt for Tarbox. "You lied to us!"

He actually chuckled, the bastard. "Did I really? Well, fancy that. All goes to prove, you can't trust anyone these days."

I backed away from him, desperately hoping I wouldn't trip and fall on my arse—or down those bloody stairs, Christ—before I had a chance to plant one on him. I didn't dare dart a glance behind me. If I took my eyes off him for a second . . .

"God, I hate poofs," Tarbox said conversationally. "Lilah, now, she's always had a soft spot for the pansy parade, but if you ask me, the world would be a better place without the whole limp-wristed lot of you."

"What about Axel?" I challenged. "Your son, remember? The one with a crush on a bloke?"

Tarbox sneered. "He's just confused. We'll get him straightened out, don't you worry. Now that ponce is out of the way."

He took another step forward—and then he swung for me.

I'd been waiting for him. I ducked under his arm and charged at the bastard, knocking him off-balance and into a display of fire irons that fell to the floor with a godalmighty clatter. I dived to grab a poker and then waggled it at him like a nervous fencer, as he clambered to his feet.

His bowler hat had fallen off, and yep, there was a bald patch. Hah.

I'd probably have enjoyed the discovery more if it hadn't been for the slight matter of my impending doom.

"Now you're pissing me off," he growled, and kept coming—then a cry came from behind me and he changed course, dodging around me. "Oi! You leave her alone," he yelled.

I spun to see Phil on his feet—thank God—if weaving a bit, holding a struggling Tallulah with one arm twisted high behind her back.

"Gerroff me," Tallulah screeched, her middle-class veneer now wholly stripped away like it'd been doused in turpentine.

"You'd better let her go right now," Tarbox snarled.

I realised no one was watching me and swung the poker as hard as I could into the back of Tarbox's knees. He went down roaring, and I nipped back out of reach sharpish, into the wooden embrace of a hat stand.

I might have yelped a bit.

"Tom?" Phil said, his voice sounding weird and wrong. "Call the police."

"I already called 'em," Lilah's voice rang out, clear and authoritative.

We all stared at her, standing at the top of the stairs like a lonely monk's vision of a pint-size avenging angel.

She put her hands on her hips. "You're going down, Brian Tarbox, for killing my man. Did you think I wasn't going to notice you turning off on the way to the hospital? I ain't daft. I knew I'd find you here."

Tarbox stopped trying to get up and stared at her as if she'd insulted his mother. "Oi, I never touched the bastard. I was with you when he died, wasn't I? That was your sister, that was. One swipe with the hammer and into the water he goes, nice and easy. And you reckoned she didn't have the balls," he added, his tone a mix of admiring and plain old smug.

Lilah looked stricken, despite this evidence of Tallulah's hitherto unsuspected testicles. "Loos?"

"Oh, for God's sake, he deserved it," Tallulah snapped, and wrenched herself away from Phil's hold. He didn't try to stop her, which was worrying.

"Yeah, uh, opinions differ on that one," I put in, taking a firmer hold of my poker and forcing myself to keep an eye on our middle-aged Bonnie and Clyde.

It wasn't easy. Phil was hurt.

Tallulah shot me a filthy glare. "Shut up. Of course he deserved it. Taking advantage of an innocent young boy's affections—I was doing you a favour, not that you'd ever care." That last was to Lilah, whose face hardened.

"My Jonny would *never* do that. One kiss, that was all it was. You tell her, Brian."

She was appealing to a flippin' murderer for a character reference?

Tallulah's colour deepened. "A kiss! That's not what Axel said—"

"Does it matter now, what he did or didn't do?" Tarbox's voice had gone all calm and reasonable. I stared at him and finally realised what was weird about his left hand. He was wearing a set of dull-grey knuckle-dusters.

Christ. My fiancé's face had been on the receiving end of those. I couldn't stop myself giving him an anxious once-over. He was leaning on the counter, and I had a nasty feeling it was all that was holding him up.

When I turned back to Tarbox, he was on his feet. Bloody hell. Lucky all his focus was on Lilah right now.

Although maybe not so lucky for her. I wished she'd get away from the top of the stairs before any accidents might be induced to happen.

"Now," Brian said, "I admit Tallulah here went off half-cocked, believing everything she heard, the daft cow." He gave Tallulah an affectionate smile that turned my stomach. "You should've got me in from the start, babe. You've always been too soft on that lad. I could have told you he was telling porkies. Giving Parrot his marching orders, now, you were on the right lines there, but if *I'd* run him out of town, he wouldn't have stopped at Camden, he'd still be bloody running. And we'd have saved a lot of unpleasantness, now wouldn't we? You gotta get over this jealousy of your sister. Using her phone like that? That ain't what family does, babe. Lilah's on your side, ain't you, love?" He turned back to Lilah and made an open-handed gesture.

My mind was reeling. Bloody hell. He *hadn't* been involved from the start? So... it must have been Tallulah who'd overheard them, and not Tarbox after all? Axel had lied to me about it? I felt stupidly hurt. I'd thought we'd, you know. Had a moment.

"What matters is," Tarbox was saying smoothly, "this is family. You ain't gonna let me and your sister go down for getting rid of a couple of woofters, are you? All we gotta do is make sure we back each other's stories up, and they won't be able to prove a thing."

I held my breath. Then I stopped holding it, because what with the shedload of adrenaline recently dumped in my system I was getting dangerously light-headed already.

"What about Tom and Phil?" Lilah asked. I wasn't sure whether to kiss her for thinking about us or yell at her for drawing us back to Tarbox's lethal attention.

He shrugged. "I'm sure we could come to some arrangement, couldn't we, lads?"

"Is that what you said to Oliver?" I shot back. "Right before you tipped him over the wall and into the path of a flippin' InterCity train? Lilah, don't listen to him."

"*Did* you kill that poor boy?" Lilah asked, stepping towards Tarbox.

He rolled his eyes. "What, Oliver? Why do you give a monkey's? You know he was your precious husband's bleedin' bum-chum, don't you? *And* he was blackmailing your sister. Threatened to tell the filth how that hammer went walkies from here the night Parrot got what was coming to him, *and* he knew why she done it, 'cos his ears never stopped bloody flapping. She was in *tears*, Tallulah was, when she told me what was up." Tarbox laughed. "He was a greedy little bugger and all. I knock on his door and tell him she's sent me with the money, and he lets me straight in, the stupid sod. He was asking for it. So don't you go harping on at me for helping out your own flesh and blood."

I'd *known* Brian had still had a soft spot for Tallulah. Okay, I hadn't known it extended to murder.

"She wouldn't have needed helping if she hadn't murdered my poor Jonny!" Lilah turned on her sister. "How could you? You knew I loved him."

"This is so bloody typical of you, Lilah," Tallulah raged. "You never take my side. Not once. It's always you, you, you. You even stole Brian from me."

We all turned as one to look at the bloke in question. He shrugged and made a face, as if to say *Women—what can you do?*

"People see you," Tallulah went on, "and it's always, 'Oh, she's so larger-than-life' and 'Isn't it amazing how well she's done despite her disability?' As if being born a little person ever made the slightest scrap of difference to you that you didn't fully exploit, especially in your so-called career." Her face twisted in a sneer. "You're just living the cliché—you know what they say about short women, don't you?"

Never having been all that interested in the subject, I didn't have a clue what they said about short women, unless it was that they wore short trousers, but I guessed if anyone knew, it had to be Lilah.

Who knows how long the family tiff might've gone on—or what might have been the outcome, with Brian still on the offensive and Phil clearly half-dead on his feet—but at that moment, we heard the door swing open, followed by the welcome cacophony of a bunch of flatfooted coppers piling up the stairs.

Thank God.

I dropped the poker and ran to Phil's side. He blinked at me, his eyes unfocussed—and slid to the floor.

CHAPTER FORTY-TWO

I suppose it made a change, me being the one sitting by the hospital bed waiting for his bloke to wake up. I was finding it anything but restful, although it was giving me a whole new perspective on his tendency to want to wrap me up in cotton wool. For Phil, I was thinking full riot gear and a three-mile exclusion zone.

Right now, Phil's jaw was making a bid to fill that three-mile radius single-handed. It'd ballooned up until he was doing a good impersonation of a hamster with a whole winter's worth of food stashed away in one cheek. The bruising was promising to be spectacular once it'd finished developing, and I wasn't looking forward to breaking it to him that he'd be on a liquid diet for the next six weeks.

He'd been lucky. Knuckle-dusters can seriously rip up your face and leave you carrying half your teeth home in a bag, but Phil had got away with a jaw broken in two places and severe bruising. Oh, and a concussion from his brain rattling around inside that thick skull of his, but at least all the scans had come up clear of internal bleeding and other nasties.

Seeing him lying there in that daft hospital gown, his poor, swollen face pale where it wasn't mottled with blood, I realised something. It didn't matter if he was better at some stuff than I was. All right, not just *some* stuff. The sort of stuff that was traditionally viewed as *manly*, like fist fights, shooting a gun, and other acts of violence. So what? He still wasn't infallible, and anyhow, that wasn't the only stuff that was important. When was the last time he'd ever found something with the power of his mind, or put together a meal with more than five or six ingredients (and the ones listed on the jar don't count)?

And anyway . . . it wasn't a competition. What mattered was that we were there for each other. Speaking of which, Phil's eyes had fluttered open, signalling his return to the land of the living.

"How are you feeling?" I asked.

"Like crap." His voice was muffled, which is what swollen lips and a jaw that's wired together will do for you.

"And they say appearances can be deceptive," I said, leaning down to kiss his forehead. "Surgery went well. They're optimistic you won't have much of a scar, which was a big weight off my mind, I can tell you. It'd be a bugger getting a stand-in for the wedding photos."

He smiled. Well, gave it his best shot, anyhow. "Love you too."

"Love you more, you daft git. What happened to always telling the other one where we were going?" I demanded.

Phil had the grace to look sheepish. "Wasn't really in the mood to give you a call." Then his eyes narrowed. "So if I check my phone, I'll see a text message from you with your full itinerary?"

"No, 'cos your phone's gonna be full up with missed calls from me and Darren. I s'pose I'm the reason it was turned off?"

"Can I plead the Fifth Amendment?"

"Not unless we move to America, no, and for various reasons, I'd rather not do that right now." I grabbed his hand and gave it a squeeze. "Think we could restrict the snits to non-life-threatening situations?"

Phil huffed. "Probably not."

Yeah, it was hard to argue with that. "*And* you turned your back on her. What were you looking at, for God's sake?"

"Social media."

I gave him a hard stare. "Let me get this straight. You nearly died because you were checking your bloody *Facebook*?"

"She logged me in to Axel's accounts. Claimed there might be something on there that could explain things."

"Huh. And that's creepy in itself, her knowing his passwords."

Phil nodded.

"Went both ways, though, I s'pose. Axel lied to protect her, even though it meant dropping his dad in it. Bit of a parenting fail on Lilah and Tarbox's part there." I moved on quickly, in case he was tempted to come out with anything like *We'll do better than that by our kids*, which I wasn't at all sure I was ready for. There's only so many stressful conversations I can handle at once, and that number goes right down after near-death situations. "You can't blame Axel too much, what with him being a kid and all screwed up about his stepdad." Phil frowned, and I realised he hadn't heard the whole story, so I filled him in on Axel's tearful confession, pointing out the bits that weren't actually true.

Phil looked thoughtful. "His real dad might blame him once he finds out Axel landed him with a fake motive for murder."

"Yeah, but maybe he knew Tarbox had an alibi? And anyway . . . Remember your old mate Wayne Hills, back at school?" It felt weird, recalling our mutual schooldays, given just how badly we'd got on in those days, and I went on quickly. "Remember how he used to get all worked up when the teachers didn't believe his excuses for not handing in his homework? Even though he'd made it all up about his granny dying, his mum having cancer, or the dog getting run over. Again."

Phil nodded. "Because like he always said, 'It *could* have been true.'"

"Yeah. Maybe Axel felt he had a right to be believed, and he was mad at his dad for, you know, *not*." I sighed. "You've got to feel bad for Tallulah, though. I mean, she was only trying to protect her nephew."

Phil huffed. "Already done that, hadn't she? When she sent Parrot packing back to Camden. She didn't have to kill him. If you ask me, she'd been waiting years for a chance to get back at her sister, and Parrot's death was as much about that as about what she thought he'd done to Axel."

"Yeah, maybe. She had to have known what she was doing when she sent that message luring Jonny-boy to the canal using Lilah's phone. Funny, though, innit? Here Tallulah is, all riled up at Lilah for, as she sees it, getting all the breaks, but it's Tallulah who ends up with everyone lying to save her from a murder charge. Well, Tarbox and Axel, anyhow. I'm pretty sure Oliver was only keeping shtum so he could blackmail her."

"And Tarbox killed to protect her from that," Phil mused. "Think he still loved her?"

For some reason it surprised me he'd said that. Was thinking about it. "S'pose he must have. Or cared, anyhow. Just not as much as she wanted him to, God knows why. He's a right piece of work.

He definitely deserves what's coming to him." Even if the man *he'd* killed had been a blackmailer covering up a murder . . .

Sod it. The only person coming out of this smelling of roses, as far as I could see, was Hazel. Poor kid. I hoped she and Axel would get over it all. "You ever see Wayne Hills these days?" I found myself asking.

"God, no."

I stifled a laugh at the force in his tone. Wayne Hills had been a vicious little shit. He'd been there the day I hurt my hip too. "Good."

I sat there holding Phil's hand for a mo. Enjoying his continued presence in my life. Also, if I was honest, putting off what needed to be said. Then I told myself to man up, and got on with it. "Listen . . . Sorry I flew off the handle about the honeymoon. I was short on sleep, I'd just had Mum and Dad bending my ear . . . Point is, I might have overreacted a bit."

"No. You're right. I should've asked you first." He gave me a weak, lopsided smile. "It really was a spur-of-the-moment thing."

"Of all the times to develop poor impulse control . . . actually, you know what? You can book a dozen bloody holidays without my input if it stops you running off to get your head smashed in."

"Same goes for you, you know."

"Oi, who's the one lying in the hospital bed with his jaw held on with wire? Some of us know how to duck."

"Don't push it, Paretski."

I gave up the struggle to keep my face straight at the way my surname came out sounding. "Wouldn't dream of it. So where are we going, then?"

"Southern Italy. Sorrento." He had to say it a couple of times. "I remembered you saying you wanted to go."

He did? I wasn't sure I could. "When?"

"Last summer. After the fire at the Dyke. We were on our way back from hospital in the cab, and you said, 'Let's go and see Pompeii.'"

Oh. Now he mentioned it, it did ring a faint bell. It'd been the early hours of the morning. I'd been weary to the bone and light-headed with exhaustion, and we'd just sorted things out between us after a bit of an iffy period. I'd barely known what I was saying. The next day—or the same day, technically speaking—had been my thirtieth birthday, and Phil had gone down on one knee and asked me to marry him.

Was it any wonder all thoughts of holiday destinations had vanished from my brain? But Phil, with his copper's mind, had been taking notes.

"And it's close to the Amalfi Coast," Phil was saying, "so we'll get to drive that coast road you see in all the car ads, and there's those blue skies and lemons trees you were after. And the beaches to laze about on when you're fed up with poking around old ruins."

My conscience got all stabby at that point, 'scuse the pun. 'Cos now I could remember going on about all that—the lemons, I mean—back when we'd been talking about Cherry and Greg's honeymoon in cooler climes. And another time, when we'd been watching the telly: I'd made an offhand comment when the car ad came on that I wouldn't mind zipping past those sheer drops and (hopefully) cheating death by a whisker on the hairpin bends, then parking up on the cliff for a Cornetto. "Oi, I'll never get fed up with you," I joked weakly. "And you shouldn't talk about yourself that way."

Phil managed a chuckle, which was more than it deserved. "It was supposed to be a nice surprise."

"Well, uh, it was. A surprise. And, you know, nice. Just not both at the same time." I kissed him again, feeling like even more of an ungrateful git. It had been a bloody touching thing to do, above and beyond the call, and I'd gone and stomped all over it in my size nines. "But, uh, thanks. For being so thoughtful, and, you know, actually listening to the guff that comes out of my mouth. You realise I'm going to be watching what I say from now on, don't you? In case it gets taken down and used as a romantic gesture against me."

"No. That's your lot. One romantic gesture per marriage."

Yeah, right. Like I believed that. "It was a good one. Despite one of us being a wanker about it. I should probably let you get some rest," I said reluctantly, because I could tell it was costing him to keep talking.

"Wait a mo. There's something I wanted to say. I know you've been thinking about us having kids, lately." Phil stopped, possibly because I was staring at him, open-mouthed.

"Me? You're the one who keeps bringing the subject up and who's suddenly acquired an encyclopaedic knowledge of Disney films." Apparently we'd be having that stressful conversation after all.

"Yeah, and you're the one who gets this hunted look every time kids are even mentioned in passing."

Oh. He meant *that* kind of thinking about it. As in, second-thoughts thinking about it. "I do want them," I said quickly, and swallowed. "But I think we ought to have a couple of years to ourselves first."

I braced myself, but Phil squeezed my hand. "We will. I'm fine with waiting. I just . . . I was worried you'd thought better of it altogether. Decided your independence was too important to you."

Heady relief made me grin. "Oi, I've got two cats. How much independence do you think I've had the last few years?"

"Kids are a little bit more of a commitment."

"I know. And I want to do that. With you. But let's get the wedding over first, yeah?"

"I never meant to rush you into stuff," Phil said. "With the moving in . . . It kept dragging on, and in the end I thought maybe you'd find it easier if I just went ahead and did it."

"Yeah, well, you're not wrong. Sometimes I need a kick up the bum, that's all. You've never rushed me into anything I didn't really want." I stroked his hand, probably looking all kinds of soppy and not giving a toss. "And I can't wait for you and me to get hitched, penguin suits and all."

"Even though you didn't get to choose the honeymoon?"

"Oh, I'm *especially* looking forward to the honeymoon." I sent him my best come-hither smile. "Well, as long as they get those wires off your jaw by then."

CHAPTER FORTY-THREE

Five Months Later

I was back in Mum and Dad's house, and my dad was helping me get dressed. It was like being a toddler again, only without the risk of impending temper tantrums and/or toilet accidents.

Although mind you, Dad *was* getting on a bit.

Gary had managed to convince us that there would be dire karmic consequences if me and Phil were to lay eyes on each other on the morning of the wedding. We'd agreed they'd mostly consist of Gary bringing it up in tones of doom and gloom every time one of us so much as stubbed a toe, but that was bad enough to persuade us to go along with it. So I'd moved back into Mum and Dad's for the night so Phil could have our house to himself, *his* mum's place not having enough spare room to fit in a hamster. Christ alone knows how him, his sister, and his two brothers managed to grow up there with both parents still alive, although I had a fair idea that his mum's wardrobe had expanded exponentially since those days. On that hopefully far-off day when she finally departed this mortal coil, Phil would probably be able to open his own branch of Primark.

At least it meant I didn't have to struggle into all the gear unaided, Dad having rather greater experience with formal wear than I did. He adjusted my cravat, gave my buttonhole a jiggle to make sure it was secure, and stood back. "You look very smart."

"Yeah, you too." We grinned at each other for a mo.

Then he stared down at his feet. As his shoes had been new for Cherry's wedding and not worn since, and had been freshly polished last night, I didn't reckon he was finding fault with his footwear. He coughed. "I want you to know, it never made any difference to me."

"Uh, it didn't?" That was what I said out loud. Inside it was more like, *What? That I never went to university? That I'm gay?*

"That you're not . . . Well. Who your real father is."

Oh. That. "You are," I said, my voice coming out a bit thick for some reason. "You're my real dad. You're the one who brought me up. Taught me how to shave and . . . and all the other stuff. You're my dad."

I wrapped my arms around his shoulders, which felt bonier than you'd think in his posh suit, and squeezed him tight.

Only for a moment, mind. Then we both backed off and cleared our throats while checking out the carpet.

"Shouldn't we—" Dad said, just as I started with, "Think we'd better—"

Then we both looked up, and I'm assuming my face was as red as his. "Right," I said decisively. "Here we go, then."

So we went. Down the stairs, out the door, and into the posh car with a ribbon on the front that'd take me to get hitched. Picking up Mum on the way, obviously. She'd have been a bit miffed if we'd left her at home.

What can I say? If you've been to a wedding, you know what it was like.

We were having the ceremony outdoors, in the very extensive Cottonmill Hall gardens—they'd assured us they had contingency plans for the likely event of rain, but for once the British weather smiled upon us. Chairs were set up in the traditional his and his sections, divided by an aisle, down which we would be walking any minute now towards a gleaming white gazebo housing a beaming (and also white, as it happened) registrar.

Phil was waiting for me at the back of the chairs. Always easy on the eye, in that suit, on our wedding day, he was . . . bloody hell, I had to pinch myself to be certain it was all real. That this bloke, Phil Morrison, my crush since I'd been a spotty teenager and he'd been so deep in the closet that his best mates were talking animals, was actually getting married to me.

I kind of wanted a time machine so I could go back and tell both our past selves about it. Then I thought better of it—past me wouldn't believe it, and past Phil would probably throw a punch at me.

"You look gorgeous," present Phil, the one I much preferred, whispered as I joined him.

"You too," I said, my voice hoarse. There was only the faintest trace now of where Tarbox (currently banged up awaiting trial, where I hoped they'd throw the flippin' book at the bastard) had hit him. He filled out his posh togs like he'd been born to wear them, top hat and all.

"Ready for this?" he asked, with a hint of a smirk.

"Whoops, no, changed my mind—joking, all right?" I swallowed down a stray bit of sentiment and added, "Never been more ready in my life."

It seemed to go down pretty well.

Greg, being a Church of England bishop-elect—yeah, he'd got that promotion—wasn't allowed to officiate at a same-sex wedding, which he'd been good enough to apologise for. Weird to think he was now in a position where he might be able to do something about that. So instead, we had the Deputy Registrar for St. Albans come out to do the honours. She was a jolly middle-aged woman who dressed like the Queen: everything matching and everything thirty years out of fashion but still looking lovely on her.

Mum sat in the front row in her brand-new Country Casuals frock, dry-eyed but smiling, holding Dad's hand. Cherry, wearing something shapeless and navy blue, bawled her eyes out, which was frankly worrying, while Greg held *her* hand. Phil's mum (tight pink skirt and matching jacket) blew her nose loudly, while Leanne (who was in a posh white dress and got herself mistaken for the nonexistent bride more than once) did that flapping motion women do to try to stop their mascara running. It worked, which goes to show the benefits of professionally applied makeup.

Phil's brothers, Jase and Nige, were squeezed into M&S suits and clearly uncomfortable—whether with the formal wear or the occasion in general, was hard to tell. We hadn't been certain Nige would come all the way back from his North Sea oil rig to watch us get hitched, but we hadn't reckoned with Phil's mum. *My* brother looked like he'd shined his bald head especially for the occasion, but fair dues, it was pretty warm. Mike Novak and his wife and son were sitting in the row behind Mum and Dad, which I'm sure didn't make the two women involved feel uncomfortable in the slightest. Their ramrod-straight posture was almost certainly down to some particularly vicious shapewear. Mike and Dad, of course, had greeted each other like old friends. Maybe by the time I'm attending *my* kid's wedding, it'll have stopped weirding me out.

Phil and I didn't go in for any of that write-your-own-romantic-novel vows bollocks, because we're way too British for all that. And there were no words I could have come up with would have done justice to how I felt. This was it: me and my bloke, standing up in front of all of our family and friends, and it was the act, not the words, which was important. We kept it simple, promising our commitment to each other in a few short sentences and swapping the rings over from our right hands to the left.

Okay, I might have thrown in an off-the-cuff "I promise to always come and rescue you when you go off to get yourself murdered," and Phil might possibly have added, "What he said."

There was a loud sniff from Cherry's direction at that point, and she disappeared entirely into one of Greg's voluminous hankies when we turned round after being pronounced "Husband and husband" (we'd reckoned *partners for life* didn't have enough of a married vibe).

Then it was confetti and photos. And further photos. I suspected Dad of having a word with the photographer, quite aware he'd never get me this well-dressed ever again. Although some of it could have been down to the ridiculously photogenic venue.

Nobody asked why Mike Novak appeared in half the family groupings, so I guessed they'd all quietly got the gossip at Cherry and Greg's do. I made a mental note to appreciate the two of them more in future.

I got started on this after the photographer had finally allowed us to slope off for the wedding breakfast. "So what's with all the waterworks?" I asked Cherry as we ambled into the hall.

She gazed mistily at Greg. He beamed and patted her hand.

Phil huffed. "Got an announcement to make?"

"Oh, we wouldn't dream of trespassing on your joyous occasion with our own happy news," Greg boomed out with a definite twinkle in his eye.

I stared. "Bloody hell, Sis, are you up the spout?" I mean, I'd noticed she'd put on weight, but I'd thought that was just Greg's cooking.

"Yes! Isn't it fantastic? I know you're both going to be wonderful uncles." Cherry's eyes weren't merely misty now; they were threatening to drown the whole wedding party.

"That's great. Congrats." I was trying to wrap my head around the idea of my big sister being a mummy, and failing dismally. "Uh, you planned it, right?"

"Honeymoon baby," Greg put in with a smirk and, ye gods, an actual wink.

I managed not to shudder, but come on, mate. This was my *sister* we were talking about.

"Still, no danger of that for you two," he went on, looking between me and Phil. Then he burst out in a hearty guffaw.

Catching sight of Raz, my sort of honorary step-cousin (long story) who happens to be trans, spurred me on to say, "Oi, some blokes are capable of getting knocked up."

"Ah, but I'm quite certain that's not the case for you, Tom. Don't forget, we've shared a bed." Greg winked again and nudged me painfully in the ribs. I manfully held back a wince. I wasn't sure if it was the winks, Cherry's subsequent giggle, or just the memory I'd up till now been doing a decent job of repressing that traumatised me the most.

Mind you, the horrified looks sent me by Phil's brothers made up for a lot.

"I don't understand it," I muttered to Phil after Greg and Sis had tripped blissfully off together, the glint of impending parenthood in their eyes. "She hasn't fainted, she hasn't been rubbing her stomach with a dreamy look in her eye, and if she's been chucking up at the drop of a hat, I haven't flippin' noticed."

Phil huffed a laugh. "Right, because every pregnant woman behaves like they do in *EastEnders*. If you're expecting the baby to pop out in ten minutes flat in a taxi on the way to hospital, be prepared for a disappointment."

Mum had insisted on a formal receiving line, so we got to shake everyone's hand as they went in. Luckily she'd also insisted we all have a glass of bubbly before we had to deal with forty-seven variations on "Don't you both look handsome?" and "Haven't we been lucky with the weather?"

Hazel Lovett was wearing an outfit her mum clearly hadn't picked out for her: a high-necked lacy blouse tucked into a full skirt that covered her down to her ankles. It showed she had a figure without actually revealing anything, and she could have been an extra from *Downton Abbey*—the early series, before Lady Mary chopped her hair off and started looking like she ought to be off running a chocolate factory. Okay, it wasn't remotely like the sort of outfit your average nineteen-stroke-twenty-year-old would be seen dead in, but the whole look suited her, down to the wispy little fingerless mitts.

Pete, on her arm and appearing even skinnier than usual in his drainpipe trousers and dapper waistcoat, seemed to have more colour in his chops, most likely because Darren had found him a job with a mate working days. Of course, Darren's mate being in the market trade, *days* actually started in the wee small hours, but it was a step in the right direction.

We still hadn't found out if Darren's insistence on taking a paternal interest in Hazel was due to him *literally* having a paternal interest in her—after all, if it was down to a work-related incident, maybe he didn't know himself, so Phil reckoned it'd be rude to ask—but it'd seemed safest to send her and Pete an invite just in case.

She'd even brought a dainty parasol, so if nothing else, she'd raised the tone of the wedding pics a notch.

"How's it going, Hazel?" I asked her. "Business doing okay?"

She'd started her own designer knitwear company, the Smithy having closed for the foreseeable on account of all the rest of its staff and management being either dead or in jail.

"It's early days, yet, but yeah, it's doing okay. And Axel's doing really well," she added, which had been going to be my next question. "Mum's hired someone to help with the business and she's been spending loads more time with him. They've been seeing a counsellor too." She'd probably clocked the doubt on my face as to whether Lilah spending time with her son would actually help him in the slightest, based on what I'd seen of them together. "She's really trying."

"Yeah? Good to hear it."

"And congratulations to both of you. You both look so handsome. Oh, and I'm going by Lorelei, these days. Or Lola." She beamed at Darren, who flashed his gold tooth at her fondly in return.

"She's a chip off the old block, this one is, ain't you, babe?" he said.

Yeah, but which block, mate? That was the question.

I didn't ask it, obviously.

The conservatory, where we were eating, was a picture. They'd done us proud, Cottonmill Hall had. Everything was decked out in white with a forest of greenery to set it off, and the tables were in serious danger of making me feel underdressed.

I'm sure the food was delicious, but I'm buggered if I can remember what we ate. Too busy looking at the ring on my finger and the husband by my side. Yeah, I know. But if you can't be mushy on your wedding day, when can you be?

Me and Phil both stood up to speak, but we kept it short and sweet. Or, as Darren might have put it, I was short and Phil was sweet. We'd used Phil not having a dad still alive as an excuse to avoid the whole Mike/Dad question for my side of the family, but then his mum insisted on standing up and saying a few words anyhow.

It wasn't *too* embarrassing. Although Leanne, Jase, and Nige all squirmed in their seats when she made a pointed dig about wanting to know when she was going to get to buy a hat for *their* weddings, seeing as here was Phil on his second one already and wasn't it way past bleedin' time they all pulled their fingers out?

Okay, Phil might have looked uncomfortable at that point too. She ended on a high note, reminding us all she wasn't getting any younger and it was about time *someone* made her a granny. Dad, who's never had much of a head for bubbly, interrupted her with "Oh you're far too young to be a grandmother," and she was so gobsmacked she sat back in her chair, lost for words. Phil gave Darren a nudge, sharpish, to stop her getting any ideas about standing up again.

Our best men, Gary and Darren, had been firmly (and repeatedly) instructed to keep it clean when it came to the speeches. They managed—just—and Darren in particular did a bang-up job of the traditional best man's task of (a) entertaining the masses and (b) embarrassing the grooms. All in good fun, mind. DCI Dave, who was wearing the suit he kept for court appearances and funerals, and bouncing the littlest Jedi proudly on his knee, certainly seemed to enjoy the anecdotes about yours truly. Actually, come to think of it, he'd probably supplied some of them.

After the speeches, the tables were shifted to the side to make way for the band. Some people danced (mostly Gary, Darren, and Phil's mum in an unholy trinity), some glued themselves to their chairs for the foreseeable (Mum and Dad and the rest of the pensioner brigade), and some spilled out through the French windows into the gardens to enjoy the evening sunshine (the rest of us). It was pretty bloody idyllic. I was almost sorry when it was time to leave to get changed for our flight.

Seeing as we were heading off in a taxi, there was none of this tying tin cans to the bumpers malarkey, and although Darren was seen lurking with a can of spray snow, Phil managed to catch him before he spray-painted the cab with *Just Married* (or, knowing him, something much, much worse).

Everyone came out the front to wave us off. I might or might not have had recourse to the silk hanky in my top pocket.

"Don't forget to see Naples and die," Gary called after us, which I personally found less than encouraging.

Still, I couldn't wait to be on honeymoon with my—get this— *husband.* Two weeks of hot sunshine and even hotter . . . well, do I have to spell it out? And not a dead body in sight. And, okay, maybe I was tempting fate there, but whatever went wrong in sunny Italy?

Apart, obviously, from volcanoes erupting and swallowing Pompeii; the Mafia; the fall of the Roman Empire . . .

Nah. We'd be fine.

Definitely.

Explore more of The Plumber's Mate Mysteries:
riptidepublishing.com/titles/series/plumbers-mate-
mysteries

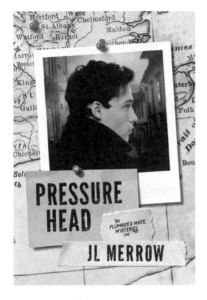

Dear Reader,

Thank you for reading JL Merrow's *Lock Nut*!

We know your time is precious and you have many, many entertainment options, so it means a lot that you've chosen to spend your time reading. We really hope you enjoyed it.

We'd be honored if you'd consider posting a review—good or bad—on sites like **Amazon, Barnes & Noble, Kobo, Goodreads, Twitter, Facebook, Tumblr,** and your blog or website. We'd also be honored if you told your friends and family about this book. Word of mouth is a book's lifeblood!

For more information on upcoming releases, author interviews, blog tours, contests, giveaways, and more, please sign up for our weekly, spam-free newsletter and visit us around the web:

Newsletter: tinyurl.com/RiptideSignup
Twitter: twitter.com/RiptideBooks
Facebook: facebook.com/RiptidePublishing
Goodreads: tinyurl.com/RiptideOnGoodreads
Tumblr: riptidepublishing.tumblr.com

Thank you so much for Reading the Rainbow!

RiptidePublishing.com

ACKNOWLEDGEMENTS

With thanks to Kristin Matherly, Susan Sorrentino, Stevie Carroll, and Jennifer Bales, and to Sue Brown, for fun, brainstorming, and research in Camden Market.

ALSO BY
JL MERROW

ABOUT THE AUTHOR

JL Merrow is that rare beast, an English person who refuses to drink tea. She read Natural Sciences at Cambridge, where she learned many things, chief amongst which was that she never wanted to see the inside of a lab ever again. Her one regret is that she never mastered the ability of punting one-handed whilst holding a glass of champagne.

She writes across genres, with a preference for contemporary gay romance and mysteries, and is frequently accused of humour. Her novel *Slam!* won the 2013 Rainbow Award for Best LGBT Romantic Comedy, and her novella *Muscling Through* and novel *Relief Valve* were both EPIC Awards finalists.

JL Merrow is a member of the Romantic Novelists' Association, International Thriller Writers, Verulam Writers and the UK GLBTQ Fiction Meet organising team.

Find JL Merrow on Twitter as @jlmerrow, and on Facebook at facebook.com/jl.merrow

For a full list of books available, see: jlmerrow.com/ or JL Merrow's Amazon author page: viewauthor.at/JLMerrow

Enjoy more stories like
Lock Nut
at RiptidePublishing.com!

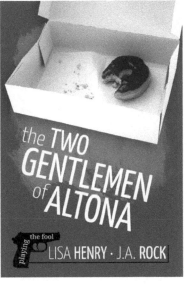

The Best Corpse for the Job

Tea and sympathy have never been so deadly.

ISBN: 978-1-62649-192-2

The Two Gentlemen of Altona

Mischief, thou art afoot.

ISBN: 978-1-62649-219-6

CPSIA information can be obtained
at www.ICGtesting.com
Printed in the USA
LVHW04s1616010518
575556LV00003B/653/P